Bad Magic
and
Whiskey

I love you mom.

Chapter One

THE PIG IS DYING, and there isn't a damn thing I can do about it.

I crouch in the mud beside the fallen animal, its sides heaving with labored breaths. Poor bugger should be happily munching breakfast with the rest of the passel, charming little pigs resembling the pudgy, short-legged illustrations in Ylva's fairy-tale book.

They had been easy keepers. Until about three months ago, around New Year's, the whole lot of them started declining. Scrawny pigs, dying pigs, barren pigs are pigs that won't make my family a living. We sell barreled pork to mining camps to earn cash. And this little piggy is the third to succumb to the malaise this week. Short of a miracle, we'll have nothing left to sell come fall.

"Is it gonna die, Auntie?" Ylva's small voice comes from behind me. I glance back at her blonde braids catching the weak morning light.

"I reckon so, little wolf." My voice is steady, though disappointment and frustration boil. I'd been hanging onto the hope that Gudrun's latest tonic, administered with the waxing moon, had stemmed the illness. I guess not.

Ylva crouches beside me and reaches out to soothe the pig. Her tiny white hand is almost lost in its black hair. At eight years old, Ylva takes after Gudrun with her knack for animals.

"Go fetch Mama Gudrun, ask her to meet me inside. Tell her we got another one down."

Ylva nods and sets off across the muddy ground, coat flapping open, despite the chill. Little bird legs skip nimbly through the muddy mess. I glance around the empty pen. No one in sight. Just me and a dying pig.

My fingers twitch. One touch. That's all it would take. I could almost feel the pig's life force, its Vitae, ebbing, almost taste its Animus Mortis waiting to be released when it died. Power I hadn't tapped in nearly a decade, right at my fingertips.

"Yum yum, if you have a penchant for pork."

I jump, recognizing the mocking voice. Damn Johnny Reb's staring at me from across the languishing animal. Great, just what my morning needs, a wrathy ghost. Thought he had finally moved on, but no, here he is.

Bastard's been haunting me since Gettysburg, shimmering gray uniform tattered as the day he died, kepi cap pulled low over his eyes. Most shades want to move on once they figure out they're dead. This fella stuck around, nursing a grudge.

"Ain't none of your business what I do," I mutter, snatching my hand back.

"Thought you were respectable now." His voice is taunting. "What would dear departed Caleb think?"

I stand abruptly, wiping my hands on my trousers. My face flushes in shame. "Caleb would expect me to save the damn farm."

The words are true enough. The homestead had been my husband Caleb's dream. But he's been gone for nigh on three years, taken by the plague of '77. He died expending the last of his power to pull my sister, Julianna, through the sickness. Caleb's death was my personal extinction event. My hopes for our life together burned to ash, everything flat and gray like this cold March morning.

Most days I feel as insubstantial as my Reb.

Turning on my heel, I retreat, leaving the ghost to the dying pig.

The shade's laughter follows me as I stalk toward the cabin.

Chapter Two

WHEN CALEB AND I arrived in Trinidad almost ten years ago, lumber was scarce, with a price tag to match. We spent the first summer living in a dugout. By fall, it had evolved into a single-room, sandstone-walled cabin with a peaked roof and a fireplace. After my sister's family joined us, we added two adobe brick rooms for sleeping and a coal-burning stove. Nothing made Caleb prouder than the final addition of four glass windows. One in each bedroom and two in the main room.

I pause on the cabin's porch to clean my boots before entering. I don't relish facing Julianna's wrath for tracking muck inside. Bracing my shoulder against the pine door, I push hard, and the bottom scrapes across the packed dirt floor. The scent of herbs underlaid with vinegar lingers—Julianna's cleaning tonic.

Inside, Julianna is at the stove, her movements rigid as she stirs a pot of porridge.

"Another one?" she asks, not turning. Ylva must have told her about the pig.

Beautiful Julianna could have been a model in *Godey's Lady's Book*—perfectly oval face, wide-set gray eyes, and golden-brown hair. But the years on the frontier marked her with her lye-roughened hands and calico dress.

She never expected to end up on her older sister's homestead raising pigs and vegetables to sell to miners. Our parents presented Julianna to Indianapolis society the year the war ended. She loved the parties, dancing, and flirting that came with being a debutante. Before Christmas, she was married to the son of a burgeoning rail baron and was poised for a life of soirées and charity boards. Her expectations took a turn when his rail stock crashed, and he ran off to South America.

"Yep." I hang my hat on the peg by the door and pull off my coat and gloves. "That's five this month."

Julianna exhales, her shoulders slumping slightly, and turns to me, her eyes tired. "We can't go on like this, Mary Catherine."

"I know." I sigh, gathering the newspapers and magazines scattered across the table. Gudrun's hunger for news and gossip compels her to collect periodicals from all the neighbors. I stack them by the fireplace before sitting down. "Maybe Gudrun can try another charm?"

Like many folks around these parts, Gudrun, Julianna's wife in every way that counts, is a Small Magic user, crafting herbs, charms, potions, and spells. She has a particular affinity for animal husbandry, which served us well up till now. I figure maybe one in twenty folks can turn a spell or charm to help with the laundry or banish flea beetles in the tomato patch, but Gudrun's skills are a notch above.

As if summoned, the door bangs open and Gudrun blows in, blue eyes shining, cheeks ruddy from the spring wind, Ylva at her heels with a milk pail in hand. Gudrun's face is grim as she peels off her scarf and hat.

"Ylva says we lost another," she huffs. "And the damn cow's milk's light. Her calf's gonna need all she can give."

Pausing in her tasks, Julianna gently grabs Ylva's head and places a kiss on her crown before turning to help Gudrun shrug out of her coat. Seeing them together lightens my mood despite the news of the cow.

Gudrun will never grace *Godey's* or *La Mode*; her sturdy face and form more suited to farm life than magazine covers, but she's perfect for Julianna.

"We can't be the only homestead losing livestock?" I ask, hoping for some insight or clarity, any explanation.

Gudrun shakes her head. "That's just it. I asked around when I was at the Ramirezes' yesterday. Nobody else is losing stock. The Cordovas' sheep are fat as ticks, and old man Baca's bringing on extra men to help with the lambing."

"It's just us, our pigs, our cow affected by whatever this is," I mutter, the weight of that sinking in.

Gudrun fixes me with a steady gaze. "Did you try...?"

"No." I glare at her, tilting my head in Julianna's direction, willing her to shut up. I had carelessly thrown out the idea to Gudrun that *maybe* my old talents could help with the livestock problem. "I promised Julianna, remember?"

Julianna turns from the stove, her face tight. "And we're grateful for that promise. The last thing we need is you slipping back into old ways."

An uncomfortable silence falls. Gudrun slinks to the table to join me. Ylva looks between us, confusion plain on her face.

"What old ways?" she chirps. "What could Auntie do?"

"Nothing," Julianna says, setting down bowls of corn porridge sparingly dotted with salt pork. The spoons rattle as each bowl plunks to the table. "Your aunt doesn't do that anymore." Julianna sits, primly spreading a clean rag on her lap. "I suppose grace is too much to expect?"

Gudrun chuffs softly. "We're nearly broke, Jules. The garden won't produce for months—"

"No," Julianna answers firmly. "We're not risking it. We have no reason to believe Mary Catherine's special abilities could make a difference anyway."

"Jules is probably right, Gudrun. What do you expect me to do about a hog die-off?" I shovel a spoonful of breakfast into my mouth, then continue, "I'm a nice, old widow woman. You're the pig expert."

"Old? You're forty-two, you got all your own teeth, you ain't too old for nothing," Gudrun snorts, losing the smile and lowering her voice. "You used to know *people*."

"No good came from those people," I counter.

Ylva's eyes are saucers, practically popping out of her head. Julianna glares at both of us, her porridge untouched.

"But you have power, yes?" Gudrun says. "You're the biggest toad in this puddle." She slaps her spoon down. "If you weren't so enamored of being the sad widow woman... There must be something you can do or someone you know who can put things right..."

Gudrun's grasping at mist. I haven't used my power since Caleb and I said, "I do." And I definitely don't run with that crowd anymore.

But...thinking back to the pig earlier, the temptation to taste just a little of the magic, my heart flips. "Maybe—"

"Enough!" Julianna snaps. "I don't want to hear another word. Finish eating, then you two will go and take care of that poor creature while Ylva helps me in the house. You can take the carcass to Elsbeth's—"

A sharp knock at the door cuts her off. We all freeze, exchanging glances. Our neighbors are unlikely to visit this early. We must have missed the sound of hoofs while we argued.

Gudrun moves toward the shotgun hanging by the door, while I go to the window. Recognizing the well-fed mule standing near the porch, I wave Gudrun back. "I got it."

Nestor, Robert Tallmadge's hostler, stands outside the door, hat in hand, shifting nervously from foot to foot.

"Morning, Miz McClellan," he says, ducking his head respectfully. I open the door wider to wave him in, but he shakes his head. "Mr. Tallmadge sent me. Asked if you could come see him. Says it's urgent-like."

"What's this about, Nestor?" I ask, warning prickling along my spine.

"Don't rightly know, ma'am. He said there's someone in town asking after—" he lowers his voice— "Mick Kelly."

I feel the blood drain from my face. Behind me, Julianna gasps. I haven't gone by Mick Kelly for a decade, not since Alan Pinkerton helped me bury that woman. Least that was the story we put about.

"Tell Robert I'll come by at one," I say, my voice steadier than I expect. "Got some chores I gotta take care of."

Nestor mounts up and leaves before I turn to find Julianna and Gudrun watching me, worry etched on their faces.

"You can't go," Julianna says immediately. "If it's the BMI—"

The BMI, Bureau of Magical Investigations, was institutionalized by Abe Lincoln during the war, and he appointed Alan Pinkerton to lead it. The Bureau's official mandate is to find, contain, and eliminate foreign and domestic magical threats to the United States. Unofficially, it keeps magic, especially Big Magic, hidden from the general public. "Normies" we like to call them.

Based on services rendered, Alan and I had an understanding. I disappeared quietly into the frontier and in exchange he wouldn't arrest, conscript, or execute me.

"Of course I have to go. And hopefully it *is* someone from the BMI. Nobody else should know Mick Kelly is alive," I cut in. "But first, we're gonna take care of the animals."

"You go put that hog out of its misery, no hocus-pocus." Julianna's voice is flat, brooking no argument. "You promised, Mary Catherine. Never again."

"Jules—" Gudrun begins.

"No!" Julianna cuts her off. "I won't have it in my home. Not after what happened." She turns to me, eyes pleading. "Go see Robert if you must. But don't do that. Please."

I nod slowly, not trusting myself to speak. The disappointment in her eyes cuts deep.

Ylva's still at the table, apparently hoping that if she stays quiet, no one will notice her listening. Catching my eye, she silently mouths "Hocus-pocus?"

I shake my head once at her, then start bundling up again to head outside.

Chapter Three

GUDRUN AND I HEAD to the north pen to see about the pig. The March light is flat and gray, the sun veiled behind a fortress of clouds. In no time, my ears ache from the chill wind. It's cold enough to dull the pig smell but not cold enough to solidify the mud. Damn pigs.

My nerves are on a tightrope. Julianna's fears are well-founded. My judgment has been known to skip a cog, but straits are dire and we need to *do* something.

The poor hog hasn't moved since Ylva and I fed the herd earlier. The subtle rise and fall of its breathing show it's reaching the end.

We pause at the fence.

"Ain't this cozy," the Reb drawls from his perch a few rails down. "Two ladies just innocently setting out to slaughter a hog. Hocus-pocus the farthest thing from your innocent little hearts."

I ignore him, though heat creeps up my neck.

Tucking my hands into my pockets, I try not to fidget. "Any chance your tonics might still work if we give it more time?"

Gudrun shakes her head. "I've tried three already. The last one even had some of that expensive cinchona bark from my cousin in San Francisco."

"Weren't you telling me about some Norwegian remedy your grandmother swore by? The one with the molasses?"

"That was for colic, not wasting sickness." Gudrun slips through the fence rails with practiced ease despite her full skirts. Her movements are gentle as she crouches beside the pig, running her hands along its sunken flanks.

The animal doesn't even grunt. It looks even worse than it did an hour ago. Patchy skin is stretched over protruding bones, cloudy eyes, labored breathing.

"See how the skin puckers?" Gudrun points to an area near the pig's shoulder. "And its gums are nearly white." She places her palm flat against the pig's side, closes her eyes briefly. When she opens them, her expression confirms what I already believed.

"It's exactly the same as the others," she says, standing. "I don't know why they're failing."

Studying the animals in the adjacent pens, she continues, "We feed them well, they forage, and that distiller's mash should put weight right on." She comes back through the fence, scowling. "I can almost taste the edges of something...hovering like a fog, but I can't quite put a finger on it." She shakes her head as if to clear it. "I'm probably just being fanciful. The kindest thing now is to end its suffering."

"You sure there's nothing else?" The words catch in my throat. It's not just about this one animal, it's about what comes next.

"Nothing *I* can do," Gudrun says quietly.

My eyes dart to the Reb drifting closer, hovering just behind Gudrun's shoulder. I thought the bastard had finally moved on around New Year's. I hadn't seen him since he serenaded me with all seven verses of "God Rest Ye Merry Gentlemen" for an entire week. But here he is again, today.

His head cocks to the side, rubbing his chin in faux contemplation. "Mighty convenient excuse for what you're fixing to do, ain't it?"

I clench my jaw and look away from him, back to the pig. Each shallow breath it takes seems more painful than the last.

"No sense letting it suffer," Gudrun says, reaching for the long knife sheathed on her belt. "We'll make it quick."

I nod but hesitate. "Before we do... I was thinking..."

Gudrun pauses. "Yes?"

"Maybe it would help us pin down the problem...if we knew for sure what we were dealing with—natural disease or mystical..."

"That something you can do?" Gudrun asks carefully. "I don't quite understand what a Va—Vorator is, just that its Big Magic."

"'Mortis Vorator' is the fancy name. I just say 'Gleaner.'" I rush on. "Didn't Juliana explain it to you? I've had the Gleaning since I was a kid."

Gudrun never asked about my history. I assumed we all kept mum out of consideration for my delicate feelings. Was Jules ashamed to tell Gudrun about me?

"Juliana never talked about your past." She raises her hand and ticks off on her fingers. "I know you were recruited by Pinkerton's BMI during the war. After the war you ran in some powerful company. And I know your...special abilities aren't discussed in polite society." Gudrun drops her hand, looking sheepish. "When Julianna and I met, she said you were as good as dead." She fiddles with her belt, looking away. "She was embarrassed to discuss your problems. I thought your big shame was whiskey."

I roll my eyes, shaking my head. Of course Julianna didn't disabuse her of that notion. Drinking seemed a safe, normal, problem. Truth was, back in the day, I often liberally applied whiskey to the hollow spaces between Gleanings. Used it to ease the gnawing emptiness that came when the power was spent. Whiskey kept the shades like my Confederate at bay. Too long between deaths was like having my skin peeled off an inch at a time. The booze soothed. But the bottle wasn't my real demon.

Whenever I rode a death, the world blazed with perfect clarity, every color brighter, every sensation sharper. But after? The doldrums could drag me into a pit so deep I couldn't see daylight. Got so bad I became less discriminating about Gleaning, took some folks who maybe didn't need taking. My last job for the BMI marked the moment I truly passed beyond the pale. I haven't ridden a death since. But Gudrun needn't be privy to all that.

"You're familiar with life force, right? Vitae Essence?" I ask, watching her face.

"Of course. Healers work with Vitae." She nods, practical as always. "Injury and disease drain Vitae."

"Well, Animus is the other side of that coin. Think of Vitae as the power that keeps a heart beating, but Animus is what makes each creature itself. The unique pattern, the soul.

"A being's Animus is tethered to its physical self by mystical chains. When something dies, those chains snap." I snap my fingers for emphasis. "That breaking releases energy—Animus Mortis. That burst, that exact moment of transition from life to death, is what my power comes from."

"Like necromancy?" Her brow furrows.

"Not even close. Necromancers scavenge the leftover Vitae from corpses, like picking through cold ashes. What I do..." I pause, searching for words. "Animus Mortis is an explosion, all at once. I catch it, store it inside me, use it later as pure force. I can shatter doors, flip wagons, stop bullets."

Gudrun frowns. "You can move things? How's that gonna help our pigs?" Frustration edges her voice.

"There's more to it." I lean closer. "When something dies and I'm connected to it, its Animus—its memories, experiences—flow through me. Like drinking from a stream that carries everything the creature ever was." I struggle to explain the knowing that comes with it. "If something unnatural is killing these pigs, if there's a curse or a hex, I might taste it in the death. See the pattern of whatever's draining them."

Gudrun looks unsure. "That sounds like what Julianna's afraid of, you getting a taste again."

"No, no," I say quickly, raising my hands. "For this I won't ride the death. I'm just talking about witnessing it. When I call on my Gleaner sight, I can see the fabric of Vitae and Animus. A natural disease would only drain the pig's Vitae, If something's tugging on both..." I let the implication hang.

Gudrun studies my face, her blue eyes sharp as ice picks. "So, you're just looking...?"

"Just looking," I confirm, meeting her gaze. My heart hammers against my ribs. And I mean it, I think. It's not really breaking my promise. Just bending it a little.

The Reb snorts. "Like a drunk having a sip."

My teeth grind, willing him silent.

Gudrun glances toward the cabin. A curl of smoke rises from the chimney. "Jules still won't like it." She sighs, then straightens her shoulders. "But I want answers."

"Maybe my sister doesn't need to know?" I drop my head, hiding behind my hat brim. The silence stretches, broken only by the pig's labored breathing.

Gudrun chews her lip. A crow calls overhead. She brushes her hands on her skirt, the sound like sandpaper in the quiet.

"Let's get this pig killed." Her voice flat.

I release my breath.

She leads the way, ducking back through the fence. I follow, feeling the heartbeat in my throat is going to choke me. Fear or excitement? I whisper softly to the pig as we approach. I don't think it knows we're near. Its ear twitches as I crouch behind its head. Its eyes are half closed, its breathing shallowly and fast.

The Reb crouches by its tail. His hat is gone, the breeze ruffling his blond hair. Grinning at me, he nods at the pig. Ignoring him, I look up at Gudrun. "Do you think we need to stun it, or do you figure it's far enough gone?"

Gudrun tilts her head and squints at the prone animal, then gently touches its half open eye. It doesn't blink. "I think it's far enough gone but let me pass a charm over just in case. Don't want it to suffer, and my nerves can't take screamin'." Gudrun leans over the pig, whispers an incantation, and taps it between the eyes. The pig shudders slightly, its legs kick, then it goes still.

"All right," I say to the waiting woman, "give me a minute to connect with its Animus and then when I say go, you can start bleeding it."

"Don't dawdle. The stun will only hold for a minute or two."

I remove my gloves, fingers clumsy with cold with...anticipation? Fear? I shove them in my belt.

"Hurry," Gudrun whispers, knife ready. "It's fading."

My hands shake as I place them on the pig's shoulder. Its skin burns hotter than I expect. Bristles prick my palm.

Deep breath in. Out slowly.

I reach for that part of myself I've kept locked away for years. The key turns in a rusty lock. Something inside me stretches, wakes.

Purple and blue lights dance across my vision. The Reb leans in, watching hungrily.

One heartbeat. Two.

There.

The world shifts. Colors bleed away until only the faint yellow glow of Vitae remains. My fingertips tingle, pins and needles spreading up my arms. The thin yellow mist dissipates like dandelion fluff.

I reach deeper, searching for Animus. Should be clinging tight and smooth to the body.

But it's ragged. Torn in places like a moth-eaten blanket.

The color's wrong. Not bright, hot pink, but muddy puce, the color of infection, of rot. A part of me knows I could try to smooth it, knit the frayed bits back together. Caleb used to talk about work like that, healers tugging at broken patterns instead of just pouring life in. But my touch is built for ripping, not mending. I pull back.

This confirms the malaise is mystical. But I need to spend more time here, it's been so long since I've opened myself to this power. Focusing on the pig's heartbeat, I signal Gudrun.

She murmurs something in Norwegian as she bends with the knife in hand. The hog doesn't stir as she slides the razor-sharp blade into the base of its throat, where it meets the chest. She pushes the handle back toward the pig's tail and then plunges it in almost to the hilt and withdraws it with a squelch. A torrent of blood follows the knife. I feel the pig's racing heartbeat increase first to a staccato rhythm and then begins to slow as its blood flows, creeping toward my boots. My own heartbeat pounds.

I close my eyes and slip deeper into the connection, surrendering to the familiar pull. The pig's dream envelops me: warm sunshine on its back, the earthy smell of its siblings nearby, the contentment of rooting through soil. For a moment, I'm there with it, safe, far from the cold March day and the knife in its throat.

My vision fractures.

Darkness—flashes of something twisted, writhing, skeletal things with hollow eyes. A thick purple miasma washes through everything. The pig's terror becomes my own, choking me. Something ancient and hungry slithers through its dying thoughts.

Pull back. Pull back now.

But I don't. The promise of power, even tainted power, calls. And I'm going to answer it.

The pig's heartbeat stutters—once, twice—then stops. This is the moment that's haunted my dreams for a decade; the transition from life into death, that perfect instant when Animus breaks free from flesh. My body remembers, craves it.

I feel the Animus crest, delicious despite the corruption. It brightens to a sickly fuchsia shot through with veins of violet. It thickens, gathering itself, preparing to break free. My hands tingle with anticipation. Just one taste. Just this once. No one will know.

I steady myself for the plunge, the rush, the burst but... it's gone. Nothing, nothing at all, no heartbeat, no breath, no pig dreams, nothing. Confused, I open my eyes. The hog is dead, nothing but a slab of meat. The Reb prods it with a spectral boot, then winks out. I stand and brush my hands off on the sides of my pants. My cheeks burn. I was gonna ride that pig's death as soon as I felt its power, promise to Julianna forgotten.

"Well?" Gudrun says. "What did you see? Or feel, or whatever you do?"

I stare at her, speechless for a second, searching for words to explain. But she doesn't understand what I tried to do, and I ain't gonna tell her.

"N-nothing," I stammer.

"Nothing?" Gudrun says. "I felt power rising around you."

"Not, nothing...the Animus was wrong, it was...ravaged. But something else took it, something stole the Animus..."

"God help us." Gudrun's face pales, her accent thickening with fear. "What creature could do that, besides you?" She clutches the small wooden cross at her neck.

Her words chill me. Snatching Animus is rare magic. Gleaners like me are one in a million. Vampires feast on Vitae or Animus, but America doesn't have a Vamper problem since Washington drove the Hessian bloodsuckers out a century ago. I suppose there are lesser creatures that would enjoy a sip of Animus, sure, but nothing that works from a distance. And why target livestock? Human life force is much tastier, more power, more memories. Pig souls don't have the same kick.

I stagger over to the fence and lean my forehead against the rail. My mind is spinning. What killed that pig?

Chapter Four

THE TWO-HOUR TRIP TO town gave Robert's urgent message plenty of time to gnaw at me. Someone asking for "Mick Kelly" doesn't bode well. That name belongs to another life, one I'd buried. Seems conveniently timed now that Gudrun and I confirmed something magical is killing our pigs. Someone from my past surfacing as unnatural death creeps through our farm. I don't like it.

Despite my itch to get to Robert, I've kept Sampson at an easy pace. Can't let him work up a sweat—that thick winter coat of his will trap the moisture, and these temperatures ain't kind to a damp horse.

Sixteen hands and solid, he's more of a saddle horse than a carriage horse, but everyone earns their keep on the homestead, including him. Downright annoyed about being dragged out of the pasture this morning, Ylva and I had to put up with his piss and vinegar getting him between the traces. He pretended he had never seen the wagon before, shying at the harness and spooking at crows that came to watch the show. Sampson will stand his ground in the face of cannon fire but spook at a few stupid birds for entertainment.

I'm freezing my tail off with all this wind whipping through the buildings on Main. Cold as it is, there are still folks and horses packed in everywhere you look. Tall ones, short ones, dark ones, pale ones all elbowing past each other on wooden walkways to keep outta the muck below.

Sampson, the big showoff, loves coming to town. His pace quickens from a dogged walk to a slow jog. His droopy ears perk and swivel, taking in all the activity. He arches his neck and prances a little, flirting when a gorgeous team of matched bays going in the opposite direction pass him. I think he's bored at home with only Gudrun's mules and the milk cow for company. The mules are clannish.

Every step Sampson takes in the muddy street squelches and plops with the one, two rhythm of his jog. His legs are covered in muck, splashing up to his belly. He'll get a good rub down when we get home.

I'm glad it's cold. I don't stick out with my hat yanked down and all these shawls wrapped around me. Not that I'm hiding or nothing, ain't like I got a bounty on my head. But Trinidad gets all kinds of people coming through, being right on the Santa Fe Trail. Never can tell when someone I crossed in my old life might pass through.

I head south on Culver Street past the Grand Saloon, a two-story Italianate in the fancy style imported from Chicago. It's strangely silent, the curtains drawn and the front doors shut tight. I'd expect to hear rowdy music. The Grand should be booming in booze, prostitutes, and hot meals for miners and travelers of all ilk. It keeps its doors open seven days a week. I can't figure what to make of it sleeping on a Saturday morning.

A small cluster of miners stands outside, grumbling among themselves. One pounds on the door, only to be turned away by a man I don't recognize. Something about his bearing raises the hairs on my neck. Looks too formal, official even.

Robert's office is smack dab between Main Street and the train depot, at the crossroads of commerce and freight travel. He always seems to have his fingers in everyone's pie. Robert is a lawyer, the county land agent, occasional mortgage holder, and general acquirer and distributor of goods and information. It's fair to describe him as an honest opportunist. I don't believe Robert is a magic user, but his position as town gossip monger puts him firmly "In the know."

I Pull into the yard and hand Sampson off to Nestor, Robert's hostler, with an admonishment to Sampson to be good.

"Don't you worry." Nestor grins at me. "Mr. Sampson and I have an understanding." He's already slipping horehound candy to Sampson from his pockets.

I smile back. "His affection is cheap. I'll be quick."

Nestor's smile falters slightly. "Lots of strangers in town this week," he says, voice lowered. "Fancy folk asking questions."

"That why the Grand's closed?"

He nods, eyes darting toward the street. "Best be careful, Miz Kelly."

I head through double doors to the main office of the single-story brick building. A bell over the door tinkles as I enter. Across from the door, a polished counter, cluttered with a cash register, a large ledger, different-sized scales and weights runs the length of the room. The intervening space is filled with mining equipment, surveyor's tools, furniture, machine parts, musical instruments, steamer trunks, and cases of liquor. Shelves overflowing with claim documents and leather-bound ledgers run behind the counter. Bags of beans, flour, and corn are stacked on pallets to the right.

"Well, good afternoon, Mary Catherine McClellan." Robert's friendly voice booms across the overstuffed room. "I appreciate you so promptly attending me at my humble establishment."

Humble, my ass. Robert owns eight city blocks, has interests in the railroad, several coal mines, and a pub on the east end of town. His mistress and partner, Louise Demarara, is one of the most celebrated madams this side of the Continental Divide.

Smiling tightly, I pick my way through the jumbled inventory to the counter. "What's this about? You sent Nestor to my cabin, said someone was asking about Mick Kelly?"

"Yes, yes, let's have some privacy." Robert lifts the bar flap near the cash register, allowing me access to follow him behind the counter. "Come on back and have some coffee. We've got a lot to discuss."

I follow him, noting the swish-clump of his fancy new prosthetic leg against the pine boards. Seems business is good enough for upgrades.

Robert's office is a stark contrast to the cluttered storefront—polished wood, organized shelves, and a coal stove radiating welcome heat. I remove my hat and start unwinding the layers of shawls from my face and neck.

"Who's been asking for me?" I press as he gestures to a chair near the stove.

"Coffee first," he insists, pouring from the pot on the stove. "This isn't a simple answer."

It smells delicious. I wrap my hands around the hot ceramic, sitting down as he settles into the chair opposite.

"Town is knee deep with Pinkerton BMI. They brought an entire detachment." His mustache twitches. "And yesterday they closed the Grand."

"A BMI detachment here?" I grip my cup more. "I didn't notice agents on the street. Are they uniformed?" There are forces in the BMI that strongly disagreed with Alan Pinkerton's decision to exculpate me and wanted me under their yoke. Robert knew I avoided contact with the BMI, even if he didn't know why. "Are they asking about me?"

"Don't fly off the handle just yet." He settles deeper into his chair, taking an unnecessarily long sip of coffee before continuing. "A few days ago, some junior agent stopped by, asking for Mick Kelly—"

"Hell no," I snap, standing so abruptly my chair threatens to topple. "You told a BMI agent where to find me?"

"Will you listen?" he counters, balancing his cup on one knee while his eyes dart briefly to the window. "I don't think an entire detachment being here has anything to do with you. You're yesterday's news, Mary Catherine." His fingers tap against the cup. "And the kid's nobody important, just mentioned hiring you for some job down south."

I narrow my eyes. "Since when is BMI business 'nothing important'?"

"Let me start at the beginning. A couple of months ago, you heard tell of a flu that swept through Denver, killed twenty-eight people and made another hundred sick as hell for weeks?"

I nod. I remember Gudrun telling me about the news story.

"Same thing happened later in Leadville and again in Georgetown this month." Leaning closer, he continues, "Marguerite Henley just came through town on her way to Santa Fe and said the same happened in Cheyenne, all the way up in Wyoming Territory."

"So, what does any of that have to do with me or the Grand or the BMI?" I shrug, head tipped to one side.

Robert rushes ahead, "Colby Thatcher, Senator Richard Thatcher's son, was one of the men who died in Georgetown. Colby was in Trinidad the week before he died and Alma Pierce, one of the Grand's frail sisters, traveled to Georgetown with him."

It annoys me that Robert refers to the woman as a "frail sister." Alma was anything but morally frail, but I nod at him to continue.

"The senator raised such a ruckus, President Hayes ordered a Pinkerton investigation and they found dark magical residue on Colby." He sits back and sips his coffee as though watching me for a reaction.

I just stare right back at him, knowing damn well the Pinkertons can't pin Colby Thatcher on me. "Well," Robert goes on, "once Thatcher caught wind it was magic-related, he pressured President Hays to assemble an actual task force of BMI Marshals, all charged with cracking his son's murder case."

"Okay, so some rich senator's son dies and there is a national crisis?" I scoff, relaxing in my chair. The BMI's presence in Trinidad really has nothing to do with me. "Colby could have been playing with things best left alone. "

"Might have," he acknowledges, "but it's bigger than that." He rises suddenly, crosses to the window, and peeks through the curtain before turning back. "BMI tested all the men they could find in Georgetown who had fallen ill and found magical residue on every one of them."

"Magical residue?" I repeat, sitting forward. The familiar itch between my shoulder blades crawls up my spine—the same feeling I get when death lingers nearby. "What kind?"

Robert gestures vaguely. "That's just it—they're being tight-lipped about details. But they've closed every high-end saloon those men frequented." He returns to his chair, lowering his voice. "They suspect it's a magical clap transmitted by the soiled doves."

I rest my cup on the arm of my chair. "They're off their nut. Are the ladies sick?"

"Not a one." Robert glances toward the door. "But that hasn't stopped them from focusing on the women. Kate Warne's old detachment is assigned to Trinidad—you remember Kate?"

The name lands like a stone in my gut. "Of course." She had been one of my greatest friends and mentor. She died before I had a chance to set things right between us.

"Since most of the prostitutes are women, I think the idea was her team could make more ground." He puts his elbows on his knees to lean closer. "The thing is, Mary Catherine, there's more to this than just some disease investigation."

"What aren't you telling me, Robert?"

His eyes meet mine, then flick away. "Elizabeth Van Lew has command of the Trinidad investigation."

My skin prickles in alarm. Van Lew was the most vocal opponent to Alan's pardon of Mick Kelly. Just hearing her name makes me want to check my flanks for ambush.

"The BMI dispatched agents to Denver, Golden, Pueblo, and Cheyenne to see if events there follow the same pattern. Large detachments are here and in Georgetown. They closed the Grand and the other parlors in town to test all the workers for contagion curses before they're allowed to resume business."

"How the hell are they explaining the shutdown? All the miners from the company towns come here for companionship. The BMI is supposed to keep magical calumny secret."

"They're calling it a venereal disease and justifying it as a public health and morality mandate." Robert sighs.

"Sounds like horseshit wrapped in fancy paper." I gesture to the coffeepot and cross my legs. "But what do I know? Hayes can't keep his own cabinet in line, much less the country. Still, even trigger-happy BMI boys don't mobilize without something putting fire under their asses." I pause, studying his face. "How is Louise dealing with these events?"

Robert pours us both fresh cups, his movements too casual. "The Grand is supposed to reopen in two days. Rumor is the BMI will be around for a while after." Raising his eyebrows comically, he sips his coffee. "Until they pull out of town, they requisitioned Holiday House to quarter agents."

I snort and about choke on the coffee finding its way around a laugh. "They quartered agents in Louise's sanatorium?"

When the railroad came through town a few years ago, Louise made a deal with the town fathers. She financed the town's trolley system, which so happens to run right through the heart of the red light district, and in exchange the town subsidizes a "rest home" for the brothel workers, Holiday House.

He chuckles along with me, but his eyes keep darting to his desk. "Right now there are only a couple ladies in residence, so she has extra rooms. She seized the opportunity to offer accommodations for all twenty-six agents, room and board, at a fair market rate." He winks. "Plus, it lets her keep an eye on their goings-on."

"I still don't see how any of this connects to someone asking for Mick Kelly," I say, setting my cup down hard enough to slosh coffee onto the table. "And if Van Lew's running things, I'd sooner walk into a bear trap than put myself at her mercy."

"Well, I think it might help mend fences with the old battle ax if you take the kid's contract. Plus, it gets you out of town while they conduct the local investigation."

"I want nothing to do with the goddamn BMI." My fists clench. "She wanted to put a collar on me, make me bend to her every whim. If it weren't for Alan, I would be a lifer—"

"Mary Catherine, that was ten years ago. Things have changed. And I don't know how to break this to you, but I doubt most of the folks over there even remember you."

"Doesn't matter. Any BMI business is trouble I don't need." My finger traces the rim of my cup. "I've got real problems at home, Robert. Since around the end of last year, something has been infecting our pigs. Almost one of five just lies down and dies."

Robert's eyebrows rise. "That sister-in-law of yours can't do anything?"

"No, nothing Gudrun's tried helped. I had hoped you might have heard about other folks having trouble and how to stop it."

"No." His face is grim, lips pressed flat as he runs a hand over the top of his head and rubs the back of his neck. "So, come slaughter in the fall, you are gonna be cash poor going into winter."

"Yup." I sigh. "That about sums it up." I swallow hard, straightening my posture. "I need to find out what we could sell the homestead for."

"I don't know..." His hand drops to his lap. "The economy is still not what it was back when you made the claim. Silver prices haven't rebounded, iron is still weak..."

"I'm not selling silver or iron," I say, my voice sharp. "I have title free and clear to 160 acres, with a cabin, a stout barn, and a well. Taxes are up to date."

I look into his concerned eyes, considering. Sure, I suspect that sometimes Robert operates a little close to the margins, but he's been a good friend to me over the years. He wouldn't prevaricate about the value of the homestead. He gave us the last load of corn draff at a discount. It's like I'm failing everyone by even suggesting selling the homestead. "This is a bad idea." I stand again to leave.

Robert holds up his hands. "Don't go stomping off." He rises, clumps over to his desk, and starts sorting through papers. "This might fix your cash problem..."

He extracts a cream-colored card from between pages of a notebook and props his good hip against the desk. "The BMI pays real cash money."

"No, Robert..." I collapse back in the chair, my head hanging.

"I'll make you a deal," he says, his voice softening. "Go speak to this agent, see what he has to say. While you're gone, I'll have Nestor load your wagon with another ton of the distiller draff."

My head snaps up. "I thought the supply had dried up?"

"Luckily for you, I received an unscheduled load on last night's train." He winks, too smooth.

"What's that gonna cost me?"

"I'll let you have it for the promise of three more hams and a gross of Gudrun's worming tonic. Shep swears by it for his cattle."

"Make it two hams and you have a deal," I say, hauling myself out of the chair and crossing to the desk to pluck the cream card from Robert's hand. The card stock is flimsy but reads:

Lt. Edison Colt

Bureau of Magical Investigation

My stomach tightens as I read the name. "Where will I find this Edison Colt?" I'm already regretting this plan, but a ton of draff will get us through another month.

"He's part of the crew staying at Holiday House. If you go right now, you can catch the Main Street horsecar trolley, east to Fletcher."

"Sending me straight to the lions' den." I tuck the card inside my shirt pocket. "If I'm not back here in two hours, you have to explain what happened to Julianna."

"You'll be back," he says with too much confidence, "and if not, I will personally pry you from the lions' teeth. Far better than facing an enraged Julianna."

I cram my hat down on my head and stomp out of his office. "Have my wagon ready in an hour."

Chapter Five

GODDAMN PIGS. GODDAMN EDISON Colt. Goddamn Robert Tallmadge.

I stomp down the boardwalk, hat pulled low, scarf high to
hide my scowl, fists jammed in pockets. Passersby skitter out of
my path like I'm a snarling dog. Tempted to growl at 'em, just for
spite.

Slumping onto a bench, I wait for the trolley. Main and
Fletcher, Robert said. My knee bounces, boot heel drumming
the wood planks. This is a mistake. I should turn around, march
back, tell Robert where he can shove this favor.

The sleek cherry-red trolley car rattles into view, pulled
by a pair of matched roans. Their harness bells jingle merrily
as they clop to a halt. The contrast with my black mood nearly
makes me snort.

Hopping aboard, I plunk a nickel in the coachman's hand,
ignoring his cheery grin. Settling onto a padded bench, I stare
out the window as buildings slide by.

Instinct says this is a shit idea, but my brain keeps whispering Robert's magic words: "real cash money." Money for new
boots for Ylva. Money for Gudrun's tonics. Money so Julianna
doesn't have to darn socks till her fingers bleed.

I close my eyes. I'm a fool. A desperate fool. But I owe it to
my family to hear this out. Then I can tell this Edison Colt to go
piss up a rope.

The car jerks to a stop and my eyes fly open. There it is.
Holiday House, with its gables and gingerbread like a gussied-up

saloon girl. The front porch swarms with dark blue uniforms. Goddamn. Looks like a kicked anthill.

Trying to stay incognito, I pull my scarf up to my chin and slink up the porch steps and through the door. Sideling up to the cadet manning a makeshift reception desk in the foyer, I tug my scarf down an inch. "Name's Mary Catherine. Here to see Edison Colt."

The cadet blinks vapidly. "Edison who?" Her finger traces down a list before her. "You sure you got the right name, ma'am? I don't see no Colt here."

A muscle ticks in my jaw. Robert, you sonovabitch.

Digging in my pocket, I produce Colt's card and slap it on the desk. "He gave me this. Said to come find him here."

She picks it up, squinting. "Oh. Well. Guess you better...wait here?" Rising, she disappears into the hustling crowd of agents.

I huddle against the wall, pulling my hat brim down till it meets my scarf. The foyer buzzes like a damn beehive with agents passing through, up and down the stairs. No one gives me a second look. I glance into the front parlor on my left; desks overflowing with papers line the perimeter. Louise's flocked wallpaper is hidden behind maps and photos tacked to the walls. The clacking telegraph machines punctuate snippets of conversation floating by.

"...testing all the soiled doves..."

"...Senator Thatcher breathing down our necks..."

"...never seen a contagion curse like it..."

"Ma'am?" The cadet's chirp startles me. "Agent Colt's out back. Bunking in the barn with the other juniors. If you go out the front door, there is a path to the left."

I stare. The barn. They stuck him in the goddamn barn.

"Much obliged," I mutter. Spinning on my heel, I stalk off the porch.

Rounding the house, I stomp through the kitchen garden, nothing but a few herbs daring to sprout in the cold. Chickens scatter, squawking their outrage. Good. I ain't the only one having a shit day.

The barn door creaks as I yank it open. Weak spring sunlight filters through grimy windows. It smells comfortingly of hay and horse apples. A dozen stalls, each with Dutch doors, march down the central corridor. Looks like half house horses, and the other six are being used to bunk agents.

"Edison Colt!" I holler. "You in here?"

A clatter from the first stall. The door bangs open and a gangly figure stumbles out, currycomb in one hand. Straw sticks out of his hair at lunatic angles. I spy a bright, sorrel pony behind him.

"Y-yes, that's me!" He gapes, eyes wide behind crooked spectacles. He brushes his hands through his hair to shake out the straw, straightens his shirt, and looks me up and down. "Who wants to know?"

I sigh. "Mick Kelly. You left a card for me at Robert Tallmadge's office."

"You're Mick Kelly?" He looks surprised.

I snort. "In the flesh. Now what's this about—"

"The Mick Kelly," he gushes. "I'm familiar with all of your assignments from when you were working for Lafayette Baker. You single handedly took down the necromancer Three-Legged Tom Barstol. And..." His voice drops to a whisper, "Blasted Billy Lee Wonder even when he begged for his life."

I open my mouth. Close it. Well, shit. This pup's done his reading, even if some of the particulars are wrong. His recitation of my crimes fires my ego just a hair, bringing back the excitement of the not-so-good old days. Something about this kid tickles my memory, but I can't pin it down.

"Yup, that's me. Regular legend of the West. Most folks know me as Mary Catherine McClellan. Mick was my moniker after the war." I push my hat back, fixing him with a flat stare. "Now, you mind telling me why BMI's sniffing 'round for Mick Kelly?"

"Oh! Right, of course." He closes the lower door of the stall. The sorrel moves to stick her head over to watch our exchange. The pony is quality with beautiful, bright eyes and a delicate face underneath her shaggy winter coat.

Edison draws himself up, straw drifting from his shoulders. "Pleased to meet you, ma'am. Edison Colt, just like the six-gun." He sticks his hand out.

Grasping his soft palm in my calloused one, I give it a firm shake. "Yeah, I got that from your card. So?"

"I'm lookin' into reports of mystical trouble down in Las Vegas, New Mexico territory. Need someone to ride with me who ain't afraid to do what needs doin', legal or otherwise." Big talk from a fella with hands that ain't seen much work.

"How 'bout you just tell me exactly what kinda mess you're pokin' into," I say.

"Two, uh, ladies of the evening"—a blush creeps up Edison's cheeks— "were attacked at the Imperial Saloon. One didn't make it." He lowers his voice. "The other gal, a shifter, claims she can't transform no more."

"Sounds like someone's slinging dark magic." I lean forward, my interest piqued. Ain't too many spell slingers out there with the juice to pull off something like that.

"According to the report, the... uhm... ladies were entertaining two local men when some kind of altercation broke out." Edison's freckled face goes pale. "Witnesses say one of the women just dropped dead, not a mark on her. The shifter lady was beat up, but she survived, except she can't shift no more."

"And you have reason to believe that story is true?" I press.

"Well..." His face scrunches and he bites his lip. "The local BMI agent documented it but couldn't identify how the shifter's abilities were damaged without killing her outright. Reported it to the Santa Fe office but...well, they don't put much stock in that agent's word."

"And they put stock in yours?" I can't keep the disbelief from my voice.

He flushes, but his eyes go hard. "Ma'am, I am a fully commissioned agent of the BMI."

I blink at him, nonplussed.

His bravado wavers and he lowers his voice. "Not as such. But my C.O., she took it seriously. Gave me leave to investigate, seein' as everyone else is occupied with the, uh, Thatcher situation."

"Uh-huh." I lean against the stall door, arms crossed. "And where do I come in?"

"Well, ma'am, you're one of the only folks around with practical expertise in that kind of Big Magic." He grins. "My uncle, Pete Zigala, said he ain't never seen nothing like your abilities."

For a moment, I'm transported back to a campfire in the Arizona territory, '67. Pete passing a bottle of whiskey, eyes wide as I demonstrated my power by pulling the Animus from a dying rattler. I used that energy to light our fire with a snap of my fingers. His whoop of amazement. Morgan's low chuckle.

Simpler times. Before everything went to hell with Lafayette.

I stand with my hands on my hips, staring while my brain catches up to his words, "Jesus, Mary, and Joseph, you're Pete's sister's kid!" The resemblance hits me. They've the same eager eyes, same quick smile. Pete rode with me and Morgan back before I got hitched, spinning tall tales around campfires and getting us into more scrapes than I care to count.

Seeing Pete in this boy's face makes refusing harder, but I still ain't interested. "Sorry, kid, I ain't in that line of work no more. Hung up my spurs, so to speak."

"I reckoned you might say that." He takes a step closer, and damn if he hasn't mastered Pete's puppy-dog look. "But Uncle Pete says you're the best of the best, Miz McClellan. We gotta find out if someone is messing with powers of life and death. If anyone can help me get to the bottom of this, it's you."

His freckled face is unlined, fresh as a peach. I grimace and sigh. "You can't believe everything you hear, especially from a rascal like Pete."

"I got leave to hire specialists, and the BMI's willing to pay top dollar."

I stare at him, my jaw clenched. Goddamn Robert, putting ideas in my head. Goddamn pigs, wasting away no matter what we do. Goddamn world, serving up hard choices every which way I turn.

◆——■——◆

"How much?"

"I'm authorized to offer two hundred a day, plus expenses. I figure ten days total." The words race out of his mouth, like he's afraid I'll bolt before he's done.

I let out a low whistle. That's...well, hell, that's more cash than I've seen in a long while. Could set the homestead to rights and then some.

"No offense, ma'am, but you ain't a spring chicken. Couldn't hurt to have a little something put by." Edison's watching me, a furrow between his brows. He looks so painfully earnest. So green he's likely to sprout leaves. "Sorry 'bout the confusion earlier, but you look different than I was expecting from your photograph."

Yeah, fifteen years older. I exhale. No, I am no spring chicken. I am a dusty old hen. And this hen isn't going to go gallivanting across the mountains to investigate a murder with a partner barely out of short pants...but that fee is more than I could hope for.

"You got leave to hire specialists, plural?"

He blinks. "I reckon so if the case calls for it."

"And if I wanted to bring on a partner? Someone who knows the territories, got my back in a scrap?"

"If you vouch for 'em, I don't see why not." His gaze sharpens. "You got someone in mind?"

I shrug. "Might do. Fella name of Morgan Jackson." My old compatriot resides near Trinidad. His courage and character pulled us through many a tight spot back in Lafayette's day. And he possessed an uncanny instinct for avoiding magical trouble...skills that might prove useful. I don't tell him Morgan's the closest thing I got left to kin, 'sides Julianna.

Edison nods eagerly. "Pete spoke highly of Mr. Jackson, said he's a crack shot. You know where he's at now?"

"I might get word to him."

"Maybe I could pay you both 225 dollars a day if you can bring him in?"

Damn. That's a year's income in one go. Enough to get us through till next year, even with the sick hogs.

I'm a fool. A damn fool. But I'm a fool who looks after her own.

"When you looking to ride?"

"Day after tomorrow, first light." He grins, sudden and blinding. Sticks out a hand to shake. "We got a deal, Miz Kelly?"

I stare at his hand. Soft and eager. Shit.

"You guarantee 225 dollars plus expenses, and I'll think on it."

He beams like I gave him a damn Christmas pony instead of a maybe. "Fair enough. I'll get the paperwork drawn up."

I trail after Edison as he natters on about supplies and trail routes. Let him talk. My mind's stuck on what went down in Vegas. Betcha the local agent is trying to make their stripes, turning a couple rough johns beating on working girls into something bigger than it is.

Walking into the yard, a flicker of movement catches my eye. There, in a second story window, a pale face is peering at us. Eyes meet mine, flinty gray and razor sharp.

I stumble. Commander Elizabeth Van Lew.

Edison's still yammering, but my attention's on Van Lew, one of the few folks in this world who can make me squirm like a sinner in church.

Her gaze bores into me, sharp and assessing. Then, slow as molasses, she raises a hand. Crooks a finger, beckoning.

"Uh, Edison," I interrupt his chatter. "I reckon your boss wants a word."

"Oh!" He blinks, following my stare. "Right. Yes. We best head in." He sets off at a trot, leaving me to follow.

Edison picks his way carefully between the chive sprouts. Inside, the house is too warm and close, packed with too many bodies.

Edison leads me through the house, back to the foyer, then up the grand staircase. The plush runner muffles our steps. We pass door after closed door till he stops at one at the end and raps quick and sharp.

"Enter," comes the crisp reply.

He swings the door wide, gesturing me in. The room's all lace and pink velvet, a fancy parlor turned war room. And there, in the center, sits Commander Van Lew on a rose embroidered settee. An orderly stack of documents occupies the low table in front of her, next to a half empty coffee cup.

I snatch my hat off my head and straighten my posture. I feel like a cadet about to be disciplined.

Twenty years my senior, Van Lew is a true legend, the most successful Union agent of the war. Operating out of her Richmond mansion, she ran her own spy network, sending critical intelligence to the Union, all while providing food and succor to inmates at the infamous Libby prison.

But Van Lew vehemently disagreed with Alan's decision to keep my involvement in Baker's assassination a secret, let alone letting me go free after. She believed power like mine needed hands-on management.

"Agent Colt," she says, not rising, her gaze crawling over me. "Mrs. McClellan. Or do you prefer Kelly, still?" Her voice is Virginia-sweet, sharp as a bayonet.

I incline my head, jaw tight. "McClellan's fine, ma'am."

"Of course." She gestures to the settee across from her. A command, not an invitation. Edison and I perch like wary sparrows.

My Reb ghosts in and makes himself comfortable right next to the commander on the settee. He pulls out a string and seems intent on a game of cat's cradle.

"You have accepted agent Colt's offer to assist with our Las Vegas situation?" she says, lacing her fingers. The Confederate drops his game to watch her intently.

"I'm considering it," I allow. "If the money's right."

Her lips twitch. Amusement or annoyance, hard to say. "The BMI is prepared to be quite generous. Shall we say, 200 dollars a day?"

I lean back and cross my ankles slowly and deliberately. "Edison here said 225 dollars. Each. For me and my partner."

Her brows lift. "Partner?"

"Morgan Jackson, ma'am," Edison pipes up. "Mick—er, Mrs. McClellan says she can bring him in."

"Can she now?" Van Lew's eyes cut to me, frosty. "And what makes you think the BMI needs the assistance of yet another...independent contractor?"

I meet her gaze squarely. "Way I hear it, BMI's spread thin as a flattened penny, what with this Thatcher business. Seems to me you could use all the expert help you can get."

We stare each other down, the air crackling. I'm keenly aware of Edison fidgeting beside me, but I don't break eye contact. I've faced down worse than Elizabeth Van Lew.

She sighs and drops her gaze to smooth a nonexistent wrinkle in her skirt. "Very well, 225 dollars per day, for each of you, assuming you bring actionable intelligence. No rumormongering, proof positive there's a Big Magic practitioner operating in Vegas. But, Miss McClellan..." She looks up, eyes glinting. "I trust you understand the gravity of this situation. The necessity for discretion and restraint?"

My hands clench on my hat in my lap. It's not a question, it's a warning. A reminder of my history, the blood, and betrayal. The parts of myself I've tried to bury.

"I ain't looking for trouble, Commander. Them days are long behind me."

"I certainly hope so. For all our sakes." She stands. "Well then. It seems you and Agent Colt have much to prepare. I won't keep you."

A dismissal, clear as a slap. I stand, Edison scrambling up beside me. The confederate puts his string away but remains seated.

"Pleasure as always, Commander," I say, tipping my hat before setting it back on my head.

She doesn't smile. "The pleasure is all mine, I'm sure. Oh, and Miss McClellan?" She waits till I meet her eyes. "Do remember, the BMI deals quite harshly with those who...overstep."

My stomach drops.

"Like that poor bastard in Cumberland," the Confederate says, examining his translucent fingernails. "What was his name? Willoughby? Necromancer fella. Heard they kept him in a box so small he couldn't stand nor lie down. For years."

My skin goes cold. Van Lew can't see the Reb, but her eyes narrow as if she can read my thoughts.

"I appreciate the opportunity, Commander," I say, forcing steadiness into my voice. "But I need to consider all angles before committing."

Van Lew's smile doesn't reach her eyes. "Of course. But don't consider too long. The clock is ticking."

Outside, Edison follows me into the yard. "You and your partner meet me at the Purgatoire crossing, day after next?" Edison says, determinedly chipper.

I look at him, this bright-eyed boy so eager to prove himself. To make his mark on the world. I know, sudden and certain as a bullet to the brain, that I can't do this. Can't let the BMI sink their claws in me again, no matter how good the money.

"Edison," I say, slow and careful. "I appreciate the offer. Truly. But I'm afraid I gotta decline."

He opens his mouth, closes it. Frustration rolls off him. "Is it the money? I can talk to the commander, try to get you more."

I bark a laugh, short and harsh. "It ain't about the money. Well, not just about the money." I take off my hat and run a hand through my hair.

"But your powers, your experience—"

"Are a curse," I snap. "A damn curse that's brought me nothing but misery. You seem like a good kid, Edison. You got a bright future ahead of you. Don't let the BMI twist you up like they did me."

His shoulders slump, the fight draining out of him. "So that's it then? You're just gonna walk away?"

I turn to go. Each step heavy, weighted with regret and relief in equal measure.

"Coward," the Reb hisses in my ear, his uniform fluttering despite the lack of wind. "You're running again."

I ignore him, jaw clenched.

"That boy's gonna die," the Reb drawls. "Green as spring grass, facing something he don't understand."

"Not my problem," I mutter.

"Sure it ain't." His laugh is hollow.

He fades as I reach the street.

"Wait!" Edison calls. "I'm gonna wait for you at the ford until nine a.m., day after tomorrow."

I don't look back, just raise a hand in acknowledgment. Idiot child.

Then I'm walking, striding, damn near running. I don't stop till I'm back at Robert's, panting like I ran from the devil himself.

Maybe I did. Maybe the devil's inside me and always has been.

✦————•••————✦

Robert looks up when I burst through his office door, brows raised. "Well, that was quick. How'd it go?"

"It didn't," I growl. "I turned 'em down. Told that kid Edison to stick his job where the sun don't shine."

"You what?" Robert sputters, half-rising from his chair. "But the money—"

"Ain't worth it." I cross my arms. "Not for what they're asking."

He stares at me, and something flickers across his face. Too much concern, too quick. "Mary Catherine, this could've solved everything. Your family—"

"Since when are you so keen on me working for the BMI?" I step closer to his desk. "Thought you knew better than to trust those bastards."

Robert spreads his hands. "I just hate to see you struggling, is all. You got a family to support, a homestead to save—"

"The BMI don't help people like me, Robert. They use us up and spit us out." I watch his eyes. "So why are you pushing this?"

He's quiet for a long moment. Then he reaches under his desk and pulls out a ledger. Flips it open to a marked page. "Got a wire from a contact down in Las Vegas. Said a bunch more people have died than the ones reported to the BMI."

My pulse quickens. "Hold up. Edison made it sound like they weren't even sure this was magical business. Van Lew acted like it was routine." I lean on his desk. "Now you're telling me you got sources confirming deaths the BMI don't even know about?"

Robert shifts in his chair, just slightly. Most folks wouldn't notice, but I've known him too long, played too many hands of cards together. "Information has a way of finding its way to different people at different times."

"Or someone's playing games." I straighten. "The BMI, you, or both. What's your stake in this, Robert? Really?"

He meets my eyes, and for once there's no charm in them. Just something hard and urgent. "The deaths down in Las Vegas...they're all women. Prostitutes. Nobody's going to care enough to dig deeper."

"What kind of deaths?" My voice comes out rough. Women, it's always women.

"That's just it." Robert taps the ledger. "Nobody knows. They just...waste away. Like something's eating them from the inside."

Cold spreads through my chest. I've seen this before. Felt it.

The twisted purple energy in that dying pig. The way its life force leaked out like water through cupped hands.

"Twisted animus," I whisper.

Robert leans forward. "You've seen this before."

I think of Chickamauga. The Chicago fire. Other things I don't let myself remember. Big Magic leaves scars on the world that don't heal right. And when someone starts stealing the very essence of life itself...

My hands are shaking. I grip the edge of his desk.

"How many magic users can do what you do?" Robert presses. "How many in all the world can see what you see, understand what's really happening? This is happening right in your backyard. If not you, who?"

"I need to think." I push away from the desk. "Need to talk it over with Julianna and Gudrun."

"Don't think too long." His voice follows me to the door. "The BMI's going in there, with or without you. And if you're not there to watch his back..." He pauses. "I fear for what might happen to that boy."

I stop with my hand on the doorframe. Think of Edison's eager face.

"I hear you," I say quietly.

Then I'm out the door, into the spring wind. It cuts right through my coat, cold and sharp.

Nestor is waiting with Sampson, buckboard loaded with the hog feed. I grab the reins, swing myself up, and set off for home at a bruising pace.

Dead women nobody cares about. My pigs dying. Something eating life itself.

And Robert Tallmadge, my oldest friend in Trinidad, pushing me toward the BMI with a ledger full of secrets he shouldn't have.

I have a choice to make, a path to choose.

But the truth is, somewhere between Robert's office and the edge of town, I already know what that choice will be.

Chapter Six

When I got home yesterday afternoon, the family was itching for gossip from Robert. I delivered the disappointing news that he couldn't shed any light on the malaise. I smoothed Julianna's worries about folks asking for Mick, just told her a half-truth about Pete's nephew wanting to look me up. I kept my mouth shut about Edison's offer. Had to sort it out in my own head before I dumped it on the family.

I tossed and turned all night, a nagging feeling eating at me that the clock was ticking. Robert's Vegas tip—if it wasn't just hot air—weighed my thinking. Like I could even be the gunslinging Gleaner that kid asked for, even if I said yes.

The morning started out well enough. The wind had eased and bright sunshine promised a respite from the chill. Then Ylva and me went to feed the animals and found two more pigs down. Got one back on its feet, but the other one, one of our breeding sows, was done for.

Standing over that spent sow, I know I'm out of time for dithering. We need money, and we need it soon.

That's how I end up in the clearing behind the cabin once Gudrun and Julianna leave to take the dead pig to Elsbeth's for butchering. If I'm riding south into trouble, I need to know if this old body can still back my mouth up.

I exhale slow, relaxing my shoulders as I sight down the barrel of my old service revolver at the Arbuckles' coffee can propped on a rock twenty-five feet away. It's heavier than I remember. The scent of lamb tallow from the lubricant makes my nose twitch. I ease my finger onto the trigger and fire.

The barrel jumps. My shot goes wild, nowhere near the can. Behind me, Ylva giggles from her patch of shade by the cabin.

"Quiet, you," I hiss, more embarrassed than mad. I take a deep breath and fire off two more, both lost in the scrub.

"Are you sure you know what you're doing, Auntie? Momma says we can't afford to waste bullets."

Her words sting more than the recoil.

"Of course I do," I snap. "I've shot plenty of things before."

Ylva squints at me, unconvinced. "Really? I've never seen you shoot anything. You don't even kill the pigs. You always get Quincy to do it."

I'm standing here with a revolver in my hand. A revolver is for killing.

My hand drops. Chagrin pricks under my skin. In her lifetime, I've avoided firearms and slaughter both.

I roll my head, easing the tension cording up my neck then line up the target and it clicks, the moment knowing this shot will be true.

My grayback coalesces behind the can, grinning maliciously. "You've gone soft, Mick," he taunts as a bloody hole blooms in his chest. "Lost your touch."

What that hole means, what comes after pulling the trigger, hits me all at once. The ground heaves under my boots like a ship deck.

The next thing I know, I'm flat on my back, staring up into Ylva's concerned face, hair haloed by the bright sky.

"Are you okay?" she exclaims. "Should I get Momma?"

"No." My voice comes out thin. I drag in a breath. "Do not tell your mother anything about this."

Ylva's brow furrows. "Which one?"

"Either. Both." I slowly sit up, pressing my right palm to my clammy forehead. The sick vertigo subsides to a dull throb behind my eyes. "Especially not Julianna. She'll skin me alive."

"Why?" Ylva plops down beside me in the scrubby grass. "What happened? One minute you were staring at that can, and the next minute you just...fell over. Was it the vapors? Momma said fine ladies often get the vapors."

I huff out a laugh. "No. Women in our family do not get the vapors." The Johnny Reb cackles maniacally from behind Ylva.

She considers that, then nods solemnly. "Good."

I grunt, let her tug me the rest of the way to my feet. My legs feel rubbery but they hold. Definitely not the vapors. I let myself remember how easy it was

"I'm doing this," I say, more to myself than her. Standing, I clear my mind of visions of dead men. The revolver slides smoothly from the holster and I fire off three shots. Fast and clean. The damn shade dissipates when the can flies through his belly. Ylva whoops.

"There," I say, a little breathless. "Still works."

Ylva comes to stand beside me, chewing on a piece of oat straw. "Did you kill people?" she asks.

"What?" The question hits like a thrown rock. I look down at her serious little face, trying to decide how much truth an eight-year-old ought to carry.

"In the war," she clarifies, unbothered. "Momma says you were very important, even though you're a woman. She says all our family believed in Mr. Lincoln." She tilts her head. "Did you hurt people?"

For a long moment, I can't find my voice. Old memories crowd in: the tang of powder, the slick of blood under my boots, men's eyes going glassy as the Gleaner opened wide. My hands shake like I'm ninety.

"Yes," I say finally, hoarse. "I hurt people, Ylva."

She slips her small hand into mine and squeezes. "Was it because you believed in the Union?"

The simple faith in her voice twists something in me. I pull her in against my side for a quick hug.

"You're absolutely right, my little wolf cub," I say. "I fought because I believed the Union needed to hold. Because I believed Mr. Lincoln was worth following. And because when you can do something to help, sometimes you have to, even when it's dangerous."

I don't explain how idealism soured into hunger for the rush, how I slid from righteous killing into something meaner. She doesn't need that ghost yet.

Ylva leans her head on my arm. "I don't think you should take a shooting job," she says softly.

I sigh, watching the breeze stir the scrub. "We need money," I admit. "Doing some work for old friends might help us get through the year. Maybe even start over somewhere better. Somewhere like San Francisco."

Her fingers tighten. "But what if you get hurt? I don't want you to go."

"Nothing's decided yet," I say. "I promise I'll be careful. And I won't make any choice that hurts our family." The words come quicker when I see the worry in her eyes. "You are the most important thing, always. If going seems too risky, if you and your moms truly don't want me to, then I'll stay. I promise."

She brightens, though some of the fear lingers. "You pinkie-swear?" She sticks out the littlest finger.

I laugh and hook it with mine. "I pinkie-swear. No choice without your blessing."

She grins, gap where she lost her tooth showing. For a moment—with the sun catching in her braids and a smear of dirt on her cheek—she looks so much like Julianna at that age my throat goes tight.

"I'm gonna have to talk to them both tonight," I say. "Your moms. Tell them about the job. See what they think."

"Will we still have biscuits?" Ylva asks, transparent as glass.

"We got just enough flour for a batch," I say. "We'll make 'em special. How about you help me fetch water and I'll see what I can do?" I slide the gun into its holster and hold my right hand out to her.

She grins. "Race you to the pump!"

She takes off at a sprint, skirts flying. I follow slower, the weight of decision settling back on my shoulders. Guns might not be enough. Magic might not be enough. But sitting on my hands while my family starves sure as hell isn't an option.

Tonight, I'll have to convince Julianna that Edison's job offer is the best bad chance we've got. And I'll have to do it without promising myself I can keep both hands clean.

Chapter Seven

"You go clean the chicken coop, please," I say to Ylva. She nods and heads out, no complaints. We had finished dinner and it was time to face the music, tell Julianna and Gudrun my plans before we all got pulled into the afternoon's chores. I sit facing them across our family table.

No use dancing around the subject.

"I didn't tell you everything that happened at Robert's. While I was there, I was presented an opportunity that could solve our money troubles," I say. Gudrun eyes me skeptically. The staccato tap of her boot against the table leg is distracting.

Taking a deep breath and avoiding Julianna's eyes, I relay the details of young Mr. Colt's offer, emphasizing the fee and the imperative to investigate an innocent woman's death. I don't mention Robert's assertion suggesting multiple victims and a power similar to mine or Edison's youth and inexperience. Gudrun's tapping stops halfway through.

Julianna blanches and leans forward. "No, Mary Catherine, you can't work for the BMI. We can find a different remedy."

Gudrun chews her wind-chapped lips. She looks from me back to Julianna. "Julianna, slow down. I think we should consider this. Money will keep the wolves from our door."

I reach across the table for Julianna's hand. "Jules, money aside, this is a chance for me to do some good in the world. They want me because I am one of the only experts in this kind of magic. They want my knowledge, not my power."

Julianna rolls her eyes.

"I agree with Mick. That poor girl deserves justice," Gudrun murmurs.

Glaring at Gudrun, Julianna shakes her hand free of mine. "Then let someone else deliver it." She shoves her chair back, stands, and retreats to face us from the fireplace. "There's no reason it has to be Mary Catherine. Sounds to me like the BMI has it well in hand."

Gudrun joins Julianna and wraps an arm around her waist. "I know the thought of Mary Catherine in danger frightens you. But it's past time to acknowledge the moment for half-measures has passed." She spears me with her intense blue eyes. "This contract may be our miracle."

Julianna shrugs off Gudrun's arm. Coming from Julianna, it's like a slap. "You are my partner, and I love you, but you don't understand my sister. She WANTS to go off and have an adventure. She's done this since we were children—make people believe her self-serving choices were for the greater good." She sneers, "They're not. This decision is for her. An excuse to start Gleaning."

Julianna knows me so well. I want to be close to the action. I want to understand what happened in Las Vegas and if there is another magic user with power like mine. But maybe I really can do some good, maybe start to make up for my past. "Jules, I share your fears. Sometimes I doubt the strength of my wherewithal to resist temptation. But I promise I will not lose myself. Providing for this family may mean getting my hands dirty, just this once."

"I thought trying your power on the pig was 'just once,'" Julianna spat, "so now it's just twice?" Ignoring us both, gazing through Caleb's glass window, arms wrapped around her slender frame, I can see her jaw clenching.

Gudrun's brow furrows, settling hands on generous hips, "Wife, Mary Catherine is a woman grown. She is neither a fresh cadet facing her first battle nor a victim of battlefield neurosis any longer. You need to trust her to govern herself. The livestock fails no matter what I try. Soon we will have naught left to sell. Even if the summer is kind, the crops from the kitchen garden will not be enough to fill our mouths come winter. "

I glance at Julianna. Her eyes shutter at this harsh truth. Gudrun gentles her tone but drives the point home. "Do not discard this opportunity. We are a single hailstorm from complete ruin."

I read unhappy acceptance in Julianna's face. After a pause, I ask, "Then it's decided?"

Julianna closes her eyes, releasing a shuddering breath. She's always been the pragmatic one, under her lady manners. At length, she straightens her back, eyes downcast, and turns to me. "Forgive my harsh words. You face impossible choices for all our sakes. But the thought of you becoming that thing..." She trails off, blinking back tears.

I stand and close the distance between us. "There is nothing to forgive. You're right. I do want to take this job, as much for myself as for the chop." I lay a hand on her shoulder. "But I can do this, Jules." Smiling, I offer an olive branch. "I got leave to invite Morgan to accompany me."

Her face lightens. "If you can convince Mr. Jackson to ride with you, his level head will do you good." She smiles. "That would ease my mind considerably."

"And my sister Vilde's in Vegas," Gudrun offers. "She's the business manager and lady's maid to the star. She'll be able to give you a hand."

Julianna takes her hand and squeezes in thanks.

"I'll look her up first thing," I say. "I'd like to get the lay of the land from someone on the inside, without a BMI agenda."

Gudrun nods. "Vilde Swenson, at the Imperial. Should be easy to find her."

I'm jolted. Gudrun's sister is working at the same saloon where the murder occurred? But she didn't mention it to Gudrun. Maybe Vilde's afraid of worrying her.

Julianna releases Gudrun's hand and starts clearing the dinner plates left on the table. "When do you have to head out? I could make you some Johnny cakes for the road."

"I need to leave now, as soon as possible, to get to Morgan's before sunset. I'm supposed to meet the agent at the Purgatoire Ford tomorrow morning."

Julianna pauses to glare at me. "So, no Johnny cakes then. Fine, Mary Catherine." She looks disappointed.

I kiss her cheek. "I'll be home by Easter Sunday. Don't fret 'bout provisions, Jules. I'll just grab a can of tomatoes and some cornmeal. Plenty of places for grub along the way and the BMI is covering expenses. I'm gonna visit Caleb before I tack up Sampson. Need to be on the trail before two."

"You best get to it then," Gudrun says. "I'll help with the dishes. I've got a batch of worming tonic to cook."

I thank her and head outside to say goodbye.

Standing in the scrub grass, near the simple wooden marker over Caleb's grave, I release a shuddering sigh. I trace the letters of his name in the graying oak. First thing I'll do when I get home is buy a stone marker.

I speak as though he can hear, but I know Caleb didn't linger. His shade will never haunt me. I didn't ride his death. He went alone into the dark. "I promised you to put the bad magic away. I wanted the homestead to be a new start, a way to forget my past mistakes. But I struggle without you. This was your dream. I believed with my whole heart it would become mine."

Stroking the grave marker, I try to explain what's in my heart. "I need to move forward. Promises to a dead man can't keep me in a hole forever. You didn't want me to lie down and die amongst the pigs. It doesn't have to be like before."

The wind gusts suddenly, and I behold my Reb soldier's shade standing solemn behind Caleb's marker. His muted grays remind me of battles where I first unlocked my gifts, riding deaths, arbitrary as cannon fodder.

The soldier's empty eyes meet mine. "Can you deny yourself, Mick? Death grants you power. You refuse his gift?" His whisper echoes in my head.

I raise a hand to still his voice. "Gifts come with a cost. I'm done payin'."

He dissipates in the breeze. He knew me in the beginning, saw me unleashed amid carnage. Unbound, I reveled in the thrill... Staring at Caleb's weathered marker, I can't ignore the ember of power smoldering inside me.

I lay my hand on the pale oak. "I'm not gonna lose my way again..."

The ember of power smolders inside me, familiar and demanding. BMI money will save the farm, and hunting a killer feels righteous enough. If the Reb speaks the truth, my powers are as innate as the seasons.

I turn toward the cabin, wondering if my choice is truly about my family's survival—or if I'm just fleeing widowhood's bleak reality.

Chapter Eight

I NEEDED TO CONVINCE Morgan to come with me to Las Vegas, but first I needed to convince Sampson to get me there. Sampson wanted none of it.

It was a promising start. He nickered softly and came to the corral fence as soon as I called, eager for a head scratch or treat. But as soon as I slipped the halter over his head, his ears went back and his head went up and he planted his feet in the mud.

"For heaven's sake, Sampson, this will be fun." I tug on the lead and try to maneuver him out the gate. This is our game. I want him to do something and he shows me he would prefer not. He'll cheerfully comply after running the gamut of pets, treats, scolding, and exasperation. It's mostly stuff and nonsense. "Hey," I scold as he narrowly misses my foot when he shoulders his way through.

The mules, Sally and Bert, watch disdainfully from across the corral.

I tie Samson to a ring on the side of the barn. He worries the knot idly with his teeth, picking it up and dropping it to make a knocking sound. I select a currycomb and, starting up behind his ears, work my way across his body. I work in small circles, massaging every bit of him as he relaxes, bobbing his lower lip in rhythm. Pulling a hoof pick from my back pocket I start the Sisyphean task of cleaning his feet. Mud will pack back into his hooves as soon as we hit the road.

Shoes for Sampson are a luxury that will end if we don't get our finances straightened out. Gudrun keeps the mules' hoofs trimmed and filed on the regular. She can nail on a pre-made barrel shoe if needed, but as a rule, I keep Sampson's feet professionally shod from spring through fall when he's working.

I get the saddle and saddle blanket off the rail. It's custom-made specially for him and me. He's slab sided and high-withered with long legs; looks more like a racehorse than a cow pony. I found Sampson in Kentucky. He cost me a quarter of my separation pay after the war. He's a handful but ridiculously brave, with enough heart to carry me through the proverbial flood.

Sampson dances sideways like the saddle is an unwelcome surprise. "Quit," I say, reaching for the back cinch. Damn it, he is gonna act a fool. I dread the ride ahead. Grimacing, I slap his neck affectionately. "You and I are too old for these hijinks. If I eat gravel this mornin', your next stop is the knackers."

I secure my war bag. It holds a change of clothes, full ammo box, extra gunpowder and papers, playing cards, bill of sale for Sampson, and a simple garrote—because you never know. I slide the shotgun into its boot on the right side of the saddle. My service revolver is belted around my waist. Panniers hold my grub and oats to supplement whatever Sampson can forage on the road. I reckon we'll be gone no more than fourteen days, on the outside.

Sampson didn't make a fuss about the bridle at all. Maybe yesterday's trip to town burned off a little fire? Or he's plotting.

One more pass to check the cinch and a quick prayer. "Please, Lord." I put my left foot in the stirrup and heave myself up. Sampson jumps right. Damn horse. I swing my right leg up and over to find the stirrup quickly. The watermelon under the saddle tells me trouble's brewing.

"All right, buddy," I murmur hopefully, projecting confidence, "let's get cracking." I nudge him, hoping we can walk this out.

God bless Ylva, who chooses that moment to burst out of the cabin, door slamming with a bang. She's shouting her head off, waving something that flies in the breeze. "Wait, wait! You forgot your scarf."

This is horrifying to Sampson's equine sensibilities. Down goes his head and he's crow hopping around the yard. I keep my seat until the sneaky asshole drops his shoulder and bucks for real; both hind feet shoot for the sky. I fly right over his head, landing face down in the mud.

Ylva stands, clutching my scarf, shaking with horror, or more likely a giggle. I can't tell which. "I guess Sampson don't want to be a saddle horse today?"

I correct her from the ground, "Sampson *doesn't* want to be a saddle horse." Covered in mud from my knees to my face, I feel the wet starting to soak through my clothes. Good golly, that hurt.

"Are you okay? Should I get Ma?" Ylva approaches me, Samson trailing behind her like a puppy. Idiot horse seems surprised to see me on the ground. With his ears pricked forward, eyes bright, I would swear he chuckled.

"No need. Get the currycomb and help me scrape the muck off." The last thing I need is my sister's disapproving gaze. Damn horse should be tired at his age.

"Mama J says you weren't always kind to animals and children, and Sampson is your just reward."

"Sampson is probably punishment and more reward than I deserve." Sighing heavily, I gain my feet. "I'd turn him into glue, except he'd probably refuse to stick."

Ylva helps me clean up and I am finally on the road to Morgan's homestead.

⁂

Three hours later, I'm closing in on Morgan's ranch. My body is screaming. My back aches, my thighs hurt, and even Sampson seems wrung out. I haven't spent much time in the saddle the last few months. How the hell am I going to ride days on a job when a few hours in the saddle has about done me in?

Maybe the warmer weather will hold, but March can be a fickle bitch. I can't count on her promise of spring.

Must be near five before I glimpse Morgan's low-slung adobe through the scrub. Corral in front near the pump and livestock trough. One of the reasons Morgan bought this spread was because of the well. He bought the claim outright from some Germans who gave up after drought took their first crop.

Morgan is nowhere in sight, but his wife, Maria Bylilly, is at the corral, slinging hay to four horses. Maria's long braid swings with her movement. She glances my way. I nod and am greeted with a scowl.

She turns back to the horses. Maria never liked me much. Morgan met her the last year we rode together and after the Kansas City crash he decided that she was the one for him. It was harder to convince Maria that he was the one for her, but eventually, Morgan won her over. He swore she kept him on the straight and narrow.

"Good afternoon, Maria," I greet her as I pull Sampson to a stop a few yards away.

She pauses in her labor and faces me. "Morgan's not here. You should ride on." And then goes back to feeding the horses. I know the fat bay mare is Morgan's favorite.

"Come on," I cajole, "I came all this way. And I see Muneca in the corral," pointing at the bay.

Maria continues pushing hay through the corral fence as though I ceased to exist.

Sighing, I dismount. My thighs and hips scream at me as though we galloped the whole way here instead of a leisurely jog on flat ground. I drape my arm around Sampson's neck. "How about if I wait for him, then?"

"Suit yourself." She marches into the house, letting the Sears and Roebuck screen door slam behind her. I don't blame Maria for her low opinion of me.

Morgan and I met Maria at the market in Taos. She was selling vegetables in the square. He and I stumbled out of the Fancy Cat saloon after an all-nighter and stumbled into her stall, sending calabacitas and beans rolling. After jawing at us to within an inch of our lives, Morgan convinced her to come back into the saloon with us and have a beer. I will never forget drinking, playing cards, and laughing that morning away. It seemed we would all be friends.

Then I claimed the pot on a royal spade flush and Maria turned to him and said, "Leave this one," pointing at me. "Your death rides her shoulder."

Morgan laughed like his head would come off and teased that she was a sore loser. Maria claimed to have seen his doom in my cards. I don't *think* I believe her.

Shaking off the memory, I lead Sampson to the trough, loosen the cinch, and let him get a drink. I slip off his bridle and tie him to the hitching rail near the corral by his halter. He can court Muneca to pass the time. I take a seat on the porch steps to wait. Maria and I have engaged in this dance before.

Hearing Morgan's raised voice behind me, I turn to see his lanky frame coming out the door. "You old cayuse!" Morgan exclaims. "Why are you sitting out here all hang dog?"

I scramble to my feet, feeling the pull of every tired muscle. I try to smile at him, but it comes out as a wince.

"You're getting old, Mick. You saddle sore? After that itty-bitty ride here?"

I haven't seen Morgan since before Christmas. I look him up and down. "What's that on your face? Did a muskrat lose its way and die?" I tease. His hair is a little grayer and a little thinner, his lined forehead a little higher than the last I saw him. He still has the same twinkle in his merry brown eyes.

"Hey now, Maria likes it just fine," he retorts, stroking the new mustache. "Looks like you lost a few pounds, Mick. You're getting scrawny. Isn't your sister feeding you?"

"Makes it easier on Sampson." I climb the porch steps and pull him into a hug. I feel his sinewy strength beneath his spare frame. "It's good to see you."

He claps me on the back and steps away. "All right now, come inside and sit. Maria will fix us supper."

"You don't think she'll poison me?"

"From the looks of you, it wouldn't take much."

"Flatterer. You always know what to say to make me feel like a delicate lady."

"Lady?" He chuckles. "I can hardly think of you as married and grown, certainly not a lady."

Morgan's been my friend and protector since the war. Ten years my senior, he and I served together during the last year of the conflict. Afterward, I convinced him to join Lafayette's organization with me. I had thought I was doing him a favor, but looking back, I know I did it so I would have someone I could trust at my back.

"If we're gonna set and chew the dog, let me get Sampson taken care of. Can I put him in the corral?"

"Muneca would enjoy a gentleman caller." He grins. "Come on through when you're done. I'll see if I can get her sorted," he says, gesturing toward the door. "Seeing you puts her all on end."

I return to Sampson and pull off the tack and saddlebags and take them up to the porch. I can hear the snip-snap of Maria and Morgan arguing. I give Sampson another drink before turning him loose in the corral with Morgan's mares. I grab another few leaves of hay from Maria's wheelbarrow and toss them over the fence to help grease the equine social wheels. Watching the horses for a few moments, it becomes clear the mares are enjoying getting reacquainted, with Sampson at the center of everyone's attention. Just as he likes it.

Hat in hand, I follow Morgan's path into the house and admire how much more civilized the adobe is than our stone and mud cabin. The kitchen is separated from the parlor by a wall and a wide arched doorway. Bedrooms branch off from a main hallway. All the floors are Saltillo tile instead of hard-packed dirt. I walk through the parlor to the spacious kitchen. A large oak table surrounded by six chairs fills the room.

Maria is stirring a pot of something bubbling away on the coal stove. It smells delicious. She glances at me and then dishes up two bowls of lamb with red chili and slaps them down on the table, followed by a bowl of tortillas wrapped in a towel. Two spoons follow, skittering across the table. Casting Morgan a hurt look, she stomps out the door, her long skirt swishing. While I remove my gun belt, Morgan eyes me speculatively.

"She all right?" I ask, hanging my belt and hat on the hooks on the wall. I cross to the table and sit catty-corner from Morgan.

"She'll be fine, but what's with the sharps?" he asks, looking at my gun belt. "You're all tricked out like you're headed for a long ride." Long ride's what we used to call jobs for Lafayette.

"Well, now I suppose in a way I am. I'm joining up with a dude named Edison Colt, working a job in Las Vegas, down in New Mexico territory."

"Protection for some snobbish merchant?" Morgan frumps, picking up his spoon. "Vegas is hopping with rich greenhorns since the train went through last year."

"No, nothing like that." I reach for a spoon. "This is an investigation. A couple of saddle tramps killed a local line girl."

"That's mighty sad." Morgan leans back in his chair, eyes narrowing. "You working with law enforcement then?"

"Well...actually, it's a BMI job."

Morgan's eyebrows climb almost to his hairline. "What the hell are you thinkin'? Don't you have the sense God gave that broom-tailed nag of yours?" He clanks his spoon down on the table. "Why would you get tangled up with them again?"

"Jaysus, Morgan, it's a short-term contract," I snap. "I'm not getting into bed with them. I'm working with Edison Colt, Pete Zigala's nephew. You remember Pete?"

"Of course I remember Pete. Tarnation, girl, I'm not the one spouting loco shit." He huffs. "Why?"

"Truth be told, I'm scuppered, almost down to the blanket." I play with my spoon, my cheeks burning. "Caleb left me pretty well set, but the last couple of seasons have been tough and this job pays real cash money."

My shoulders slump further. "We lost most of our market vegetables last summer, what with all the hail in July. We had savings. But then our pigs. Lost one in five since New Year's. They just keep failing. We're gonna be broke."

Morgan sits back and scowls slightly. "I thought Juliana's wife was good with that kind of thing...what's her name?"

"Gudrun," I reply. "She's at the end of her rope. Whatever it is, it ain't natural. Something's sucking the life right out of them."

Morgan's spoon freezes halfway to his mouth. "What do you mean 'not natural?'"

I stare into my bowl, avoiding his gaze. "The usual signs..."

"Mick." His voice carries that stern edge I know too well.

The silence stretches between us, heavy and accusing, until I crack. "I... uh... I sorta rode one of the pigs' deaths."

Morgan sets his spoon down with deliberate care. "You promised Juliana you wouldn't—" He stops himself, leans forward. "And you're certain? Your pigs are being magically assaulted?"

I nod grimly. "Something twisted the Animus. Never seen anything like it."

"Jesus, Mick." He frowns, mustache curling down to his chin. "You heard tell of anyone else having trouble with die-offs?"

"Not yet. No one in town, at least. Maria heard any rumblings 'bout death mages in the region?" Maria has a knack for knowing things, mystical and otherwise.

"Nope, and my woollies are doing just fine." Morgan and Maria run about 500 head of sheep and goats with her family.

He reaches for the bowl of warm tortillas. Peeling back the towel, he grabs one, dropping it beside his plate before handing the bowl to me. "This here stew is made with spring lamb. Have a taste."

I take a bite and moan. "Jiminy, that's good." Rich, fatty lamb braised in red chili bathes my mouth, so different cooking at my homestead. Neither Julianna nor I are a dab hand in the kitchen, relying on whatever pork bits and dry goods we have. It's supplemented from the garden in warm months. Gudrun sometimes offers reconstituted fish that I have yet to develop a taste for. Maria's cooking is a treat. I gotta convince Julianna to add chilis to our garden. I'll tell her they fight off scurvy.

We eat in silence, savoring the spicy stew, until Morgan asks, "Any chance someone's coming after you? If no one else in the area is losin' livestock, maybe it's a you problem. You weren't very popular back in the day."

I consider that for a moment, then say, "I left with my share of enemies, but why would someone target me and leave you alone?"

"Pshaw, no one remembers me. I was just the nice man with the horses. But you, everyone knew you. You were the only woman in Baker's ring. *You* were always the loudmouth—had to prove a point about the weaker sex, drinking, picking fights, couldn't let an insult go unchallenged." He pauses to take a bite, chewing slowly. "Your signature was all over the KC crash. If there was anyone left who cared, they'd come after you."

"Maybe so." I put my spoon back in the bowl. "But why a decade later, and why something so pissant? I don't see what anyone with that kind of power would gain murdering twenty pigs. And sure, it's a hardship for my family, but it doesn't seem like much of a revenge, all things considered."

"Aye, you're right. If they were coming for you, it would be more of a brouhaha than a few hogs."

I know he's right, but I can't shake the feeling my past is gaining on me. My grayback popping in for a visit, the pigs dying and then the BMI pulling me into their web feels like too much for coincidence.

Apparently following my train of thought, Morgan asks, "Why did the Beemers finger you for this contract? And why do they give two figs for a dead saloon girl? Seems below their notice."

I push the empty chili bowl away and bite my lip before answering, "Some Washington bigwig's son died after visiting a saloon in Georgetown. Appears to be a contagion curse moving through some of the high-end brothels. The BMI is throwing all their resources at that case, so they're short-handed." My throat feels suddenly tight. I avoid Morgan's eyes.

Morgan nods. "All right, and...?"

I rush ahead. "Two women were attacked in Vegas. The one who died, the agent on scene reported one or both of her attackers sucked the life right out of her. The other lady is damaged. She was a shifter. Lost the ability. BMI is concerned they got a bad actor using Big Magic."

"Hold on...sucked the life right out? Like your pigs? 'Cept this girl died fast instead of wasting slow."

"No, not the same...wait." Shit. How did I miss that? "Someone laying their hands on the girl and killing her is different than the power it would take to drain the pigs—over distance, over time. Can't be related. Besides, the Vegas thing might not even be mystical. Could just be hysterical reporting."

Morgan squeezes his eyes shut. "Jesus wept." He scrubs a hand over his stubbled chin. Eyebrows raised, he asks, "They want you to do what exactly?"

"I'm just gonna confirm the attack was magical. If it's mundane, it's out of the BMI's jurisdiction. They want me for my expertise on the subject. I'm one of the only living Mortis Vorators—"

"You're the only sane one," he interrupts.

I sigh. "Either way, I'm the only one in the area with Agency experience."

"At the end of the day, they don't give one wit for a dead bit of calico and a broken shifter. They're worried someone with your kind of power is acting outside of their control." He pushes his chair back, "I'm guessing you didn't swing by here just to say hello and eat some of Maria's cooking. You got another iron in the fire?" He eyes me suspiciously.

"Don't be coy." I grin at him. "You know perfectly well I want you to join up with me."

"Don't you think we are too old for these kinds of shenanigans? Leave it to young folk like this Colt kid."

"Oh, come on, we aren't old. We are in our prime. And think of those poor girls. We can get 'em justice—"

"How much they paying?" He cuts me off.

I smile. He's hooked. "Two hundred and twenty-five dollars per day, plus expenses. Expect ten days."

He whistles. "Decent bit of chop." His eyes dance around the room until they land on the Winchester rifle hanging over the door.

"Can you still shoot the spots off a die at a hundred paces? Or did your eyesight escort your hairline off the premises?" I tease.

"I see the way you are moving after your little trip over here. I wouldn't be casting stones if I were in your glasshouse, missy."

"Imagine," I cajole, "one last long ride. You and me doing some good in the world. A little freedom from the wife. And with Edison along, you have a brand-new audience for your tarradiddles."

Morgan looks thoughtful, and then clapping his hands, stands. "All right, we go, see if Bad Magic is the root, and let the authorities handle the rough stuff. Then we head home. No monkey business?" He stares hard at me, hands on hips.

"You mean my Gleaner?"

"Yeah, I do. You promise you aren't planning on jumping back into that mix? I don't want none of that kind of attention from people drawn to that malarkey. You're just there as an expert in the field, right?"

"You always came out fine where magic was concerned." My hands clench, but I pooh-pooh him.

"That wasn't any of my doing directly. That was luck." Morgan isn't magical, per se, but he has an odd knack that could send magic used against him off-kilter. The man can dance with disaster and end up leading the waltz.

"It's more than luck." I scoff, standing to help with cleanup. "But truly, I promise, no Gleaning. Won't need to, not if you're there with your Winchester."

Morgan starts clearing the table. "Yeah, fine, I'll hold you to that. When we heading out?"

"We gotta meet Edison by nine tomorrow at the Purgatoire Ford."

He pauses, looking toward the back of the house where Maria retreated.

"Why don't you let me finish cleaning up"—I volunteer—"and you go take care of personal business?"

He nods. "Yeah, I best get her sorted. Make sure her brother can help out while I'm away. You can bed down in the spare room."

I finish tidying the kitchen with a lighter heart. With Morgan at my back, everything is going to be just fine...right?

Chapter Nine

I WAKE IN THE gray light of dawn, momentarily disoriented. Memory rushes back—Morgan's agreement to join me on young Edison Colt's investigation. The thin mattress creaks as I stretch, assessing the aches from yesterday's ride. Not too stove up, I reckon, though my backside may have words with my saddle later.

Splashing water on my face from the washstand, I brace for the day ahead. Morgan's words from last night circle my mind like vultures. "Why do you want to get tangled up with the BMI again?" Fair question. I'm spouting loco shit. But the money, the pigs dying, the chance to do some good for once... I gotta try.

The scent of coffee lures me to the kitchen. Maria stands at the stove, stirring a pot of porridge. She acknowledges me with a curt nod, pouring a tin mug and sliding it across the table without a word. I murmur my thanks, wrapping my hands around its warmth.

Morgan stomps in from outside, shaking droplets of melted frost from his boots. "Mornin', ladies," he greets, snatching a mug for himself. "Mighty fine day for a ride into mayhem, eh, Mick?"

I snort. "Just another Sunday social."

Maria's spoon clangs against the pot, her silence pointed as a blade. Morgan sighs, slipping into a chair beside me. "Look, Mick, I gotta ask once more...you sure about this? Workin' for the BMI, pokin' dark magic?"

I stare into the black mirror of my coffee. Memories swirl in its depths—blood and gun smoke, the giddy rush of stolen Animus. "I ain't never gonna escape what I've done, Morgan.

Might as well put the skills to use. 'Sides, we need the money somethin' fierce."

He shakes his head. "Skills like yours, they got a way of hugging you tight, like a hangman's noose. I just don't want to see you swingin', is all."

I shrug, feigning a nonchalance I don't feel. "Dunno. Maybe. Untangling dark workings in Vegas might give me insight into my own troubles. And if someone's comin' for me..." I swallow. "Rather meet it head-on than wait to be bushwhacked."

He's silent for a long moment, assessing me. I hold myself still, resisting the urge to squirm under his scrutiny. Finally, he nods. "All right then. We ride together. But you promise me, Mick, any hint of magic messin' with your head, any hankerin' to tap that old wickedness, you come to me?"

I cough. "Yea. I promise."

Maria plunks two bowls of porridge before us, her dark eyes flash. "Crazy fools," she mutters, stalking off.

Morgan watches her go, a wistful smile playing about his mouth. "That woman's got more spine than you an' me combined." He tucks into his breakfast. "This kid we're meetin', Edison Colt, he worth his salt?"

I consider as I chew a mouthful of the bland mush. "Hard to say. Wet behind the ears, for sure. But he's part of Kate Warne's old squad, and Commander Van Lew is runnin' this show. They don't pick their ponies for prettiness."

"Van Lew?" Morgan's spoon pauses halfway to his mouth. "Thought that old battle axe woulda hung up her spying ways by now."

I huff a mirthless laugh. "Not before she sees me to the devil."

He eyes me, regret and anger mingling in his gaze. "She always was harder on you than the menfolk. Held you to a different standard."

"I gave her plenty of cause." The old shame licks at my skin. I push it down, focusing on the warm clay of my bowl, the solid planks of the table.

Morgan reaches over to pat my shoulder, quick and gruff. "All the more reason to step carefully here. Don't give Van Lew any cause to screw you over on account of old sins."

I nod, gaze fixed on the shadows playing across the tiled floor. We finish our meal in silence, each lost to our own ponderings.

Soon enough, it's time. Sampson's loaded up, stomping eagerly in the morning chill. I check and recheck my tack, my guns, stalling. Morgan waits patiently beside Muneca, reins looped loosely in one hand.

No more delaying. I swing onto Sampson's back, wincing at the pull in my thighs. Morgan mounts up lithely and easily beside me, damn him. I tip my hat to Maria, who's watching stonily from the porch.

"Ma'am," I offer. "I'll bring him back in one piece."

Her lips thin. "You won't darken my door again otherwise."

I sigh, gathering the reins. Morgan gives her a jaunty salute, his eyes soft. "Te amo, querida," he murmurs.

Then we're off, Sampson falling into a mile-eating trot as the little adobe shrinks behind.

⋄⊶——⊷⋄

The ride passes peaceably enough. We don't jaw much, just let the creak of leather and the thud of hooves fill the space. My mind drifts, sifting anxiously through the ways this scheme could go tits up.

Couple hours later and thankfully the weather holds, hinting at warmth. Sampson and Muneca trot along the trail leading to the river, ears pricked and eyes bright. The sun has thawed the frost so that the trail's slick with mud. Near the river bottom, cherimoya and scrub give way to more grass and cottonwood trees. I glimpse the early morning light glinting off the water and call back to Morgan, "He should be waiting on the other side."

Morgan interrupts his singing to reply, "Aye, yup." Once I convinced him to come, he embraced a venturesome spirit and has been serenading me with a blasted song about the educated Mary Ann all morning.

We come around a large boulder to the ford. I bring Sampson down to a walk. The bank is churned from hooves and legs—cattle tea. Ice sheets the puddles. Someone drove cattle through in the last day. They always leave a mark.

I settle deeper in the saddle and point Sampson across the river. A quick prayer and a gentle push with my heel to get him moving. Sampson's attitude toward water is notoriously unpredictable; he'll splash in a trough, he's been known to enjoy bath on a hot day, but I never know how a water crossing's gonna go. Some days he'll waltz through. Today is not one of those days.

Sampson creeps right up to the edge of the river, stops, puts his head down, and snorts. I feel him quivering beneath me like he expects an alligator to be waiting for him. Of course there are no alligators or horse-eating river beasties of any sort. He plants his hooves and refuses to budge, no matter how I chivvy him. Muneca moseys past us, plopping into the shallows calm as you please.

"We'll show him the way," Morgan calls over his shoulder.

"Much obliged," I respond. "Come on, Sampson, you don't want to be shown up by a lady, do you?" I remind myself to relax. Funny thing with horses, they sense your expectations. Pretend everything's just fine and sometimes they believe you.

Muneca blithely wades chest deep into the water. She pauses to drink and pats the current a couple of times with her chin to make a splash. No doubt deciding it's too cold to play, she hurries across, her tail dragging behind.

My big sissy is trembling like an aspen leaf. Kicking him again, Sampson takes a couple steps forward, then starts dancing left and right. Muneca's about halfway across. Sampson looks at her longingly.

"Come on, you yellow-bellied nag—" I'm cut off as Sampson launches himself into the river. In two splashing bounds, he's practically climbing Muneca's tail. My head snaps back with the leap, forward with the landing, slamming into Sampson's neck. I see stars and taste blood. The saddle horn punches me in the gut. I'm grateful I'm not taking a bath. Goddamn. I really oughta know better by now than to let this horse take me unawares.

Muneca lays her ears back at his ninny-headedness, threatening to kick his teeth in, clearly not appreciating being crowded by the big dummy.

Morgan soothes her and turns in the saddle. "You all right there, Mick? Reckon your technique could use some polish."

"Shut your gob afore I polish it for you."

I check my nose for blood and wipe my streaming eyes on my sleeve. Damn, I hate getting hit in the face. I spit pink into the churning water, glowering at Sampson's pin-pricked ears as he dances onto the far bank.

"So where is this partner of yours?" Morgan asks, scanning the brush. Even in early spring, the leafless branches are heavy on the river bottom. I can't see more than a few yards ahead.

"He said he would wait until nine. Let's head up the trail and see if we catch him."

Morgan and I follow the trail west, Sampson in front. A few yards in, we see the leftovers of a fresh campsite within a cottonwood stand. Morgan points at it and nods.

A sharp crack splits the quiet—BANG—followed by a flurry of wings as birds explode out of the brush ahead of us. A second shot rings out, thudding into the trail ahead. Something small and brown darts for cover.

"What the hell!" Morgan curses. He grabs his Winchester and we both roll off our horses and crouch in the long weeds. "Who's taking potshots?"

Two more shots ring out in rapid succession. Neither one particularity close to us or the horses. A third shot cracks, followed by a triumphant whoop.

"That ain't aimed at us," I murmur, peering through the brush. "Sounds like someone's huntin'."

"Don't matter. I don't appreciate bullets zitting anywhere 'round my person," he answers. "Trail's right here. River's right here. That fool could punch a hole clean through someone he never even saw."

The brush rustles ahead. I catch a flash of sorrel hide and the bob of a wide-brimmed hat.

"Hold," I whisper. "Someone's comin' out."

Edison Colt emerges from the trees, spectacles askew, both pistols in his hands. He's grinning like he's just won a prize at the fair.

"Damn quick little bastards," he mutters to himself. Then, louder: "Ha! Nearly had—oh!"

He freezes when he spots us.

"Well I'll be—?" He squints hard, leaning forward until his nose practically points at me. "Mrs. McClellan! I didn't reckon you'd be here so early."

I step out from the weeds with my hands visible, though my fingers hover near my gun belt. "Edison. You might try checkin' what's beyond your target next time."

He blinks, then flushes. "Rabbits," he explains, a little too eagerly. "Plumb thick along the river this mornin'. Thought I might scare one into supper."

Behind me, Morgan rises to his full height, Winchester leveled squarely at Edison's chest.

"You might also scare yourself into shootin' a man," Morgan says flatly. "Trail's ten paces from where you're firin'."

Edison finally notices the rifle. His eyes widen. Both Colts dip and wobble dangerously as he gestures.

"Oh! Sir—I—no offense meant. I was keepin' my fire downrange." He waves one pistol toward the brush, the other drifting far too close to his own boot. "Didn't see anyone else about."

"Put. Them. Away," Morgan says, each word landing heavy. "Before you shoot your foot or mine."

Edison fumbles, cheeks blazing red, nearly drops one Colt before managing to jam both into their holsters.

Morgan snorts and lowers the Winchester. "This is Pete's nephew, for real?"

"Hey now. We're all friends here," I say, stepping forward with my hands raised between them. "Yes, Morgan Jackson, this is Edison Colt, the Bureau's bright new hope.".

Edison's face cracks into a wide grin. Like a wind-up toy, he bounds across the space separating us, his mouth running faster than his feet.

"The Morgan Jackson? I am right pleased to meet you, sir!" He skids to a halt before us, nearly tripping over his own boots. "Uncle Pete admired you and your shootin' skills something fierce. Said you could shoot the eye out of a hawk clean through a gale" Edison points excitedly at Morgan's rifle. "Is that the Winchester Pete was so envious of?"

Morgan studies him for a long beat, eyes sharp, then lowers the barrel. "It is."

Edison exhales in visible relief.

Oh me, this child is green as spring grass.

"Betwixt the two of us," I say, eyeballing Edison, "we're going to need a sharpshooter." What was Van Lew thinking sending this greenhorn out alone?

"All right!" He grins again. "This is just like one of Pete's yarns. We have ourselves a storied gang!"

"This ain't no gang," I correct him. "Just a few folks getting together to right a wrong. Me and Morgan are gonna earn some tin, then we all go back to our regular lives."

"Fine, whatever you say, ma'am." Edison's still grinning.

"Now," Morgan continues, "I'm gonna need your solemn promise you won't go shootin' at anything you can't clearly see. That includes rabbits you ain't sure won't put a bullet somewhere foolish. Especially if that somewhere's me."

"Yes, sir," Edison says at once. "I promise." He thrusts out his hand. "Wholeheartedly."

Morgan takes it, grip firm. "No harm done," he says. "This time."

"That's good enough for me," I cut in, already turning back toward Sampson. "Let's vamoose before you decide to hunt squirrels."

Edison's fancy sorrel prances through the mud.

"That's a fine-looking little mare," Morgan says, leaning down from his saddle to run his calloused hand up the white blaze on her face. "What's her name?"

"Abigail." Edison straightens his spectacles and pats her neck with a lovesick sigh. "I named for my mam because she is tough and beautiful just like Mom."

Morgan and I roll our eyes at each other as we start down the trail. This child is still naming his horse after his mama?

"It's not like that," Edison corrects from behind us, having caught our exchange. He ducks under a low-hanging branch, tipping his hat off to one side. "My mam owns Calpurnia's. Finest watering hole on the San Francisco waterfront. Raised me and my sister right there among the sailors and stevedores."

A woman running a bar is pretty rare, much less near the Port of San Francisco. How is Edison so darned soft? I'll guarantee his mother ain't.

"Hold up," I say, twisting in my saddle to squint at Edison. "You're tellin' me your ma runs a saloon? On the Embarcadero?" I whistle low, startling a sparrow from a nearby bush. "That's a rough crowd for a passel of young'uns. Can't imagine it was easy, woman alone and all."

Edison adjusts his grip on the reins as Abigail picks her way around a fallen log. His face sobers. "No, ma'am. It wasn't. But my ma, she's tough as a two-bit steak. Had to be, after my pa lit out for the goldfields."

Morgan clucks to Muneca and moves ahead of us as the trail narrows between a rocky outcropping. Over his shoulder, Morgan grunts, "Sounds like a hell of a lady. But if you were raised in a San Francisco barroom, how'd you end up a BMI boy? Ain't a natural progression."

The trail widens again, sunlight dappling through the trees. "That's a bit of a yarn, sir. See, when I was about twelve, there was this yellow fever epidemic." He pauses to remove his hat and wipe sweat from his brow. "Ma got it in her head me and my sister had to get outta the city, away from the miasmas. So she packed us off to Uncle Pete and Aunt Conchita."

Morgan barks a laugh, the sound echoing off the rocks. "Mick and I thought Pete was crazy, running away to join a traveling show."

"It ain't just a road show. It's a genuine European style circus," Edison supplies, standing in his stirrups. "It was wondrous! Acrobats, wild animals, magic users of every stripe. That's where I first discovered my own, ah, peculiar talents."

I slow Sampson to fall back next to Edison's Abigail. "Talents, huh?"

The kid flushes, two spots of color on his freckled cheeks. He adjusts his glasses again, a nervous habit. "Of a kind. More of a knack I can read magical signatures, sorta decipher the intent of the spell, sometimes track it back to the caster. No Big Magic like your gift, Ms. McClellan."

"Gift?" Morgan snorts, leaning down to avoid a thorny branch. His voice carries on the breeze. "More like a damn curse. Power like hers, it ain't to be trifled with."

Edison frowns, eyes darting between us. "Anyhow," he continues, scratching Abigail's neck, "Aunt Conchita helped me enroll at the Boston Metaphysical Academy. To learn to put my knack to good use, protecting folks from things that go bump in the night."

"That's all well and good," I allow, shifting to relieve my muscle soreness. A jay scolds us from overhead. "But that don't explain how come you're out here with us, chasin' soul crafters and spirit botherers."

The kid ducks his head, abashed. "That's Uncle Pete's doing. He used to tell me stories, y'see. 'Bout his adventuring days. 'Bout the heroes he rode with." He darts a glance at me, shy and fierce all at once. "He told me about you, Ms. McClellan. Said you were the best Gleaner he'd ever seen, bar none."

I blink, nonplussed. It's been a long time since anyone spoke of me with anything close to reverence. Wariness, sure. Fear, often. But admiration? Respect? Nope.

"Pretty sure I am the only Gleaner he's ever seen," I say gruffly, nudging Sampson forward. "Pete always was silver-tongued. Can't believe half of what he says."

"I don't think he was exaggerating, ma'am." The kid's voice staunch as he urges Abigail to keep pace. His spectacles slip down his nose again, but he doesn't notice. "He said you were powerful and pragmatic, a killer when needed. And I aim to show you and Mr. Jackson and the whole damn Bureau that I'm ready to ride with the big guns. I can hold my own against any black magician or demon-raiser the frontier spits up."

Morgan, several yards ahead now, twists in his saddle. His eyebrow arches eloquently as our gazes meet. Muneca flicks her tail at a persistent fly. I give Morgan a minute shrug in return and make a mental note to set the record straight on some of Pete's taller tales. Let the boy see the hard truth behind the dime-novel shine.

But for now, I nod and give Edison a half-smile. "I thought I told you to call me Mick?"

The kid keeps yammering like a jaybird, peppering me with questions about Sampson's breeding and the finer points of quickdraw technique. I let him prattle, keeping a weather eye on the horizon.

I wonder, not for the first nor last time, what the hell I've gotten myself into. What dusty phantoms and bone-deep regrets I'm riding to meet.

I shove the doubts away and fix my gaze ahead. I got a job to do.

Chapter Ten

LORD LOVE A DUCK, Morgan has moved on to John Phillip Souza. Wasn't so bad when he was just whistling while he started the fire, but now he's belting out the chorus as I ease my aching body to the ground.

What is wrong with that man? We spent ten hours in the saddle today and it feels like twenty. My legs, derrière, and back scream with every movement. And there he is, all lah-de dah like it's all a frolic in the meadow.

We've made camp in a hollow off the trail and should reach Vegas the day after tomorrow. Only the thought of the paycheck soothes my screaming back.

"What's up with the sour puss, puss? You goin' soft on me?" Morgan asks, firelight casting his face in high relief.

"Why aren't you suffering? You've got at least ten years on me."

"Clean livin'." He grins. "Plus, I spend every seven days out of ten riding with my sheep while you laze around with your pigs."

Edison returns with an armful of branches. Earlier, Morgan turned up one good-sized, dry piece of pinion that's firing the cook fire, but most of the fuel is wet. He maneuvers a cast iron skillet over the fire and gives the beans another stir, releasing the heavenly scent of lamb, cumin, and chili.

Edison peers into the skillet. "Beans? Why're we having beans? I coulda shot us a rabbit if I'd known."

I pluck a pine cone from the kindling and lob it at him. "Sure, if a three-legged rabbit lay down at your feet, promised to hold real still, and gave you three tries."

Edison brushes pine needles from his shirt, indignation spreading across his face.

"Rules of the road, boy," Morgan says, not looking up. "Never insult the cook."

Edison's shoulders slump. He has the grace to look abashed as he settles onto the ground beside me, mumbling an apology that's half-swallowed by the crackling fire.

I elbow him gently in the ribs. "I would rather eat Maria's cowboy beans than a fancy dinner any day of the week." I stare longingly at the pot. My stomach growls loud enough for both men to hear. "Wait till you taste them. Morgan and I will fight over your share if you pass." I lean forward, warming my hands over the fire. "We only got them for tonight. Back to canned rations and anything you shoot until we get to town."

Morgan dishes out our meal. Edison hesitates, dipping just the tip of his spoon in his bowl and gingerly licking it clean. His eyebrows shoot up in surprise. The next moment, he's shoveling the chili into his face like a savage.

For several minutes, the only sounds are the pop of the fire, the clink of spoons against tin, and occasional appreciative grunts. When we finish, Edison collects the dishes and washes them in the creek.

"There's hope for the kid yet," Morgan observes, feeding another stick into the fire.

When Edison returns, Morgan places the skillet over the embers to dry. We all settle near the fire, boots toward the flames, saddle blankets around our shoulders. I'm hoping the cold will keep the scorpions away.

Edison turns and, rummaging through his saddlebag, produces a parcel of papers bound in string and waves them at me.

"I've prepared a case dossier," he informs us, pride tinging his voice. "Contains copies of our agent's reports and anything I could find about the town. Figured we could review it after supper tonight, strategize our approach for Vegas."

I take the proffered bundle. The kid sure don't lack for enthusiasm, I'll give him that. "How...thorough," I manage, glancing at pages of tiny handwritten text.

Morgan grunts noncommittally.

I consider Edison's request for a minute. "Why don't you put these away for now." I toss the dossier back to Edison, who fumbles it against his chest. "I'm too worn out to wrap my head around this scribbling and won't be able to read shit in firelight, old eyes."

Edison looks abashed but tucks the bundle away.

"Eyes ain't the only thing old," Morgan says, pulling out a flask. "But I got a remedy."

He takes a swig and passes it to Edison, who coughs—of course—after his swallow. When it reaches me, I study the engraving and hand it back.

"Not even on the trail?" Morgan asks.

"Too much bad mojo tied up in spirits for me," I say. "You go ahead."

Morgan confesses, "Maria won't let me keep it in the house. Only break it out for special occasions. Gonna hunt bad guys, visit a brothel, and head home with full pockets."

Edison's eyes go round. "Mr. Jackson, sir, the BMI can't sanction sampling the wares at the whorehouse." He flushes and fiddles with the flask's lid.

"You sample too much." I laugh. "And no one's pockets are gonna be full. Don't lead this boy into perdition," giving Morgan a hard look.

"You're one to talk," Morgan says. "Remember you and the stevedores down in Charleston?"

Edison chokes on his whiskey, avoids even looking in my direction, and tosses the flask to Morgan.

"Well, that was different," I say, leaning back with my hands behind my head. "I'm a respectable widow woman now."

"Mick, that is absolute humbug," Morgan corrects me, taking another swig and passing it again to Edison. "You're the same old roustabout you ever were. You're just wearing a cloak of respectability."

"Pish-posh," I say, settling my shoulder more comfortably against my saddle. "I am respectable. No stevedores, no whiskey, and no magic."

Edison takes another long pull from the flask, then confesses with a slurred voice, "Never actually been to a brothel, myself. Uncle Pete said I should wait till I'm eighteen. 'Course, that's only a few months off now."

Morgan and I exchange glances. I mouth, "Seventeen?" at him and he raises an eyebrow.

"Hang on." I lean toward Edison. "How old are you exactly?"

Edison's face flushes crimson. "Turned seventeen last fall," he mumbles into the flask. "Told Van Lew I was twenty-one."

I stare at Morgan in disbelief. Seventeen? Christ on a cracker, they've really have sent us out with a child.

"Don't look at me like that." Edison straightens defensively. "Uncle Pete rode Pony Express at sixteen. Age don't matter none if you got the skills."

Morgan is looking increasingly uncomfortable, jaw tight, shoulders tense. His eyes meet mine with that look I know too well, the one that says we've stepped in something deep.

I try to soothe him. "Morgan, he's got a point. And we're gonna run this gig straight, just like we agreed, no monkey business."

"Wait," Edison interjects. "No magic from you," he says, pointing at me. "But no magic from you either?" He dramatically points at Morgan. Looks like the booze is lubricating his gestures.

"Morgan doesn't have magic," I explain.

"Magic don't really work on me," Morgan clarifies. "Not immune. It just doesn't do what the fella casting it expects."

"What about your shooting? The way Pete describes it, I thought you had a bit of mystical help."

"Nope, just years of practice and an eagle eye," Morgan says.

"Is the other stuff true?" Edison glances at me, taking another pull from the flask. "I heard you shot the Wonder brothers in Dodge City. Even when Billy Lee begged for his life."

"It was Fort Dodge," I answer flatly. They'd been raiding wagon trains, executing entire families. "And I didn't kill Billy Lee Wonder." Which is true. There wasn't enough of his mind left when I finished with him to make killing necessary.

"Whoo-hee, Uncle Pete told true. You are a cold killer." Edison takes another long drink. Morgan glances at me with a worried expression. Worried for me or for his whiskey, I can't say.

"Hey, boy, give that." Morgan waves at the flask. "That's all we got for the road."

"I've seen your service record, you're one of the only US Mortis Vorators," Edison slurs, stumbling over the Latin. "I was taught MVs die or go loco by forty. You don't seem crazy."

"Who taught you that nonsense?" I ask, irritated.

"Professor Townsend. Expert on death magic at the Academy." Edison nods vigorously, then sways.

Morgan's head tilts. "Samuel Townsend? Tall fella with a pronounced limp?"

Edison's eyes widen. "You know him?"

"Worked a job with him in '71. Shapeshifter case in Missouri." Morgan leans forward. "Strange, though. Sam always said that age limit nonsense was superstition. Said he'd known Mortis Vorators in their sixties still sound as church bells."

Edison's face flushes. He stammers, "Well, perhaps I misunderstood his lecture."

"Perhaps," Morgan says mildly, catching my eye. "Or you never took his class."

Edison suddenly becomes very interested in the fire. "I learned more about death magic in general from Uncle Pete than I ever did in school anyhow. He says you kill people and eat them," he harrumphs, changing the subject.

"I don't kill people and eat them." I sigh. "When a person or critter dies, a burst of energy is released—Animus Mortis. I absorb that energy. I don't eat them."

"But Pete says when you kill people you own their souls?"

"No, if I absorb a person's Animus their shade haunts me." I sigh. One day on the trail and I am well and sick of what Pete says. "Sometimes briefly, sometimes for a long while. If I use my powers to do the actual killing, I can be stuck with those shades almost forever."

Edison leans forward, eyes bright despite his drunken state. "You do kill people and eat them. That's what we're gonna need in Vegas! Someone's using death magic to kill women." He gestures enthusiastically with the flask. "You could stop them in their tracks.

"Think about it," he enthuses, warming to his subject. "We identify the culprits, build a case, and when the time comes"—he mimes drawing a pistol—"justice is served! Uncle Pete said you were the best hunter the BMI ever had."

"Edison, you ain't making sense. 'Besides Van Lew was clear, this is reconnaissance," I remind him. "Confirm whether or not the attacks were even magic."

"But that's just...bureaucratic caution," Edison blathers. "With your experience and my"—he gestures vaguely—"knowledge, we could solve this. Catch the killer. Make a real difference."

"That ain't the deal, boy," Morgan says firmly, prying the flask from Edison's fingers.

"But wouldn't you rather"—Edison leans forward, eyes bright with alcohol and ambition—"be the ones to bring justice? Not just file a report and let someone else get the glory?"

I keep my face neutral, but something stirs inside me. The old hunger. The thrill of the hunt.

"Stick to the mission, kid," I say, avoiding Morgan's eyes. "Just like Van Lew ordered."

Morgan studies me a moment too long.

Edison's eyes flutter closed. "Promise not to eat me?" he slurs as he tucks his glasses away.

"I promise," I say.

A soft snore escapes Edison. Morgan continues to study me from across the fire, his lined face somber in the dying firelight.

Morgan moves to sit beside me.

"The kid never took Townsend's class," he says quietly. "Doubt they even met him."

"Seventeen," I mutter. "Barely old enough to shave."

"That's not what concerns me." Morgan's voice drops lower. "I saw your face when he talked about bringing justice. You want more than reconnaissance too."

I poke at the embers with a stick. "I promised you. Just fact-finding."

"Uh-huh," Morgan says, unconvinced. "Just make sure you remember that when we get to Vegas and things get interesting."

We watch the gutting fire in silence until finally he asks, "Did the dreams stop?" A question he's avoided asking me for the last ten years.

"Mostly," I say. "Quitting the booze helped. Caleb helped."

"And the shades? Anyone still lurking?"

"Not many." I pause. "My Reb popped up last week."

"Is *he* around?" Morgan says as he pokes at the embers. "He" being Lafayette Baker. Morgan was there the day the train went up.

"I used to see him in my dreams." I shake my head. "But I don't think it was a haunting, just memories and fear."

"Small blessings," he says.

"Amen to that."

The Reb stares at me from across the fire, silent and still. I turn my back to him, seeking sleep. Everything should be fine once we get to town. Edison's agent is waiting for us. I'll get in touch with Gudrun's sister to hear the local skinny. We'll figure out if a death mage killed the girl or just bad men. Should be home within ten days with my pockets full. I'm sure it will be fine.

✦━━━━✦

I wake to Morgan's god-awful baritone voice. He's standing above me, singing "She's a darling. She's a daisy. she's a dumpling, she's a lamb." But he can't stop there. Dear Lord, it continues, "You should hear her play on the piana, such an education has my Mary Ann." At least it's not Souza.

I grind my eyes shut and take stock. I am still all kinds of sore, with a rock under my left hip. I deserve to be sore. Running around in the middle of nowhere with an old reprobate and an armed child.

I peel my eyes open and the singing stops. "Up and at 'em, Mary Ann." Morgan grins at me, nudging my foot with his boot. "We gotta get movin' while the sun shines."

Groaning, I haul myself to my feet. "I'd rise easier if we cut the serenading."

"You're just jealous," Morgan teases, "'cause you have a tin ear." He hands me a steaming cup. "Drink this. Edison's already watered the horses, waiting for you to tack up."

I eye them both, waiting to see if last night's revelations will hatch eggs this morning. Morgan continues his fool-ass grin, still humming that Mary Ann tune under his breath as he quenches the fire and packs his gear. No problems there.

Edison's avoiding eye contact. He turns and heads to the creek to fill our canteens.

Morgan nods in Edison's direction. "He's fine. Just a touch of barrel fever."

"From that little bit of hooch?" I ask, folding blankets as I go.

"I told you the kid couldn't handle his liquor. When I was his age, I coulda drunk twice what he did and nary felt a thing the next morning."

I snort at him. "That's because you would still be drinking the next morning."

Morgan laughs. "Now that is the sound on the goose."

Edison returns and I have to agree he looks green. "Could you kindly keep your caterwauling to a minimum?" he pleads. "My head is pounding like a drum. Musta slept wrong."

"Just remember this next time someone is passing a flask." I cuff him affectionately on the shoulder. "Let's mount up. Morgan, you figure we can make it to Vegas tomorrow?"

"Maybe," Morgan says, throwing his saddle on Muneca. "If you can stop riding like a greenhorn, we could pick up the pace a bit."

"Trail on the murder is growing colder every day," Edison says, arms full of gear. "But I understand if you need to take it easy, ma'am. Seeing your age and being of the fairer sex and all."

"Watch your mouth, kid," Morgan warns. "Those are fight'n words to any woman you meet out here, much less a strapper like Mick."

I give them both the evil eye. "All right, I'm the logy member of the party, slowing everyone down." I start tacking up Sampson. Morgan is older than me and he's acting like he is headed to a Sunday dance. I can do this. Some roostered-up child like Edison is not gonna get under my skin.

We all mount up and start following the trail south.

Chapter Eleven

We're topping a low rise when a noise like distant thunder hits me. Cattle. Running hard.

When cattle put it in their heads to run, sometimes you just get out of the way and let them go. But sometimes you gotta intervene so they don't do harm to themselves.

From the ridge I can see them, a brown-black river churning across the valley floor, dust smoking up around their hooves. Three cowboys ride the edge of the mess, trying to keep the leaders from breaking. The lead cowpoke's buckskin pony looks ragged. Beyond them, the land falls off toward a dark slash of a ravine.

"If they go over that," Morgan says, reining in beside me, "you're lookin' at busted legs and busted cowboys."

Edison squints under his hat, open-mouthed. "Can't they just...turn them around?"

"You can't stop a full-tilt run," I say. "You gotta mill 'em."

"Milling?" he echoes.

Morgan jerks his chin at the circling riders. "Since you can't stop thousands of pounds of snorting, sweating beef, you get 'em going in a circle, let 'em blow themselves out. That singing you hear?" Now that he says it, ragged, tuneless, yodeling notes drift up to us. "If you can hear your partners, you know they ain't gone down under a steer."

One of the riders' songs carries clear in the cold air. "Oh, the Rio Grande is muddy and the trail is awful hard..."

Down below, the lead rider's buckskin is lathered, head down, flanks heaving. He's not gonna last much longer. Two rangy moss-heads at the front keep testing the edge of the circle, angling toward that ravine.

"Reckon we should help?" I ask.

"Charitable thing to do." Morgan sighs, adjusting the ties on his bedroll. "Don't like cows, that's why I run the sheep. But I like buryin' cowboys less."

"Well, that and your land ain't rich enough for beef," I add. "Let's see if we can lend a hand." I shift, checking my cinch.

Edison nudges Abigail forward. "What can I do?"

"Seeing you've never worked cattle before you stay here, if we get up in a tighter mill you can jump in and help with the cleanup."

"I'm not afraid of cattle, pshaw."

"Course you ain't. But you and Abigail are new to cow-punching; plunking you down in the middle of a stampede is likely to do more harm than good."

His face falls, but he nods. "Yes, ma'am."

Morgan and I kick our horses down the slope. Sampson's ears prick and he surges forward, delighted to have real work. Working cattle is one of Sampson's favorite pastimes.

When we hit the flat, the ground rumbles from the steer pounding the earth, a turbulent sea of hoofs, horns, and hide stretching across the valley in front of us. I kick Sampson into an easy canter on an intercept to the lead buckskin. I raise my right hand, showing I'm not flashing a gun. The buckskin is spent, chest and neck lathered, nostrils distended.

I swing in beside the lead rider. His hat's jammed down, his dark hair plastered to his skull with sweat. He keeps singing between gasps, barely glancing over.

"You want help?" I shout, riding knee to knee and trusting the horses to find safe footing. I wave back at Morgan, indicating there are two of us.

"Do I *look* like I don't?" he hollers back. "We got two bastards up front tryin' to break off toward the gulch. If they go, the whole damn herd goes with 'em."

"We'll take the point," I say. I wave to Morgan, and he peels off toward the far side of the circle, Muneca already reading the cattle.

Heart racing, my focus shifts to the horse pounding below me, the cattle pounding beside. Sampson and I pour on enough speed to slot in front of the lead cows. A big steer with a broken horn starts banking right, thinking about cutting us off. I clap my hat at his nose and Sampson snakes his head, ears flat, snapping at the brute's shoulder. The steer drifts back into the tide.

We work like that for another circuit, crowding the leaders, keeping the circle tight, letting the ones in the middle run themselves out. Sweat stings my eyes; dust grits on my tongue. The herd's gallop eases to a hard trot, then a crippled shuffle as they finally blow.

The riders' singing roughens, turns to laughter and hoarse whoops as horses drop to a walk to match the cattle. Someone takes up another verse just to hear his own voice echo off the hills.

When the last cow drags from a run to a walk, I haul Sampson around, letting him prance. The herd's restless, blowing and bawling, but the danger's passed.

The lead rider brings his buckskin alongside us. The horse's chest is white with salt, flanks heaving but he's walking nice and loose. The kid on his back can't be more than twenty. They're almost always young for this kind of work. His gear's seen hard use but good care.

"Obliged," he says, tipping his hat. "Thought those old boys were gonna get the best of me," he winks.

I adjust my scarf to hide my warming cheeks. With those big, dark peepers, I'm guessing he's got his choice of lovers. "You had 'em headed the right way." I roll my shoulder to release the tension. "Just needed fresh horses."

Our horses pace shoulder to shoulder. Sampson knows the business of cows. Anytime one drifts our way, he pins his ears back and snakes his head like a band stallion.

"That 'hoss of yours has cow sense," the young man says, eyeing Sampson appreciatively.

"He likes to be boss." I sigh, giving Sampson a firm pat. "Good with cows but brings its own challenges."

He chuckles, tugging his hat lower against the cooling breeze. "The good ones always have quirks."

"I'm Mary McClellan." I give him my married name so as not to raise alarm. Hopefully, he doesn't have an Uncle Pete to tell him about me. I hook my thumb toward my companions. "My compatriots are Morgan Jackson and Edison Colt."

He grins, even teeth flashing in his dusty face. "Lucius Haygood," he offers. "Those boys are Juan Hermosa on the grullo and Frank Baumlin in the red shirt. We're drivin' Caesar Hermosa's beeves down to Fort Union." He looks past me to the herd, and the grin fades. "Or what's left of 'em."

I follow his gaze. Up close, the cattle are ragged, bunching tighter together as the temperature drops. Ribs show on animals that ought to be fat on early spring grass.

"Wonder if we're in the same boat?" I say, frowning. "My pigs have been wasting since fall." I tap nervously on my saddle horn. "They get lethargic and just lie down and die."

Lucius straightens in his saddle, sudden interest lighting his eyes. "Exact same with our cattle. Nothing wrong with their innards when we butcher." He gestures toward the gaunt herd. "Caesar figures we better sell what's left for beef 'fore they all die on the range."

I say slowly. "You hear of anyone else in the same boat?" Nothing about Lucius suggests he is "in the know," I don't share my thoughts about it being a magical malaise.

"Just our herd." He wipes his face with a filthy sleeve. "We've tried about everything, even supplementing with special feed Ceasar's been getting in Trinidad." He jerks his chin toward a low butte. "My sister's holed up yonder with a lame horse. She's on chow duty. You and your friends are welcome to grub. I gotta swing around, see about any strays."

"My crew can sweep for strays," I offer. "Your horse is spent." I wave Morgan and Edison over. "An hour of work is more than a fair trade for a meal."

"I accept gladly, but you haven't tasted Edith's cooking yet. You might be sorry for the trouble!" Lucius grins, tips his hat at Morgan and heads toward the butte and his sister.

I watch him ride away. Yup, I gotta get off the homestead more. Julianna would be scandalized if she knew the thoughts I was having about this cowpoke half my age. Shoot, I'm scandalized by my own self.

An angry bawl interrupts my thoughts. The big moss-head with the broken horn throws his head, spins, and breaking out of the herd, hooves churning straight for the ravine.

"I'll head him!" I yell. Sampson is already surging forward, ears flat. Morgan curses behind me. "Don't bust your fool neck, Mick!"

The steer hammers across the flats, bleeding dust and snot. He veers north straight for a muddy pothole about twenty feet across. Spring rain and snow run off fill the basin. He barrels straight into the pond, chest-deep in mud and cold water and bogs to a halt, bellowing pitifully.

Looks like the nasty beef is well and truly stuck. Sampson pounds up to the edge of the pond and stops, feet sinking past his pasterns in the heavy mud. I consider options, being neither equipped nor skilled to rope the bastard. I glance back at Morgan riding up behind when providence strikes.

The crafty devil wasn't stuck at all. Without warning, it bounds toward me, and Sampson, who doesn't take lip from dumb beef. Ears flat, teeth bared, Sampson scrambles to block the cow. His hind legs slip on the slick bank and he pitches sideways, twisting like a cat to save himself.

I am not a cat.

The world flips. Freezing water slaps every inch of me at once, stealing my breath. Mud sucks at my boots as I flail up, soaked to my scalp.

By the time I haul myself onto the bank, where Sampson's standing, blowing like it was all *my* idea, ears pricked.

"You all right there?" Morgan calls.

"Fine," I snap, wringing water from my sleeves. I'm shaking so hard my knees knock. "Thought I was due a bath." Teeth chattering, I slip and slide around the rim of the pool to grab Sampson.

Morgan reins Muneca in away from the mud, face tight between worry and mirth. "If you're done showing off?" He holds out his duster. "Here, this will keep the worst of the chill off."

"Thanks." I pull my sodden coat off and tie it to my saddle, then slip Morgan's duster on. Chill settles in, stiffening my hands. I struggle checking my saddle's latigo before I mount. Giving Morgan a wet, muddy wave, I leave him to the stray and head toward the yellow firelight of camp.

Camp's tucked against the lee of the butte. By the time Sampson and I trudge in, my teeth are knocking loud enough to spook the cows all over again. My clothes squelch with every step.

Lucias's sister, a pretty woman with the same dark eyes as her brother is already at the fire, stirring what smells like a pot of red chile. My mouth waters. Glancing up as I approach, she takes one look at me and clucks her tongue.

"Get over here," she orders, pulling blankets from some hidey hole in the chuck wagon. "You're gonna freeze solid." She orders one of the wranglers to take care of Sampson.

"I'm fine," I lie.

She snorts. "You look like a boiled owl." She wraps a blanket around my shoulders anyway, shoves me down on a crate by the fire. Then handing me a tin of steaming chili. "Texas style, no beans," she says with a dimpled smile. "I'm Edith."

The heat of the fire bites before it soaks in. The chili chases some cold from my middle, but a deep ache spreads through my back and limbs. I finish just as Lucias returns from his tasks.

"Little brother," Edith orders, "seeing as I cooked, cleanup is your charge." He gives me a conspiratorial wink as he gathers the dishes.

Edith reaches into her saddlebag and pulls out an amber bottle. The firelight flickers over the glass as she holds it up. "I've been saving a bottle of The Imperial for a special occasion. Reckon this here counts, seeing as y'all saved our hides today."

Morgan's face lights up when he spies the whiskey. "Imperial? We've business to attend to at the Imperial Saloon in Vegas. Are they distilling?"

"They are, but they haven't been distributing local. Had to get this from our cousin up in Denver." Edith smiles. "It's supposed to be extra special, made from high-altitude corn or some nonsense."

Morgan happily accepts the bottle from Edith and takes a hearty swig, sighing with satisfaction. "Mighty fine whiskey, ma'am, mighty fine." Ever the flirt, he gives Edith his most charming smile, but she just snorts and shakes her head at his foolishness.

The bottle makes its rounds. I refuse, a sense of unreality clouding my mind. The dunking has triggered the ague I've battled since Charleston.

When the bottle comes back around to me, Edith cajoles, "C'mon now, it'll chase that chill right out."

I peer at the label in the firelight. For a moment, leering skulls and dancing bones seem to writhe among the script. I blink hard and it resolves to ordinary lettering. Fever playing tricks.

I ain't drunk whiskey in a long time. Not since I swore off the bottle with Caleb. But I'm still shaking in this damn blanket, and the fire doesn't seem to be touching the chill sunk into my bones.

"Just one," I say, mostly to myself.

Edith pours. The whiskey hits my tongue like fire, then blooms warm all the way down. For a heartbeat all the sharp edges of the world blur and soften. I close my eyes in spite of myself.

And fall.

Not into sleep exactly. Into something else.

◆———◆

Pigs, slick and fat, bellies opening like split grain sacks. Corn spilling out, except the kernels are little glass beads, each one holding a tiny, flickering face. A tower looms above, copper and steel, throbbing with violet light as the beads run down its sides like rain. Something in the dark below drinks that light and laughs.

"Mick?" Morgan's voice is far away. "You with us?"

I jerk upright, breath sawing in my throat, cup rattling in my hands. The fire's burned low. Edith and Lucias watch me with matching frowns.

"You went away there for a minute," Morgan says. "Looked like a snake bit you in your sleep."

"Just a bad dream," I lie, wiping sweat from my neck. But the taste of that whiskey lingers, oily and bitter behind the sweetness.

I struggle to rise, groaning at the pain in my joints.

"Easy now, you need to rest. You have a fever," Edith murmurs. She readjusts the scratchy blankets around my shoulders.

I lick my dry, cracked lips. "The whiskey...something's wrong with it..." I rasp.

Edith tsks softly. "You're feverish. Was just a chill. Sleep now."

Exhaustion tugs at me, but I resist its pull. "Please..." I grasp Edith's hand with feeble urgency.

Her dark brows knit in concern. She gives my hand a comforting pat. "Rest now. No more dark dreams."

Reassured, my eyes slip closed. My thoughts scatter into darkness.

I drift in and out of uneasy dreams, unable to gain any real rest. Lucius and Morgan's murmured voices stir me. Dawn light filters through my gritty eyelids. The tantalizing aroma of coffee teases. I pry my eyes open with some effort and struggle to sit upright. My body feels like one giant bruise, but my head is clearer.

Edith passes me a steaming cup. I wrap my hands gratefully around the warm tin and breathe deep the restorative vapors.

"You had quite the night," says Lucius somberly. Morgan nods, his usual joviality subdued.

I sip the hot brew, scalding my tongue. "I apologize for causing a ruckus. Wasn't nothing but fever dreams." I remind myself my dreams haven't been inhabited by Baker in years. 'Twas just the ague playing on my worries.

Morgan's eyes hold a shadow of worry. "None of us slept easy after your fevered ramblings...anything we should know?"

"Just dreams." I stare into the swirling grounds muddying my coffee. I rub my sternum, unsettled by the visions. Past or future, no way to know.

I finish my coffee under Edith's watchful gaze. I'm still feeling mazy, but we can't dally. "We best be getting underway if we're to make Vegas before nightfall," I say, getting gingerly to my feet. A full day's ride awaits, giving ample time to worry my dream like a loose tooth.

Chapter Twelve

THE RAIN POUNDS A merciless rhythm as we approach Las Vegas, each drop hammering my fever-addled brain. I've been drifting in and out of consciousness most of the day, haunted by last night's dream and the persistent ague that's settled in my bones. Sampson's steady four-beat gait—squish, squish, squish, squish—lulls me into a daze beneath sodden clothes that never dried from my dunk in the cattle pond.

Even Morgan's spirits have drowned in the downpour. He and Edison ride ahead in silence, their hunched shoulders telling the same miserable tale. I let Sampson follow Muneca, glad he's paying attention. My mind can't focus on anything beyond the violent shivers wracking my body.

When Sampson stops abruptly, I force my head up. Through rain-blurred vision, a wooden sign emerges: "Welcome to Las Vegas / Bienvenido a Las Vegas."

"Do you see that?" I croak, my throat sandpaper-rough.

Edison peers closer. "You mean the runes?"

"Yeah." Below the painted *welcome*, mystical symbols are burned into the wood. Certainly invisible to ordinary folks but clear as day to those of us who know what to look for. "No Magic in Town Limits By Order of the Sheriff," I translate for Morgan's benefit.

Edison runs his fingers over the runes, his brow furrowing. "Most sheriffs post warnings like this. None can actually enforce it, so it shouldn't affect our investigation." He pulls his hand back with a slight frown. "There's a magical shadow, though, probably just concealing the runes." He drops his hand and straightens in his saddle. "I reckon we head to the Imperial, find our agent?"

"Then a room?" I groan. "I'd trade Morgan for a hot bath right now."

Morgan snorts from ahead. "Buck up, Mick. Don't think anyone would take you up on that offer. But I wouldn't turn down a warm bed myself."

"Not Mick," I remind him sharply. "I'm Mary Catherine here. Don't want anyone connecting me to the past."

Las Vegas spreads before us like two separate worlds stitched together at the seams. The newer section sprawls outward from the railroad tracks—a hasty arrangement of eastern style wood frame buildings thrown up since the railroad arrived last year.

Across the Gallinas River, Old Town waits with its weather-worn adobes and newer brick territorial style buildings. The town's position at the crossroads of the railroad and Santa Fe Trail makes it a bustling hub where cowboys, ranchers, traders, and travelers converge by the thousands daily. Perfect for three strangers to disappear into the crowd.

We cross the bridge into Old Town, the horses' hooves clattering on wet planks. My fever makes the journey seem endless as we navigate the crowded Main Street toward the Imperial Saloon. The plaza's windmill stands sentinel over the churning mass of street vendors hawking their wares despite the weather.

Finally, the Imperial looms ahead—a two-story adobe with a wraparound portal and balcony. Even through my fever haze, I notice the distillery compound behind it stretching toward the foothills. That's new since my last visit.

Bright yellow light leaks through heavy curtains along the portal, and the sound of a piano accompanied by raucous male voices stirs me from my stupor. Just a little longer, I tell myself. Find Vilde, secure a room, and maybe—just maybe—this fever will break.

"Come on, Mick, let's get inside. I'll see if there is a hostler." Morgan ties his horse in the yard. I know I should be doing something. Probably getting off my horse.

I heel Sampson up to Muneca and dismount. The ground seems an awful long way's down. My knees buckle when I land on the wet ground. Morgan steadies me.

My hands fumble to tie the release knot. I gotta shake this off. We've got business to conduct.

"Let's get this show on the road!" Edison shouts, practically buzzing with excitement. Somehow he's already halfway up the stairs leading to the front door of the saloon. He swings it open and marches through. I punch lethargy down. I just gotta find Vilde and then we can rest.

I almost collide with Edison, who's stopped just a couple of steps inside, staring like a yokel around the large hall. The noise hits me like a sledgehammer, adding to the fever cacophony in my head—conversation, yells of glee, curses, clink of glasses, the scrape of chairs on a wooden floor and piano music are mashed together.

Gaslights spaced along the wall and a couple of large chandeliers hanging over the main hall, the bar and the card tables throw a cheery light around the room. A mahogany bar with an actual brass foot bar runs almost the entire length of the left wall. Behind the bar is an eight-foot painting of a naked woman reclining on a green chaise, with dogs or coyotes lounging beside her. Card tables run the right side of the room opposite the bar, under a second floor balcony.

The center is almost open, like a church aisle leading to a small stage opposite the front door. The stage is elevated and illuminated by shell lamps around the foot and a third chandelier hanging over top. A piano player is set off to the left, but I'm only hearing the occasional note over the din of the crowd. Men and boys are seated two or three to a table. Ladies of the line in various shapes and sizes move among the seated men, delivering drinks and conversation. I don't see any female patrons, only entertainers. The stage is framed by heavy gold velvet curtains.

Morgan crowds in behind me and we shake off the rain. Just being out of the weather lifts my spirits.

On the stage, a short mustached man steps onto the apron and raises his hand for quiet. He's wearing city clothes, dandified with a brocade red vest and a gold tie clip. Burning brown eyes and a perfectly spun handlebar mustache highlight his aquiline features.

The crowd noise drops and the piano player clinks out a staccato intro.

"Gentlemen and not so gentle men." He smiles, smooth words delivered in a flat, clipped accent typical of New Mexico Territory. "I am proud to present to the patrons of the Imperial, Paloma Noruega!" The audience hoots and pound tables enthusiastically. He continues, "Sit back and witness the forbidden, the exotic, Danza de la Paloma."

The curtains part, revealing a strawberry-blonde woman posed center stage, surrounded by wrought iron perches. She's wearing a floor length, gossamer cape, split up the sides. Her bare arms are outstretched and wrapped in pink ribbon. Five white doves perche along each arm clinging to bows woven through the ribbons. The crowd's excited hollering suggests this is more than a simple animal act.

As the pianist whips the music into a habanera, Paloma begins to move. Her shoulders and hips ripple in time to the syncopated beat, the birds bobbing along as she rotates. The audience falls silent, spellbound.

Something about her nags at me I can't quite place. With a purse of her lips, the doves on her shoulders flutter across, pull the ties of her cape, and return to their perches. The cape drops, revealing a translucent chemisette over a pink corset that pushes everything northward. Her backlit legs ghost behind a translucent skirt.

Another cue to her birds and they pull the bows at her waist. The skirt falls, leaving her in bloomers, bare from the knees down. I've seen leg shows before, but this is a new one to me.

Morgan and Edison stand slack-jawed beside me.

"Close those before you catch flies," I hiss.

Morgan snaps his mouth shut, looking chagrined. Edison just blinks, eyes still fixed on the stage.

The act continues, growing more risqué by the minute. Edison's acting like he's never seen a woman's thigh before despite his time with the circus. That boy is wet enough behind the ears to water a cactus. He stumbles into an empty seat, and I let him go. The show should keep him occupied while Morgan and I handle business.

"Come on." I gesture toward the bar. "Let's see if we can find Vilde."

I size up the crowd, calculating our approach. Asking outright for Vilde might draw attention. Better to start with something ordinary—a drink—and work our way around to it. The key is to be unremarkable, just another customer with a parched throat.

He tears his eyes away from the stage and shrugs. "I am powerfully parched. I wouldn't mind another snort of that Imperial whiskey."

"Every one of Luke's crew complained about feeling poorly this morning after drinking last night. Why on earth would you want more?"

"It's fine whiskey. They just got spooked by your episode."

"I don't think that whiskey is a good idea," I grouse, leading the way to the bar.

"If you listen to my wife, no whiskey is a good idea," he mutters. "But I am free of her consideration for the present."

A large bunch of backcountry types in their Sunday best cluster around the pour station like they're paying court at a cotillion. I elbow my way in, ignoring the perturbed looks. Luckily, nothing armors you for the disdain of others quite like being a woman of a certain age. Disdained or ignored are two states in which I have much practice. Morgan hangs back. Good thing no guns are allowed in the bar or I think we might have to deal with a showdown, and my shooting ain't up to snuff.

Reaching the bar, I understand the bill and coo coming from the plow chasers. The barmaid is attractive enough to give Paloma a run for her money. Plus, she is slinging beer and whiskey, many a man's dream woman. Tall, dark-skinned, with natural wild hair. She is thundering exotic even for the cosmopolitan culture of these crossroads. Her fine looks are emphasized by a fringed buckskin vest over a calico blouse. Turquoise drips from her ears and around her neck. A heavy chatelaine holding a knife, a corkscrew, and various other bits and bobs draped over a voluminous skirt with pockets. Shit, she's prepared.

I lean up to get her attention. "Hey there."

"Excuse me, boys, I'll be back in two shakes." She slinks away from her admirers to me. "Hey yourself," she purrs in a cultured voice. She sounds like the product of an Eastern boarding school. "What's your poison?" She looks me and Morgan up and down.

"You got any of the Imperial Whiskey?" I ask, scanning the bar shelf. "Heard it was manufactured right here."

"Sorry, bud," she responds, leaning on her elbows on the bar top across from me. "It's too good for this rabble. Hoodoo only serves it to special guests."

My heart drops to my toes. She can't mean Hoodoo Jones, Lafayette Baker's most trusted lieutenant. I flash to a memory of Hoodoo's cadaverous face grinning as he animated a fresh corpse outside Richmond, making the dead soldier dance while still wearing Union blue. "Who's Hoodoo?" I stutter, my mouth dust-dry.

"Big boss, owns the distillery." She taps her fingers on the bar, then gestures at the bottles on the back shelf. "Second choice?" The way she's searching my face sets my teeth on edge. Last thing I need is to be recognized here. I've never seen this woman before. There's no way she knows me. She's way too young to be from the old days.

Paloma's act must end. The piano music stops, the quiet flooded by a wave of clapping and whistles.

Ignoring her intensity, I continue, "You know where we can find Vilde?" I pitch my voice low, hard to be heard over the din.

Her gaze follows the length of the bar, stopping at the mustached emcee at the end. He glares spikes in her direction. She turns back to us, picking up a bar rag. "If you're not spending, you need to get along."

Ole Mustache stops glaring when he notices my attention and starts whispering furiously into the ear of a small dark man seated in the corner. The smaller man turns, and something about his profile—the sharp nose, the hollow cheeks—sends an icy finger down my spine. I shift my position, using Morgan's bulk to block their view.

I lower my voice, pull a dollar out of my pocket and place it on the bar, keeping it under my fingertip. My other hand pulls back the front of my coat to rest on my Colt. "Point me to Vilde and I'll get outta your hair."

"Who wants Vilde?" she asks, polishing the bar top with the rag and keeping a side-eye on mustache.

"I've got a message from her sister."

I watch the barmaid freeze, her gaze locking with mine for a heartbeat or two. The gears of her mind grind away behind amber-colored eyes. Something clicks and her face lights up with understanding. "Ah, I see." She nods, the tension draining from her shoulders. A smile spreads across her face as she sets aside the bar rag and reaches under the counter for two glasses.

Confused, I ask, "You gonna tell me what I need to know?"

She pours three fingers in each and slides them toward me. The smell adds to the existing smoke, stale beer, and sweat, making my stomach polka. "You here on account of the murder, right?" She nods.

I'm missing something, but I can't see my way clearly. Finally, I nod back.

She leans in. "Wait fifteen minutes for him to clear out." She tips her head at Mustache. "That's Vicente. He runs the bar. Head to the top of the stairs, last door on the right. Let Paloma know Leona sent you. She can put you in touch with Vilde." Stepping back, she taps the bar with her knuckles and lets her voice carry. "That'll be two bits."

"Keep the change." I slide the dollar across the bar and grab the whiskey. The dollar disappears in her skirts. She winks and immediately turns to resume her chat with her coterie of bumpkins.

Turning to Morgan, I hand him both glasses and grab him by the elbow to pull him away from the bar.

"My, my, she is a looker." His head swivels to keep her in his sights, his view of her lost behind the crowd. "Did she give you what we need?"

"I think so," I say, fussing with my kerchief to cover my chin. "According to her, someone named Hoodoo owns the distillery."

"Hoodoo Jones?" Morgan's head whips around, his voice dropping to barely a whisper.

"She didn't clarify and I didn't ask. Didn't want to seem too interested." The fever spikes suddenly, cold sweat breaking out across my forehead. Just the name conjures a chill worse than any ague.

"Shit." Morgan's hand drifts toward where his gun would be if we hadn't checked them. He scans the room with new intensity. "If he's here..."

"Naw, he'd stand out like a redheaded stepchild in this crowd. Let's find Edison."

We collect Edison, who's still moon-eyed over Paloma's performance. He assures us he left a message in code for the agent to meet up with us tomorrow. I'm relieved to not have to deal with any BMI nonsense tonight. Making nice with some straitlaced, hoity-toity agent is beyond my endurance. Morgan and I don't mention our concerns about Hoodoo. Plenty of time to discuss once we're clear of the bar.

The damn fever washes through me fresh, setting my legs and back to aching. Thankfully, we're able to snag a table in a dark corner to wait for Vicente to clear out. Edison and Morgan pass the time sipping the whiskey shots and reminiscing about Paloma's act with the Johnny Reb listening raptly. I think about chasing him off, but I can't quite muster the gumption. I'm just so happy not to be on a horse. I think I fall into a doze. Next thing I know, Morgan's shaking my shoulder. "Mick, the emcee's gone."

I force myself to stand, gripping the table's edge against a wave of dizziness. The room tilts and rights itself as I take a steadying breath. "Let's move before he comes back."

We make our way toward the stairs. With each step, my fever pulses behind my eyes, turning the gaslights into halos of pain.

"You sure you're up for this?" Morgan murmurs close to my ear.

The stairs loom before us—a mountain in my condition. Edison bounds up first, eager as a pup, while Morgan stays close beside me, ready to catch me if I falter.

I pause halfway up, clutching the banister as sweat beads on my forehead. Below us, the barkeep Leona catches my eye and makes a subtle hurrying motion with her hand.

"Come on," I rasp, forcing my leaden legs to climb faster.

Chapter Thirteen

EDISON KNOCKS ON THE first door on the right. "Hello, the barmaid sent us up. We're looking for Vilde."

"You may enter," a female voice responds with a hint of a familiar accent.

We step into a combination of a boudoir and a dressing room. Bed to the right, vanity to the left. All manner of feminine costumes hang against the wall and bird cages cluster in each corner. A window looks out to the alley below over a wide balcony and the air is filled with the soft cooing of her birds.

My head is spinning and all I can think of is lying down. Riding wet and exhaustion have taken their toll. Ever since the assignment in Charleston, I'm prone to these fits of fever. They come on fast and leave slow. Morgan gestures to an armchair to the left of the bed. I collapse gratefully. He takes a spot seated on the trunk at the end of the bed and Edison reclines against the wall by the window.

Paloma is sitting before her vanity, her face and form reflected in the triptych mirror. She is wearing a pink silk dressing robe. Apparently, pink is her signature color. "Give me just a moment to remove this war paint." She's dabbing cold creme on her face and rubbing it off with a handkerchief.

Seeing her from profile it clicks. I exclaim, "You!"

She looks over her shoulder. "Me?"

"You're Gudrun's sister!" I accuse. "Vilde."

"How do you know Gudrun?" She turns to face me.

"I'm Mary Catherine McClellan. She's my sister-in-law."

A smile breaks over Vilde's face, and she rises and crosses to me. "So we are sisters too. How lovely." Her face glows even behind the thick, splotchy makeup and cold cream. Bending, she pulls me into a warm hug. "Mary Catherine, I have longed to meet you!" She steps back and puts a hand on my head. "You're very hot. Are you ill?"

"Nothing to worry about," I say. "Just an old war wound, not contagious."

"Yeah, I heard you were a great hero. Julianna spoke so proudly of you when I saw them in Kansas City."

"Well, that's kind of you to say." I pause, feeling a little awkward. "Neither one of them mentioned you were Paloma Noruega."

"I have been touring, darling! My family doesn't approve of my art form. You know how it is." She winks at me and then turns to take in Edison and Morgan. "We will catch up on all the family gossip later. You must tell me who these two beauties are."

"Vilde Swenson, may I present Morgan Jackson and Edison Colt."

Vilde offers her hand like a duchess.

Morgan steps forward and takes her hand gently in his and passes his lips over her knuckles. "The pleasure is mine, ma'am." He steps back.

Edison nods at her and flushes. "I enjoyed your...dancing...ma'am," he stutters. "I like your doves." He fusses with his belt buckle.

"Thank you, darling." Vilde winks at him. "Just between you and me, they are pigeons. Much tougher. But the 'Norwegian Pigeon' doesn't have quite the same ring. Appearances are everything.

"So, gentlemen and Mary Catherine," Vilde settles herself back on her vanity stool. "What brings you here? I assume you aren't here just for my act or a roll in the hay?"

Edison blushes and stammers, "Uh, no, ma'am, we wouldn't presume."

"No matter," Vilde hums, straightening a pink lace stocking. "Most of the business here is of the fleshly variety. Very nice girls. I am not one to judge. But I'm not one of the daily specials."

I suspect Vilde isn't above being kept. She just isn't a nickel a roll.

My head pounding, I cut in, "Vilde, we're looking into the death of Ada Salazar. What can you tell us?"

"Oh, that is a dark business. You need to stay clear of management," she coos. Turning back to her mirror, she resumes ministrations to her face. "But I can help you. Mads Brown and Elmer Ottoson killed Marisol's sister Ada and beat up Delilah so bad that she can't shift to her coyote form anymore."

Morgan glances at me, a storm brewing in his eyes. "Who are Mads and Elmer?"

She raises her eyebrows, meeting Morgan's eyes in the mirror. "They are supposedly in charge of whiskey distribution." She turns to face us, "And this isn't the first incident. Vicente has done nothing."

"Vicente is the proprietor?" I ask.

She grimaces. "Ugh, the loathsome toff emcee." She gives her face a final scrub. "And he bought the Sherriff's election."

"Who's his buddy, creepy little man sat at the end of the bar?" I ask.

"Darling, that is the mysterious Múcaro. None of the girls are allowed to even talk to him. He is deep in cahoots with the owner, Hoodoo Jones." Morgan glares at me but I focus on Vilde. "They disappear for days sometimes to the caverns under the distillery."

"What's in the caverns?" I pull the thread.

"Distillery stuff, darling," she says, waving her hand dismissively. "The rumors suggest they have a tête-à-tête, but I don't see Múcaro as the romantic type."

"Stop!" Edison cuts in. He's pulled a notebook and pencil out of his breast pocket and starts scribbling urgently. "The murder, what exactly happened?"

"Ooh, I love a man on a mission," Vilde croons. Then catching Edison's frown continues, "Right, no gossip. Back to business." Hands on her knees, she leans forward and drops her voice conspiratorially. "Bad things happen to good people whenever Mads and Elmer are in town for business. Girls get sick. Ada isn't the first woman who died. Marisol told me another lady, Mary Beth, passed mysteriously after servicing Mads about three months ago."

Morgan starts to interrupt, but Vilde waves a finger at him. "You've been around long enough to know life is hard for working girls, but this is worse. Sometimes the girls who service those two are sick for days. Two others lost their ability to shift. Delilah is the only one who hasn't died yet."

"If these men are responsible, why wasn't something done?" I'm horrified by the abuse of the women, but Vicente's business depends on his stable. "Losing hostesses must be costing him a fortune."

"Exactly!" Vilde cries, standing. "But he's barely lifted a finger. Until Delilah, he was telling everyone they all succumbed to 'excited delirium,' such gumsuck." Crossing to her wardrobe, she pulls a pink dress and holds it against herself, checking the length. Tilting her head, she continues, "The ladies and gentlemen of the line are almost all shifters. They're tough and heal fast. When the ladies raised a ruckus, he fined Mads and Elmer and banished them from the saloon until after the Solstice." She rehangs the dress and turns back to us, expression serious. "Those boys ruined Delilah and they're responsible for Ada and Mary Beth's deaths. Something has to be done and Vicente hasn't done enough."

"What does Delilah say happened? Was there a ritual or a spell?" Edison asks eagerly.

"No, nothing out of the ordinary. Well, except for death and disfigurement." Vilde grimaces. "Delilah is one of the new girls. Ada was showing her the ropes, entertaining Mads and Elmer.

"Delilah was extremely inexperienced and didn't understand how to handle a man's...ego." Vilde swaps her silk wrapper for a flannel hanging over her chair. "Apparently, she laughed out loud when Mads dropped his trousers. As you can imagine, he didn't take kindly and she said he decided to teach her a lesson. Instead of just knocking her around, he pulled his knife and sliced up her face good." She pulls the flannel tighter around her shoulders. "With the screaming and the blood, Delilah didn't see what happened to Ada. I wasn't there, but Marisol said Ada was dead on the floor, not a mark on her when she busted in the door."

Morgan and Edison cringe, but Vilde hadn't finished. "Afterward, Delilah tried to change to her coyote form to heal her face—shifters are so lucky that way—but she couldn't. Somehow Mads damaged her Essence. No shifting means she hasn't been able to earn. Clients pay extra for a shifter, but most of them don't want a scarred up face. She's losing all the way around."

"Any idea what Mads did to her?" Morgan winces.

Vilde shivers. "The other girls say Mads power sucked her, slurped her all up."

"Some kind of a Gleaner?" Morgan gives me a hard look. I rack my foggy brain for possibilities. Only Gleaners or Vampers can steal Animus from a live woman. But maybe a device or a spell?

"Don't be dramatic, darling. Mads is no Big Magic user." Vilde rolls her eyes. "The poor girl might be suffering from hysteria brought on by the violent attack."

I find that unlikely but remain silent.

"Where did this happen?" Edison cuts in.

"Why does that matter?" I chide. Between the fever and the pounding head, I'm eager to end this interview. We need to talk to the victim and find the bad men, and I need to lie down.

He sighs and looks at me like I'm an idiot. "Because we *need* to see the scene of the crime to investigate."

"Delilah's room, next door," Vilde answers, gesturing toward the wall with the bed. "Her headboard is right on the other side of mine. But I can't get you in there. Vicente's got it locked tight."

Edison moves to a corner of the room next to the bed, closing his eyes. A faint glow surrounds his hands, and the air in the room chills. His face tightens with concentration.

"What are you doing?" Vilde hisses, rushing over.

"I'm trying to see if there's a magical signature, confirm a magical attack," Edison whispers, his face screwing into a grimace.

"No, stop…damn it, you don't understand." Vilde tries to pull Edison's arm away from the wall.

He lets his hand drop, looking chagrined. "I ain't getting much," he says low. "Just listenin' along the plaster. But it's some kind of major death magic was worked in that room. Same shadow we saw on the runes on the town's sign."

"The sign you didn't bother reading?" Vilde snaps. "Damn men, can't follow a simple direction."

"The warning for no magic?" He scoffs. "Sheriffs post that for show."

"In most towns, maybe," Vilde fires back. "Here, Hoodoo laid real spellwork over this place. There's a ward watching for anyone throwing magic around."

"My knack won't set anything off, it ain't spell-slingin'. It's like the girls' shifting, just how I'm made."

Vilde starts to argue but she's cut off by a pounding on the door.

A tiny red-haired woman bursts in, slamming the door behind her. "Quick, you gotta get out. Vicente's on the warpath," she pants. "He heard Vilde had strangers up here, and he's coming to check for himself."

Vilde rounds on Edison. "See? I told you, a whiff of power and he's at my door."

"Ain't me he's smellin', ma'am," Edison mutters looking sick and clutching his notebook.

Marisol lowers her voice, eyes darting to the hall. "He's jumpy as a cat, worried about the law sniffin' around. Don't want no trouble tied to his girls."

"Well, hell," Morgan gripes. "We better clear out."

Vilde springs into action. "Out to the balcony!" She waves toward the curtained windows. Turning to the redhead, she says, "Marisol, show them the way down."

Morgan's eyes meet mine. "Take Edison," I say. "I'll slow him down."

Morgan nods and runs to the window where Marisol waits, Edison on his heels. I confirm they are safely out and make my way to the door, where I ask Vilde, "Will you be all right?"

"Yes, I'll be fine." She pushes me out the door. "Vicente won't harm a hair on my head. I pack this place."

I race down the hall to the stairs. Vicente meets me on the landing.

"Evening. Enjoying your little powwow?" His eyes bore into mine, suspicion palpable.

"Just visiting an acquaintance," I respond, my breath held.

His eyes narrow. "An acquaintance among the whores. You don't look the type." Sucking his teeth, he says, "Word downstairs is you and your pals have been stirrin' things up. Didn't you see the sign? No magic in town." Shit, did Edison's little read activate the ward? I keep my voice steady. "No trouble here, just a friendly chat." I start to brush past him to continue down the stairs.

Vicente's hand shoots out, seizing my arm. His gaze slides down over my coat, my trousers and scuffed boots, lip curling like he caught a bad smell. "I reckon your kind don't listen so well. Women forgettin' their place. There are consequences to actions."

Men like Vicente only got room in their world for two kinds of women: the ones they can buy and the ones they can break.

I wince as his grip tightens, but Morgan and Edison need time to escape and I'm too worn out to pick a fight. Forcing a smile, I try to defuse the tension. Whether he actually felt Edison's power or just liked the sound of his own rules, I couldn't say. Either way, he'd found his excuse.

"I apologize for the misunderstanding, mister. I didn't intend to cause offense. I admit I tried a wee charm to carbonate my beer. No need for trouble."

His laughter is harsh. "Trouble's already here, darlin'." With a swift motion, he twists my arm and flings me down the last few stairs. I land face down with a resounding thud.

Pain blossoms across my jaw. I bit my lip in the fall. Struggling to rise, fever and violence burn through me. I long to smack that toff right in the teeth. The gathered crowd swims in my vision as I roll onto my knees. My grayback crouches near my head and sighs in my ear. "You gonna take that from the little weasel?"

Vicente looms over me, his face contorted with anger. "Don't let me catch you bothering the performers again, or next time, I won't be so gentle."

"Don't get your dander up," I slur through swollen lips. "Just gonna get my check."

Vicente motions for two men in the crowd to drag me out to the muddy street. The damn Confederate laughing is the last thing I see before my eyes fall shut.

Chapter Fourteen

I JERK TO CONSCIOUSNESS. At least I think I'm conscious. Hard to tell. Fever plays tricks. Curving dry stack stone walls surround me, sunlight pouring through an arched doorway and windows high on the wall. Moaning, I take stock. My body's sluggish, wrung out, but there's no pain. Hallelujah.

I ease myself into a sitting position and look around, blinking sleep out of my eyes. Yup, the fever's left. I've no idea how much time has passed since my drubbing at the Imperial. Rolling to my knees and then my feet on the sandy floor, I get my bearings. I seem to be in the middle of a giant stone beehive. On shaky legs, I move to the door, drawn by the scent of coffee and bacon. My stomach rumbles.

The sun's full shine slaps me upside the head. Shielding my eyes from the glare with my hand, I try to figure out where the heck I am. The scene outside raises hopes.

Edison and Morgan are busy around a fire. At least three women are with them. Could one of them be the "unreliable" BMI agent? Gazing past the group, I spot another five of these stone beehive shapes built in a line. Ahh, we're at some old coke ovens. Must be near a bust coal mining operation. Brush and trees surround us, providing additional shelter. I spot the horses grazing near a creek. And mercifully, no visiting shades.

"There she is!" Morgan calls when he spots me. "Come have some grub."

Approaching the fire, I'm more steady with each step. Morgan smiles and hands me coffee and a tin plate overflowing with flapjacks and a hunk of bacon staring back up at me. "The ladies were kind enough to bring some supplies. Edison has been interviewin' them. Fortify yourself and we'll bring you up to speed."

I grin and grab a seat on a log. I shoulder up to the red-haired girl, Marisol, who helped Morgan and Edison escape the saloon.

Glancing around, I don't see Vilde, but I recognize Leona, the barmaid. She's watching me intensely. The last woman is standing near Morgan with a bonnet pulled forward on her face.

Morgan gestures toward her. "That there is Delilah. She told us what she remembers about the night Ada died. Edison took notes. And you remember Marisol and Leona."

I nod at each of them before shoving a huge bite of flapjacks in my piehole. Chewing quickly, I swallow and look around the group expectantly. "How long was I down?"

"Just the night," Edison replies, licking his fork clean. "I figured you for a goner the way you were sweatin' and groanin', but Morgan had faith you'd pull through."

I continue shoveling food in my mouth. Morgan's seen me taken with the ague before. He knows the drill.

"Did I miss anything important?" I ask between bites.

Edison rattles off a list of details, including the fact that Ada's body has been disposed of, so we're down to witness accounts as far as our investigation.

"Vicente thinks he chased you off," Marisol pipes in.

"That's helpful," I say, reaching for my coffee.

Leona leans forward. "I don't think Vicente would be so cavalier if he knew who you are."

That makes me start, the cheerful comradery of breakfast cut short. Is that a threat? Morgan places his coffee mug down, his eyes sliding to the Winchester beside him. Edison and Marisol just look confused.

"I'm not sure what you are getting at, Leona." The coffee's suddenly bitter in my mouth. I keep Morgan in my peripheral. He'll have my back if needed.

Leona looks smug. "Sure you do. You're Mick Kelly, Pinkerton BMI War Hero and sometime wanted outlaw."

Marisol gasps. Morgan slides the rifle to his lap.

"My name is Mary Catherine McClellan," I answer calmly, looking her up and down, daring her to say different. No reason for a stranger to know me as Mick.

"Kate Warne, my foster mother, had cabinet cards of your likeness. I know who you are."

My grip on the plate eases.

It seems like all the ghosts of my past are stopping in. Kate was a Pinkerton detective and a dear friend. She did have a foster daughter I never met. But here, now?

"Vicente doesn't know your face from Eve, but I reckon he'll know your name." Leona shifts forward. "And Hoodoo Jones is sure to recognize both."

Shit, Hoodoo is Hoodoo from my past. In the excitement last night, I lost track of that nugget. I'd hoped I had seen the last of him when Lafayette died. Could it be a coincidence that he's mixed up in this mess? I ignore Morgan shaking his head, muttering under his breath. "Goddamn Hoodoo Jones. I told you no monkey business or I was out...damn it...Maria's gonna skin me..."

Edison stands to get attention. "Hold up, Leona. What are you getting at? Mrs. McClellan is here under official contract for the BMI."

Leona turns to him fiercely. "Typical bureaucratic cockup. Didn't you read my reports?"

'Reports' echoes in my head. Leona is our Vegas contact?

"I understood you would be operating undercover. The message from the Santa Fe office said Van Lew was sending an agent to confirm the magical attack before BMI would take any action. As if I need someone to check my work. YOU bring HER. Hoodoo hates her."

Edison flushes. "I reviewed everything I could get from Santa Fe," he retorts, pushing his spectacles up his nose. Leona is shaking her head vehemently as Edison speaks. Losing confidence, he asks, "Wasn't he Lafayette's number one? The way my uncle Pete described it, Mick and he were compatriots. Why would he hate her?"

Leona presses her lips together in a hard line, looking at me expectantly. Delilah huddles like a mouse across the fire.

I exhale a long breath. "Hoodoo and me had a falling-out over the KC crash that took Lafayette," I explain. "He believed I had something to do with it."

"Hoodoo blames you for Lafayette's death?" Edison asks, more than a little surprised.

"Admittedly, I wanted Lafayette dead." That shuts Edison up for the moment.

"Why?" Leona counters. "From all accounts, you were neck deep in Lafayette's gang, making money hand over fist. Did you kill him?"

"I don't owe you an explanation. My past is my business." Looking around, I pause. No one but Morgan knows the truth. BMI agent or no, I'm not airing classified information.

Morgan is still muttering to himself. I move to sit next to him and keep my voice low. "This doesn't change the plan. We keep our heads down, find evidence of bad magic, and collect the coin."

"I don't want nothing to do with Jones," Morgan says, gripping his rifle to his chest. "Dollars to doughnuts, he's the one who took out Clyde in Cheyenne."

"You said yourself that was a barroom brawl."

"The brawl where Clyde's head went missing? Knowing Hoodoo is near makes me feel differently. I think we should run home and hide under the bed."

"But Hoodoo doesn't know we're here. If he doesn't find out, nothing's changed. We aren't even after him."

"But now four more people know who we are," Morgan says, tightening his grip on the rifle as he points at each face around the fire. "Three can keep a secret if two are dead. And Clyde already ended up that way."

Leona's eyes flash as she cuts him off. "None of us will breathe a word. I've spent two damn years building this case." She jabs a finger toward the women. "Delilah needs her shifter ability back. Marisol's sister is dead. We all want justice."

She looks at Edison, studying his boot tips. He looks up. "What are you looking at me for? I'm also a duly sworn agent of the BMI." Gesturing at me and Morgan, "You're my crew, I'm not gonna spill our business to Jones. Criminy."

"One last job," I remind Morgan, squeezing his shoulder. His face remains skeptical.

"Hoodoo's dangerous, Mick," he says quietly. "And he brings out the worst in you."

I swallow hard. He's right, my contempt for Hoodoo puts my temper on a hair trigger. "Just expert opinion. No monkey business."

"I'll hold you to that," he replies, eyes hard.

Pointing at Leona, I ask Edison, "so she's our contact?"

"Yes, I'm the agent he was supposed to meet," Leona snaps, standing with arms crossed. "You shouldn't even be here."

Edison adjusts his glasses, pulling out his notebook. "Agent Freeman, Mick is the foremost expert on life force manipulation and extraction in the region."

His condescending tone makes me want to slap the cherubic expression off his face. I notice Leona's jaw tighten as she watches him scribble notes.

"The magical wards in town," Edison pauses to chew his pencil, "were those in your reports that Santa Fe ignored?"

A muscle works in Leona's cheek. "That explains your idiotic spell-casting attempt in Vilde's room."

"There was no spell casting, just my knack." Oblivious to her anger, he leans forward. "But how does it work? An entire town warded?"

"The source is in the distillery," Leona says, kicking a stone into the fire where it cracks loudly. "I reported it when the ward activated. Never even got confirmation my report was received." She meets my eyes. "I've been screaming into the void for months."

Typical BMI nonsense. Probably dismissed her because of her gender or race or both.

"Vicente, Hoodoo, and Múcaro all know when someone tries casting," Marisol adds, leaning forward. "The wards went up last Easter, long before Ada and Delilah were attacked."

I frown. "So how could there be a magical attack with wards in place?"

"That's the part that scares us," Marisol says. "Ward slaps down anybody else pokin' at power, but Mads and Elmer seem to do what they please in town and never pay for it. Vicente don't say how, and we don't ask."

Edison looks up. "We need to confirm Delilah's symptoms are magical in origin—"

"What is there to confirm?" Delilah's whisper cuts through the air as she raises her head. "My shifter ability gone, my face ruined." Behind her sunbonnet, bruises swell purple and yellow against her skin. "What more evidence do you need?"

Leona cuts in, heat in her voice. "Shifting's not some parlor trick you call up with a spell. It's baked in. I can still shift just fine inside Vegas city limits, the wards don't change that." She looks at Delilah, jaw tight. "If she can't change, something took her very essence. That's a magical attack."

My teeth grind at what was done to Delilah.

I stand, keeping my voice calm. "But we don't understand what parts are magical. Edison, can you do that thing you did in Vilde's room, look for a magical signature?"

"I can't read people. I can only read inanimate objects. This is where you earn your commission."

"Mick." Morgan stands at my shoulder. "I don't care for this idea."

Edison wants me to use my Gleaner sight, exactly what I was supposed to try on our pig with Gudrun. It's barely magical, certainly not Big Magic. The sight is a natural part of being a Gleaner. But I promised Morgan.

"Edison, I told you I wasn't that woman and I would not be using my powers for this job. You insisted you just wanted my expertise." There. I sound resolved and mature, but my fingertips tingle in anticipation of touching power.

"Ah, c'mon Mick," Edison cajoles. "You're not gonna eat anybody. Just a little peek to confirm the cause of Delilah's symptoms. A shifter's ability to shift is tied up in her identity, her Animus. Either it's damaged or her problem is psychosomatic."

Leona loudly sucks her breath over her teeth at Edison's suggestion Delilah's problem is in her head. But he blithely prattles on, "You confirm and I've got justification to take Mads and Elmer to Trinidad. Can't otherwise. It's not a BMI matter unless it's magical."

"Mick," Morgan whispers urgently in my ear, turning me away from the group. "I see you considerin' this, thinking it's just a taste, but you best be concerned this isn't opening a floodgate."

"I agree with Edison," I hear Leona from over my shoulder. "If we have the means to understand what happened to Delilah, we need to seize the opportunity."

I pinch my lip, staring into Morgan's face without seeing him before reaching a decision. Dropping my hand and meeting his eyes, I say, "Morgan, this could give us everything we need to wrap this business up. Then we can head home, okay?" Turning back to the group, I glance once more at Morgan, seeking approval. He scowls but finally nods at me. I will summon the Gleaner sight to examine Delilah's Animus. I look to Delilah. "If you give leave, I can see the web of your life forces. Maybe see what's what?"

Edison exhales loudly in relief and readies his notebook.

"Will it hurt?" Delilah asks, wide-eyed.

"Not a bit," I say, projecting a confidence I don't feel. Circling the fire to reach her, I grasp her hands in my trembling ones. "Ready?"

She nods. I take a deep breath to steady my nerves and call my power.

It's just like it was with the pig. The power's somnolent. Rusty from sleep, it takes a minute to focus. I close my eyes and let the Gleaner wash through me. It's lethargic and thirsty. It hasn't been fed well in years. First the pale yellow of Delilah's Vitae, like an old calico washed too often. A shifter's Vitae should be blaze, like sunshine. The Gleaner fully wakens. I feel it lunge toward Delilah, but I pull it back. Sweat rolls down my face. Opening my eyes, I see the woman in front of me bathed in a patchy pink mist, Delilah's damaged Animus.

Hers is thin in spots, leaving a violet nothingness that should be covered in the vibrant pink of life. Something bored fist-sized holes through her essence, leaving her Animus leaking like water through an old bucket. It's not drifting away. It seems to be being siphoned. Watching it for a moment, I consider how delicious it would taste. I could just reach out.

No. If I had the right kind of skill, I could maybe pinch those leaks shut, braid fresh strands across the gap. I can *see* where the weave's gone thin. But I've never learned how to tug without tearing. One wrong pull and I'd rip out what she's got left.

Dropping her hands, I close my eyes to banish the Gleaner and step back. Nausea washes through me and a longing for more. When I open my eyes again, the group is staring raptly at us, Edison's notebook forgotten in his lap.

Leona recovers first. "Satisfied?" She goes to Delilah and guides her to sit.

I glance around our camp. I'd expect my brush with power to summon the shade, but the kepi hat is nowhere in sight. Looking at Edison, I answer, "I've never seen anything like that. It's like something's...mining Delilah. There are holes punched through her Vitae Essence into her Animus."

He chews the end of his pencil for a moment. "What could do that?"

"Whatever it is, that explains the other two deaths," Leona says. "Vilde told you there were other shifter women, besides Ada, who lost their ability after servicing Mads? Both of them eventually died."

"Does that mean I'm going to die?" Delilah's high, sweet voice cracks. Marisol takes one of Delilah's hands in hers and squeezes. "Maybe I'm already dead. Without my coyote skin, I am...lost. Not woman nor beast. I'm trapped in a half life." I ache for her, for the violation of her body, her identity ripped away. She shakes off Marisol's hand, and her wide eyes implore me.

"You've got power, Big Magic. You can help me be whole again. Can you get my shifter ability back?"

"I don't think my ability works that way," I tell her gently. It's consumptive, not restorative. Do I tell her how tempted I was to slurp up her Animus, to push her into Death's embrace, to release her Mortis Animus? She wouldn't look to me for aid if she understood what I am.

The nightmares that haunted me during the fever hinted at something larger than Delilah's trouble alone. A sense of impending danger lurked, a foreboding I couldn't shake. "It's not just about what power I have, Delilah," I said softly, my voice tinged with resolve. "It's about what it costs me...and others."

Silence hangs between us. I glance up. She reminds me of Julianna, cultured voice and willowy form hiding toughness. But her yellow eyes are all shifter. I can't let her die, but I don't know how to stop it.

I can't stop it, I remind myself. I'm here for the money. Leona can figure out how to save Delilah. It's not my problem.

"Well," I say, standing and brushing dust from my pants, "we've confirmed what we came to find out. Something magical is happening to these women."

Edison jumps up, eyes bright with barely contained excitement. "This is exactly what we need! We've got magical evidence now." He flips frantically through his notebook. "With confirmation of Animus extraction, we have full jurisdiction to apprehend the perpetrators."

"Slow down, Edison," I warn, though something inside me sparks at the prospect of action. "We came for information, not to hunt men."

Morgan rises beside me, his eyes never leaving Delilah's face. "For once, I side with the boy." His voice is quiet, measured in a way that always means trouble. "What do you propose we do, Mick? Just write up a report?"

"That was the agreement, Morgan. Fact-finding only." I give him a pointed look while my pulse quickens traitorously. "You were clear about not getting tangled up in anything more."

Morgan's jaw tightens, gaze shifting between Delilah's bruised face and my eyes. "I know what I said. But seeing this..." His voice drops. "Some things can't be witnessed without demanding action."

"Morgan—"

"They're stealing her very self, piece by piece," his voice rough with emotion. "We can't just walk away."

A thrill runs through me that I desperately try to hide. Those holes in Delilah's Animus are just like my pigs. Whatever's causing this is something new, something powerful. My fingers tingle with the memory of the Gleaner stirring within me.

Edison nods vigorously, misreading Morgan's solemn resolve as endorsement of his own eagerness. "Exactly! This is our chance to bring in real criminals! Uncle Pete always said—"

"This isn't about Pete's lies," Morgan cuts him off, though not unkindly. "It's about what's right."

I school my features into reluctant consideration, but inside I'm already mapping possibilities. What kind of wizardry could bore through Animus like that? Is it related to the pigs? If so, how? The mystery pulls at me like a physical force.

"We round up Mads and Elmer," Morgan says firmly, "and take them back to Trinidad for Van Lew's crew to question."

Edison nearly bounces with anticipation. "I'll telegraph for backup—"

"No," Leona interrupts sharply. "Jones owns the telegraph. We need to avoid notice."

"I've been watching them," Delilah says, leaning into the conversation. She smooths her skirt across her lap. "I might be able to help. Since I lost my coyote form, the men talk freely around me. They think I'm broken." Her fingers trace the edge of her bonnet. "Their mistake."

A slight smile crosses Morgan's face at her spirit, while Edison scribbles frantically in his notebook. I feel my own lips curve, there's something satisfying about the wounded turning the tables.

"I overheard Vicente tell the porters to get a whiskey shipment together," she continues. "He's sending the boys to Dodge City tomorrow."

"Why ship it out instead of selling local?" Morgan asks.

"I have the exact same question," Leona says. "Working at the bar, we never get the Imperial. It's always distributed elsewhere."

"They'll have to go through Devil's Gate Canyon," Delilah adds. "Too much snow in the pass. Vicente's furious about the delay."

Edison practically vibrates with excitement. "That's perfect! We can intercept them in the canyon!" His hand instinctively hovers near his pistol. "I've been trained in field apprehension techniques—"

"You've been trained to trip over your own feet," I mutter, but Edison's too caught up in visions of heroism to notice.

I exchange a look with Morgan. I recognize the iron in his expression. There'll be no talking him out of this. If we're changing course, at least we're doing it together. If I'm honest with myself, I'm eager.

"Sounds like a plan." I sigh, feigning reluctance while my blood sings with anticipation. Action at last.

The women help Edison gather the cooking supplies while he chatters about proper arrest procedures. I grab Sampson's currycomb and head to the horses, hiding my face so no one sees the fierce smile I can't quite suppress. Some quiet time with my ornery mount might help me sort through the mess we're diving into and the exhilaration I have no business feeling.

Chapter Fifteen

HEAVY, LOW CLOUD COVER intermittently blocks the moon. The ponderous sky matches my mood as we ride along the canyon trail. I slouch in the saddle, hat tilted over my eyes. My heart's pounding out of my chest, nerves so rattled I can barely grip Sampson's reins for the sweat rolling down my palms. I was always nervous before a job, and especially tonight with no magical backup, just guns and smarts. Thankfully, Edison agreed to follow Morgan's and my lead, "bowing to our superior experience," he said.

Morgan's silent, no serenading as we close on the target. His face is grim under his hat's brim. Edison seems immune to the tension, unconsciously flowing with Abigail's easy walk along the trail.

Up ahead, laughter and firelight echo off the canyon walls. Mads's team is closer than expected and still awake. They sound drunk as lords, probably on stolen whiskey. Hoodoo has the county so wrapped up it seems they're fearless, not believing themselves targets for outlaws despite a wagon full of premium whiskey. I'm happy to disabuse them of that belief.

Before narrow walls open into a wider gully, I rein Sampson to a halt and motion the others to do the same. Mads's gang is no more than fifty yards ahead.

Morgan clears his throat. "No need to get fancy. I'll circle across the top, get eyes on them, make sure nobody's on watch." He dismounts. Muneca obediently ground ties, rooted to the spot despite the dangling reins.

I give a curt nod as he fades into the dark. Edison's leg jitters with nervous energy. Or maybe just too much coffee. "Knock it off," I hiss at him. "It's quiet time now."

"Sorry," he whispers back. "I'm excited. It's happening like one of my uncle's stories, except I'm the law."

"Try not to shoot yourself in the foot, kid."

"I got this." Edison pats his holster. "You wait and see."

I bite my tongue. The child has no idea. We have surprise and sobriety on our side, but we'd only succeed with a big helping of luck.

Morgan slips back, practically silent. A former scout in the army, Morgan can still move like a ghost. And I would know. I chuckle to myself, nerves getting the best of me.

Morgan motions for Edison and me to dismount and pull us close. "Four baddies, four horses on the picket line, two for the wagon, two for riding guard. All them 'pokes full as ticks around that fire. None are bothering with eyes on the horses or lookout."

"Can you tell which are Elmer and Mads?" I ask.

"Called each other by name. Elmer is the big one. Moves slow, gray hat by the wagon. I think Mads is the little guy at the end. Got his pants all tucked into fancy turquoise boots."

"I go straight up the middle, tell them I'm taking them in. Pigs could fly and they'll come quiet like."

"You," Morgan breathes, looking at Edison, "sneak back and cut the picket. When the action starts, you are gonna spook the horses. I'll circle up behind with the Winchester to keep anyone from running until Mick has the boys."

"I can do more than let the horses loose." Edison protests through clenched teeth.

"You better," Morgan responds. "You gotta send them mounts running into the canyon. Can't leave the gang with transportation. We're counting on you. I'll owl hoot once I am in position. That's your signal to let loose the picket."

"No, not an owl," I say. "Owls are bad luck."

"Fine, a whistle then, whippoorwill."

"Let's get to it," I say. We hobble the horses just off the trail. Morgan heads up the game track to the top of the canyon. Edison circles around with him. I wait for the signal, listening to the nonsense coming from the men around the campfire.

I hear a whistle. I guess that's a whippoorwill. Close enough. Breathing deep, I square my shoulders and move toward the firelight. My boots on the rocky ground sound like firecrackers to me as I stride toward their camp.

At my approach, the cowboys scramble up from their spots lounging by the fire. I only count three, none with turquoise boots. Shit, where's Mads? Elmer sways as he rises, face ruddy from drink. The other two men stand easily, not looking worse for drink. The sound of crickets seems loud in the pause.

"Who the hell are you?" Elmer slurs, hat perched on the back of his head, rifle clutched in both hands across his chest.

I stop a few yards off, hand hovering near my holster. "You are wanted for questioning by the Bureau of Magical Investigation in the death of Ada Salazar and the assault of Delilah Hughes, ladies of the Imperial Saloon," I say. "Come quiet or things will get ugly."

Elmer hawks and spits. "They weren't no ladies." The other men laugh. Assholes. Swinging his rifle up, Elmer shouts, "Get!"

Seeing Elmer line up a wobbly shot, I throw myself to the left an instant before a bullet whizzes by. My Colt is in my hand even as I hit dirt. One loud crack later and Elmer's shirt blossoms red. He stumbles backward and falls. Surprise paralyzes me. I can't shoot worth shit. How did that happen? Shit, shit, shit, killing them was not the plan.

A pause, then Elmer's screaming starts and gunfire erupts, bullets stripping bark off the trees around me. The burnt toast smell of gunpowder rises into the night. I hear Edison whooping, chasing the horses from the gunmen's picket. Better late than never. I scramble behind a stump, peeking out to track the two other men diving for cover. Edison appears behind Mads's camp, staring dumbly, not even drawing his weapon as bullets pepper the ground in front of me.

"Get down, you idiot!" I bellow.

He doesn't move, battle-stunned. I lean out and snap off two quick shots, driving Elmer's companions down to the ground before they notice Edison. They both move like professionals, within the cloud of gun smoke. I'm no match for them. Where the hell is Morgan? My eyes cut to the lump that was Elmer, chest pumping, his shirt staining crimson but still alive. At least his screaming stopped.

Just then Morgan's rifle cracks from above. One of the gunnies screams. Morgan's bullet found its mark. His cries echo long and loud against the canyon walls. Edison finally ducks low, self-preservation kicking in.

Within seconds, silence falls across the canyon. Peering around the stump, I size up the field. Elmer lies moaning in the dirt. Screams from the gunnie Morgan shot fade out. He's crawling through the trees, trailing blood. I think the other man escaped up the gully. I rise, brush myself off. Morgan half-slides down the steep trail from the butte, rifle clenched in both hands.

"Everyone all right?" He looks from Edison's white face to the body sprawled on the ground. "Kid?"

Edison nods, chest heaving like he'd run ten miles uphill.

Morgan grimaces. "Hell's bells, greenhorn. Next time keep your head down or someone will blow it clear off."

"That's Elmer." I point at the unconscious man. "Where's Mads?"

"There were only three horses on the picket," Edison breathed. "I came to tell you, then the shooting started."

"Shit, bet he's headed back to town. We gotta clear out."

"No, we gotta provide what succor we can to these men," Morgan says, striding over to the shooter in the trees. He gazes down at the inert form. The gunnie swims in a pool of his own blood. "Mick, can anything be done here?"

The Johnny Reb stands beside Morgan, beckoning me with his index finger.

I kneel by the man and place my palm on his chest. His essence crawls up my nose and into my brain. I see everything through the pink mist of death transition. "Ain't nothing I can do for him. He is on his way out." The Gleaner presses the edges of my awareness. My skin tingles, pulse loud in my ears. Just a little sip? Could come in handy later.

The moment is broken by Morgan pushing me away. "Don't you even think about it." Kneeling, Morgan takes the gunnie's hand and snaps over his shoulder at me. "Go see what you can do for Elmer." The Lord's Prayer starts pouring from his lips in a hushed baritone.

"C'mon, Edison." I push the still dazed kid and make our way back to the fire.

Elmer is struggling to sit up, six-shooter firmly in his grip. "Don't come any closer," he growls. His shirt is damp with blood but looks like I just winged him. "I don't know who you are, but I'm getting get out of here before Mads comes back, and you're gonna help me."

Dumbfounded, I look at Edison then back to Elmer. "Okay, sure. Our plan is to take you to Trinidad, let you explain every-thing to the BMI. That work?"

"That's fine by me. I just gotta get clear of Mads."

Huh, this is a twist. "Okay, mister, put the pea shooter down and we'll get you out of here. Did Mads hightail it because we were coming?"

"No idea. Wanders off sometimes. Wherever he is, sure he heard the shootin'. I got a chance to run and he's gonna be none the wiser. We gotta go now." Elmer battles to his feet. Blood gushes through his shirt and he stumbles.

"Sit down," I tell him. "We're gonna try to slow the bleeding or you won't make the ride. Edison, go get the horses." I push Edison toward the trail and shout into the trees. "Morgan!"

I rummage through the equipment scattered around the fire, looking for something to use for a bandage. I find someone's shirt and pass it to Elmer. "Hold this tight against the wound." Then I grab a bridle and cut the reins to bind the field dressing. We can't leave a blood trail.

Morgan joins us, face stern. "The gunnie passed."

"Morgan, this is Elmer. I shot him a little bit and we need to get a move on. Turns out Elmer is eager to get away from Mads."

Cheerful whistling and the clop of horse's shoes cut through the gloom. Edison rides into the dying firelight, Sampson and Muneca trailing Abigail. The kid has shaken off his stupor and got a second wind. He sits straight in the saddle. Surveying the three horses, I try to figure out how to account for Elmer in our getaway.

"Edison, will Abigail ride double?" I call out.

"No way," Morgan says. "Elmer is huge, more than that little filly can bear. Tie his hands and put him on Muneca. She has the most sense. I'll ride with Edison. You'll have your gray beast to yourself."

With a frustrated growl, Morgan and I each clasp Elmer under a shoulder and half drag him to Muneca. We toss his leaking body over her back. His trembling hands smear red over the saddle horn as we tie his wrists together. Morgan and Edison riding double will slow us down. But assuming Abigail can keep pace, we should still reach camp before dawn.

"And now," Edison cries, "we beat a hasty retreat from the forces of evil!"

"Settle, kid, at least one man lost his life back there," Morgan chides.

"Pete says life is cheap on the long ride. I say we're above ground for another day and we got our suspect. Those are reasons to celebrate."

"If you wanna keep breathing," I say, "you will shut it and get moving. Mads and at least one more gunnie are out there and we are easy targets."

Transportation sorted, we mount up and start the ride back to camp.

Chapter Sixteen

STARLIGHT KISSES THE TREES as we ride into camp, my eyes scanning every shadow. Elmer trails on Muneca, slumped and pale. The moon's set now, marking maybe three hours since the ambush. Not much time before Mads reaches town, and Hoodoo sends men after us.

It's been a long day of hard riding, and we need to hole up until dawn. The horses are spent and Elmer won't quit bleeding. Come morning, we'll strike south to Santa Fe, wire Van Lew from the BMI office there. With luck, we'll be gone before Hoodoo's men pick up our trail.

Weariness settled on my shoulders once the adrenaline faded hours ago. I dismount gingerly, strained muscles protesting. Even Morgan slides from his horse with a stifled groan. His back slumps with exhaustion. Only Edison bubbles with youthful energy.

"Hot diggity! That was some adventure," crows Edison, hopping to the ground. "Did you see when Morgan shot that guy? In the dark, through the trees, POW! Saved the day. Mick and I woulda been goners for sure!"

Morgan shoots the boy a dark look, the thrill of violence clearly lost on him. "Taking a man's life is nothing to macarize, son. Best pray you don't come to learn it firsthand."

Edison's grin fades at Morgan's stern tone. "I hope I can do the same someday. Pete says 'ruthless in service of the mission' is the highest compliment, and I aim to live up that sort of operation." He scuffs the dirt, unabashed.

"Just tend to the horses, Edison," I say wearily, helping Elmer dismount. Edison hasn't ridden sufficient miles to understand the cost of ruthlessness. Life would come for him soon enough. At twenty, I had danced with death with a light heart. But the war and all that came after taught hard lessons.

I squeeze Elmer through the domed opening of the coal oven we were using as a bunkhouse. Inside, we're protected from the wind and as snug as we sad desperadoes could expect. I settle Elmer on a horse blanket against the far wall. His youthful face peers at me. Pain etches lines around his eyes and mouth. He looks so ordinary, just a foolish kid, fallen in with the wrong crowd. "You gonna be square with us, Elmer?" I ask, studying him intently. "Why you running away from Mads?"

He refuses to meet my gaze. "Ain't nothing good for me there, not no more. Mads is crazy and Hoodoo…" Elmer shudders. "I just wanna get free of them, start fresh."

I remain silent, turning over his words. I believe he is telling the truth, but I got enough experience to be wary. I'll keep a skinned eye. First thing, though, is to check his wound.

"Lie back and let's take a gander at that gunshot."

Elmer complies, squeezing his eyes against the pain.

I remove the temporary dressing and eyeball his abdomen. Looks like the bullet passed straight through his side. A two-inch chunk of meat was carved away but doesn't look like it has entered his belly.

His position also gives me a chance to study his belt buckle, pot metal with a piece of crudely scrimshawed bone about three inches across. I don't like the look of it.

"What's the story with that buckle?" I ask casually.

"You like it? You take it," he says, reaching to undo his belt. "Mads gave it to me when I joined up. I don't want anything to do with it." He struggles to pull it through his pant loops, face contorted and grunting in effort.

"Easy now." I try to calm him. "I'll help you." I reach for the buckle and nausea sweeps over me when my finger touches the scrimshaw. I sit back. "Is that spelled?"

"I don't know nothing about no spell. Just don't want it near me."

"Well, I'm not touching it again," I say. "You'll just have to leave it for now."

"No, no, I can't die with it on me. Please help get it off me." His panicked wail echoes off the walls of the shelter.

"Easy." I clap him on the shoulder. "Assuming infection doesn't take you, you ain't gonna die."

He stops squirming and opens his eyes to look at me gratefully. "You really don't think so?"

"I really do. You get some rest. I'm gonna have Edison put a clean bandage on that wound and later you and me are gonna discuss that buckle." We'll see if Edison's ability can make sense of it.

Morgan's got a small fire going in the center of the dome, just enough to ward off the March chill and heat water for coffee. The beehive coke ovens came ready made with a chimney hole in the top, but I still watch the smoke anxiously. Even with the moon set, a wisp of smoke might give us away. "Coffee'll be ready soon. It'll shake some life back into those weary bones, come sit afore it gets cold," he calls.

I sink to the ground near him with an appreciative sigh. The bitter aroma is already reviving me. Edison enters, dragging our saddles. Still oblivious to everyone's fatigue, he starts prattling. "I was thinkin'...maybe we can go after Mads in the morning? I bet he's holed up at that claim the ladies told us about. We can ambush him, get the upper hand...I probably should have set after him last night. Not sure runnin' was the best idea."

Morgan silences him with a glare. "Boy, do you recall what you did when the bullets flew? Standing in the open with your jaw slack? What makes you think you would have survived another showdown last night?"

Chastened, Edison kicks sullenly at a scattering of charred coal fragments. Morgan hands me a steaming cup. I take it with a grateful nod, allowing the warmth to seep through my aching hands. Kid needs to learn patience.

"Edison," I say, wanting to turn his energy in a productive direction, "how about you see to Elmer, get a fresh dressing on his wound and let me know your thoughts on his fancy buckle?"

"Fine." He sighs. "But don't know why I'm playing Florence Nightingale."

"Because I need to see if your expertise can tell us anything about that buckle. Didn't feel natural to me."

"About time you recognized I can do more'n water the horses. I am the lead agent," he gripes. "You got any carbolic?"

"There's some muslin and carbolic in my saddlebag, left side," I tell him and turn back to Morgan. "Edison's right. That gunman would have had us both if you hadn't taken him out when you did."

Morgan runs his hands over his balding pate. "I know that," he says, "but this doesn't feel like the old days. Holding his hand while he passed, I saw them all, all the men I killed. Some for good, some for profit, they're all in my head."

"Aye, I know what you mean." We're both silent, each chewing our own reveries of misdeeds past. I hear Edison tending to Elmer.

Morgan continues, "I told myself this was an honest job, helping women, working with the law for once, but the truth is, I wanted to get loose of the homestead, whoop it up a bit. I forgot how bad the killin' makes me feel."

"There wasn't supposed to be killing, just investigating."

"And I believed that lie, that it was a simple job. Or I lied to myself." He takes a deep breath. "I know you didn't lie a'purpose. I'm old enough to know anytime you mix guns and money someone ends up dead. Is that gunnie any worse a human than we were back in the day?"

"We never signed up for a job to profit off innocents," I reply.

"But there were plenty of innocents caught in the crossfire." he responds. "And who the hell are we to make that judgment? That entire last year with Lafayette, we were operating in the gray at the best of times. Who's to say we were any better than Elmer over there?"

"No one's gonna say that," I answer. "Least of all me."

"I don't know." Morgan sighs. "I'm not wanting any more of this."

"Morgan, something terrible is going on here. It's not just Ada and Delilah. Other women have died. Even them drovers with the sick cattle, hell, my pigs, are part of a bigger picture. I think taking in Mads and Elmer is the right thing to do. We are on the side of the law this time. We don't have to fix it all. We just gotta do our part. And earning the BMI fee will let me put my family straight."

"Right? I don't know if I trust your judgment 'bout right. You called the Gleaner to read Delilah. I know I agreed, but that opened a door. I saw you when that gunnie was dying. You practically licked his face before I pushed you away. I've known you long enough to recognize the signs."

"Ouch!" Edison's pained cry breaks our confabulation. "It bit me!"

"The hell you griping about now?" Morgan scolds.

"This," he says, coming to join us at the fire, buckle wrapped in muslin. "It bit me."

"Whadaya mean bit you?" Morgan says, squinting at the dull metal.

"I don't know how else to describe it. I was calling up my sight and when I touched the bone, it felt like teeth taking a chomp out of my finger." He gingerly touches the edge like a hot burner. "Huh, nothing now that it's off Elmer. But look." He holds his reddened finger out for inspection. "It still burns."

"Did you learn anything?" I ask.

Edison sits down, staring at the chunk of silver. "I don't recognize the signature of whoever made this, but it's similar to the spell on the town sign and Ada's room. Same muddy color. I can't tell what this buckle does. But it's... hungry?"

"What do you mean, hungry?"

"I mean it wants to eat. This here"—he points at the scrimshaw—"it's like a prisoner, banging on his bars 'cause he's starving. I bet old Elmer knows plenty." He turns hopefully toward the blanket where Elmer huddles silently. "C'mon, Elmer, what is this thing?"

Elmer refuses to meet Edison's entreating look. Before he presses further, Morgan interjects, "Leave the prisoner be. A man who betrays his fellows says more 'bout his own soul than those he rats on."

Elmer raises his head defiantly. "I ain't no rat! Mads is plain crazy, him and Hoodoo both. A demon's got into them. I seen it with my own eyes. It ain't natural!" He shudders, hands worrying the blanket clenched in his lap.

"What do they do?" Edison leans in, excitement and wonder plain on his face, notebook forgotten.

Elmer looks down at his hands and shifts on the blanket, wincing at his wound. "It sounds crazy."

"Crazy or no, go on," Morgan encourages him.

"The buckle... it's like a tool for stealing bits of soul. If I touch the buckle with one hand and touch a person with the other, it steals Animus, just little bit, like a leech." Elmer could be an automaton, staring into the fire. "The power flows through us back to the Imperial, to the caverns below."

Edison scribbles frantically. "But people don't notice when you take their Animus?"

"At first, we just collected on the road...going anyplace with enough folks so we could blend in. Told people we were setting up distribution for the whiskey business." Elmer's voice turns bitter. "Vicente backed us up with money to buy rounds. We were always the life of the party, popular everywhere we went. I hated being friendly with people while stealing from them. Mads loved it. Said he was happy the suckers were getting what's coming to them."

The fire pops, making Elmer jump. He clutches at his wound, face going pale. "I didn't think we were doing serious harm. Just a little sip from some dude at a bar didn't seem like a big deal. They'd go home and sleep it off. Didn't seem any worse than whiskey." He finally looks at me entreatingly. "But them buckles can hurt people bad. Mads likes to use them that way."

"Where did these buckles come from?" I ask, studying the crude scrimshaw on the bone inlay.

"Múcaro." Elmer's eyes dart to the shadows. "Two years ago, Hoodoo brought him on, said he was a master distiller from Mexico. He came with these trunks, set himself up in the caves. Nobody allowed down there. I seen him take stuff out—jars of powders and oils, old bones and such. He'd lock himself up for hours, working on his 'recipes.'"

A log shifts in the fire, sending sparks upward. Elmer's eyes grow distant. "Few weeks later, right before Easter, Hoodoo and Múcaro did some ritual and...something came over Hoodoo. He wasn't himself no more. Started spouting craziness about finding his power. Showed us visions I don't never wanna see again. Blood and gold and rotting corpses." His voice drops to a hoarse whisper. "That's when he gave the five of us the belt buckles. Said we were special. Said we were never to take them off... Said they were made from the skull of the first betrayer."

Morgan and I share a look. Cursed objects binding his henchmen together. What was Hoodoo's plan? Cold fingers of dread creep over my scalp.

"Is that what happened to Ada and Delilah?" I ask, keeping my voice steady despite the rage building inside me.

Elmer's words come faster now, like he needs to get them out. "Me and Mads were back in Vegas, between gigs. Mads wanted some companionship and he asked for Delilah 'cause he ain't had her before. She was new."

He stops, swallowing hard. The wound in his side has started seeping again, a dark stain spreading across the bandage. "Vicente said Mads could give her a run, but Ada needed to come along, keep an eye on things. I always liked Ada, had a beautiful singing voice. I was happy to spend the evening with her."

"What went wrong?" Morgan's voice is hard.

"Ada and I were drinking and snuggling by the stove when I heard Delilah laugh. Then Mads hit her, and she screamed, so he hit her again, but she wouldn't stop screaming, so he kept hitting her."

My fists clench, and I press my lips together, holding back accusations, but I manage to keep my tone even. "What were you doing while Mads beat Delilah?"

Elmer seems to ignore me. "Ada went to help. Mads screamed at me to hold her. Then she started screamin' too. He kept hitting Delilah till she was knocked out. Ada threatened to bring in Marshals, said she had a cousin...said she would see Mads swing in the square. He grabbed her and drained her dry before I could help... He was gonna drain Delilah dead too, but I pulled him off. Then the other ladies busted in the door." Elmer's head dropped to his hands, covering his eyes. "It all happened so fast. I shoulda done more..."

"Yea, you should have." Morgan looks away, shoulders slumped, and pokes at the fire.

Mads needs to be stopped. Shit, this whole operation needs shut down, but something's missing from Elmer's story. I say, "Elmer, I don't understand. The buckle's powered by magic, right? How could Mads use the belt buckle in town?"

Edison straightens, his earlier enthusiasm returning despite the horror. "How's that possible with the ward?"

"Anyone castin' through a buckle, the ward treats 'em as 'house magic,' lets the spell fire. Everybody else gets slammed. But there's a price," Elmer adds, his voice dropping even lower. "If you use the buckle inside the ward, power can flow both directions. Hoodoo...he can take your Animus. Vicente says it gives Hoodoo insurance against betrayal. That's why I don't want it near me. It's like he's got an invisible straw straight to my soul."

I mull that over. A damn skeleton key. Hoodoo's men get to break the rules because they're wired into the engine that enforces 'em. All we gotta do is get Elmer and his buckle to Van Lew and our contract is done, unequivocal evidence the women were victims of a magical attack. But this entire cabal needs to be stopped. And maybe there's still a way to help Delilah, return her stolen soul.

"Could that much stolen Animus power a ward this size?" Edison asks, turning to me.

I rub my temples. "Maybe. You said yourself it's gotta be Big Magic to cover the whole town. That means life or death..." A horrible thought strikes me. "Elmer, when did you start collecting Animus? Was it around the time the ward went up?"

He nods. "That's about right."

Morgan frowns. "If they're powering the ward with stolen souls, what's the point? Why stop magic in town just to use these cursed buckles?"

"I don't think it's just the ward," I say thinking it through. "That much power... Hoodoo's got bigger plans."

"All I know is there's something hungry down in them caverns," Elmer whispers. "Something that feeds on what we collect."

Edison stands abruptly. "I gotta get word to Van Lew."

Elmer cuts in, "You'll never get word out." He tries to sit up straighter, wincing. "And you promised to get me out of here. Won't do me no good if you go and get yourself shot."

I reach for my forgotten coffee, gone cold now. "We gotta give the horses a chance to recover and Elmer needs to lie still. We should be safe here for the night. We lost Mads clear on the other end of the valley."

Morgan sets his cup down. "If it weren't for the horses, especially Muneca riding double all day, I'd say we should abskize. But all things considered, I agree. We wait."

Edison puffs his cheeks and lets the air slowly escape. "I suppose. But I don't like it."

I stand with effort, exhaustion deepening. The weight of what we've learned sits heavy on my shoulders. Something worse than a ward is brewing in those caverns, and we're the only ones who know. "I'm tuckered out."

Morgan nods. "I'll keep first watch. Dawn's only a few hours away."

I drift toward my bedroll, casting one last probing glance at Elmer, still crouched miserably on the blanket. For now, I sink onto my bedroll, but sleep won't come easy with visions of Hoodoo's soul-stealing operation haunting my thoughts.

Chapter Seventeen

THE CRACK OF A rifle shot pierces the air, jolting me awake. I bolt upright, peering through the small opening of the arched door. Another shot rings out, followed by shouts and horses whinnying. We are under attack.

"Get up!" I yell, shaking Edison awake. "We've got company!"

Edison scrambles to his feet, blinking sleep from his eyes. Morgan already has his Winchester in hand, crouching near the door. Edison fumbles for his pistols in the darkness. Our captive, Elmer, cowers in the shadows of the oven.

I creep to the narrow doorway and peer out. Through the starlight, I can just make out armed riders closing on our camp. Our horses tug nervously against their picket, too far away to reach before the riders close.

"Is it Mads?" Morgan growls, pressing against my back to look through the arch.

I squint, trying to make out faces in the dim light. A tall rider directs the others with sharp hand gestures. Recognition slams me in the face.

"It's Hoodoo Jones," I whisper, "and looks like he brought friends."

Morgan hisses a curse. "Dammit, I warned you about coming to Hoodoo's attention. Mads must have made it back to him."

Now Hoodoo and his gang are attacking us under the cover of darkness. Elmer whimpers, I grimace. "Bet he's here for the boy."

Elmer has a buckle and knowledge of Hoodoo's operations. That makes him a dangerous loose end. One Hoodoo seems intent on tying up.

"Like hell," Morgan mutters, clicking back the hammer on his rifle. "He'll have that boy over my dead body."

Nope, not gonna come to that, not if I have any say. I count the men closing on us, and the new ain't good. We're outgunned eight to three. Morgan's a crack shot, but neither Edison nor I are worth a damn. This old coke oven provides pretty good cover. Hope it's enough.

Morgan's eyes dart across the clearing where the horsemen gather. "If they stay in the open, I can pick 'em off." His eyes glint like steel.

The riders venture cautiously toward our camp, scouring the dark for any signs of life. We hold perfectly still, breath held. They surely can hear the pounding of my heart.

After an agonizing minute, Hoodoo's reedy voice cuts through the silence. "Well, lookee here, boys. Seems we got some late-night campers after all. Why don't y'all be neighborly and invite them to join us for a spell?"

On some invisible signal, pistols and rifles erupt with flashes of fire. We throw ourselves to the ground. Our little shelter reverberates with the force of the gunshots, stone chips zipping through the air, peppering the soft ground outside. Only a few shots make it through the narrow windows and door, bouncing off the curved walls harmlessly for now. Hoodoo's men either hope to drive us out or gun us down direct. But luck is on our side. The stone dome pits under the fusillade, but the thick walls hold.

When the barrage stops, Morgan eases up to one of the narrow vent windows. Raising his rifle with steady, practiced hands, he draws a bead on the tall, slender figure beyond the gunmen. I hold my breath. The clean crack of Morgan's shot echoes, but somehow Hoodoo senses the attack. He dives from his saddle as the bullet whizzes through the space previously occupied by his head, striking a raider behind him.

One down.

"Damn." Morgan growls. Hoodoo's men are returning fire while their leader rolls for cover. It can't be long before they overrun us.

On my left, Edison fumbles with shaking hands to load his revolvers. Why weren't they already loaded? His eyes shine white and wide through his smudged spectacles. I hope the boy doesn't do something stupidly brave to prove himself. Packed overfull of Pete's lies and expectations, but sorely green around the edges yet when it comes to confronting armed men. I send a quick prayer to anything listening that he survives the night.

Outside our shelter, Hoodoo regains his feet, barking orders at his men to advance. We're rapidly running out of options. Flight isn't possible. Morgan is lethal, but I'm not sure he can take them all down before they're upon us. I've half a mind to release Elmer to his fate and hope these hellhounds let us be. One look at the young man's gaunt face, stretched by pain and fear, halts that line of thought. He's too similar to the soldiers I'd seen butchered by the thousands during the War. Elmer begged us for protection and I mean to give it.

That leaves one option. The one that turns my veins to ice and makes my soul sing. Dark power simmers inside me, sinuous and seductive. Hoodoo's gunman lies dying right outside. If I could reach him, I could ride him, harness that power and stop those hunting us. Hunger coils in me, prodding for release. The Johnny Reb appears at my shoulder, stroking my cheek. I can almost understand his whispered words. A breath to unleash it...

A cry rings out, shattering my thoughts. Morgan lurches backward with a yowl, grazed by a bullet across his shoulder. Blood, black in the dim light, splatters the sandy floor. He collapses to his knees. My heart seizes in panic. No!

I react on instinct, rousing my somnolent Gleaner, and reach for the dying gunman's Animus. Psychic fingers fail to catch hold. I'm old and weak, and he's too far away. Glancing at Morgan's prone figure, my fear and adrenaline ratchet higher. With a surge of will, I prime the Gleaner with a sip of my own life force and reach again. Grasping the gunman's stuttering heartbeat, I shove him into death. No gentle ride into the pink mist for this sucker.

The explosion of his freed Animus jars my senses, and rainbows of hot color wash over my sight. With a scream, I amass the energy and thrust it into the night. Air ripples as energy explodes from my core and cannonballs into our attackers. Two men go flying as if punched by a giant fist. They crash limply to the dirt, spines broken on impact. Before they draw their last breaths, my Gleaner is on them too, greedily harvesting them as they pass from living to dead. Visions of broken bodies and purple fog swirl around me from their memories. My blood sings with power, sated after years of longing. This is what I was born for.

The night shadows lean closer, caressing me like old friends welcoming me back. I shudder, revolted and enthralled. A cold wave descends on me, raising gooseflesh. The shades of the gunmen stare at me across the clearing. My Confederate joins them and leads them through the trees. I start to follow before a sharp cry yanks me back. Morgan attempting to rise, blinks at me in dismay. "Dammit, Mick," he pants, pressing a hand to his bleeding shoulder. "What did you do?"

Shame floods through me, dampening the pleasure. What have I done? I promised never to call on that wicked energy again, never to play reaper-goddess feasting on the throes of Death. Just last night Morgan said he doubted the Gleaner inside me could stay caged. Yet at the first taste of battle, I slip my leash to answer the hungry whispers in my blood.

There will be a price to pay, there always is. But that bill will have to queue up behind bigger problems—we still face Hoodoo and his surviving men.

Too late, I sense movement in the darkness. One of Hoodoo's lackeys bursts around the oven's door, pistol leveled at Morgan's back. There's no way he'll bring his rifle about it time. Panicked, I thrust out my hand and slam an invisible hammer into the man's chest, stopping his heart instantly. He collapses mid-stride, eyes rolling up white.

Enraged, Morgan wheels on me, oblivious to his own near-death. "Will you STOP that?" he thunders. "I'd rather take a bullet than pour more blood on your hands! We fight clean, without your damned powers." He turns away, hefting his rifle, the stock stained with his blood. "Where is that slippery son of a bitch Hoodoo?" he scans the darkness. "I've got a bullet with his name on it for old times' sake..."

I fall back, his words piercing my heart. Morgan's right. But in that moment, there was no other choice. The Gleaner wasn't gonna be leashed when peril closed on my partner. I am its creature, bound by a thousand scarlet threads. My stomach twists sourly.

"Parley!" a voice calls from the darkness, the word stretched into two distinct syllables. "Let's talk this through like civilized folk, shall we?"

Morgan's rifle doesn't waver. "Ain't nothing civil about ambushing folk in the dark, Jones."

"Now, now, Morgan Smith." The voice draws closer, honeyed and dangerous. "That's mighty rich coming from you. Besides, seems to me your friend there just sent three of my men to meet their Maker in ways that weren't exactly...sporting."

"Show yourself then," I call out, "if you're feeling so diplomatic."

"Ain't this just the sweetest little reunion," an amused drawl accompanies Hoodoo as he saunters from the darkness, blood-speckled hands gripping a lantern. His cadaverous face splits into that too-wide smile I remember, revealing teeth that gleam in the lamplight. He strokes his luxurious mustache with one long finger, a gesture I've seen a hundred times in Lafayette's war room.

He tilts his head, studying me like a curious vulture. "I declare our old warhorse Mick Kelly risen from the ashes like Lazarus himself. Must admit it's a shock seeing your face after all these years." His voice lilts with exaggerated courtesy. "I had believed you perished in that awful wreck, burned to a crisp trying to save my Lafayette." His mouth twists in a mockery of grief. "We all mourned you after, even held a memorial service for those poor souls sent to fiery judgment. Imagine my delight when I learned you still counted among the living?"

The familiar wash of despair almost drowns me. I nearly died that dreadful night. Dozens of innocent lives extinguished, their agonized shades haunted my nightmares for years.

My voice rasps across the intervening yards. "The reports of my death were greatly exaggerated...though I'm sorry I can't say the opposite of you, Jones."

He tilts his head, that smile widening. "Ain't that just the sweetest thing," he purrs. "You always did have more mouth than brains. My Lafayette always did admire that about you..." He gestures lazily toward Elmer. "Give that boy here, and we can all call it a night."

"Kid asked for my protection and I reckon I'll stand by my word." My thumb caresses the grip of my revolver.

Hoodoo throws back his head and barks a laugh that sounds like bones rattling. "Bless your heart, playing at being decent folk. Tell me, does your friend Mr. Smith know how many souls you harvested? Does your boy know what his hero really is?" His amused look darkens. "We're cut from the same cloth, you and I. Lafayette's cloth. He baptized us both in blood and power. Difference is, I don't pretend to be something I'm not."

Anger flashes, steadying my nerve. "There is NO comparison," I grit my teeth. "Even then I spilled blood to save lives from monsters like you!"

Hoodoo shrugs. "Still hear those screams sometimes, don't you? All those poor souls trapped in those burning train cars while you rode their deaths like a Ferris Wheel. Lafayette calling your name as the flames took him."

My fists clench. Morgan intervened that awful night of fire and fury, pulling me from the ashes. I emerged transformed...or so I desperately wanted to believe. Desperately needed others to believe about me—that I was not in fact the monster Hoodoo named me. My wandering gaze falls on Morgan glowering beside me, fresh blood staining his shoulder. Shame chokes me.

"And here we are." His voice turns ugly. "Providence smiles and I find myself with the bitch who murdered my boss and rode off with nary a look back."

Understanding crystallizes—Hoodoo wants revenge as much or more than to claim Elmer. Resolve firms my heart. Over my dead body... I would not fail the boy.

Slowly, I straighten, power thrumming just beneath my skin. I lock eyes with the taller man, seeing only a predator who would tear the world apart to sate his appetites. My voice emerges cold as tomb ice. "Walk away now, Hoodoo, and I'll let your current devilry be. Come at me, and I vow only one gets clear of this field alive."

He scowls, trembling lip telegraphing his dimming confidence. Hoodoo always feared me. The night itself presses close around us, responding to my coiling power. His men shift in the lamplight. Hoodoo again rallies his bluster.

"You and what army, bitch?" He sneers. "One tired blue-belly and a teen pup hardly make for house odds. Last chance—throw me the whelp and we leave you be. Otherwise, ain't a power on this earth gonna save you, darlin'."

I slide my gaze sideways to Morgan. His mouth is a hard line, but he gives a sharp nod. I look at Edison beside him and he nods, glasses askew and pale face practically glowing in the dark. We would make our stand together. I hear Elmer praying behind me.

I turn back to Hoodoo, contempt dripping from my words. "Hoodoo, I didn't think much of you back then. Lafayette's yellow lap dog. Can't say my opinion has improved. If you want Elmer, you go through us."

With a shriek, Hoodoo smashes the lantern to the ground outside the doorway, casting flickering light into our shelter. One of Hoodoo's men takes cover beside a log, rifle trained on the doorway. Guns roar, muzzle flashes punctuate the darkness. Morgan curses roundly even as his rifle fires and one man falls.

A bullet zips over my left shoulder, taking Elmer in the head. Even as he falls, Hoodoo and his last henchman melt into the trees.

Chapter Eighteen

DEATHLY SILENCE DESCENDS. I sag to my knees, spent. The Gleaner drained me to the dregs, but the cost is a small price for our lives. That bill will come due.

The Reb stirs, rising with the recent dead I've consigned to oblivion. Thin wisps of shade-stuff coil around me. The remnants know me, reaching with smoky fingers to stroke my soul in dreadful intimacy. Revulsion and self-loathing choke me. Oh God, what have I done?

"On your feet, Mick." Morgan's rough voice cuts through the gathering spirits. "Ain't no time to feel sorry for yourself. Hoodoo could be back with reinforcements before the sun fully rises."

I shudder back to myself and look up dully. His expression holds no comfort or gratitude, only contempt. He turns away, mouth twisting bitterly as he scans the gruesome aftermath. Happy whistles and chirps of early morning birds contrast harshly with the rotten egg scent of gunpowder.

The ground outside our shelter is littered with the bodies of Hoodoo's henchmen, dark lumps in the false dawn's glow. Three victims of my magic, one from Morgan's rifle. The shades of the three whose deaths I rode skitter around the bodies. Their energy roils inside me. I gleaned little of their memories upon their death. They were focused on killing us, but especially Elmer. Why did Hoodoo want Elmer dead so badly? Was there anything left he could have told us?

I feel the dead men's Animus seeping into my own, filling fractures with mortar. Despite the shame, it's comforting and familiar.

I lurch upright as Edison creeps from cover, eyes round with shock behind his spectacles. He edges toward us like a skittish colt, wide gaze darting between me and Morgan.

"She had to," he whispers hoarsely. "He woulda killed you, Morgan. Wasn't nothin' else to be done." He looks desperately at the older man for reassurance.

Morgan says nothing for long moments, jaw tight, fighting some internal battle. When he turns back, whatever war had raged behind his eyes resolved. "Road to hell's paved with good intentions and cold necessities," he rasps darkly. Cutting his gaze from Edison, he leans down to carefully cover a dead man's face with his poncho. The tremble of Morgan's hands causes shame to cascade over me. Doubtless this grim reminder of our past ripped open old wounds. Sickness roils in my gut. I should have found another way...

Morgan barks, "We gotta clear out of here lickety-split. Ain't time to bury these men properly." He gestures to the gun-man with the poncho. "Edison, grab this feller's feet. We'll drag them into one of the ovens and block the door. Might keep out animals out long enough for friends to find them and bury them proper like."

I stop myself from correcting him. These men likely didn't have friends who cared one way or the other about the disposition of their mortal remains. Instead, I take hold of the smallest body by the shoulders and drag him to the nearest oven. With time short, we should leave them where they lie, but if Morgan needs to assuage his conscience, I ain't gonna fight it.

I return to the oven where we camped to care for Elmer's body, still slumped on the blanked by the firepit. What secret earned him execution? Death eased the lines around his eyes, making him look even younger. This poor kid survived one ambush only to lose the next. I failed him too. At least he didn't die with that accursed buckle on. I wrap Elmer's body in the blanket and signal Edison to help me haul him to the others.

We rush to finish the sobering labor. When Morgan straightens from shoving the last piece of brush over the door of the charcoal oven, his face is granite. "I ain't built for this no more," he bites out. "Killing's a young man's trade. I'm going home to Maria before my number's up for good." He turns to gathering his gear. "We've got what the BMI wanted—proof. No reason to dally."

"Morgan, you heard what Mads did. I think we gotta bring him in." I look at Edison.

"Mads has gotta face justice for killin' Ada," Edison says, wiping his glasses with his shirt tail. "And with Elmer dead, he's our only witness to Hoodoo's goings-on. No one is gonna believe us otherwise. You heard what happened with Leona's reports." He places his glasses back on his face and straightens his hat. "Between the ward and the buckles, this could be the biggest case in BMI history, and I'm the agent on site. I gotta see it through."

"Leona's still in town, you remember." I roll my eyes at his hubris. "She's been the agent on site for a year."

"That's why we gotta bring in Mads." His eyes are shining. "Give the higher-ups proof they can't ignore."

Morgan shakes his head. "You both got more ego than sense." He bends to pick up his saddle. "This is like the old days, Mick. You never could pass up a fight, never could walk away from a bully. I'm headed home, with or without you."

My heart fractures. There's truth in his words. Seeing Hoodoo's smirk when he called me a killer—it lit something I thought buried. I crave to wipe that smile clean off his smug face. That's why Morgan turns away from me even more than from the bloody remains of our stand. In saving his life, I lost my friend. Proved his faith in me misplaced. I am the monster Hoodoo named me.

I stride after him. "Morgan, please!" My voice breaks wretchedly. "You would have died too." I would breathe fire to prevent that, no matter the cost.

Morgan turns and his eyes gentle. "I know, Mick. I should never have come on this job. I knew full well what you are, and I love you for it. Expecting you to be different ain't fair."

Silence falls between us. He swings his rifle over his shoulder and heads to the picket line to tack up Muneca. I trail behind. Face etched with sadness, he continues, "My long ride days are done, Mick. I'm too old to travel this road any farther. I can't bear your magic. The killin' is hard enough, but when you use your powers, I feel like I'm being sucked into a pit. If you're determined to stay, this job's too dangerous to do without your special abilities. I saw that last night. But I'm out."

I busy myself preparing Sampson, searching for words to make things right. Morgan leads Muneca a short distance away from the other horses. I remain mute.

Edison hurries over. "Here, sir." He hands Morgan a cloth-wrapped buckle and an envelope. "Give the buckle and my report to Commander Van Lew. She'll see that you are paid for the entire ten days as per our agreement."

"Morgan..." I start but give up. Then stare at my feet. "Please be careful. Hoodoo's gonna be looking for all of us."

"Yup, you better keep him too busy to bother with me." Morgan scratches Muneca's neck. "Me and Muneca are gonna try to board the northbound train at La Junta. My friend Bill Koenig's got a spread up there. I might call on him to put us up." He looks at Edison. "I'll be adding the ticket price to my expenses."

"Of course. Yes, sir," Edison squeaks. "Whatever you need."

Mounting his mare, Morgan touches his hat brim in a final salute and tips his head at me. "Find Mads. But stay alive." Then looking at Edison, he says, "Son, you won't have a storied career if you're dead before twenty."

"Goodbye, Morgan." Edison touches the brim of his hat. "I'll stop by when I get back to Trinidad and have some more of Maria's beans."

"Yeah, you do that," Morgan calls back. "Remember, your uncle Pete's livin' into a ripe old age. Follow suit."

Wheeling Muneca, he casts me a long look, then rides away without a backward glance. Something shrivels inside my chest, a light snuffed out. I stare after until the forest swallows him whole.

A small scuffing sound recalls me to the present. I turn to consider Edison. The boy hovers nervously, hat in hands, eyes large behind smudged lenses. But not afraid, I realize. Not of me, even after witnessing the devil let loose.

He squares his narrow shoulders with a stubborn set to his chin. "We're still goin' after Mads. Gotta finish the job proper?" At my mute nod, he jams his hat back on his head. "Pete says a crew worth their salt don't leave a job half done. Not a patch on Morgan, but I reckon we've got work to do."

Dear Lord, more Pete. I hope Pete's philosophy doesn't kill this boy. "You heard what Morgan said? Pete's happily toddling into his dotage. No matter his stories, he survived his youth."

He rolls his eyes at me. "I ain't some kid who needs protecting. You're my partner in this, and we've both got goals here."

I manage a brittle smile. "Well then. Let's get out of here before more guests drop in."

He grins eagerly back. Edison grunts, tightening Abigail's cinch. "You used your power on a few of those guys. You get anything about their plans?"

"I know they powerfully wanted Elmer caught or Elmer dead." I pause to check Sampson's bridle. "And I know the one that came for Morgan was more scared of Hoodoo than he was of dying... He had a sweetheart in Georgetown." I sigh. "But not much else."

"Any chance you can talk to them? Figure out where we'll find Mads?"

"Sometimes folks that go fast like that aren't interested in conversating. But they're still lurking around, keeping company with another shade from the war."

"They here now?" His voice climbs an octave as he mounts Abigail, head swiveling around, eyes darting everywhere. "I don't want to be riding with no ghosts."

"Relax, kid." I settled on Sampson, checking my shotgun in its holder. "They won't bother you. Don't Pete have something to say about shades?"

"Ironically, Pete says to leave the past in the past." His teeth flash in a smile in his grimy face. "I don't imagine he would approve truck with ghosts."

I chuckle back and head Sampson off at an easy jog, Abigail beside us.

He says, "I reckon we head west around Vegas, bivouac today, reconnoiter and try to locate Mads?"

"That camp of his must be somewhere in the mountains," I muse. "We don't know if he has run to ground there or if he's sheltering in town. He must've told Hoodoo we had Elmer." The thought of Hoodoo makes my mouth dry—seeing him tonight was like looking into a mirror of my darkest days. Another bully drunk on death magic who needs stopping.

"With what we learned about those buckles, this case is huge!" Edison's eyes shine with ambition.

"Easy there, kid, we're just helping finish what Leona started."

Edison's ears redden as he shifts uncomfortably. "I know. I don't mean to cut her out of the credit none. Between her investigation and what we've uncovered, we can bring Mads to justice for Ada. Maybe even stop Hoodoo before he hurts anyone else like Delilah."

The memory of Delilah's damaged Animus flashes through my mind. With what Elmer told us about the battery in the caverns, maybe there's still a chance to help her. To save someone instead of just ending them. The thought eases my guilt over tonight, just a touch.

Side by side, we ride on into the night, leaving behind the ambush and the loss of Morgan. The future remains uncertain and my own redemption doubtfully attainable.

Chapter Nineteen

MY THIGHS ACHE FROM hours in the saddle as Edison and I pick our way through another rocky draw west of Vegas. Since dawn, we've been searching these hills for Mads's hideout. But so far, we've found nothing but empty caves and abandoned prospects.

The night's chill retreated with the rising sun, leaving the air crisp and cool, but by early afternoon, the temperature climbed, leaving both riders and horses sweating. When we reach a meadow around midday, I signal a halt. "Horses need water," I say, nodding toward the creek. "And we could use a bite ourselves."

We settle in the shade of an aspen grove, keeping watch while the horses graze. Edison pulls tortillas and jerky from his saddlebags, but his mind's clearly elsewhere. He fidgets with his hat, glancing my way several times before speaking.

"Morgan left his whiskey," he says softly, pulling out the flask. "You want a snort?"

"No, we gotta keep our heads clear." What is he thinking? I shift, pulling my coat tighter.

"Why'd he get so riled up about your magic? I mean, I know he didn't like it, but enough to send him off?" Edison tosses a pebble, we watch it skitter down the slope.

"'Cuz Morgan's seen what could happen when it goes wrong," I say. "Up close and personal-like."

"What's that mean exactly?" Edison prods.

I stare at my boots, jaw working. Talking about the crash...it comes hard. Like poking at an old wound, never quite healed. But Edison deserves to understand what my power can do.

Haltingly at first, I begin. "Our last job together was a shit show. Because of me." I rub a hand over my face, feeling the years etched there.

"That the Kansas City crash?"

I sink low to lean against my saddle. "Yes, the Kansas City crash. See, there was Confederate gold on that train. Lafayette wanted it. A gunrunner was trying to set up shop in California, keep it from the federal government. The plan was to decouple the cars and blast the armored freighter, confiscate the gold."

I hang my head, old anger and sorrow welling up. "But that ain't what happened. I convinced Morgan and Clyde we needed to take out Lafayette. Permanently. He had plans for that gold we couldn't let fruit. Things went sideways real fast..."

Edison gasps, but I ignore him and stare up at aspens swaying in the spring breeze, seeing again that hellish night. "Clyde got the cars decoupled all right. But the dynamite blew early, in the wrong spot. Stopped the engine dead on the tracks. Then..." I swallow hard. "Then the passenger cars accordioned right into it. Crumpled like tin cans. Fire everywhere, people screaming..."

Edison makes a low sound, horrified.

I barrel on. "I rode into that chaos, gathering deaths like strawberries—even folks who weren't ready to go." I can still taste the metallic tang of panic and smoke. "Once the killing started"—I tap my chest—"the Gleaner in me woke up hungry. Pulled so much power I nearly burned out like a spent match."

Edison leans forward, face pale beneath his freckles. "Morgan pulled you back?"

I nod once. "Dragged me free." I pick up a stone, turning it over and over. "Over a hundred dead. Morgan always said half woulda made it if I hadn't..." My voice trails off. From the corner of my eye, I spot the Reb watching, nodding along, ghastly smile wide.

The kid swallows hard, but there's calculation alongside the horror in his eyes. "And Lafayette was worth that price?"

A bitter laugh escapes me. "I was runnin' with his crew for months after Belle nursed him through typhus. He came back...different. I should've known something wasn't right. But

I was on the edge of control... Lafayette had me using my power all the time. It's addictive... The more I use, the more I want... I was addled half the time between the Gleaner power and the whiskey."

Somewhere in the trees, the jay scolds us. Edison waits, silent.

"It all went to hell when I overheard him with Belle one night." I meet Edison's gaze directly. "They thought I was out cold, as usual, but I heard them. Lafayette hadn't survived the typhus... Belle had turned him, made him a vampire—"

Edison jolts upright. "That's—" His hand flies to the silver cross at his neck. "That can't—"

"Can't be true? The Continental Congress banished all vampires?" I give him a mirthless smile. "Turns out Miss Boyd slipped through. And a necromancer like Lafayette, once turned? Twice as dangerous."

Edison's brow furrows in concentration, pieces falling into place. "The gold he was after... it wasn't just money."

"Smart boy. Lafayette needed it for a ritual, some kind of mystical secession, nonsense he picked up down in Mexico." I draw a circle in the dirt with my boot heel. "Planned to turn half of Galveston into his personal feeding ground."

"You sent for the Bureau?"

"I sent word to Alan Pinkerton by way of an informant, but I couldn't wait around for an answer." I scrub my hand across my face. "That train was coming, whether the Pinkertons were there or not."

Edison's face shifts through several emotions before settling on reluctant understanding. "So Morgan and Clyde agreed to—"

"To put down a monster, yes." I lean back against my saddle, suddenly bone-tired. "And that's why Hoodoo's so hot for revenge. He worshiped Lafayette, no doubt wanted the same power. Probably expected being turned himself someday."

Edison's eyes widen. "He's a necromancer too."

I nod slowly. "And they make powerful vampires."

"But it's been what, ten years since the crash?"

A crow caws overhead, drawing my gaze upward. When I look back at Edison, his eager face reminds me how young he is.

"Originally, he didn't know I survived. Morgan and Clyde let the gang believe I died trying to save Lafayette." A mirthless chuckle escapes me. "Alan Pinkerton himself turned up in the aftermath. Smoothed over the investigation, quashed any mention of Yours Truly." I grimace. "Even put about the story to the public I'd perished, then expunged my official record."

"Pinkerton covered for you?" Edison asks, brow furrowed.

"In a manner of speaking," I say carefully. "The BMI takes a dim view of vampires setting up shop on American soil. Lafayette's demise was real convenient for them."

I touch the brim of my hat, shadowing my eyes. "But it came with a caveat. My name was never to cross the Bureau's desk again, and then you show up."

Edison digests this, clever mind spinning, "Doesn't seem right," he mutters. "You did what needed doing. What they couldn't. That's why Van Lew was so cagey."

"Commander Van Lew understands down to her core what I can do given the wrong circumstances." I shrug. "The BMI ain't in the habit of leaving loose ends."

The wind picks up, rustling through the aspens. Edison stares at his hands, thinking. When he looks up, his eyes are troubled but determined.

"It's not right," he says, pulling on his ear. "I'm sorry I dragged you back into this."

I reach over and squeeze his shoulder, surprised by my own gesture. "We all carry our ghosts, kid. I'm trying to do some good this time."

He grips my hand. "Well, I'm right pleased you're on this case with me, Mick. Ain't nobody I'd rather have at my back." Embarrassed by his earnestness, he flushes and settles his hat more firmly.

We startle at a soft scuff and clatter of shale sound downslope. Has Hoodoo sniffed us out? My hand flies to the shotgun. Edison slides silently into firing position atop a large boulder, pistol tracking toward the sound. I hold my breath, straining to identify the intruder over the pounding of my heart. I can't separate shadow from movement as the trees shift and dance in the wind. The "chick-a-dee-dee-dee" song of birds stops and the horses are still on their picket.

Movement flickers in the shadows. My finger tenses on the trigger.

◆—■—◆

Then the gleam of tawny fur, in the sun... I blink in surprise as the largest mountain lion I ever laid eyes on slinks from the tree line. She moves purposefully, not bothering to hide her presence... which hadn't spooked the horses. Something's off.

I prepare to fire a warning shot, scare her away, but something in the cougar's demeanor gives me pause. Her ears prick toward us without fear, tail twitching with curiosity rather than aggression. Was that a smile lurking around her whiskered mouth? Anxiety trickles down my neck that has nothing to do with facing down a hundred-odd pounds of fang and claw.

The lioness sits back on her haunches, tail coiling around her paws. Impossibly, shimmering like heat-haze, her form blurs and shifts. Resettles into the unmistakable curves of a naked woman crouched in the dirt.

Recognition slams through me, staggering in its impossibility—Leona. And unless I've gone completely crackers, she's sprouted herself a lion's shape.

Unperturbed by guns pointed in her direction, she straightens. "Well met, sister." Her cultured throaty voice breaks the silence.

After searching for a few seconds, I find my words. "I don't know I'd call us sisters..." I look her up and down.

She shrugs, unabashed.

Behind me, Edison makes choking sounds. I fight back a hysterical bubble of laughter at the absurdity of debating sorority with a cat-woman on the side of a mountain. "Seems you've been holding out on us."

Leona tosses her hair behind her shoulders, teeth flashing white. "Girl's gotta have some secrets in this trade."

I snort, lowering my gun. Secrets are one thing. Turning into a great goddamned cat is something else entire.

I cut a look at Edison, who's doing his best impression of a stunned trout. Remembering himself, he spins around, facing away. His ears burn crimson. "Miss Freeman, I—you never mentioned—"

"That I'm more than just a barmaid with good ears?" She smiles. "The Bureau prefers I keep that particular talent under wraps."

I gesture toward our packs. "There's a spare shirt if you want it."

"Obliged." She strides over, unfazed by her nudity, and pulls out a shirt. "Good thing I tracked you when I did. The way Hoodoo rode into town this morning, spitting nails about Elmer..."

Edison turns back cautiously once she's covered. "You followed our trail?"

"By scent." She taps her nose. "A lioness never forgets a smell." Her eyes narrow. "Where's your other partner?"

Edison's face falls. "Morgan took off. Had enough after..." He glances at me.

"After I used the Gleaner," I finish flatly. "Crossed a line for him."

Leona's expression sharpens with interest. "So it's true what they say about you." She studies me with new eyes. "Explains how you took down three of Hoodoo's men."

"What else happened in town?" I ask, eager to change the subject.

"Hoodoo banished Mads to his old claim. Trying to clean house." She settles on a rock. "Vicente's furious—bad for business, leaving him short-staffed—but he's not crossing Hoodoo these days.

"Then Hoodoo started squawking at Múcaro about you besting him. Don't know what Múcaro can do." She adjusts the borrowed shirt across her shoulders. "Take it your arrests didn't go to plan?"

I give Leona the shorthand version of capturing Elmer and our exhausting trek back to camp, followed by Hoodoo ambushing us. I lean forward. "Elmer told us something before he died. Those belt buckles Hoodoo's men wear? They drain Animus, feed it somewhere."

Leona goes still, eyes widening. "I knew it," she breathes. "That explains the ward." Her gaze sharpens. "What else did he say?"

I shrug. "Not much. But it's plain as day Hoodoo's up to his eyeballs in some nasty devilment. Edison confirmed the buckles are enchanted."

Leona cocked an eyebrow in Edison's direction. "What's your power?"

"It's barely a power," Edison explains. "Just a knack. I feel castings, recognize the signatures. If it's strong enough, I can track the spell."

"Practically a mystical bloodhound. That seems like an ability the BMI would value." Her voice hints at a growl. "And what do you see in the buckles?"

"The magic is purple and...ravenous. It's the same color as the runes on the town sign, so it comes from the same source. It all points back to town."

"No shit," Leona harrumphs. "Don't know what good that does us." She pulls on the cuffs of her borrowed shirt. "That hole Mads opened in Delilah seems to be killing her faster every day." Her voice tightens. "This morning, her eyes were clouded over, like she's going blind. Whatever that belt buckle did..."

"She got any family?" I ask, checking my revolver's chambers mechanically while the Reb looms behind Leona, studying her with suspicion.

"Just the girls at the Imperial." Leona paces the small clearing, catlike even in human form. "Vicente won't pay for a doctor. Says she's—" Her voice breaks. "Says she's not worth the expense."

I holster my weapon, remembering those holes I'd seen riddling the girl's Animus like buckshot. "That magic is still feeding on her. Like a slow poison that's spreading."

Edison fidgets with his notebook. "Could you... could your abilities help her?"

"No." I shake my head. "I only know how to take energy, not how to fix it."

"But maybe the BMI could," Edison blurts, straightening abruptly. His thin fingers drum against his thigh. "That's brilliant! With Mads, his belt buckle as evidence, and Delilah showing the effects—our research division would have everything they need to understand this magic."

I bark out a harsh laugh. "You're suggesting we hand that girl over to your butchers?"

Edison's face flushes red. "It's not like that! They're healers too. They'd help her."

"Like they 'helped' those Navajo Dators in '67?" I spit into the dirt. "Half of them died.'"

"That was before my time," Edison protests. "Things are different now."

"BMI doesn't change its stripes, kid."

Leona's head snaps up, eyes flashing. "And what's your solution, Kelly? Leave her to die?" Her fingers curl into fists. "I've watched three girls waste away this year. Delilah's the only one still breathing."

A hawk screams overhead, circling on the thermals. We all fall silent.

"Whatever Hoodoo's doing with that stored Animus," Edison says quietly, adjusting his spectacles, "it's getting bigger. More buckles, more victims." He kneels, drawing a pattern in the dirt with a stick. "If the ward and buckles are connected, he could be building toward something catastrophic."

"We focus on Mads," I counter. "We can't split our attention."

"We're taking Mads to Trinidad anyway," Leona argues, crouching to study Edison's diagram. "What's one more passenger?" Her eyes meet mine, challenging. "Unless you're planning to kill him and be done with it?"

I look away. The temptation hovers, silent as the Reb's knowing smile.

"Delilah won't last another week," Leona presses. "Not the way she's failing. And she might know things about the operation."

Edison nods eagerly. "She's both witness and victim. Commander Van Lew would consider her invaluable evidence."

I stare at the distant mountains. The BMI using a dying girl as a research subject turns my stomach. But leaving her to die feels worse.

"Fine," I growl. "But I want your word, Edison—your personal guarantee—that she'll be treated with dignity. She's a person, not a specimen."

Edison's earnest face lights up. "I swear it. I'll personally oversee her care."

"And what if she doesn't want to go?" I challenge, watching Leona's reaction.

Something haunted flickers across Leona's face. "She's desperate enough now." She studies her human hands. "Last night she asked if I'd...end things for her, if it gets worse."

That silences us all.

"I'll talk to her," Leona says. "But first, we need Mads." Her expression hardens. "Edison's right about one thing—time's running out."

"Then we move tonight," I decide, hating how the BMI is now tangled in our plans. "Mads first, then we collect Delilah before dawn."

"What if I joined you tonight?" she cuts in. "Now that you know what I can do...between my tracking abilities and your experience"—she nods to me—"we could surround Mads before he knew what hit him."

Edison's eyes light up. "Three of us would be perfect! Your abilities change everything."

"No." The word leaves my mouth before I fully consider it. Both heads swivel toward me.

"But, Mick," Edison protests, "a shapeshifter would give us an enormous advantage! She could scout ahead, flank him—"

"And expose her cover if anything goes wrong," I counter. "She's more valuable as our eyes and ears at the Imperial."

Edison's face flushes. "That's—you can't just—"

"She's right." Leona's voice cuts through, though frustration laces every word. "Damn it all to hell." She runs a hand through her hair. "As much as I'd love to help take that bastard down, I'm playing a longer game here."

Edison deflates. "But your abilities—"

"Will remain my ace card." Her eyes meet mine with grudging respect. "The moment Hoodoo learns what I am, my usefulness in town ends."

"Precisely." I meet Edison's gaze. "We gotta hang on to every advantage we have."

The disagreement settles uneasily as Leona provides detailed directions to Mads's claim. "He's only got two men with him. Thanks to you, Hoodoo keeps losing muscle and they're spread thin." She smiles wickedly.

"I'll document everything we have," Edison says, still looking disappointed. "For the official report."

Leona fixes him with an intense stare. "Remember me in that report, Mr. Colt. I've been gathering evidence for months while Santa Fe ignores my warnings. Cracking this case is my chance too."

I grimace. Damn fools, ignoring their best agent in the field.

Edison's expression softens with understanding. "We wouldn't be here without your work, Agent Freeman."

We plan to meet at an abandoned grain mill on the North end of Old Town after Edison and I grab Mads. We'll collect Leona's reports and hit the trail.

She nods, her human features blurring. "Watch yourselves. Hoodoo's desperate now."

I touch two fingers to my hat brim. "Happy hunting, Miss Leona. Don't go gettin' dead."

A rumbling chuff, almost like laughter, emanates from the big cat. Then she turns and vanishes among the trees.

As the lioness lopes away, Edison stares after her, wonder evident on his face. "A shapeshifter," he whispers. "Working right under Hoodoo's nose all this time."

"She's a good agent." I smile. "Perhaps she'd be willing to give you lessons once we're done here."

"You really don't think we should bring her along tonight?" Doubt creeps into his voice.

"I think keeping her secret is worth more." I meet his eyes.

His face contorts. "I just want to get this right, Mick." His narrow shoulders square. "I know I've got what it takes."

"You'll get your chance. But keep your head clear. No heroics."

"Partners, right?" he says, a hint of a smile returning.

"Partners," I agree, surprised to find I mean it.

As we ready ourselves for the hunt ahead, I feel that familiar darkness stirring inside me. The thought of confronting Mads stirs something hungry, a whisper of power and violence singing in my blood. I nod at Johnny Reb watching from the shadows, his knowing smile a challenge to my restraint.

Chapter Twenty

THE WANING MOON SET a couple of hours ago, leaving Edison and me with frosty starlight. We creep through silvery darkness toward the distant pinprick glow of a lantern in the fold of the hills. Our target ahead: Mads's mining camp. The Norwegian gunman is lying low. With Elmer dead and many of his cronies scattered by our last clash, Mads is isolated and vulnerable. The perfect chance to capture him.

We pause to get our bearings. We are on the eastern slope of the gully, facing the camp. The mine's main shaft, visible only as a pitch-black hole in the mountain faces eastward. Rusted bits and bobs of machinery lie scattered around the compound. I can make out a dilapidated hoist beside a crumbling ore cart. Its pulley squeaks in the breeze. Nearby, a series of battered wooden troughs trace the flow of water from a small spring nestled among the rocks.

My fingers brush the handle of my revolver, taking comfort in its solid presence. Guns and magic—weapons on this hunt. Though one is proving treacherous to my fraying conscience. The memory of the exaltation of riding Hoodoo's men into oblivion flickers on the edges. I couldn't have made a different choice, could I?

I force the uneasy thought away. This is no time for doubt. We need to get Mads to Van Lew. I need the contract money. Even if capturing our quarry taps my Gleaner, the ends justify the means. Don't they?

Edison's harsh whisper interrupts my brooding. "What do you see?" He pointed toward the distant camp, practically wriggling with excitement.

I follow his gesture to the crude bunkhouse hunkered above the talus slope. Lantern light spills through a single grimy glass window. A lone sentry patrols its perimeter, rifle resting casually over one shoulder. Sloppy overconfidence on Mads's part—must believe Hoodoo scared us off. Exactly the break we need.

"A single guard. Can you see him?"

Edison pauses sheepishly. "Not so much, but I can see something moving."

I nod. "Your plan is good, even if your eyesight ain't." Edison fairly glows under the praise. Turned out Edison learned a trick or two about fireworks from his time in his uncle's traveling show. His simple plan relies on some oily rags, a little gun powder, the Arbuckles' can and a spark... I pat the haversack on my hip. It contains my garrote and extra rope. Edison's matching bag holds the rest of the necessities and a box of Lucifers, wicked phosphorus matches, sure to get the job done.

I whisper quick final instructions. "You circle wide and come in from the southern flank on the mine side. As soon as I take out the sentry, you hit them with the smoke—that'll flush 'em out straight into my arms for a nice surprise."

Edison grins fiercely before melting into the pines. Worry churns my gut watching him disappear. He handles himself beyond his years, but our last attempt at an arrest turned into a shit show. I don't wanna tell Pete I got his nephew killed.

No. This will go smooth and clean, as we planned. Mads will be easy pickings once rousted into the open night. I pat my pistol reassuringly, heartbeat steadying.

Picking my way around the camp to the north, I circle to approach the shack's door. The sentry has his back to me, lazily scanning the surrounding hillside. I ghost up behind him and slip the garrote around his neck. His startled yelp dies to a rasping gurgle. He spasms violently in my grip, clawing at the cord. I hold for all I'm worth, pulling him backward, teeth gritted with effort. After an endless few moments, he falls to his knees. A few seconds more and he's out.

I bind him awash in a rush of satisfaction. It's easy to tell myself that I do this for Delilah, for my family, or the mission—yet the tingle of his life in my hands stirs an unsettling sense of triumph.

The Reb's beside me, his gray uniform almost silver in the starlight. "Still good with knots," he drawls, crouching to inspect my handiwork. "Getting yourself a taste for it again?"

I ain't got time for reflection at the moment. Ignoring him, I move to a position by the door. Risking a glimpse through a grimy window, I spot turquoise boots propped on a table— Mads's trademark vanity. One other shape moves in the lantern light. Seems they're passing a bottle between them.

A muffled snap of a twig carries through the darkness. I freeze, listening. Edison moving into position? My pulse races scanning for him. With a deep breath, I draw my pistol and slink to the rough door. Up close, raucous laughter and a language I vaguely recognize as Norwegian. My lips curl in a feral smile. Your last easy night, Mads, my lad...

Edison's signal comes. The crash of breaking glass followed by the Arbuckles' can flying through the broken window. Black powder smoke billows through the cabin. I lift the revolver and pound the door with its butt, yelling, "Open up! Pinkertons!" I dive to the side.

Gunshots explode through the door, splintering wood where I'd stood. Two figures stagger through the doorway, coughing and cursing.

The larger man stumbles directly into my path. I drive my knee up hard, catching him in the groin. His forward momentum does half the work. He folds with a choked whimper, retching into the dirt. A quick strike with my revolver butt to his temple drops him flat.

Then I spot those damned turquoise boots.

"Hold it right there, Mads!" I bark. "Hands high where I can see 'em!" For one breathless instant, he gapes at me. Shock and fury war across his bearded face in the smoky air. With a roar, he charges, fists swinging wildly.

I dodge right, but hands close on my gun arm, nearly yanking it from its socket. We crash together, grappling. "Ack!" He was freakishly strong for all his short stature. We reel, my boots scraping for purchase in the vomit-soaked earth. Mads swiftly gains the advantage. Bearing me down, I feel his belt buckle hot through my coat. Pinning me with one arm across my neck as I claw his face, he reaches down to rip my shirt open. I panic and pound his face with my fists. He shoves my left arm under his knee as I reach for my power.

But the buckle's burning hot against my ribs. I try to gather Gleaner power to blast him off me, but it doesn't rise to my call. Dark violet fog starts wreathing his hand where it grips my throat. The same magic he'd used on Ada. Damn it.

I feel my strength tearing away where the buckle touches, my own Animus being ripped out through my flesh. Panic swells. I can't access my power. He's stealing it faster than I can gather it.

Fetid breath bathes my face as he leans in, growling curses I can't understand. Scared, my free hand claws frantically at his eyes. I fight for breath as his weight on my chest compresses my lungs. The glowing mist thickens between us. Where the hell is Edison?!

As though in answer, a sharp retort splits the night. Mads jerks sharply, his snarling face going slack with shock. Dark blood blossoms in his side. He jolts upright, surprise shifting to rage, then two more shots boom out. Both bullets punch neat holes in the man's side, spraying crimson. He stares down incredulously, then topples motionless to the dirt.

I scuttle free, sucking air in ragged gasps. My eyes cast desperately about until they light on Edison. The boy stands frozen at the shack's corner, revolver level in a white-knuckled grip. His eyes enormous behind skewed spectacles. Mads twitches, blood spreading beneath him, seeping toward his ridiculous turquoise boots. Shot by Edison's panicked hand.

"Oh Lord, I... I didn't mean to... He was on top of you. I thought he'd..." The boy's voice climbs hysterically. "Oh Jesus, what've I done?"

"Hush now!" I stand and cross to grip his shoulders. "You did what was needed. You saved me."

He shudders, pale beneath his freckles.

"But I k-killed him. I ain't never..." Tears well, spilling down his cheeks. "What do we do now?" he whimpers.

My own pulse thundering fit to burst, I squeeze my eyes shut, forcing calm. Fear becomes rage at the memory of Mads's hands on my body. His preternatural weapon pillaging my Animus to enrich his master's. My gaze snags on Mads's belt buckle glinting in the fire glow. The grayback coalesces sitting atop Mads's chest, beckoning me.

I turn back to Edison, voice harsh, no time or inclination to offer comfort. "Get that other bastard tied fast, then fetch me a blanket. I'll deal with this mess."

Confusion creases his young face, but he stumbles to obey.

As Edison trusses the moaning gunman, I kneel beside Mads's motionless body. Dark blood oozes from the wounds. His eyes hold only flatness, but I detect a pulse.

The Reb leans close to my ear, "Did he find you, sweet Mary Catherine?"

I bare my teeth as magic crackles eagerly under my skin. "You would steal from me?" I snarl into his slack face. "Time to plumb the void, love."

The Confederate crouches by my shoulder as I reach for Mads. Ravenous for skin-to-skin intimacy of riding his death, I rip the bloody remains of his shirt apart to press my hands into his chest. Behind me, a muffled gasp as Edison grasps my intent before my awareness is subsumed by my power. Then I'm falling through darkness, unearthly cold buffeting my phantom body.

My focus narrows to the pulsing knot of energy tethered to the ravaged husk of Mads's mortal coil. His spirit thrashes and wails, rejecting the inevitability of his death. My will closes on him hungrily, shoving him into oblivion despite his panicked resistance. The moment his heart stops, his Animus Mortis is mine. I gulp it, barely aware of the flashes of Mads's life playing like chronophotography; Nightmare images of a cave, filled with oceans of purple poisoned energy, decomposing bodies, surrounding a brass and steel tower. The same vision I'd glimpsed riding Hoodoo's man, but clearer now—I could make out figures moving around the tower's base, feeding it somehow, the purple miasma pulsing with each offering.

With a final hiss, awareness snaps back to my body. I sway upright, exultant with stolen power racing through my veins. Mads's essence writhes inside me, trapped by my magic. Without thought, I turn to the tied henchmen.

It would be stupid to leave these men alive. They will surely set Hoodoo upon us. The one I strangled teeters on the verge of death already. I kneel beside him, reveling in the rapid thrum of his heartbeat. Running my fingers through the fuchsia mist of his Animus like a lover's hair, I reach to unbutton his shirt. But Edison's voice stops me, "Mick, don't. You're not a monster."

A wave of shame douses the ecstasy. Face flushing, I throw myself back from the downed man. What the fuck was I doing? Morgan leaves and I become the creature?

I turn to Edison huddled behind me, revolver still clutched in his hand as silent tears roll down his face. My heart wrenches. Have I destroyed Edison's faith in me too?

"This ain't right." He raises his Colt in my general direction, hand shaking. His voice firms, "I represent the law. I won't let you do this."

I raise both hands. "All right, Edison. But remember, you said you wanted ruthless. These men could ruin our escape. It might be us or them."

"You ain't being ruthless. This ain't in service of our mission." His voice is hard now. "I saw you take Mads. That was lust."

My head drops to my chest. He has the right of it. The intimacy of Mads's death satisfied a part of me that wasn't slaked by the impersonal deaths of Hoodoo's gunmen. Euphoria sang through my veins that I hadn't felt in a decade.

"And I ain't no better than you." Edison drops his hand holding the Colt to his side. Lifting his tear-streaked face, eyes pleading, he says, "I ain't a killer, Mick. I didn't want...not like this." He gestures helplessly to Mads's empty body. "We were supposed to take him alive. But in that moment, I wanted him dead... I shot him and I kept on shootin'." His voice is a rasping whisper. "Beyond necessity."

I stare at him, pushing my unnatural feelings aside. My partner needs help. Finally, I say gently, "Hush now, lad. 'Twas him or me." I crawl to his side so I can squeeze his shoulder. "You saved me, Edison. Could be Mads didn't leave you much choice in the heat of the moment."

Edison scrubs the back of one shaky hand across his wet eyes, leaving a smear on his cheek. "Don't know how I'm supposed to live with this."

My voice catches. "One day at a time, lad. Same as the rest of us sorry bastards."

We sit in heavy silence, the night pressing close. The acrid scent of gunpowder and blood mingles with the cool night air. Part of me still yearns for that dark hunger, that twisted ecstasy I felt riding Mads's death, tempting me to reach for that oblivion again until nothing else remains.

"It's done, Edison," My voice sounds far more confident than I feel. "We can't change what happened. We gotta move forward. We'll take Mads's buckle to Van Lew. With the one Morgan brings, it will be enough to convince her to take action. You completed the mission."

Edison nods slowly, though his eyes are still haunted. I can see the specter of Mads lingering in his thoughts, a shadow that would follow him not unlike my own shades. I can't promise that it will ever fade.

"Come on," I say. Standing, I hold out my hand. "Let's take care of them so we can get moving."

He stares at my outstretched hand for a long moment before clasping it. I pull him up and he sways into me briefly, a choked sound escaping him. "You're not gonna...?"

"Nope, we do it your way." I pull my revolver. "Night's getting cold. You get them into the cabin, while I cover you."

As we approach, the gunnie Edison secured eyes us with a mixture of fear and defiance. The one I garroted is unconscious, his breaths shallow and labored.

The gunnie spits at my feet. "You think killing us will save you? Hoodoo will hunt you down. You're dead walking."

I lean down, my voice low and dangerous. "Maybe. But right now, you're alive because of my partner's code. Don't make me regret it."

The man shrinks back from my glare. Edison steps forward, his face a mask of determination despite the tears still wet on his cheeks. He removes their guns, then half drags them into the cabin.

He pauses to grab ratty blankets piled near the door. He freezes, eyes like saucers. Moving the blankets revealed a wooden crate, lid askew, marked "HERCULES." And there, nestled in straw, are several sticks of dynamite.

"Jesus," Edison exhales, "I coulda killed us all..."

"Maybe." I smile. "Or maybe it won't even pop. TNT is mighty unpredictable when it's abused. Leave it. Let's get going."

Ushering Edison out the door, I stop to meet the gunnie's eyes. "Take care of your partner," I tell him, trying to keep my voice steady. "We're taking your horses. You can start the long walk back to town as soon as you can get free. Should be a right pleasure explaining to Hoodoo how we got to Mads on your watch."

He swallows hard.

"I hear Taos is awfully nice this time of year. If you take my meaning," I say. "Especially with the way this place is gonna be crawling with BMI."

He nods as I pull the door shut behind us.

I make damn sure to cut that cursed buckle off Mads's belt and wrap it in a rag. We round up the henchmen's horses from the corral before collecting Sampson and Abigail. They're excited by the new additions.

The night's chill has settled deep in my bones, or maybe it's the memory of that nightmare vision from Mads's death of a cavern filled with purple poison, the brass tower surrounded by decomposing bodies. We killed another man tonight and I rode another death. We are no closer to helping Delilah or any of the other women. The death weighs on Edison's conscience, but the hunger in me has only just woken up.

All I have to show for our trouble is a cursed belt buckle and another shade to haunt my dreams, but part of me is already hoping to do it again. And that terrifies me more than Hoodoo Jones ever could.

Chapter Twenty-One

I crouch on a crumbling rock wall within the old gristmill. The soft shifting and murmur of the horses signal they are dozing in the predawn stillness. I wish I could find such peace, but my mind churns like millstones, thoughts gritty as moldering grain. I've kept my Gleaner chained for a decade, but now it's prowling under my skin, eager for another fix. I need to get clear of this mess; temptation keeps knocking and I keep opening the door wide. Between the buckles, Delilah, and everything we witnessed, we got plenty to bring the BMI down on Hoodoo's head. Van Lew should be satisfied. Even if she blames me for all the dead bodies.

Beside me, Edison sits hunched over his infernal notebook, pencil scratching even in the gloom. The boy should be grabbing some shuteye before Leona arrives, but he scribbles on, brow pinched in consternation. Documenting the night's grim work, I reckon. My shoulders tighten at the memory—Mads's blood dark on my hands, the unholy thrill of riding his death.

I shift, joints popping, and wish for some of Morgan's coffee. But instead, I reach for my canteen. The water is cold, settling my nerves some.

"Want a drink?" I rasp, proffering the canteen.

Edison starts, head jerking up from his furious scrawling. He blinks at me. "What? Oh. Yeah, thanks." His Adam's apple bobs as he gulps, face screwing at the alkaline finish.

Smudged spectacles can't hide the shadows lurking in his eyes, the new wariness tightening his mouth. My heart twists.

I'd give a lot to rewind the night, unsee what we've both seen. What we've both done in the name of the mission.

"You did what you had to, Edison." I venture into the brittle silence. "With Mads. He didn't give you a choice."

He hunches in on himself, thin shoulders climbing to his ears. His fingers trace nervous patterns on his notebook cover. "I know that. In my head, I mean. But it don't make it easier."

"No, it surely don't." I sigh, wincing as I stretch my bruised ribs.

"Does it get easier?" His voice is small and lost, eyes fixed on a dark stain on his cuff—Mads's blood.

I take another pull from the canteen, buying time. The faces of the dead parade through my mind, too many to count. Some righteous kills, some I'd give nearly anything to take back. Finally, I say, "The killing should never be easy. The living part, well, try to do better, be better. But you don't forget. You carry them with you, the ones you...the ones who are gone on your account."

He's quiet for a long moment, pencil forgotten. "I wish..." He trails off, swallowing hard. "I wish it felt like Pete's tales, you know? Wish it felt like...like justice served. Mostly seems like some mad fever dream." He pauses, rolling a shoulder against remembered recoil. "I ain't sure I got the stomach to make a habit of it. Mostly all I feel is sick."

"Good." The word hangs between us, harsh truth. I gentle my tone. "Means you ain't numb to it. That's important, Edison, don't go numb. Without the pain, it's too easy to convince yourself the ends justify the means."

He nods jerkily, looking impossibly young.

I finger Mads's buckle in my pocket, its magic a dull throb against my palm. "Well, with Mads dead instead of captured, reckon we need to figure our next move."

Edison closes his notebook with unusual firmness. "We get Delilah, we hightail back to Trinidad. Present our findings to Van Lew." His voice wavers. "The buckle, the ward, the deaths... It's enough evidence to warrant a full BMI operation."

I study him, surprised. Just yesterday, the boy was all fire and vinegar about making his mark. "Thought this was your chance to prove yourself."

He adjusts his spectacles and won't meet my eyes. "It is. Was. But after tonight..." He swallows hard. "This is bigger than us, Mick. We need proper backup, proper authority."

Part of me knows he's right. Lord knows I'd welcome the excuse to put distance between me and the sweet song of my Gleaner. But Delilah's fading Animus haunts me. What is Hoodoo up to? By the time the BMI cuts through their red tape...

"You think the Bureau will move quick enough?" I keep my voice neutral. "They're tied up with that senator's boy, and Van Lew ain't known for bein' hasty."

"They have to!" Some of Edison's earlier passion flares. "An anti-magic ward this size..." He flips his notebook back open, like the answers are hidden in his cramped writing. "If we document everything properly, present a solid case..."

"Bureaucracies move slowly, Edison." The words come out hard. "And Morgan's probably already there with your notes and Elmer's buckle."

His shoulders slump. "I know. But what else can we do? Just the two of us, three with Leona, against Hoodoo and his whole operation?" He gives a hollow laugh. "I already killed one man today. I'm not sure I'm ready for more."

Ahh, his ambition got squashed by the reality of killin'. That I can understand. I'm not sure which dog I'm backing in this fight. A part of me just wants to go home, pack my pistol and magic away for good. But another part needs to bring Hoodoo down.

"Say," I muse, deliberately casual, trying to lighten the mood. "What're you gonna do when this is all over?"

Surprise flickers across his face at the change in topic. "I got leave coming. Reckon I'll visit my mam and sister in San Francisco."

"Bet she'd be right pleased to have you underfoot again."

A ghost of a grin rises to his lips. "Yeah? Reckon she would like that. Been too long since I saw her and my sister." He spins his pencil, considering. "It'd be nice to get away from...all this for a spell."

"Oh really," I say. "What's Uncle Pete gonna think of that?"

"I'm not sure how much I care what Pete thinks," Edison says. "Don't think I believe his stories anymore." Edison's brow lowers. "I done seen the seamier truth behind Uncle Pete's tall tales." His gaze darts to me. "Ain't quite the fantasy he spins."

We both freeze at the sound of footsteps on gravel. My hand drops to my revolver, body tensing as I slide into the shadows beside the doorframe. Edison follows suit, pressing himself against the wall with surprising stealth.

Leona slips through the doorway, Vilde close behind. Both look haggard in the predawn light that filters through the mill's damaged roof.

I ease back into view, tugging my coat closed to hide the fresh blood splattered across my shirtfront. Leona's nostrils flare slightly—can she smell it? Somehow divine how I'd glutted my twisted magic on Mads's soul?

My pulse quickens as I scan the doorway, waiting for a third figure that never appears. I step forward, boot crunching on shattered glass. "Where's Delilah? Thought you were bringing her."

Leona's face hardens, her posture stiffening. Exchanging a look with Vilde, she answers, "She's gone," voice low and tight. "I went to get her when my shift ended and her room was empty. Vicente's claiming she's helping Múcaro with a special project."

"I thought the girls were forbidden from even speaking to Múcaro?" I answer.

"Exactly." She grimaces. "He wants her for something terrible. Vilde and I learned our enigmatic friend Múcaro is more than he appears." She lowers her voice conspiratorially, her eyes sparking. "He's a wanted man. A Central American death mage. President Porfirio Díaz issued a bounty for Múcaro's head."

Vilde shudders. "The last girl Múcaro took for his 'special project' turned up dead three days later."

"Death mage. Special project." The words hang in the air as understanding crashes over me. "Son of a bitch...that's why

Hoodoo's flinging around power he shouldn't have. He ain't the real threat. Múcaro's been the puppet master all along." And that project ain't gonna end well for Delilah. "We've got to get her back."

I finger the buckle in my pocket, remembering the dying pigs back home, their Animus corrupted and drained. "And we need to find out what Hoodoo and Múcaro are up to with stealing Animus from folks. This ain't just about Vegas anymore. If they're draining souls on this scale..." I don't finish the thought.

Edison's eyes widen behind his spectacles. "You think it could be connected to your homestead?"

"Don't know for certain," I admit. "But my pigs' Animus was damaged, and here we find a death mage collecting Animus through these buckles. Seems mighty coincidental."

Leona nods grimly. "Even more reason to get inside the distillery. We need to rescue Delilah, yes, but we also need to see what Múcaro's operation actually looks like. How far it reaches."

"Vicente's Spring Soiree kicked off last night with the early arrivals," Leona says. "But the main event starts tonight—Friday. Elected officials, ranchers, and mining tycoons from all over the territory are already pouring in. Most of them will stay through Saturday."

Vilde wrinkles her nose. "Absolutely dreadful lot, but Hoodoo is desperately keen to impress them."

My pulse jumps in anticipation. "Tonight's our chance then. With Hoodoo occupied, we could infiltrate the distillery. Find Delilah and get an eye on Múcaro's operation."

The Reb whispers in my ear, "And you're conveniently glutted on Mads's death. Been a while since you unleashed that Gleaner. Too bad about the ward."

I brush my ear, shooing him away.

"We don't dare go in daylight." Leona checks the position of the rising sun. "Too many comings and goings, and distillery workers are everywhere. But every hour Delilah spends with Múcaro puts her in more danger."

"Tonight's perfect. Vicente's shindig means most of the guards will be pulled inside for security." Vilde leans forward, lowering her voice. "Plus, me and the girls prepared a special performance. We've created the most spectacular European extravaganza, darling! With bunnies so divine even the angels would weep. It will be, how you say, a tour de force of distraction."

I can't begin to imagine.

Vilde settles back, a calculating gleam in her eye. "All the important guests, and half the territory's lawmen drinking themselves silly, hardly anyone will be in the yard. I can get you a good twenty minutes, maybe more." She winks roguishly.

Edison's brow furrows. "But how did you come by this information? Mail and the telegraph are under Hoodoo's thumb. You got another informant?"

A sly smile tugs at Vilde's lips. "Darling, haven't you figured it out? I told you my doves were really pigeons." She winks. "They're carrier pigeons. They can get a message to Santa Fe in less than two hours."

"The birds in your act? The ones that..." Edison flushes crimson, adjusts his spectacles. "I mean to say, the doves that assist with your...performance?"

"Those very ones," Vilde says with a dramatic flourish of her wrist. "Who'd suspect a showgirl's props? Certainly not our dear Vicente, though he inspects every scrap of mail that comes through town."

"Well, I'll be damned. Here I was thinking those birds were just for show, helping you..." I clear my throat. "Handle your wardrobe."

The scratching of Edison's pencil on his journal competes with early morning birdsong. "Fascinating! The application of avian assistance for covert communication..." He pauses, pencil hovering. A pigeon coos somewhere in the rafters, making him glance up nervously. "Though I suppose all the details needn't be included in my official report."

"Might be best to leave out the specifics of Vilde's act entirely." I pat his shoulder. "Some things are better left to the imagination."

"Right." Edison's ears burn red as he carefully tears out the last page, crumpling it into a tight ball before stuffing it deep in his pocket.

I clear my throat. "You need to know." I take a steadying breath and rush ahead. "Mads is dead. Edison had to shoot him. Things went sideways. We did get his buckle."

Leona's eyes widen fractionally, but she maintains her composure. "Explains why I didn't smell him. The rest of his men?"

"Two henchmen still breathing. We left 'em trussed up at the camp. I don't reckon they're gonna be keen to tell Hoodoo they lost Mads."

Leona nods. She doesn't seem shocked by the revelation. I didn't volunteer to explain how my lust overcame me and I rode Mads into death.

"That magical ward has been the bane of my existence, blocking me at every turn. Between that buckle and your special gifts..." she muses.

"Can anyone use them?" I pull Mads's buckle from my pocket, keeping it wrapped in the bandanna. Its dull metal absorbs the weak dawn light.

"Actually..." Vilde's voice drops low, her fingers tracing patterns on her skirt. "Some of the girls shared interesting tales about those buckles. Seems Hoodoo's men took liberties, let the girls handle their fancy accessories."

Edison perks up. "They let them touch the buckles?"

"More than touch." Vilde's lips curl. "Mads especially loved showing his off. Most of the girls are shifters—helps with the special requests." She waves her hand dismissively. "But Mads likes to watch. He'd get all excited having them transform back and forth while wearing it. Afterward they were always bone-tired."

My stomach turns. Mads used the buckles on the women of the Imperial for fun to feed whatever horror Hoodoo's got in that distillery.

"Ain't that rich," drawls the Reb from behind Leona. He adjusts his tattered gray kepi, eyes gleaming hot. "You're squeamish about some trinket when you just feasted on a man's dying breath?"

I ignore him, but my hands tremble as I hold the buckle out. The echo of Mads's death still pulses inside me, sweet and terrible.

"Mick," Leona's eyes narrow. "As last resort, this buckle gives us an edge. Maybe double edged, since Hoodoo will know if you use it, but it's something."

Anticipation and dread war within me, the tantalizing promise of answers dragging me forward even as every instinct screams to cut and run. But I think of the dead women, of the dark magic Elmer related. I can't just turn away.

Edison shifts, something like defiance flickering across his face. "Now wait just a minute. Shouldn't we inform Commander Van Lew first? Get official sanction?"

Leona arches a brow at him, closing the distance between them with two deliberate steps. Her fingers tense at her sides. "And how long do you estimate that bureaucratic process would require, Mr. Colt? I suspect weeks at minimum, potentially months." She huffs out a frustrated breath. "We both know the Bureau will hem and haw, 'evaluating the situation' while Hoodoo's darkness festers." Her mouth twists bitterly as she taps the floorboards with her boot. "People are suffering. Delilah may die. We can't tarry."

"All right. We do it your way. But I'm noting my objections for the record." He straightens his shoulders, resolve hardening his face. "And we should at least send word to Van Lew about what we've found and what we're planning. If this goes toes up, the Bureau needs to know what happened."

A tight smile plucks at Leona's lips. "Fair enough. Vilde can send a pigeon to Santa Fe, asking them to wire Van Lew."

We huddle together as dawn creeps through the broken roof, spinning our dangerous plot. "Leona will fetch me and Edison at ten tonight. We just need to stay out of sight until then."

A queer sort of peace settles over me once Leona and Vilde leave to return to the Imperial.

I lean back against the crumbling stones, Mads's buckle a pulsing weight in my pocket. Power calls to power. I've too many sins to my name to resist its siren song for long. The thought of Delilah in Múcaro's clutches eats at me, but beneath the concern lurks something darker—anticipation. A righteous cause to unleash what I'd kept caged for so long.

The Reb sits beside me on the crumbling wall, translucent in the growing light. "Been a spell since you let yourself off the leash."

I don't answer, but my fingers twitch with the memory of power.

"Watching you work is something special." His spectral hand passes through my sleeve. "Like watching a thunderstorm roll in. Terrible beauty."

"I ain't doin' it for the thrill," I whisper, too low for Edison to hear.

The Reb smiles, all teeth and no mirth. "Keep telling yourself that, Gleaner."

Beneath my breast, my power prowls in anticipation, a beast scenting blood.

Closing my eyes, I breathe deeply the cool air. Weariness drags at my bones. But I'm ready. For a chance to shine light into the darkness, however briefly.

Chapter Twenty-Two

BLOOD THRUMS IN MY ears, I'm counting down the moments to Leona's arrival. Beside me, Edison fidgets with his pistols while scanning the darkness.

She finally ghosts through the mill's doorway. Instead of her corseted bodice and petticoats under a full skirt, she's wearing a simple calico skirt and blouse with no jewelry. Her bare feet whisper over splintered boards.

"I came around the south end to ensure I wasn't followed," Leona murmurs.

I'm a mite trepidatious about sneaking into Hoodoo's lair, but we're committed. Finding Delilah is our priority. Vilde's information about her being held in the distillery caverns might be our only chance to save her before Múcaro uses her for whatever his dark plans entail.

"Edison, you got the horses' picket secure?"

"Mick, for heaven's sake and the third time, yes. They're snug as bugs. We're only gonna be gone a couple of hours."

Hopefully, I add silently. I fret over leaving Sampson and Abigail hidden behind the mill with the extra mounts from Mads. If we don't return, they'll have to get themselves loose.

"You got the buckle?"

"Jesus, Mick!" Edison pulls the amulet from his deep coat pocket. "Yes, I STILL have the damn buckle."

"Give me that." Leona rolls her lips at our exchange and huffs through her nose at our bickering. "I don't want you lighting yourself up like a signal flare."

Edison hesitates, then hands it over. Leona strings the buckle on a heavy ribbon and slings it around her neck. "We keep it off you until last resort." she explains, adjusting it beneath her clothing. "Don't need to tell everyone what we're up to." She straightens her blouse, the slight bulge of the buckle visible below her collarbone.

With the buckle secured, Leona's demeanor shifts to all business. "You two follow my lead," she dictates. "Stay low and stay quiet. We're gonna go roundabout to get to the back side of the Imperial. Our goal is the small warehouse by the grain bins. It houses the entrance to the caverns. Vilde says it was built over some old cave to age the whiskey and that's where Hoodoo and Múcaro disappear to. You got it?"

Edison and I both nod. I slam my hat on my head and without further words, the three of us slip into the night toward town and the bright lights of the Imperial. My heart races double time despite stern warnings to settle down.

When we get to Main Street, Leona leads us through a narrow alley behind the post office. The moon hasn't risen yet. She moves like smoke, blending into shadows and sliding between buildings. Edison and I do our best to match her stealth. Our best ain't that great.

The Imperial is rollicking. Even from six blocks away, I can see light spilling from every window and hear piano accompanied by off-key singing. Vicente's party seems to be a success. Vilde has probably completed at least her first set by now, keeping Hoodoo distracted while we attempt to rescue Delilah.

We creep along an alley parallel to the Imperial to reach the compound behind the saloon. Leona leads us between rows of grain sheds elevated off the ground to keep the rats out. Our target, a small warehouse, hunkers right up against the foothills about fifty yards west of us.

Edison freezes, his face going pale. "Mick, Leona," he breathes, pointing at one of the sheds. "There's something in there, same signature as the buckles."

"We don't have time," Leona growls. "The guards make rounds every fifteen minutes. We've got seven minutes to reach the warehouse before they circle back."

"This is important," Edison insists, already moving toward the shed.

I grab his arm. "Delilah's our priority. She could be bleeding out while we're standing here."

Edison's jaw sets stubbornly as he shakes my arm off.

I exchange a glance with Leona, her frustration mirroring my own.

"Quick. You've got two minutes," she agrees tersely.

He darts over to the shed and releases the bolt catch on the wide door. It swings out, the first couple feet of the interior visible in the low light. It's filled with dried corn, a huge pile against the back wall. Escaped kernels litter the floor. Edison bends to pick up a handful of the golden grain, then yanks his hand back with a whimper.

"It's enchanted," he confirms grimly. "It feels like fire ants. It's stealing tiny drops of Animus."

I stare at the innocuous pile of corn, revulsion rising in my throat. "Why curse the corn?"

"Later," Leona cuts in sharply, eyes darting to the shadows between buildings. "Guards will be back any minute. We need to move. Now."

Edison uses his kerchief to wrap a few grains and stows them in his pocket—evidence for the BMI. His delay has cost us precious minutes, and Leona's tension is palpable as she urges us forward with quick, impatient gestures.

Voices echo between the buildings. Leona yanks us behind the shed as two of Hoodoo's men trudge down the alley, guns on their shoulders. They're close enough that I can smell tobacco and whiskey on them. I scarcely dare breathe, pulse loud in my ears.

"Don't know what this hullabaloo is," the taller one grumbles. "I was gonna catch Paloma's special act, heard she's doin' something with rabbits."

"I dunno what gives," his partner responds. "But Jose said Vicente want extra eyes tonight. Something happened at the old mine."

Leona draws us farther into the narrow space between two sheds. We're boxed in—grain shed walls on two sides, a stack of empty barrels behind us, and the open alley in front. Leona loosens the buttons of her blouse. I press my back against the rough wood, heart hammering. The men pause less than ten feet from our hiding spot. The shorter guard strikes a match, the sudden flare casting long shadows into our corner. I hold my breath, feeling Edison tense beside me.

"You hear that?" the taller guard asks, head cocked.

Footsteps approach from the south. More guards. We're trapped between them.

"Miguel! That you?" calls a voice from the southern approach.

"Yeah, me and Bill. You boys see anything?"

"Nah, ain't nothin' to see. Vicente's got a stick so far up his ass, wants us checking the perimeter every fifteen minutes."

The guards from the south draw closer. One of them kicks something that skitters across the dirt, coming to rest at the entrance to our hiding spot. The metallic glint of Edison's pocket watch catches the match light.

"What's this?" The shorter guard bends down, squinting. The other men group around him.

My heart stops. We're caught.

Making a split second decision, Leona presses into the deepest shadows between the barrels. She gives me a quick nod, eyes already glowing with transformation energy. "When I move, run for the warehouse."

She hands me her clothes and the buckle.

The air distorts around her. Where a woman stood moments ago, a massive lioness now crouches in the shadows.

Before I can blink, she bounds out from between the sheds with a bone-chilling roar, directly between the two groups of guards. Their terrified reaction is instantaneous.. Guns fire wildly into the air as men scatter in all directions, screaming about a mountain lion.

"Go!" I snap at Edison, pushing his back. With the guards fleeing in panic, we sprint toward the warehouse's side entrance, using the chaos as cover. My boots barely touch the ground as we dash across the open space between buildings.

We reach the door, both breathing hard. Edison presses himself flat against the wall while I peer around the corner. The guards are still distracted, chasing Leona's tawny form as she leads them on a wild chase away from us.

"Quick," I say, approaching the smaller door. "You sense any power on this lock?"

Edison snatches up the lock, squinting through his spectacles. His hands dart across the wood, checking every surface. "No magic on this lock, door, frame, or lintel."

"Open it!" I hiss.

His fingers fly over the lock—click, click, done. We burst through the doorway, my heart hammering. A sudden scratch outside makes me jump. I yank the door back open and Leona slips in, her leonine form still intact.

The darkness inside is almost complete, only starlight coming through small windows high on the walls. The smell at first is pleasant: yeast, maturing whiskey, old wood, and lightly damp earth. But underneath it stinks of moldering meat.

The front of the building is wood-framed, but it continues into the rock, transitioning to a cavern. Hundreds of barrels of whiskey are stacked on wooden scaffolding, marching into the darkness.

Following the first row of casks to the rock face, I spot a door in the floor girded with a heavy lock and reinforced framing. I hesitate, but Edison brushes past and lays one palm flat upon the wood. "Wait, what's this now...?" His brows lower in concentration, fingers tracing the edges.

"Those runes mean it's sealed by magics," he whispers excitedly. "This is the way in!"

We're interrupted by an urgent "chuff," from the opposite corner of the cavern. Leona joins us, growling impatiently.

I squeeze Edison's shoulder, forestalling his magical examination. "Good enough for now. Let's see what our clever kitty found us first, aye?"

He blinks, dragging his attention back from the portal as I gesture after Leona's tawny flicking tail.

She leads us past the cask piles to a craggy seam in the rock wall. It's nearly obscured behind broken casks. Cool air sighs from the deeper shadow, bearing a mineral tang.

I bend to inspect the tunnel, calling over my shoulder, "There's space to crawl a fair ways back. I feel a steady airflow."

Edison nods beside me. Mining operations necessitate ventilation shafts lest deadly gasses overwhelm those below. This tunnel might access older pits beneath the ridge.

Leona shimmers into human form and motions for me to hand her her clothes. "If this is a hidden way in avoiding the upper levels, this seems ideal for covert reconnaissance, yes?"

I scrub both hands over my face. "You're sure this ain't just a smugglers' bolt hole?" I say.

Her amber eyes ignite, body coiling with anticipation. "This shaft runs deep. I can smell depths. And something else..." She pauses, nostrils flaring. "Blood. Fresh blood. Delilah's down there. I'm certain of it."

I hold up both hands. "All right, boss. Reckon you've the right of it." My voice sounds calm, but an ominous foreboding tightening my neck. I don't care for tight spaces, and this hole ain't inviting. Looking around, I retrieve a lamp from the worktable near the entrance.

Leona finishes dressing and slings the buckle back around her neck. She steps into the fissure and pulling Lucifers from her pocket, lights the lantern.

I step back, gesturing them both ahead. "I'll bring up the rear. Mind the echoes and tread soft as cat feet."

Leona bares her teeth at my joke but slips neatly into the gap without response.

Chapter Twenty-Three

THE COOL TUNNEL AIR raises prickling goose flesh beneath my shirt as we descend single file. The tallest in the group, I duck to avoid scraping my head. I focus on keeping my feet beneath me on the steep, uneven floor, with one hand braced on the damp rock wall. The shuffling steps of our passage echoes oddly, but no voices or movement sounds below. So far, our gamble's met no resistance.

We wind endlessly downward through stale murk. Gravel and shards slippery underfoot threaten twisted ankles or worse. The incline levels before opening into a rough-hewn cavern. We emerge cautiously from the narrow tunnel mouth into what appears to be a staging area with multiple tunnels, some with the glow of kerosene lanterns, branching into the ridge's belly. Ancient timbers brace sagging ceilings.

I try to envision the scale of this mining operation, the tonnage of rock and earth removed. The idea of the weight above us makes me queasy. Catacombs must honeycomb the ridge, dug over years. The perfect place to hide Hoodoo's twisted workshop.

Beside me, Edison says uneasily. "Mick, I don't like this. If there's a whole network of tunnels down here…"

"Then there's no telling where Delilah is being held." I finish grimly.

Leona's lips compress to a bloodless line, but she squares her shoulders. "The whole thing smells of blood. I can't follow Delilah's trail. It's too muddied. We could wander down here for days if we're not careful."

I survey the branching shafts, unease prickling my nape. Leona's right. We can't afford to get turned around in this labyrinth. And Hoodoo's sanctum could be anywhere.

"Edison, try activating your knack. If our friends are operating on this massive of a scale, might be a trail from their spellwork." I keep my voice low, barely above a whisper in the echoing space.

Edison freezes so abruptly I nearly stumble into his back. He stands rigid, head slowly swinging from side to side like a hound scenting. Leona's mouth opens, but I wave her questions to silence, watching the boy's focus turn inward.

Long moments pass before he blinks sluggishly back to our surroundings. I grasp his shoulders, peering intently into dazed eyes. "What is it, lad? You sense something?"

He nods mutely, still wrestling visibly to process. At length, he manages hoarsely, "The trail...down that way." One hand waves, indicating the dimly lit central tunnel.

I draw a slow breath and douse our lantern. Leona shadows close behind as Edison leads us into the mountainside. I can only hope Delilah is in the same direction as the buckles.

As we walk, the air seems to become charged with a quality I can't explain, but I recognize as power, magical workings somewhere ahead. My scalp tingles as I feel the Gleaner roil under my skin. I push Edison behind me and take the lead.

A mechanical thump and hiss grow louder with each step. Bright lamp light beckons from the passageway ahead. Our tunnel opens onto a stepped slope, and I halt sharply, throwing out an arm to stop Edison and Leona.

Ten feet below, a massive cavern unfolds. I crouch, pulling the others down. A monstrous tower seizes my attention, dominating the back wall, stretching upward until it vanishes into shadows. Part distillery tower, part clockwork nightmare. Copper coils snake around iron chambers that pulse with sickly purple light. Steam hisses from valves while gears and pistons pump. Gauges with needles trembling in the red zone dot its surface like bloodshot eyes. Each throb sends waves of malevolent energy through the chamber. This is the source of the ward blanketing the town, I realize with sinking certainty.

Horror and hunger war within me. The amount of Animus contained in that machine defies comprehension. My Gleaner stretches hungrily, longing for a taste, but the ward completely blocks even the hope of dipping into that reservoir. Hoodoo's horde, the power he's been pilfering, is stockpiled and greedily locked away.

The underground space stretches out in tiered stone steps descending toward a central floor. It's disturbingly reminiscent of an operating theatre I visited in Charleston. The open cavern is chopped by enormous stalactites stretching toward the floor. That rhythmic thumping reverberates like the mountain's heartbeat.

"Just a few more adjustments, and we shall be ready for the Equinox," a cultured voice echoes through the chamber.

At the center of the cavern stands a wooden table where a figure lies strapped down. My breath catches.

"Delilah," Leona whispers beside me, her body tensing like a bowstring.

Delilah is pale as death, wrists and ankles bound with leather straps.

Near her stands Múcaro, elegant in a tailored suit, a nightmare version of a surgeon. He moves confidently, adjusting glass and copper tubing running from Delilah's arms to an immense golden reliquary beyond the table. It's easily seven feet long, adorned with intricate carvings that catch the lamplight as it shudders in time to the thump. Heavy chains secure it to iron rings set in the stone floor.

Múcaro approaches the chained casket and reverently lays both palms flat upon its surface. He caresses the lid while chanting in sibilant tones, his fingers trailing over the designs like a lover. Patting it once he turns back to the table.

"Cariño," Múcaro speaks to the semi-conscious Delilah, "your discomfort pains me greatly. Truly, it does." He adjusts a valve, causing Delilah to wince. "But as I've explained, your contribution to our great work demands sacrifice."

Múcaro continues, checking gauges on an apparatus connected to the tubing. I had mistakenly remembered him as feeble. I stand corrected. Air eddies around him chasing coils of power emanating from his footsteps. "The quality of your humors surpasses all my previous subjects."

His tone shifts, becoming more intimate. "The scar on your face is no detriment to your contribution here." He touches Delilah's face like a lover. "Mi linda, I value your blood."

Blood? Gallons of stolen Animus power and he's stealing her blood and dripping it into a casket? Damn blood and Animus mean's they're playing with some kind of vampiric magic. It's the only creature I can imagine that requires both.

He turns to make notes in an ancient leather-bound book supported on a lectern. The book crouches like an evil toad. "It is a privilege to witness such fortitude. In another life, perhaps we might have been...acquaintances." A small, chilling smile plays across his lips.

Gaslights flicker along the walls, illuminating a gallery of horrors. Anatomical drawings cover every surface, repeating images of hands, skulls, flayed human chests rendered in loving, terrible detail. Photographs and tintypes of dissected body parts are tacked haphazardly between them, while rusty symbols and runes crawl across everything like infected wounds. Surgical instruments gleam dully on rough-hewn tables.

Leona presses a hand over her mouth, clearly fighting nausea.

Edison freezes beside me, suddenly doubling over. His body convulses as he retches dryly, trying to silence himself with hands over his bone-white face.

"The buckles," he chokes out, fingernails digging into my sleeve. "That's what connects them, what they're feeding...that damned casket." His trembling finger points to the reliquary. "I can see the threads."

I visually trace the network of copper piping branching from Delilah across the floor to the reliquary, then back to that pulsing tower. With each throb, purple energy surges through the pipes from the tower into the golden box.

Múcaro closes the leather-bound tome with a decisive snap. "Alas, time waits for no man, not even one of my considerable talents. Vicente requires my attention." He bows slightly to Delilah's prone form. "Rest assured, I shall return promptly to continue our most stimulating conversation."

He exits through a side tunnel, whistling the Habanera from Vilde's act.

"Now," I hiss, and we move quickly down the stone steps.

Leona rushes to Delilah, hands immediately working at the straps binding her wrists. "She's alive," she whispers, voice thick with relief and rage.

Delilah's skin has the waxy translucence of a corpse, blue veins visible like rivers on a map. Crimson symbols painted across her forehead and chest pulse in rhythm with the chamber's heartbeat.

Edison's hands are steady as he focuses on the copper lines. "These connect to that main line... I think if we pinch here and here..." He demonstrates, restricting the flow into the reliquary. The pulsing slows but doesn't stop.

"That thing's...unstable," he breathes. "It's humming, like it's over-pressured. Look there"—he points at the base, where copper piping dives into a squat iron tank—"all that flow forced through one junction. If that joint failed, the whole construct would shake itself to pieces. The backlash'd be spectacular."

"Good thing nobody's dumb enough to go kicking it, then," I say, pushing him away. "We've got other problems."

Delilah's eyelids flutter, her cracked lips parting. Her gaze wanders before finding Leona's face.

"You came," she whispers, voice threadbare. Her fingers weakly clutch Leona's sleeve.

A tune echoes through the cavern—the Habanera from Paloma's act. Múcaro is returning.

"Shit," Edison hisses, fingers fumbling as he free's Delilah from the last of the tubes.

"Let's go," I whisper, helping Leona lift Delilah's frail form. We turn toward our entry tunnel but and freeze as the sound of boot steps echo off the rocks.

Lamplight flickers at the mouth of our entrance tunnel. The silhouettes of men appear, pushing carts loaded with crates and barrels. The harsh clink of glass against glass echoes in the chamber.

"There." Leona nods toward a wide mining passage on the opposite side of the cavern—away from both Múcaro's approach and the men with the carts.

We duck behind a stalagmite formation as Múcaro's whistling grows louder. From our hiding place, I can hear men working at our entry tunnel, the grunt and thuds.

"Señor Múcaro!" a voice calls from somewhere beyond our view. "Señor, you're needed urgently!"

Múcaro's whistling stops, scowling. "I left explicit instructions not to be disturbed, Miguel."

"Yes, señor, but it's Señor Vicente. He requires your assistance with one of the guests."

"El Patán." Múcaro sighs audibly. "Very well."

His footsteps move away, but the workers continue unloading crates, blocking our original path.

"Now," I breathe. "Before they notice she's gone."

I follow Edison and Leona dragging Delilah. It's only thirty feet to the far tunnel Leona spotted.

"Intruders!" Miguel's voice cracks through the chamber. The sound of running feet grows behind us.

I turn and drawing my revolver, I snap off two shots to slow our pursuers before bolting after my companions.

Múcaro's voice joins the chaos. "Capture them!" Kinetic curses sizzle against the walls, close enough to raise blisters. An inhuman shriek shakes loose rocks from the ceiling. A blinding flash throws our shadows ahead of us, ice stabbing through my chest.

Gaining the tunnel, I pound through the darkness, the sting of magic fading. Edison tosses me one end of his bandana, the other gripped tight as light fades behind us. Our feet pound on the stone, the darkness swallowing everything but the sounds of our ragged breathing and pebbles skittering beneath our boots.

"Faster," I urge, hearing the commotion growing behind us. "They'll be after us soon."

My lungs burn as we press forward in the dark. Leona somehow manages to maintain a steady pace despite carrying most of Delilah's weight. The air presses close, thick as wet wool. My lungs burn as I struggle to keep pace. Dear Lord, I'm not sure I ever appreciated sight so much as I do right now where there's nothing but blackness. The dark seems to go on forever, maybe hours pass, maybe minutes, but we are so deep into the hillside I fear we are lost for good.

At last, a hand on my wrist pulls me to a stop. My chest heaves as I brace against the tunnel wall, legs trembling from our headlong flight. I hear Edison wheezing along beside me, doubled over.

"Wait," Leona whispers against my ear. "Listen."

I force myself to stillness, breath held, straining to catch any hint of pursuit. The darkness weighs on my eyes until spots dance in my vision. My palm stays pressed to the rough stone, anchoring me in the void.

Leona's voice breaks the silence. "Nothing." A pause. "Just the mountain settling." Her certainty steadies my racing pulse. "Light the lamp, Mick."

My trembling hands fumble pulling the tin lamp from my belt. The match flares painfully bright, then settles to a steady glow as I touch it to the wick. Warm light pushes back the crushing dark. Leona's sweat-streaked face appears in the flare, her expression intent as she studies the tunnel stretching behind us.

She shoves Delilah into Edison's arms, and snatches the lamp without a word. We continue on until the tunnel opens into a massive corridor. It's large enough to allow two fully loaded ore carts pulled by mules to pass side by side, with room to spare. Rusted rails snake into darkness.

For a moment, we pause, chests heaving as we get our bearings. The mine's scale is staggering, a labyrinthine network. Leona lifts her head, nostrils flaring as she scents the air.

"There." She points to the tracks headed off to the left. "Fresh air coming from that direction."

We find what must be the mine's original entrance, long since forsaken. The stone partially collapsed, a gap is covered by rotted planks that Edison and I make short work of, pulling enough free to squeeze out and into the fresh morning air.

It's like a blessing. My lungs expand gratefully as I stumble away from the mine, drinking in the open sky above. Stars wheel overhead, but the sun's glow peeks above the eastern horizon. We were in that subterranean hellhole for hours.

Edison drops to his knees in the scrub brush, chest heaving. "That was... that was..." He can't seem to finish the thought.

"Too damn close," I complete for him, wiping sweat from my brow. My shirt clings uncomfortably to my back, and every muscle protests our mad scramble through the tunnels.

Leona gently lowers Delilah to the ground, arranging her cloak beneath the girl's head. "She's weak. We need to get her somewhere safe."

I scan the scattered pinyon pines and rocky outcrops surrounding us. My heart's still pounding from the claustrophobic press of the tunnels. For a few terrible moments down there, I'd feared we'd never find our way out, that we'd wander lost in that maze until Múcaro's men ran us to the ground.

"Let's put some distance between us and this hole," I mutter, helping Edison to his feet. "The mill's too obvious. They'll search there first."

Leona shifts Delilah's weight in her arms, her decision already made. "My apartment. Above Wong's Laundry in Old Town. It's not far, and I've got supplies there."

I nod, checking my revolver—might come down to gunplay if Hoodoo's men catch up. "Lead the way."

The eastern sky brightens. We need to move.

As we set off across the rocky terrain, I can't shake the image of that golden reliquary, pulsing with stolen life. Whatever horror Múcaro plans for the Equinox, we've got precious little time to stop it.

Leona's apartment sits above a laundry across the river from the Imperial. The space is small but neat, with sparse furnishings that speak to a life lived ready to move at a moment's notice. We lay Delilah on Leona's narrow bed, her breathing shallow but steady.

My hands won't stop shaking as I help Leona secure the windows. The early morning air carries a bone-deep chill. Even here, I can't shake the feeling of that pulsing malignancy chained in the dark below the distillery.

Edison retches in Leona's washbasin. When he straightens, his face is ghost-white in the lamplight. "Sweet Jesus," he whispers, wiping his mouth. "That reliquary..." He slumps against the wall. "Thought we were buzzard bait back there."

Leona snaps the locks shut, yanks the curtains closed, then prowls between the window and the door. Her head jerks up, nostrils flaring wide. "Something's following us. I can smell it."

"Not following." I grip the back of a chair, fighting the pull of the Gleaner. The power I felt in the caverns is too tempting.

The Reb's been standing near Delilah, watching her doze. "That box down there's full of death. Bet it would taste mighty fine." He licks his lips.

I ignore him, but my knuckles whiten on the chair back.

"Watching," I say aloud, to Edison and Leona. "The whole damn town's got eyes now."

From the bed, Delilah moans softly. Her eyelids flutter open. "The Owl..." she whispers, voice cracked and dry.

Leona brings her water and perches on the cot next to her. "You're safe now, Delilah."

"No one's safe." Her fingers clutch weakly at Leona's sleeve. Her eyes are feverishly bright. "He killed them all... Múcaro...he liked it."

Leona holds the water to her lips. Delilah gulps thirstily and falls back. "The blood, shifter blood..." she murmurs, eyes drifting closed again. "The thing in the box...not alive, not dead...the blood preserves it."

"See, you ain't gonna win this without a fight," the Reb mutters. "You should ride this one's death. I'd appreciate some womanly company."

He's such an asshole.

Edison fumbles in his coat, pulls out the buckle. His hand trembles as he holds it out. "The magic signature on this...it's the same as in the cavern, that casket, that machine," Edison says carefully. "Same as the corn we found. Corn goes into the whiskey, right?" His voice cracks. "Does that mean they're feeding it to everyone who drinks it?"

Leona groans, clenching her fists. "The magical contagion, the flu, in Denver, Cheyenne, the one that took Thatcher's kid. It's not the working girls. It's the whiskey."

It feels like a firework going off in my head. Blood rushes across my scalp. "The distiller's grain Robert sold me. The drovers at the stampede." My throat closes as I remember Gudrun feeding our livestock. "It's not just Las Vegas. They're shipping that poison all over."

"Harvesting Animus." Edison's words fall like stones in the darkness. "Feeding it to whatever is inside that casket. We need to get this knowledge to Van Lew." Edison's knuckles whiten around the buckle. "All of it—the reliquary, the ward, the whiskey operation."

"Vilde can send a pigeon from the Imperial," I say, already calculating the time. Dawn's approaching fast.

Edison yanks his dog-eared almanac from his breast pocket, flipping pages with trembling fingers. "Múcaro mentioned the Equinox." His face pales further. "Christ, it's tonight—11:04 p.m." He taps the page frantically. "Even if pigeons reach Santa Fe by eight, it would be a horse killing ride to make it here in time."

"Meechum runs the Santa Fe office," Leona says, her lip curling. "If that pompous ass moves quick enough to wire Van Lew, her agents in Trinidad might make it by train." She doesn't sound convinced.

I check my watch. Time's bleeding away. "Then we better move now."

A soft knock at the door freezes us all. Leona smooths her dress before approaching the door.

"Who's there?" she growls.

"Mrs. Wong," comes a woman's voice. "Everything all right? Heard noises."

"My landlady," Leona mouths, before cracking the door.

A short Chinese woman in a practical blue dress peers in, her eyes widening at the sight of Delilah on the bed. Her weathered hands, stained purple from laundry bluing, grip the doorframe. She gives a short nod, the jade pendant at her throat catching the lamplight. "Trouble follows the BMI like flies on horse dung."

Leona's eyebrows rise. "How do you—"

Mrs. Wong rolls her eyes at Leona and slips inside, like someone used to navigating other people's messes. Leona lets her pass. "I've lived in Las Vegas for five years, handling everyone's dirty laundry, including yours." Mrs. Wong snorts, the scent of lye soap and herbs following her into the room. "Most things come out in the wash. I know when dark magic gathers. And I recognize BMI on sight." She produces a small cloth bag from her apron pocket, fingers deftly untying the drawstring. "Tea. For the girl. It will help stabilize her essence."

"Do you trust her?" I ask Leona, jerking my thumb at Mrs. Wong.

Leona looks thoughtful for a minute before answering. "Yes. Absolutely."

Kneeling beside Delilah, she glances at Mrs. Wong, who is already preparing tea. "Will you watch over her?"

Mrs. Wong settles into the chair beside the bed, coaxing Delilah to drink. "Go. I will keep her safe."

Leona, Edison and I exchange glances. "We'll need to be quick," I say. "In and out. Just long enough to get Vilde to send a message."

"And if she can't?" Edison asks.

"Then we're on our own," Leona answers.

Chapter Twenty-Four

We stable the horses at a livery near the train depot in New Town. Plenty of comings and goings there. Sampson and Abigail should blend right in and be easy to get to when we finish our business at the Imperial.

Leona, Edison, and I sneak through the pre-dawn stillness toward the Imperial Saloon. Keeping to the shadows, we circle the building, seeking Vilde's balcony. Heart pounding, I scan the alleys for guards. It feels off. There should be more of Hoodoo's men prowling about. Not that I'm complaining, but the lack of security makes my neck prickle. If we're caught, we're as good as dead. We lost plausible deniability with our little escapade in the caverns. I'm certain Múcaro recognized me.

The hotel remains slumbering behind its ironwork balconies. Only the glow of an upper story window hints at wakefulness within. The same window Morgan and Edison escaped from when this cursed adventure started. I exchange terse nods with Edison and Leona.

Squeezing Edison's shoulder, I wave him ahead up the ornamental drainpipe near Vilde's balcony. The boy swarms up like a spider. Ah, youth. I watch apprehensively, dreading my own attempt to follow.

Leona smiles at my envious gaze and then, lithe as her namesake, leaps to catch the railing and vaults gracefully over. No drainpipe required. She disappears from view into Vilde's suite. Thankfully, no sounds of alarm or outrage follow. Hand over hand, I haul myself skyward, thankful for every nook that helps me with a toehold. My shoulders protest the abuse of the last week.

After what feels like an eternity, with one last breath, I heave myself over the railing and slide cautiously between the parted curtains. The scent of face powder and theatrical grease-paint lingers in the closed air. Edison and Leona stand arrested within, confusion creasing both faces. I move up softly behind them, one weathered hand readying my revolver just in case. No guards meet my gaze, only Vilde, collapsed, weeping to break a heart before her gilded mirror.

She's alone amidst the lush disarray of costumes and prop cages. Strangely, I don't see any of her beloved pigeons, all the cages empty. Could they all be in the roost on the roof? My sharp inhale breaks the tableau. Vilde's reddened eyes fly up to find us in the mirror's reflection. The left side of her face is purple with fresh bruising, her eye swollen shut. Shock blanks her pretty face, then anguish twists her crumpling features anew. She turns toward us beseechingly but is unable to force words past trembling lips.

Dismay slides cold fingers around my throat. Damn it! I let my revolver's muzzle dip. Leona stalks noiselessly to check behind the patterned dressing screen while Edison drifts toward the nearest gilded birdcage, face taut. The room is empty.

I sheath the handgun to crouch beside Vilde's tiny vanity chair. She flinches as I settle gingerly on my heels. Studying her downturned profile, I keep my voice soft despite a thousand questions racing through my thoughts.

"Talk to me, songbird." She hunches tighter, long strawberry curls obscuring her face. My pulse throbs. "Where are your doves, Vilde?" I ask. No answer but to cover her face with her hands and sob quietly.

Edison shifts at my shoulder while Leona prowls the shadowed perimeter like a specter cut from moonlight. Their wordless tension wears at my composure. I keep focus locked upon Vilde until her eyes lift to meet mine.

Voice hoarse from tears, she says, "Vicente t-took my lovelies!" She gestures brokenly around her.

"What?" Edison's whisper is sharp with alarm. "All of them?" His eyes dart frantically between the empty cages.

My stomach drops. Our lifeline to the BMI, gone. The clock ticking toward 11:04 p.m. seems to accelerate.

"Damn it all to hell," I hiss, fighting to keep my voice down. "Without those birds, we've got no way to get word to Van Lew in time."

Leona's face hardens. "We're on our own then." The finality in her voice sends a chill through the room.

Wrestling composure, Vilde continues, "Last night, his thugs snatched Gabriel, Selena, all my pigeons." She swallows painfully.

I stroke her clenched knuckles, fears dancing through my mind. "We'll get the birds back," I lie. My mind races.

Vilde dashes tears away fiercely. I grasp her icy hand. "H-his men d-dragged me to his o-office," she stutters, fresh tears streaking her face.

"Go on." I hold her gaze, dreading what comes next. "Did he do that?" I gesture at her face.

Vilde touches her battered cheek. "He thinks I helped you save Delilah."

Leona comes to stand behind her and places a hand on Vilde's quaking shoulder. "Are we revealed?"

Vilde turns to Leona, her voice firmer, a trace of her old confidence. "I did not admit I was working for the BMI. He thinks I'm trying to help Mick because she's my kin. He never mentioned you at all. And he doesn't know what the pigeons really are."

"Hang on." My ears prick at her comment. "When did Vicente find out we're related?"

Vilde's face blanches. "I'm not sure... He's known my sister was in Trinidad. I might have mentioned your name..."

And that's how Hoodoo found me, was able to target me with the damn grain. I sigh, easing tension in my shoulders. Knees popping, I stand. "It will be all right. Let's get you packed up. We need to get out of here."

I'm struck speechless as this triggers a fresh round of sobs from Vilde. Leona inspects her coldly. "What aren't you saying?"

Vilde turns to look at me. She's bathed in the sunrise's crimson light. Like an unwanted presage, my Reb materializes in the corner. Vilde's frozen like a rabbit.

Leona presses on ruthlessly. "Speak!"

Chin quivering, Vilde begins, "I overheard Vicente and Hoodoo planning. After Vicente beat me, they left me on the floor. May-maybe thought I was unconscious," she takes a deep breath. "They were talking about a ritual for the Equinox, to cul-culminate the Spring Soiree tonight. They called it Ostata or Ostara... a R-ritual of Revitalization."

"We know they're planning an Equinox ritual." I sigh. I don't think we can stop it. We just need to head out, let the BMI come in after and clean up."

Vilde looks at me, tears spilling down her face, but the sobbing has stopped. "They said they had 'The Heart.'" My own heart plummets like stone, dreading her next words. She continues wretchedly, "The Heart is Morgan. Hoodoo's men captured Morgan."

I scarcely hear Edison's shocked oath or Leona's furious questions over the roaring void opening within my head. Morgan. Loyal, stalwart Morgan, who chose to return home for an ordinary life, to his wife and his sheep. Morgan wanted no more killing, no more death. I dragged him here, promising our last long ride. It can't be his last everything. Morgan, whose death Maria ByLilly prophesied all those years ago. It would be my fault.

"Where is he?" I shout over the other voices. I will ride to him this second. I have the buckle. I have power stored. Nothing can stop me. "You must know where they've got him." Vilde's soft "no" sparks spitting frustration. I pull her up and grab her shoulders, forcing her to meet my wild stare. "You heard their plans!" I shake her.

The Reb ghosts from the corner, appearing bloody in the crimson sunrise. "Scared, ain't ya?" He says with knowing eyes. "Scared you'll have to become that person again."

I ignore him, releasing Vilde's shoulders.

Vilde steps back from me, stricken, fresh tears spilling free. "I-I d-don't know." She wrings her hands. "Hoodoo left a couple of hours ago. He's got a suite at the Hot Springs, abandoned homesteads, caves, all over the valley... But they have to bring Morgan to town. The ritual has to happen in the cavern below the Imperial."

I stare at the distraught woman, breathless. She said the ritual was tonight. It's barely dawn. There's time. "This ritual—when, exactly?"

Vilde trembles, tears tracking through paint and powder. "Hoodoo said 'The Heart' has to be in place at exactly the time of the Equinox when the dark and light are in perfect balance."

Leona's voice sharpens. "After what we saw in that cavern, that ward tower, that thing in chains... This isn't just about Morgan." She paces the small space, her movements tight with tension. "A ritual of that scale, on the Equinox, with that much stored Animus...they're raising something monstrous."

Edison says, "If Morgan is the key, they'll have to keep him alive until the Equinox."

"We ride out now. I can take Hoodoo." I move toward the balcony to leave.

Leona presses me back. "Mick, we will save Morgan. But you heard Vilde. Hoodoo's got hidey holes all over the place. We don't know where to look. We need to be smart. We need Morgan alive, and we also need to stop whatever they're planning to unleash. That reliquary..." She shivers despite herself. "Whatever's in there is truly evil. The kind of thing the Bureau was created to contain."

"Even with the buckle, you really think you can take him?" Edison says. "Whatever that was in the cavern, it's more power than I've ever even read about."

"That ain't Hoodoo's power." I snarl at him. "That's stolen. And it don't matter. You don't understand... I can take him."

"What if he's got sharpshooters?" His jaw clenches. "Magic or no, they can just shoot you in the head from 200 yards."

"Not if I hide in the cavern. Vilde just said they gotta do the ritual down there. I'll just head there now and wait. I still got power stored from riding Mads."

Leona looks at me askance but says nothing.

"Now you're just talking crazy." Edison's composure cracks wide and the kid's actually yelling at me. "The cavern is THEIR base of power. You've used your Gleaner what, three times in the last decade? And you are gonna take on that machine, that monster, Hoodoo, and Múcaro? Using their piece of kit? For all you know, they can just disenchant that damn buckle whenever they feel like it." He closes the distance between us. "Then where will you be? A broken down, aging wannabe rescuer with nothing but bum knees and an old service revolver. GREAT PLAN, MICK." His eyes practically bug out of his head.

"I've got a shotgun too," I shout back.

Vilde pushes between us, pleading, "Please, hush. All is lost if you're found here now."

Leona taps her lip with her index finger. "If we can find an alternate way to alert the Bureau, they may be able to get here in time." Her tawny eyes burn. "Any ritual involving that thing in the caverns needs to be stopped!"

I dash moisture from my eyes. "How do we get the BMI here in time? It's already what, six?"

"I could ride to Santa Fe," Edison volunteers.

"It's seventy miles. There isn't enough time to get there and back. And it would kill Abigail," I snap.

"What about the train?" Vilde suggests meekly. "Unless there's snow, it's only three hours to Trinidad."

"I'm not leaving Vegas without Morgan." I cross my arms to stop the trembling of my hands.

"Of course not." Leona collapses on the bed. "It can't be any of us. We could be recognized at any station along the way."

"Marisol's little sister could go?" Vilde volunteers tentatively.

The weight on my chest eases. "If we can get her on the morning train, BMI forces could get here by tonight." I pause. "It's dangerous. Will she do it?"

Leona jumps on the idea. "Ada was Ximena's sister too. She'll help. And if we don't stop whatever is happening in that cavern, everyone in town is in danger. She is too young to have come to Vicente's notice yet, so she won't be missed."

"Good, yes." Doubt creeps into my voice. "We have no guarantee that they will act on Ximena's information."

"We'll send these with her." Edison holds out his BMI badge and a page from his notebook. "These notes summarize everything we've found so far. Van Lew will know it's legit."

"Excellent," Vilde says, wiping her face and taking the items from Edison. "I'll go to Marisol now and beg her to get Ximena on the early train." She scurries out the door.

Edison pulls a bandanna out of his hip pocket to polish his Colts.

I continue to pace the confines of the suite, mind racing but finding no surety. Only hours until Hoodoo's ritual spells Morgan's end. I have to find him, kill Hoodoo, and end this mess. But doubt niggles. Edison's right. I'm not what I used to be.

"What is this Ritual of Revitalization?" Edison asks from where he's propped by the window. "Do we know it's fatal, if it's a sacrifice?"

"Well, I doubt they rode him down and captured him just to drink some tea," I insert caustically.

Leona sits on the bed but continues watching the door, deep in thought. "It's not a classical name, is it? Sounds made up. I've never heard of a ritual named so."

Leona's eyes narrow in concentration. "Revitalization..." She taps her fingers against her thigh. "That's not classical terminology. But the timing—Vernal Equinox—that's significant."

She sways, deeply in thought, thinking aloud as she works through the problem. "Spring rituals are about rebirth. Resurrection." Her voice drops. "And with a necromancer and a dangerously powerful Death Mage involved—"

She glances at Edison, who picks up the thread, his voice tense. "They're resurrecting something."

"Or someone," Leona says. "And they need Morgan as..." She hesitates, glancing at me.

"The Heart," I finish, my voice hollow. "Vilde said Morgan is The Heart."

Leona nods. "Which means they likely already have the other components. The Head. The Hands." She gestures toward the door. "Those anatomical drawings in the chamber weren't just decoration."

I kick a bird cage and round furiously on her. "Who cares! We need to save Morgan. Until he's safe, I don't give a shit, period."

Leona looks at me pityingly. "Understanding their plan may help us save him. Knowing the type of ritual they want him for can tell us much."

Punching my leg in frustration I try to dismiss her words. But before I can respond, the door bursts open, and Vilde stumbles in, chest heaving. "He's here! Hoodoo's taking Morgan to the square!"

Vegas's town square carries a dark legacy. Sure, it serves as the heart of commerce and community gatherings. But that hanging windmill dominates the center, and it's been less than a month since Vicente's men lynched some poor bastard without bothering with a trial. And that wasn't the first time.

"Mick, wait." Edison reaches for my shoulder as I head for the door. "We need a plan. If we spook them now—"

I wrench free of his grip. "You're right. Give me the buckle." I try to fish the hateful object out of his coat pocket.

He tries to dodge around me, but I feel it in his outside pocket. Grabbing it, I try to make him see. "That's Morgan out there." My voice cracks. "I brought him into this mess."

"And getting yourself killed won't help him!" Edison plants himself between me and the door. "Think about what's in that cavern. The ward, the reliquary—"

"Move." I draw my revolver, not pointing it at him but making my intent clear. "Now." The image of Morgan captured, waiting for death, burns away all reason. I can't lose another friend to my mistakes. I won't.

Edison's face hardens. "No. I won't let you throw away everything we've—"

I shove him aside with all my strength and am through the door before he hits the floor, taking the stairs three at a time. Behind me, Leona shouts something, but I'm already gone. My boots thunder down the wooden steps as I race to reach the street.

Morgan needs me. Nothing else matters. Not Edison's protests, not Leona's warnings, not even my own doubts about facing Hoodoo. My oldest friend is out there, captured because of me. I won't let him die for my mistakes.

I burst out of the Imperial's door into the dusty morning light, my revolver ready. Somewhere above, I hear Edison's voice calling my name.

Chapter Twenty-Five

MY BOOTS CRUNCH ON the packed earth. The weight of my revolver presses against my hip, acold comfort against what awaits. I scarcely notice Edison catching up to me, walking in step down the alley toward the plaza just a couple blocks over.

Elmer's buckle scorches my palm, tension mounting behind my temples as the buckle aligns with the ward, freeing me to use the Gleaner. Between breaths, the pressure dissolves, power flows to fingertips. The buckle's power opens a door. I'm gonna use it to end Hoodoo

The half-built bank building provides no cover on our approach. I stay close to the low-slung red-and-tan stone of the Victory bar, trying to get a clear view without revealing my presence quite yet. I pause in the shadow of an apartment building to my right.

The plaza stretches before me, oddly still. No merchants hawk their wares; no children chase each other through the dust. A few townspeople gather at the edges, under the deep portals of the adobe building ringing the north edge of the square. I spot Marisol and two other girls from the Imperial watching from the shadow of the mercantile, perpendicular to my hiding spot, their faces grim. The windmill at the center stands motionless, its wooden frame casting a long shadow across the square. A gallows waiting.

Hoodoo sits beneath it on a huge, raw-boned bay. His black coat unmarked by dust. Eight mounted men flank him, circling their horses, wary of attack. Morgan kneels in the center, bloodied but alive, hands bound by a rope tied to Hoodoo's saddle horn. His hat is gone and his clothes are ragged, both knees skinned out of his trousers. Hoodoo dragged him. Sweat runs down Morgan's face in the mild spring air. I imagine I can hear his ragged breath around the rag gagging him.

Hoodoo is gonna pay.

The windmill creaks once in the rising breeze.

Hoodoo's tenor voice rings across the town square. *"Got Mr. Jackson, gonna take him to the Saloon."* He's parodying Clementine.

"Anybody wants him back better meet me afore noon.
Oh my darling, oh my darling, oh my darling Mick Kelly."

He rides forward on the last line, forcing Morgan to stumble to his feet to avoid being dragged.

None of the gathered townspeople protest.

At my shoulder, Edison gasps. "What's he doing?"

"Hoodoo always did aspire to the spotlight," I answer. "Reckon he's enjoying this, bringing me and Morgan to heel." But I'm gonna change his tune.

"Can't we just shoot them all and make a run for it?"

"Not with your skills, nor mine."

Hoodoo's got armed men, but no Múcaro. Now is the moment. Without further thought, I activate the Gleaner, calling the power stored from riding Mads's death. It coils up from my center until my fingertips and toes burn with crackling energy.

Before Edison can say boo, I step into the open, planting my feet wide. Hoodoo's men tense, hands on their weapons, but Hoodoo himself remains relaxed, a smirk playing across his gaunt face. The force builds in my hands like lightning, ready to strike. I'm gonna stop his black heart and we can all go home.

For a moment, it seems to work. Hoodoo sways in his saddle, his smirk faltering. But then, with a sharp command to his men, the tide turns.

It feels like someone jams a funnel into my gut and turns me upsidedown. My power, my very essence, is stripped, leaving me staggering. Hoodoo's laughter fills the air. Elmer warned me: cast through a buckle in town, and you open a vein straight to Jones.

I stagger and crash to my knees. The feeling is similar but ten times worse than facing Mads when his buckle tried to steal my Animus. My life force tears away in strips, hope peeling off like skin under a blade. The sensation triggers memories of the Kansas City crash, that same impotence and shame as I watched Morgan walk away from the carnage. Not again. The plaza spins as I slump toward the ground. Edison's voice is distant as he cries my name again and again.

Through blurred vision, I see several townspeople back away from the square, whispering and crossing themselves. Only a few of the Imperial's girls remain, watching with hard eyes. They've seen Hoodoo's cruelty before. Just when darkness starts creeping in at the edges of my vision, it stops abruptly. My chest heaves as I suck in air.

"Did you really think it would be that easy, Mick?" Hoodoo taunts, urging his horse closer. "Didn't Elmer tell you about my safeguards. No magic in town without my say-so. Even with a buckle."

"Whoop-de-doo, you stole some power and now you're acting like you're the tallest hog at the trough. You always were a bully." I force myself to stand, meeting his gaze defiantly. "Some cursed borrowed magic ain't gonna save you from me, Hoodoo Jones."

"Ah, Mick." He sighs. "I might have believed you once upon a time, but today I have the winning hand. Your little attack was a delectable amuse-bouche."

I glance down when Edison shifts and points at his Colt. I give the tiniest shake of my head.

"Boss, you want Jose and me to go get her?" the rider on Hoodoo's left asks.

"No, you twat." Hoodoo's tone is harsh. "Kelly is gonna come to me of her own accord. It's part of the game. Don't ruin it."

"Give me Morgan," I demand, "and we'll get outa your hair."

"No, I don't think so." Hoodoo places a hand on his chin as though in thought. "I know! You bring yourself and that stolen buckle to the Imperial at noon and maybe we can arrange a trade." He jerks the rope binding Morgan's hands, forcing him to fall to his knees. "I promised my guests an opportunity to see justice served. I wouldn't want to disappoint."

My mind races, but I agree, "Fine. I'll come with the buckle, and you swear not to hurt Morgan." Morgan's eyes find mine. He shakes his head, eyes wide. The look tears at me—same as when he tried to stop me using dark magic against Hoodoo's men. He's always trying to save me from myself. This time, though, I'm the one who needs to save him, whatever the cost.

"You have my most solemn vow, I will not harm your friend if we make the trade," Hoodoo drawls. "Be there at noon." He and his men turn and continue down main street, Hoodoo humming the hateful song. I stand and watch until they turn off Main Street, then I drop beside Edison. My heart is thundering to leave my chest.

No way we can attack them head-on. Not enough firepower or skill. We won't know if Ximena got word through to Van Lew for hours yet… Taking the bait to meet at the saloon where I have allies might be our best chance. Anything to earn Morgan free.

Edison grabs my arm as I start to rise. "You're not considering walking into that trap?"

"Got a better idea?" My voice comes out hard.

"No, but…" He pulls out his notebook, flipping pages frantically. "The Equinox isn't until tonight. Whatever Hoodoo's planning with that ritual—"

"No." I brush the dust off my pants, trying to ignore how my hands still shake. "Morgan won't last that long if I don't show."

A shadow passes overhead. A turkey vulture circles the plaza. It reminds me of something darker. Something hungry. Hoodoo may have promised not to harm Morgan, but he never said anything about what Múcaro might do.

I draw my revolver at the sound of steps rounding the corner. Leona emerges from the alley beside the Victory, her face set. She glances meaningfully at a few townspeople still watching us, then walks by me, whispering, "Meet at my apartment."

✦────────✦

"I'm not letting you trade yourself or that buckle. There has to be another way." Edison paces around Leona's spartan room. If you can call two steps in either direction pacing. Only a foot or two wider than the door, there's hardly room for both of us to stand.

After debating with him for the last fifteen minutes, I collapse on the cot. Heat and the scent of soap come from the laundry below. After moving Delilah to Mrs. Wong's room, Leona's gone ahead to report for her shift at the bar, leaving us her room as our temporary sanctuary.

"At least let me go in with you," he urges.

"Edison, Leona and Marisol will be inside with me. I'm not planning on just giving myself up. The girls are gonna sneak me in, maybe give me an opportunity to grab Morgan and run." He opens his mouth to argue some more, but I cut him off. "If I go in there, we gotta have a fast getaway. You gotta have the horses ready."

He tilts his head back and stares at the ceiling for a minute before meeting my eyes and sighing. "Fine, I'll hitch them at the smithy across the street. They'll blend in. I'll be the lookout. When you grab Morgan, I'll be ready."

"Who knows, maybe I can get in and out without Hoodoo being the wiser." Yeah, when pigs fly. I know the chances of getting both of us out alive are slim.

"I don't like leaving you to face that bunch alone." He clenches his jaw. "'Specially since Hoodoo holds you in such hateful regard."

"I won't be alone. I got the ladies of the Imperial at my back. I stand and tap his chest gently. "Get the horses set up close and then find a hidey-hole where you can see what's happening." I pause, then grin. "Reckon you will have to be VERY close for you to actually see. Maybe just listen for a commotion?"

"Ha-ha, you got the run on me." Acknowledging the joke, he sobers. "I promise I'll be ready."

I hug him tightly, then pull back to look in his eyes. "If this endeavor goes tits up, your oath to take Sampson and ride hell for leather for the back of beyond?"

"Yes, ma'am. I'll save that snuffy, broom-tailed nag if it's the last thing I do."

"Thank you."

The narrow stairs creak under our boots as we descend from Leona's room. At the rear door, Edison adjusts his gun belt one last time. "I'll have Sampson and the others ready in ten minutes. Just..." He pushes his spectacles up. "Just make it count."

"You too." I clasp his shoulder. "Remember what I said about riding out if things go wrong."

"I remember." He heads north toward the livery.

✦━━━━━━✦

Walking down the street sunshine soothes my spirits despite the ordeals ahead. This damn job seemed so simple back on the homestead—verify a little magic use, et voilà, cash to solve our money woes. Now Morgan is a pawn in Hoodoo's twisted scheming. And I led him straight into the hornet's nest. But I'm gonna set things right.

Grinding my teeth, I shove back regrets. I can't change past mistakes, but I can damn well grab destiny's reins before Hoodoo's ritual does. I'll tear that saloon apart beam by beam if I have to.

Spring comes earlier to Vegas than my home, but I don't dare remove my heavy coat because it will expose the service revolver on my hip. Nothing draws attention as much as looking like you're skulking. I'm trying to meander, just a backcountry cowpuncher taking in the cosmopolitan sites of Las Vegas, lah-de-dah. I'm retracing our steps from the previous night through back streets and alleys to the Imperial. I got my hair tucked up in my hat and my bandana high on my neck, obscuring my jaw. Because of my stride, height, and dress, there's nothing ladylike about my demeanor. I figure if Hoodoo's men are looking for a gun-toting woman with a teenage sidekick, it behooves me to appear solitary and masculine.

I circle around the plaza to get a view of the Imperial's entrance. Surprisingly, music spills into the late morning breeze. Vicente's soiree. I watch the comings and goings for a few minutes. Same gap-toothed dude at the door collecting firearms. If they dragged a beaten and tied man through the front doors, surely folks wouldn't be stopping by for a morning beer?

Mindful of Leona's intelligence—no one is working the distillery but plenty of muscle—I make my way around the back. I linger at the entrance to the alley running between the saloon and the distillery where I can see the service yard. It's basically a loading area with access to the corral and tack shed. Keeping my face lowered, I scan for any sign of Morgan's passage. The distillery is quiet. No sounds of machinery, no production workers hustling around, just the faintest smell of yeast and vinegar.

A couple of kids lead horses to the saloon's corral. Hoodoo's big bay snaps at the boy at its head. Poor beastie, belonging to Hoodoo would make an angel spiteful.

Looks like they brought Morgan in through the back, unless there is direct access to the caverns through the saloon's cellar.

I wait a few minutes, then head around the end of the building to find my allies in the kitchen. Get in, get Morgan, get out, I silently repeat like a catechism, willing myself calm against hopelessness. I'm just rounding the corner to the kitchen entrance when I spot a guard in a ten-gallon hat leaning against the door, smoking. Damn it. I press myself backward against the corner. Now I look suspicious and it's a matter of seconds before he spots me.

You got this, don't lose your head. I repeat my new refrain. Heart thundering fit to burst, I step into view, affecting bored indifference. I suppose the baby faced kid is old enough to shave. He's reed-thin beneath his too-large hat. Still, the confident hand resting on his holstered Colt suggests he knows his business.

"Hey! You." He tosses his stogie and steps my way. In for a penny. Running would cause a commotion; shooting him would be too loud.

I incline my head politely, noticing beads of sweat above his lip, and lean casually on the wall. Willing my shoulders to relax, I feel the Gleaner stirring in my belly. "Busy morning?"

"No rest for the wicked, as they say." His smile doesn't reach his eyes. "Here on...business, are ya?"

"Got an appointment with my favorite girl." I wink at him. "What's the hullabaloo? Place is hopping."

"Boss is having himself a little soiree with old friends. Invited all the important folks in the Territory to see the show." His smile fades. Eyes travel along my dusty riding clothes to my grimy face. "You don't appear to be on the guest list." His lip curls faintly.

I don't think I can take him in a fight. Facing him head-on might be a mistake.

He continues staring me down, recognition dawning on his face. "You ain't no john. You're that woman!" His sinewy hand suddenly seizes my shoulder, rank breath hot on my face. "Boss'll be mighty happy to see you."

My panic spikes as I try to break his grip.

BANG. Edison strikes the guard square across the noggin with a shovel. A clang and a soft crunch reverberate in the spring air. The poor bloke drops like a daisy.

"Holy smokes, kid." My heart's going a mile a minute. Glancing around the empty yard, I hear footsteps and laughter from the end of the street. "Quick. We gotta hide him."

We each lay hold on a booted leg and start dragging him toward the corral. The folks on the street sound like they are having their own party. *Just don't turn this corner,* I will the Universe, fighting rising tension. "Good timing, that," I murmur to Edison.

"You told me to watch for commotion," he huffs. "This fella sure has some weight for a skinny guy."

"You pulled my bacon outta the fire again." I release the body and push it tight against the leeward side of the horse trough. Not perfectly concealed, but no one's likely to notice from the saloon side.

Edison pulls hay from the nearby pile and packs it over the body. "There. Now unless someone's up close, he should stay hidden."

I nod. "Back to lookout for you, my lad."

"I hate leaving you, Mick. But I'll be ready." He takes off down the boardwalk.

I hurry back to the kitchen door and cautiously crack it open. Marisol grabs me from the other side and pulls me in by my coat sleeve. She puts a finger to her lips to hush me and glances over her shoulder. Another woman, Claudette, is chopping carrots at the scarred worktable occupying most of the space in the narrow room. A sink with a hand pump shares the outside wall with a coal stove. She smiles and motions me to follow Marisol toward the narrow, winding stairs. Marisol leads me up the back staircase that's intended for access to bring fuel or food to the rooms above without traipsing through the public areas.

Marisol and I creep up the narrow wooden stairs. There's no railing, but the passage is only shoulder width. We emerge at the farthest end of the guest room hallway overlooking the saloon, catty-corner to Vilde's door. Reaching the second floor unchallenged, I exhale.

The piano is still going in the bar below, but the crowd seems subdued. I hear the clinking of glassware and the low murmur of voices but no laughter or shouting. My fingers itch to grab my revolver, to charge down there guns blazing. But my tendency to shoot first, think later is what got Morgan into this mess. I force myself to breathe slow, steady. Morgan needs clear thinking, not blind rage.

Marisol pauses for a second to confirm there are no guards in the hallway and then drags me out of the stairway and into Vilde's room. She closes the door with a soft click.

The suite feels forlorn. All of the ornamental cages are gone, leaving a few bedraggled costumes hanging on pegs around the wall. The vanity has been stripped of her creams and unguents. No more posters or photos are tacked on the walls and her bedside table is empty but for a single kerosene lamp. Vilde is seated on the double bed, her back against the wall. Leona peers through the curtains to the street below.

"What have you learned?" I begin eagerly.

Marisol clutches my hand and urges me to quiet.

"Sshhhh, the walls are thin and I don't know who we can trust." Leona crosses to join Vilde on the bed and motions me over. Marisol picks up the tiny vanity bench and joins us to powwow.

Voice low, Leona starts, "I took up my post behind the bar as per my usual schedule. Vicente swept through and ordered me upstairs. He's handing bottles out to all the tables instead of bar service."

"He sent all the girls to their rooms and ordered us to stay put until summoned," Vilde adds. "He said we were having a special guest for lunch."

"Just a few minutes ago, I heard them drag Morgan out of the cellar up to the bar." Marisol wrings her hands. "I saw them tie him to a chair on stage." Red haze clouds my vision and I lose track of what Marisol is saying before I force myself to focus. "...the bar is packed with big wigs. Vicente promised to show them their protection money at work. He's pouring so much Imperial Whiskey down their throats, half of them are so tight, I don't know how they're upright."

They're not just drunk. Hoodoo is gathering power and sucking life from those men, feeding them Imperial. My ears start ringing as panic claws at my chest. Morgan's in there, watching those men die by inches, waiting for the ax to fall on him.

I exhale to a slow count of six and I reassure myself. I can do this. They'll keep Morgan alive until the Equinox. This is all just taunting, Hoodoo's feeble attempt at humiliation. He wants me here to watch, to break me while simultaneously demonstrating his power to a cowed audience. But they won't kill Morgan until the ritual.

I curl my fingers into fists, feeling the familiar pull of the Gleaner stirring beneath my skin. Not yet. It's all games for now, and I will beat him at his own sport. Morgan taught me patience in cards, time to put those lessons to use.

* * *

We're interrupted by heavy fists pounding the door. "On your feet, ladies! The boss requests your presence!" Rough voices repeat the message down the hallway, summoning all the women.

Marisol stifles a shriek as the harsh knock comes again, vibrating the door with its force. Leona strides across the room, expression thunderous. She wrenches the door open with a growled curse leveled at the swaggering bully across the threshold. "By damn you will wait until we are properly attired!"

Her imperious command gives him pause before yellow teeth emerge in a jeering smile. With exaggerated courtesy, he sketches a mocking bow. "Apologies, mistress, no offense intended. But the courtesy of your presence is requested at the gallery straight away." His grinning cohort waves a truncheon suggestively over one shoulder.

Leona draws herself tall, affecting detached curiosity. "Did Vicente indicate the nature of this summons?"

The guard shrugs with practiced indifference but malice glints. "Some old duffer's getting the boots, it sounds. Don't pay me to ask questions. Now get to stepping lest you keep the boss man waiting!" With a leering nod, he retreats to marshal other stragglers into the shadowed hall. We move to comply. Fear shivers Marisol's slender shoulders as we slip into procession, her head bowed wretchedly. On impulse, I squeeze her hand in passing, whether to lend courage or seek my own, I can't say. More than a dozen women grimly take their place along the upper gallery banister. I crouch behind them, hoping to remain unnoticed, camouflaged by their voluminous skirts. Glimpsing the saloon below, my breath catches at the waiting scene.

Vicente holds court upon the stage, face alight with enthusiasm. His pompadour gleams in the weak sunlight. Ranks of uneasy men fill the tables, eyes downcast. Scents of stale tobacco, stale beer, and unwashed bodies drift up. Vicente raises his hands as if to welcome friends to some convivial party.

Fear floods my veins as his voice fills the hall. "Good citizens! We gather to correct grievous wrongdoing." He paces the stage apron gesturing grandly. "As sheriff, I present despoiler and bandit, one Morgan Smith by name. Captured through fortuitous chance!" At his signal, the curtain draws back, revealing a gray figure bound in a ladder-backed chair. A small table with a single long-bladed knife is positioned behind him. Shocked oaths tear from the ladies around me and uneasy gasps sound from the crowd below.

Blood trickles from Morgan's temple, vanishing into his coarse whiskers. His clothing hangs in tattered disarray, displaying a multitude of bruises. His shoulders remain unbowed, dark gaze tracking the spectators. Vicente circles with predatory focus, leather soles slithering upon the boards. "Behold! As promised, the rogue Smith, lately accused in my own halls of capital crimes. Murder, rape, robbery—nowhere safe from his depredations."

The crowd shifts uneasily and throws glances toward the doors.

My fists ache, watching Vicente goad the reluctant crowd into his twisted drama, their muttered condemnations falling easily from uneasy lips. Vicente orchestrated this ,trial, to threaten dignity and life, justice not even a pretext. Morgan stares stoically ahead, refusing to be goaded.

Leona's hand falls on my shoulder. "Peace. The intention is to draw you out. The taking of his life must be part of the Equinox ritual. We'll have time to extract him when this masque concludes."

A nasal drawl splits the churning air. "Well, lookee at this menagerie!" Vicente looks peeved as every eye swings to Hoodoo's cadaverous form mounting the stage. He surveys the scene wearing a vulpine grin, focus landing upon the women clustered above. Searching the group, he continues, "I was expecting a special guest...there she is! Dear ol' Warhorse amongst my twittering fillies." His mocking gaze spears me, still half-concealed behind Marisol. "Mick darling, Vicente's hospitality falls shy if he neglected to include you in the festivities."

I stand to approach the railing. My heart hammers, fit to burst in rage.

The showman in his own right Vicente joins the game. "By all means, I entreat the good lady to attend us!"

Morgan shouts wild-eyed, from below. "Run, Mick, you fool!"

Leona beside me, ashen but resolute. "Wait," she hisses. "You lose all advantage from below."

My fists turn white-knuckled upon the railing. I long to vault onto that stage and tear out Hoodoo's lying tongue. Leona's hand closes on my wrist.

"You promised me a trade, Jones. Me and the buckle for Morgan. Here I am. Let him go." The crowd below has fallen to complete silence.

"Mick, Mick, Mick..." Hoodoo shakes his head. "Always trying to steal the spotlight." Hoodoo taps his index finger against his cheek as though in thought.

"Hoodoo, you crock-headed gump," Morgan rasps. "You stupid enough to think some addled piece of calico had anything to do with Lafayette's death? You don't have the sense God gave a titmouse. I'm the one you want. Let her go."

"Do you hear this, Mick?" Hoodoo moves behind Morgan's chair and grips his shoulders. "Your loyal protector, even now spinning yarns meant to convince me you weren't the one to kill Lafayette."

"Enough, Hoodoo." I hold the buckle up. "I'm the one you want. And I've got this. Let him go."

"Why don't you come down here and we can talk? Otherwise..." Hoodoo nods at Vicente, who plucks the knife from the tray and drags the edge lightly across Morgan's collarbone. Blood sheets down the older man's shirt as he twists against his bonds.

"Stop! You promised not to hurt him." I hate how my voice rises in pitch.

"And I haven't, have I? Keep your story straight, Mick. That was Vicente's hand providing a tiny reminder of who holds the power here. Bring me the buckle and maybe we can still reach an accord."

I scarcely hear him, eyes locked on Morgan's. No fear shows in my friend's bold glare, only banked fury and defiance. I should never have dragged Morgan within a hundred miles of this morass.

I start making my way to the stairs. Panic sets my blood aflame. That filth Hoodoo would torture Morgan for pleasure. My magic may be useless against Hoodoo here with the ward and his control, but my Colt isn't if I can get close enough. Leona wrenches me close as I pass her, her breath hot in my ear. "Keep your head! They won't kill the prize before tonight."

I nod and continue, tucking the cursed buckle into my pocket. Instead of clearing a path, the Imperial's women crowd down the stairs in front and behind me, drawn to the spectacle below. Two of Hoodoo's buckled henchmen climb toward the landing, pushing their way through petticoats and soft skin.

I ignore them all, my focus locked on Morgan.

I reach the landing just as Morgan's voice rises above the silence. "You too chicken to face Mick without me as a shield? She always was the better of you. Everyone on the crew saw it. Lafayette always knew it too."

"Shut up, you Aussie cunt." Hoodoo jerks Morgan's head back by a fistful of hair. But beneath his snarl, I catch something worse, the gleam in his eye when he's got what he wants. Morgan bellows furiously.

The sight shatters my self-control. To hell with the stairs. I vault over the landing railing, my body crashing six feet to the floor below. The bone-jarring impact registers only slightly through my rage.

For an instant, surprise freezes the villains to stillness. Then Hoodoo's face splits in a terrible victorious smile. In the same heartbeat, his knife slashes a wide crimson arc through Morgan's exposed neck. Blood washes his chest, spraying Hoodoo's face red. Morgan sags lifeless in his bonds, lifeblood sheeting the rough boards below.

Time stops. Morgan's head drops forward. No drama. No last words. Just...gone. Our trip here—Morgan singing his damn Souza songs while we saddled up, alive and whole and mine to protect. My anguished cry drowns in the saloon's uproar.

Hoodoo stands motionless before Morgan's corpse, knife hanging loose in his grip. Our eyes lock across the heaving crowd separating us. That same terrible smile plays across his blood-spattered face. He wanted this. Wanted me to watch, helpless. The bastard timed it perfectly.

Something in my head snaps. Bellowing, I bull my way through the roiling human sea. Pain screams from countless bruises. I no longer recognize saloon, stage, or former friend. All reality is narrowed to Hoodoo. Blood pounds. I will rend the source of my misery from existence with my bare hands.

A path clears before me. Dimly, I register skirts shifting, bodies stumbling, but nothing matters except reaching that blood-spattered monster.

With a final surge, I break free to the stage's edge. Screaming, I launch myself at Morgan's killer, hands clawing for his sneering face. Faster than I blink, Hoodoo clamps my wrist with crushing force, wrenching me off balance, pulling me toward him. He's ready for me. Has been ready.

"Not yet, my pet!" he purrs, his night-black eyes drinking in my fury. "The real game's just begun..." His grip raises bruises even as my struggle redoubles, teeth bared inches from his leering face. Not even my rage can break his hold. We sway, the saloon's chaos fading around us. His breath on my face reeks of decay.

Two sharp retorts pierce that deadly haze. Hoodoo jerks sharply, rocking sideways, losing his death grip on my arm. A crimson circle blooms dark and wet on the sleeve of his pristine white shirt. His jaw slackens with shock as he tries reaching for me with his useless arm, then falls gracefully to the ground. He always was a pussy 'bout his own blood. Leona leans precariously from the gallery, teeth bare, wisps of smoke still curling from twin pocket pistols. Her amber eyes blaze.

The spell of Hoodoo's control breaks. I reel away, gasping. A glance confirms Morgan beyond all aid.

For one mad second, I lunge toward him instead of the exit. Three desperate strides and I'm at his side, fingers scrabbling at his bloody left hand. The simple gold band Maria gave him slides from his still-warm finger. I clutch it in my fist, all I can salvage from his slaughter.

The doors, if I can just get outside to Edison and the horses...

Vicente's men raise their weapons to return Leon's fire. Raw desperation floods me. No choice. I touch the buckle and reach for my power, knowing what the ward will do. The burst of energy jams their hammers and agony rips through me as Hoodoo's magic reaches in and tears my Animus. Like hooks inside me, pulling my life force out through my skin. My knees buckle.

Through swimming vision, I see Vicente's men diving for cover as Leona takes aim again. A serving tray appears from nowhere, crashing into one guard's back. Another trips over a stray bottle. The blonde near the door—Claudette?—stumbles dramatically into the path of a third. Each "accident" precise. Christ, the women are trying to clear a path for me. Vicente will make them pay.

The sunlight blinds me as I burst outside. Edison catches me as I fall. Through the roaring in my ears, I hear shouts, running feet, the creak of leather. A horse snorts close by. Then nothing as Hoodoo's ward exacts its price, my last coherent thought a prayer that the women who helped won't pay too dearly for their courage.

Chapter Twenty-Six

HANDS GENTLY SHAKE MY shoulder. "Mick... Mick, you gotta wake up now."

My eyes slit open to Edison's face hovering above me. Disoriented, I peer around the gloomy hollow where we took refuge after escaping Hoodoo's ambush two nights ago. Our gear is piled behind me. The very rocks seem to mock me with memories of a night mere days past when the future seemed hopeful. Desolation yawns—Morgan is gone. My friend gone as if he had never been.

I turn to my side, lest Edison see tears streaking my cheeks. Numbly, I stare into the afternoon sun. How dare it shine?

"Mick, we're burning daylight." Edison's voice breaks through my fog. "Where's Morgan? We still got time before the Equinox, but we gotta make a plan."

I stare at him sightlessly for a moment, the answer crushing the breath from my lungs. At last, I find my voice. "They killed him, Edison...slit his throat like a hog to slaughter. And I couldn't..." A guttural sound tears free. "I didn't save him."

Edison sits back, color draining from his face. "No. That's not...we were supposed to..." His hands clench into fists. "What do we do now?"

"Nothing. We're done here." I press the heels of my hands against my eyes.

"Like hell we are." Edison's voice cracks with fury. "You're just going to let them get away with butchering Morgan?"

"What would you have me do? I failed. I led him right to Hoodoo's door." I stare sightlessly.

Edison sits back away from me. No doubt distancing himself from this truth. From my weakness.

I only escaped the saloon by the grace of others—couldn't even save myself.

"What's next?" Edison's fragile voice interrupts my pity party.

I sit up and stare bleakly at him. What can't he understand? "There is no next. We've lost, boy," I rasp. "Hoodoo beat me…"

Silence stretches taut between us. My thoughts churn without direction or purpose. I stir. "You should take the buckle to Van Lew. I wash my hands of this business."

Edison's expression tightens stormily.

"You saying we leave Hoodoo to his ritual, leave Morgan to rot while we escape as cowards?"

A clatter of shale interrupts our argument. Edison reaches for his revolvers. I glance around for the shotgun, no sense of where it ended up, as Vilde's voice calls out, "Hallooo." She appears through the trees, my shotgun resting on her shoulder, Leona beside her.

Despite eyes reddened by tears and bruises from Vicente's beating, Vilde looks steady. She gathers me in her arms before I can protest. "Thank God you're alive."

Stunned by her spontaneous warmth, my throat closes and tears threaten. She joins me, sitting on the rocky ground.

Leona is clothed in her usual fringed vest and voluminous skirts. She's got a bag slung across her body. She pauses to squeeze Edison's shoulder before joining those of us seated below the rock face. She sits ramrod straight, cross-legged, hands folded in her lap. All business. Leona looks at Edison. "From your face, I take it Mick told you what happened?"

"Yeah, she filled me in." Edison crosses his legs, hunched forward.

Leona shifts slightly, easing her back. "I am deeply sorry for the loss of Morgan Smith. He faced his end bravely."

I flash to Morgan's face challenging Vicente to do his worst. Did he know that was the end? Did he hope I would find a way to rescue him?

"There's no time for mourning." Her voice is emotionless, face grim. "The ward over town grows even stronger by the hour. I can feel it pulling Vitae, like a slow poison affecting everyone within its borders. We must halt the ritual. My shot barely grazed Hoodoo. It hasn't stopped his plans."

"I was just explaining to Edison that I'm done here. That ritual's outside of my care. We're headed home," I answer flatly.

"Speak for yourself." Edison bristles, posture strengthening.

"Outside your care? Vicente's men are spreading that cursed grain across three territories," Leona says, her eyes flashing dangerously. "Every death feeds whatever's growing in that cavern. And those women at the Imperial who helped you escape? Vicente will make them pay."

"I never asked for their help," I mutter, guilt stomping through my soul.

Leona's hands come out of her lap and she points at me. "You are BMI. It is your responsibility to help thwart these dastardly plans. The ritual isn't just about Morgan." Her hands clench. "That cursed grain is spreading through the whole territory."

I counter tiredly, "My BMI days are well behind me. I have nothing to offer. I only made it out of that saloon alive because of your quick thinking. I need to go home to my family."

"You will be lucky to have a family if this ritual comes to pass," she snaps. Her hair starts floating wildly around her head as her cougar threatens to emerge. I remember what passionate conviction feels like. That's how I felt a decade ago when I convinced Morgan and Clyde to end Lafayette. That's what started the chain of events leading right here, to Morgan's death. I want no part of it.

"You're Mick goddamn Kelly." Leona's voice cuts sharp as a blade. "You're giving up because of one overblown necromancer and a death mage?"

"You don't understand—"

"No, you don't understand." Edison's voice trembles. "Uncle Pete always said 'The only thing necessary for the triumph of evil is for good men to do nothing.' We're the good men...er, good people." His face crumples. "Morgan believed that. He believed in you."

I stand, unable to bear their faith in me. "I can't help you." Turning away from their disappointed faces, I head up the mountain path toward where Sampson waits. I need my friend's simple comfort, not demands for heroism I can't deliver.

Sunlight fails to warm the path up the mountainside. I become aware of a creeping sensation. Feels like the weight of unseen eyes. I raise my head, dread curdling my stomach.

"Running again?" The Reb materializes beside me, Confederate gray stark against the evergreens. "Reckon that's becoming a habit with you."

"Not now." I trudge forward, but he keeps pace easily.

"When then? After Hoodoo finishes whatever he's brewing? Funny thing about you, Mick," the Reb drawls, "spent your whole life trying to make yourself smaller. For Morgan. For your sister. Hell, even for that dead husband of yours. Reckon you got so good at it, you forgot who you really are."

"I know exactly who I am," I snap. "Old. Tired. Past my prime."

His laugh holds no humor. "That what you tell yourself? Truth is, you're stronger now than you ever were. Just scared to admit it might mean standing alone."

I whirl on him. "You want to talk about facing things? You've been haunting me since Gettysburg, refusing to move on. What're you scared of?"

"I ain't scared." His face cracks into the familiar sardonic smile. "I got a powerful curiosity, wanna see how it all turns out." He gestures behind me. "Speaking of figuring things out..."

Mads's shade stands there, blood staining his shirt where Edison's bullet found him. "You didn't hesitate," he says, voice hollow as an empty well. "Rode my death like a goddess of old. Took my power because it needed taking. And it felt right, didn't it?" His empty eyes bore into mine. "Now your friends are gonna pay the price while you pretend to be less. What choice you gonna make this time?"

The gunmen from the ambush coalesce at Mads's shoulder. "You saved yourself and Morgan that night," one says. "Used your power true and clean. No holding back then."

My legs weaken. I sink onto a fallen log, surrounded by the shades of my failures. But they're not attacking. Not condemning. They're...waiting.

"Ain't about what power does TO you anymore, Mick." The Reb crouches before me, his eyes holding mine. "It's about what you choose to do WITH it."

A soft nicker breaks through my thoughts. Sampson ghosts from the deep shade, solid and real amidst the gathering spirits. I throw my arms around his neck. Comfort from his nearness and solidity. He wraps his neck over my shoulders and we stand as I pour my guilt and misery into endless tears against his warm hide. Eventually he becomes impatient, and starts searching my pockets for a treat. That's when I notice the small hard lump, Morgan's wedding ring, shoved in my pocket when I made my escape.

The Reb stands, adjusting his kepi. "Time to choose, Mick. You gonna keep running, or you gonna stand and fight?"

I slide my thumb through the ring. It's warm like it came from a living hand. Morgan would expect me to stand. Morgan trusted me, even if he didn't trust my power. Doesn't mean I shouldn't use it. I should have tapped it to blast Hoodoo's head off the first second I laid eyes on him.

I thread the ring on a piece of twine and tie it around my neck. The gold settles against my skin, right over my heart. For a moment, warmth spreads through my chest.

"You're right," I tell the Reb, straightening. "Been hiding long enough."

He tips his kepi, a rare gesture of respect. "About damn time." The other shades fade, leaving just him. "Now what are you gonna do about it?"

I give Sampson one final pat and turn back toward the path. Toward my friends. Toward responsibility. "I'm going to finish what we started. And this time, I'm going to do it right."

The Reb's approving nod follows me down the mountain. Time to face Hoodoo. Time to face myself.

Chapter Twenty-Seven

I STRIDE TOWARD CAMP with new purpose, the Reb's words fresh in my ears. The afternoon sun casts long shadows across our little clearing between scattered boulders. Edison and Leona circle each other, voices sharp.

"...and I will not leave her alone with this!" Edison's voice cracks.

"She needs BMI backup, not a green agent who can't—"

I let them go at it while I turn Morgan's ring over in my fingers. Ten years ago I watched Maria slide this band onto his hand. The steadiest shot in the territory shaking like a kid, but his voice never wavered on "I do."

I close my fist until the metal bites. Judging by the sun, we've got less than eight hours till the Equinox. Eight hours to stop whatever Hoodoo's cooking. Eight hours to make Morgan's death mean something.

I march toward the bickering pair. Vilde stands a little apart, hands clasped. Edison's toe‑to‑toe with Leona, a terrier facing a lioness.

"Mick," Edison rounds on me the moment I appear, face pink. "Tell this feline witch I am not leaving. I got work to do here. You need me."

I clamp a hand on his shoulder. "Wait."

Leona eyes me. "Glad you decided to rejoin us." She notes acerbically. "Have you returned to your senses?"

"You all got the right of it." I meet each of their gazes. "I still got work to do. Morgan would expect me to fight." They all exhale. I scowl. "He wasn't the type to run scared because odds lengthened."

"Oh, Mick." Vilde takes my hand. "Thank you," she whispers, noticing the ring.

Edison paces, kicking at loose stones. "Why are *you* even here?" he snaps at Vilde. "Aren't you in trouble with Vicente and Hoodoo?"

"Vicente trusts me," she says. "At least he trusts that I'm too scared to move against him." She glances at the sky. "The Equinox is at 11:04 tonight. That's when Hoodoo plans his ritual."

Leona nods grim. "Which means we have precious little time. We can't count on the BMI, even if Ximena made it to Trinidad."

"So it's just us," Edison says, bravado leaking out of him as he looks at our small crew.

"There's more you need to know," Vilde says. "Hoodoo specifically wants *you*, Mick."

Of course he does. Revenge. "The train crash," I breathe, heart hammering.

"Hoodoo's cooked up payback for whoever killed Lafayette Baker," Edison mutters, twisting his hat brim.

"The rumors were true," Leona says, tapping her lip. "You assassinated Baker, and Pinkerton protected you." Her eyes fix on me.

The wind kicks dust across Leona's crude map. A hawk circles overhead, its shadow passing over the marks in the dirt.

"Yes." I straighten my shoulders. "Clyde Ball, Morgan, and I took out Lafayette in Kansas City in '70. I burned him to ash. Alan Pinkerton helped cover our tracks and keep me out of a noose."

"And Hoodoo was loyal to Baker," Leona says, voice bitter.

"Not just loyalty." I remember those years too well. "Baker promised him vampirism for his trouble."

Vilde crosses herself. "Gud bevare meg. A vampire with government power..."

Leona freezes. "Wait. Lafayette Baker was a vampire?" Her voice drops. "That's impossible. The Bureau's official line is that vampires were driven off this continent."

"Tell that to Belle Boyd," I say, tightening my gun belt. "She turned him in '68. By '70 he was planning his own little empire in Texas."

"Is there a pattern?" Leona asks. "Morgan's dead. Hoodoo wants you. What happened to Clyde?"

"Clyde was killed two years ago," I say, bitterness roughening my voice. "I thought it was a robbery gone wrong..."

"Didn't Elmer say something about the buckles being made from the 'first betrayer's' head?" Edison flips through his notebook. "Could that be Clyde?"

"Head, heart, hands," Leona murmurs, sketching three symbols in the dirt. "Clyde was the head of your little outfit. Morgan was the heart. And you—"

"I'm the hands," I finish, flexing my fingers. "I killed Baker. Ruined Hoodoo's plans. So he took Clyde, then Morgan. I'm next."

"Not just killed," Edison says. "Sacrificed. For a ritual tied to the Equinox."

"The Bureau has files on Baker's death," Leona says. "Rumors his followers collected... pieces."

I shake my head. "There was nothing left to collect. I made damn sure."

Leona looks back at her map. "This goes beyond revenge. The amount of animus they've stockpiled down there—if Hoodoo harnesses that tonight..."

"It could fuel magic powerful enough to affect the whole territory," Edison says. "The ward around Las Vegas is just a demonstration."

A sick dread coils in my gut. "What else could he do with that much animus?"

"Control it. Direct it. Weaponize it," Leona says. "The Bureau's worst fear? Somebody making a magical dead zone around Washington. Or worse, a zone where only *they* can use magic."

"And with Múcaro's knowledge…" Edison trails off.

"So it's not just about me or Morgan," I say, the weight settling on my shoulders. "If Hoodoo completes that ritual, he could threaten the whole damn country."

"Which is why we can't wait for BMI backup." Leona's tone brooks no argument. "We'd be too late."

"I still don't understand," I say. "If we're so important to his plans, why didn't he come after me sooner?"

"Hoodoo started baiting you months ago." All eyes turn to Vilde perched on her boulder like it's a parlor chair. "He sent cursed feed to your homestead. They have an agent working in Trinidad who made sure you got the grain. He called it his opening salvo."

"That can't be right. I got the feed from Robert Tallmadge. He isn't working for Hoodoo." My own voice sounds hollow to my ears.

"Tallmadge was tasked with getting you to Vegas," Vilde says, smoothing her skirt. "If you hadn't come with Morgan on your own, they were going to use me as bait. They figured if Gudrun's sister turned up murdered, you'd come." Her mouth twists. "Then Mads killed Ada, and Tallmadge used that instead to tug your strings."

My canteen slips from my fingers, water spilling into the dust. "No. I don't believe that."

Edison stops fidgeting, adjusts his spectacles. "I dunno, Mick. Tallmadge is the one told me he knew somebody could help with the Vegas business. I couldn't believe my luck when I found out it was you."

My stomach turns to lead. "Goddammit." I kick the canteen, sending it spinning. "Robert's been like kin since we settled in Colorado. He…" Words fail.

Knees wobbling, I crouch, let dry dirt sift through my fingers. "How do you know this?"

Vilde blushes. "You know the Spring Soiree? The telegraph manager was one of the guests. Vicente made me help him home after Mor—" she corrects herself—"after you left. Once he passed out, I peeked at his records. Hoodoo's been wiring Tallmadge for at least six months."

"I'll take care of Tallmadge when I get home." The odds of that seem thinner by the second. I haul myself upright. "Right now, we gotta figure how to reach the cavern before the ritual. Maybe they won't shoot on sight if they still need me for the Equinox?" I squint at the sinking sun. "I could turn myself over. Buy us time."

"That's not an assumption we can make," Leona says, watching the hawk overhead. "We were wrong before."

"We need to focus on what we can control," I say, turning to my gear. "Soon as the shooting starts, we're gonna need every edge." I pull the bandanna-wrapped buckle from my saddlebag. "We need magic to have any chance against Hoodoo."

I grimace, remembering how he turned my own power against me in the plaza. I set the buckle on a flat rock. "Within the town ward, this cursed thing is the only key to my Gleaner. Can't touch my power without it."

Edison crouches beside it, careful not to touch. "But when you jammed those guns in the saloon, you managed a burst before Hoodoo shut you down."

"Barely." The memory of that backlash sends a shiver through me. "Felt like tearing my insides out. Nearly collapsed right there."

"A risky gamble," Leona says, studying the buckle. "You're betting you can strike faster than Hoodoo can drain you."

"Seems a thin reed to hang a plan on," I admit. My hand hovers over the buckle, then pulls back. "One quick hit before he even knows I've drawn. Like a fast gun beating a slower draw."

"Except if you're too slow, he doesn't just outdraw you, he takes everything," Edison warns.

I meet his worried gaze. "Without my Gleaner, we're three people with guns against all of Hoodoo's men, schemes and Múcaro's magic. Against whatever ritual they're cooking up down there." I wrap the buckle back in the bandanna. "Sometimes the only way past a trap is straight through it."

"If you can disrupt Hoodoo or the ritual with one strike..." Leona trails off, doubt creeping into her voice.

"Then maybe we got a chance to end this before he bleeds me dry," I finish. "I'll hold off till we're right on top of 'em. When he thinks he's already won."

The weight of it settles over us—the whole plan hanging on whether I can be quicker on the draw than a man who's had months to prepare.

Leona bends over her dirt map, drawing in new lines. "If we can get into the caverns without magic, we've got a chance. Is there a way to spook them into sending men away from town? Maybe toward Taos?"

Edison drops onto a rock, ragging his pistols. "If you're sure she's reliable"—he gestures at Vilde—"why not send her back to the Imperial to feed Vicente bad information, convince him we're running?"

"That would give us surprise." Vilde rises, tightening her shawl against the cooling air. "They *expect* you to run. Hoodoo doesn't know how bad he banged you up. He thinks grief'll keep you on the back foot till the Bureau can leash you."

I study Vilde's bruised face. My stomach knots. "That puts you in terrible danger."

"Without BMI backup, we're past worrying about safe," Leona says. "A false trail pulls guns off the board. And Vilde's the only one can walk that world without raising suspicions."

I cross to Vilde, rest my hands on her shoulders. "I don't reckon sendin' you back into that viper's nest serves *you* best. We got spare horses. You could ride and not look back."

Her eyes flash, stage-regal. "Oh, Mick darling, for one thing, I can't possibly leave my birds in Vicente's clutches—assuming he hasn't butchered them yet." The lilt falls away. "Vicente and Hoodoo took Ada from us. Three other women have gone missing since I arrived. They've stolen years off every girl's life with those buckles." Her jaw hardens. "I didn't cross an ocean and build a life here just to run when monsters rattle the door."

She looks between us. "You both underestimate a pretty face, as usual." A shadow of mischief glints. "The dove bears sharpest claw when guarding helpless brood."

Leona and I blink at her for a heartbeat, then huff a laugh. She's mocking us and we deserve it.

Her smile fades. She takes each of our hands, squeezes. "Your cause is mine, of course."

"Assuming that works," Leona says, back at her map. "Any idea how many men he's still got in town?"

"I'm not sure," Vilde says, crouching beside her. "At least fifteen between his regular guards, deputies, and distillery men. Maybe I can talk him into sending half on a wild goose chase."

I rub my sternum, feeling Morgan's ring warm against my skin. "So eight men, plus Vicente, Hoodoo, and Múcaro. And there's just the four of us." I look at Edison. "Three if he leaves."

"Wait one goddamn minute!" Edison lurches to his feet, holsters slamming. "I can pull my weight same as any man in this crew!" He jabs his chest. "Don't you sideline me."

"Edison, you *are* the only man in this crew." I catch his arm. He yanks it free, scowling, but I hold his gaze. "I need you to lead some of Vicente's boys off. Make 'em think we're high-tailing east."

"You're just trying to keep me out of the fight," he gripes.

"I'm trying to keep you *alive*," I say. "If this goes tits up—and it likely will—somebody's gotta make it back to Van Lew and tell her what we found. And every gun you drag off that saloon floor helps us."

His jaw works. "You wanna make me bait."

"Exactly," Leona says. "Your role may be the most important of all."

He kicks at the dirt, studying his boots. "I suppose I could lead 'em on a merry chase."

"And you'll take Sampson," I add. He looks up, wide-eyed. "You already promised."

"The ornery cuss is more likely to kill me than the bad men are," he grumbles. "I guess the trail'll look more convincing with two horses."

He sighs, shoulders loosening. "Have Vilde tell Vicente we're riding east to dodge the weather, cut up toward Dodge City, then back around to Colorado."

Leona slaps dust over her map in frustration. "We're still too few. Three of us won't be enough. We need more hands."

She fixes Vilde with a look. "The Imperial's women helped Mick escape. Think they'll do more?"

"The women of the Imperial have as much reason as you to want Hoodoo stopped," Vilde says. "They've watched their friends disappear. They've seen what happened to Ada and Delilah. They risk their lives every day under Vicente."

"It's not just revenge," Leona adds. "As long as Hoodoo and Vicente run Vegas, none of them are safe."

I nod. "We're not draggin' them into our fight. This *is* their fight. We're just giving them a shot at it."

"Marisol's good with fire." Vilde's eyes glint. "And Jorhun—she's a pony shifter. Maybe she could lay another trail toward Taos. She and Edwardo are Ada's siblings." She glances at the lengthening shadows. "I need to hurry before Vicente takes roll call."

The hawk overhead gives a final cry and wheels away.

"Leona, meet me at the mill in an hour with Edwardo and Jorhun," I say. "Vilde, get the women set up for distraction. You and your girls pull their teeth upstairs; me and Leona'll clear the bar and head for the caverns."

I take Mads's buckle from my pocket, feel the corruption hum under my fingers. "Hoodoo expects me to use this." I wrap it back in the bandanna. "So I won't touch it till we're close enough he thinks he's already won."

"With the women of the Imperial to help us..." Vilde begins.

"We've got ourselves a proper army," I finish. "Small, but fierce."

I thumb my revolver free, the weight familiar, if not as sure as Morgan's ever was. "We'll take the fight to 'em with whatever we've got."

"It's not much of a plan," Edison says.

I spin the cylinder, liking the sound of it. "Plans are just pretty lies we tell ourselves before shooting starts." I meet his worried gaze. "Hoodoo already took two of the best men I've ever known." I holster the gun. "He don't get to finish what he started."

The others break to their tasks. I stand a moment longer, watching the sun sag toward the horizon. My hand drifts to my chest, to the ring hanging there.

"I know you're watching, old man," I murmur. "Ain't much to see—just a stubborn woman too mule-headed to lay down." The breeze cools the sweat on my neck. "By sunrise, either I'll be with you, or I'll have sent Hoodoo and his whole goddamn operation straight to hell."

For a heartbeat, I almost hear his dry chuckle on the wind.

Give 'em hell, Mick.

"That's the plan," I whisper.

Chapter Twenty-Eight

THE SETTING SUN BURNS blood-red against the crumbling mill wall at my back. I roll a twig between my fingers until it snaps, craving clean whiskey to steady the tremor in my hands. Morgan would've had a flask ready. Edison checks the saddles for the tenth time, an unusual quiet hanging between us like a noose. Leona paces, her bare feet kicking up dust with each turn.

Sampson's solid warmth draws me from the wall. I rest against his shoulder, breathing in his familiar scent. The old campaigner turns to nose my hip pocket for treats, and I manage a rough laugh.

"Greedy beggar." My throat tightens as I scratch his jaw, feeling the familiar warmth beneath my fingers. "Not this time, old friend."

Fifteen years of blood and fire we've seen together. Never flinched at cannon fire, never failed me in a fight. I press my forehead against his neck for a moment, breathing in the scent of horse and dust and home. Now I'm handing his reins to Edison and praying to whatever god might listen that they both make it out alive.

A soft wicker draws Sampson's attention. A skinny boy with coal-black curls emerges from the brush, a bay filly close behind.

"Our secret agents," Leona says warmly.

"Buenas tardes, Miss Leona." The boy tugs nervously at a frayed sleeve before gesturing at the filly. "She's shy about shifting with an audience."

Can't be more than thirteen, this Edwardo, despite the heavy calluses on his hands. The weight of what we're asking of these children makes me ashamed.

Edison wastes no time on pleasantries. "You sure about this? Ain't some grand adventure we're playing at."

Pride and defiance war across Edwardo's face before his jaw sets. "We know that. Ain't stupid." His voice drops. "Marisol and me lost family to them bastards already." He raises his chin, hand moving to a small knife at his belt. "I aim to carry my own weight 'longside any man here!"

Edison's mouth quirks up. "You and me *are* the only men here." He sheepishly glances my way. "A hawk's eye in the sky and an extra set of hoofprints will make us harder to track."

Pride lights the boy's face. "Yes, sir! I'll scout clean ahead as soon as we make dust."

"Now that's using your noggin." Edison nods. "Ought to reach Dodge City well ahead of trouble." He claps Edwardo's shoulder. "First, though, let's see if Sampson tolerates you."

"Good luck!" Leona settles against the wall, Johrun pressing close. The filly's ears prick forward, watching.

Anxiety tightens the boy's features.

"Don't fret," I say, untying Sampson's lead. "He knows his business."

Edwardo extends his hand slowly, like he's approaching a rattler. Sampson surprises me, dipping his head to bump the boy's palm. The tension drains from Edwardo's shoulders as he scratches Sampson's poll. "Ain't so fearsome after all..."

My chest aches watching them. Fifteen years together and now I'm trusting my ornery partner to a green boy. But better than leading him straight to Hoodoo.

"Time to move." Edison's voice catches as he mounts up, still avoiding my eyes. His knuckles whiten around the reins. This boy who tracked me down so eagerly, now forced to leave me behind.

Edwardo springs onto Sampson's back, light as a sparrow. The old gray doesn't even twitch. Maybe he approves of carrying less weight for once.

I grip Edison's stirrup. "Ride careful as you know how. Your legend's still unwritten." The words scrape my throat raw. "Make it a good one, far from this cursed valley. I'll see you in Trinidad when this is done."

Edison blinks hard, meeting my gaze. "We surely will, ma'am." A flash of the determined young agent breaks through. "I'll be back with reinforcements before you know it."

"No, you won't," I say firmly. "You'll take good care of my horse and get the contract money to Morgan's wife and my family. That's an order, Agent Colt."

I watch until they vanish into the scrub, dust settling in their wake. The weight of what's coming settles over me like a shroud.

Leona clears her throat. "We'll stop Hoodoo's madness tonight." She grips my shotgun across her chest. "Vicente first, then the necromancer."

I turn into the breeze, tasting copper on the wind. If luck holds, Edison will be miles from here soon. Leona and me are playing with fire staying behind. But I can't run, not before I make this right for Morgan.

"Vilde planted the bait about your escape," Leona says low. "Vicente's already sending out men to chase you down." Her mouth thins. "It leaves the girls at the Imperial to face his anger..."

I squeeze her shoulder. "They just need to hold a few more hours."

The sun bleeds its last light across the horizon. Night's coming, and with it, Hoodoo's ritual.

✦⸺▪⸺✦

Stale beer and horse shit fill my nose as I crouch behind empty barrels in the Imperial's back courtyard. Leona's shoulder presses against mine, both of us holding our breaths in the deepening twilight. A horse stomps restlessly in the nearby stable, each thud matching my heartbeat.

"We need to clear the saloon first," I whisper. "Can't risk Vicente or any of his men flanking us when we go after Hoodoo."

Leona nods. "And if we're lucky, we might find Múcaro or Hoodoo himself here. Take out one piece of the puzzle before the main event."

The smell hits before the sound. Burning corn and wood smoke billows through the yard. Right on time, Marisol.

A door slams against the saloon wall. Boot heels strike wooden planks, heading our way. My palm slicks with sweat as I ease the revolver from its holster. Beside me, Leona's muscles coil tight as a spring, shotgun ready.

Three shadows pass within arm's reach, cursing fit to peel paint.

"Goddamn better be a real fire this time…" The voice fades as they round the corner toward the smoking grain shack.

I let out a slow breath. Marisol's plan worked; fire'll keep them busy. With luck, Vicente's crew inside'll be thin.

We ghost across the yard, hugging shadows. Light spills from the back door, my heart hammering against my ribs as we reach it. Seconds stretch like hours before it creaks open. Delilah's face appears, pale between her braids, dark eyes wide.

Relief floods through me. We slip past her into the steamy kitchen. She leans close, breath hot on my ear. "End him." Simple words carrying the wish of every girl Vicente's broken.

I ease the kitchen door open a crack. Vicente sprawls at his precious mahogany bar, wearing some fool waistcoat in crimson brocade. Three hired guns ring him like guard dogs, iron on their hips. Their laughter echoes off the walls.

No sign of Múcaro or Hoodoo. Damn, I half hoped we'd find them all together. But this is better. Vicente is the weak link despite the hired muscle.

My shades press close, whispering poison. Coward. Failure. The Reb's laugh cuts sharper than the rest. I shove them back, focusing. Ending Vicente won't stop the ritual, but he's got answers we need, and I aim to pay him back for Morgan.

Three men here, three at the silo, none wearing buckles. Edison's diversion hopefully drew the rest away.

I meet Leona's eyes, reading the same steel there. Time to move.

My boot hits the door hard. Vicente's head snaps up, words dying as Leona's shotgun finds his men. They freeze, hands hovering over whiskey glasses. My revolver centers on that fancy vest.

"Well, well..." Vicente sets his drink down like he's got all night. "Thought you'd be halfway to Kansas by now." His smile's all teeth, no warmth. "To what do I owe the pleasure?"

I step closer, keeping my voice steady over the of my pulse. "Just tying off loose ends. You're gonna tell me about the ritual in the cavern."

Vicente sips his whiskey, playing at calm. "Come now, sweetheart, you're clearly outnumbered. Why would I tell you anything?"

"Seems to me we've got the advantage." Leona's growl carries the promise of violence as she gestures with the shotgun. "Your boys outside are occupied."

"Kitty cat." Vicente's smile turns ugly. "You don't begin to understand." His glass hits the bar with a sharp click. "We've got special security for vermin like you."

I ignore the bait. "Simple choice, Vicente. Tell me how to stop the ritual, or I put a hole through that fancy vest."

His laugh scrapes like broken glass. "You won't shoot. My men would end you before I hit the floor."

"Where is my friend's body?"

He spreads his hands, rings catching lamplight. "Your friend serves a greater purpose." His shoulders shake with dark mirth. "Sent him off in style! No chance of recovery now, I assure you."

I pull the buckle from inside my shirt with my left hand, letting him see what this is really about. Vicente's laughter dies. His throat bobs as he swallows, eyes fixed on the cursed metal. He looks away, then squares his shoulders to meet my gaze. But the pulse jumping in his neck betrays him. We both know his hired guns don't matter anymore.

"Last chance." My gun hand stays rock steady. "What did you do with Morgan Smith's body?"

Vicente's smile widens. "What do you care for the mongrel's earthly remains? Check the trash heap."

But sweat beads on his upper lip. "You won't use that power of yours, Miss Kelly." His eyes flick to the metal in my hand. "Hoodoo's got his finger on that buckle. He'd feel you open that door, and the backlash would burn through your mind like wildfire."

Red fills my vision. My free hand spasms, imagining the satisfying crunch of cartilage and bone... Behind me, shades crowd thicker, their susurrus murmuring like hungry locusts.

"Then let him feel it," I growl. "You done woke the wrong damned passenger, friend."

My voice rings cold as the trigger slides back. Muzzle flash halos Vicente, bullet striking him squarely between the vest's gilded scrollwork. My Gleaner leaps for him, unfettered.

Wait. The plan. One fast strike when we're right on top of him—

But Vicente's sneer burns through any trace of strategy. Morgan's body, desecrated. And I've got the buckle right here in my hand, power thrumming just beneath my skin, begging to be used.

There's no shame, no restraint slowing the plunge into Vicente's death. His Animus washes through me. Like playing cards spread before me, I discard visions of Vicente as a boy, herding sheep, playing dice. I care nothing for his story. I am the rider. I control the power.

The visions focus showing the cavern swathed in sickly pink light pulsing from the chained casket. Múcaro sways before it like a snake charmer. On a crude table lies... oh God, Morgan's chest ripped wide, cavity empty, heart gone.

I consume the rest of Vicente's fading spirit in a single gulp. Coming back to myself, I blast his deputies into the bar's walls without touching them. Hoodoo must have sensed my release of power. I brace for the retaliation, for Hoodoo's magic to come crashing down on me like a sledgehammer. Seconds tick by.

Nothing happens.

"He didn't feel it," Disbelief wars with relief. My hands tremble slightly as the power settles beneath my skin. "Either he's too deep in the ritual to notice, or...he's letting me use my power, waiting for me to walk into his trap..."

Leona gapes at me, shotgun still trained on the downed henchmen. "What the hell were you thinking? You were supposed to wait—"

"I wasn't thinking." The admission scrapes out of me. "Vicente said trash heap and I just... I broke the damn plan before we even started."

"Don't mistake luck for good sense," Leona says, voice tight with controlled fury. "If he's that focused on the ritual, it may be happening sooner. And if he's playing with you..." She doesn't need to finish.

If Hoodoo wanted me angry, wanted me using the buckle, feeding him information through every burst of power... Like a fish rising to bait, too stupid to see the hook.

Vitae is drifting from the unconscious henchmen. They're nowhere near death, but I could push them. It takes little effort to strangle a human heart. The Gleaner is insatiable, prodding me. I shove it down and release my hold on the buckle, shoving deep in my pocket.

Vicente's shade has already joined my chorus. He cowers amongst the crew. Great, I'll get to spend the next few days with Vicente following me around.

Leona eyes the brutes passed out on the floor, and pragmatically suggests, "You could go whole hog, eat them too? I hate to leave enemies at our back."

Her cold logic warms me. She sees what needs doing, no horror at what I am. "Let Claudette handle them." I sigh. "Got enough juice now for what's coming. No need to be greedy."

I take a shaky breath, the power settling uncomfortably beneath my skin. "We need to move. We were right. The casket in the cavern is somehow the target. Hoodoo's already got Morgan's heart."

"How much time?" Leona reloads her shotgun.

I check my revolver, replacing the spent cartridge. "Looked like the ritual's already started but not finished. Even they can't rush celestial bodies."

We slip out the back door, leaving Vicente's cooling body behind. The night air hits my face, stars wheeling overhead toward their appointed positions. The Equinox is approaching, regardless of what we do on Earth.

The buckle pulses against my skin as we move toward the hidden entrance to the cavern. I'm gonna stop Hoodoo and, destroy the casket, whatever the cost. The Gleaner inside me stirs hungrily, no longer a burden but a weapon I'm happy to wield.

Chapter Twenty-Nine

THE LOADING YARD'S EMPTY when Leona and I slip across it, shouts from the grain fire fading behind us. My pocket watch reads a quarter to ten. Little more than an hour till the Equinox. We're almost out of time. My heart hammers as we reach the small warehouse nestled against the rocky hill. The door opens without resistance. Too easy.

Beyond the threshold, a single lamp feebly illuminates the maze of whiskey barrels. Humid air clings close. Silence descends as the door clicks shut behind us, leaving nothing but the sibilant hiss of the lamp's wick.

We head for the secret entrance Leona found earlier, moving as quiet as we can. Our footsteps seem loud. Before we've gone more than six feet, shuffling footsteps scrape the grimy floor behind me.

I spin, gun up. The thing that stumbles into our light might've been a miner once. Now it's just moldy rags hanging off bones, deep pits where eyes should be. No mind left in the ruined skull, just hunger.

Bile rises in my throat. Dead creatures don't frighten me overmuch, but this is an abomination. Hoodoo's cheap necromancy animated this poor bastard. I reach for its Animus, hoping to shut it down, but there's nothing to grab. No Animus. Whatever's driving it pulses sick purple, nothing my magic can touch.

I back away as it inches closer. My back is soon against the nearest mountain of casks, I'm out of space to retreat. It closes the distance between us. Bracing my left forearm against its gnashing teeth, I fight revulsion at its graveyard stench. I plant the revolver beneath its whiskered chin and squeeze off a single shot, hoping to stop it. The bullet bursts wetly through the back of his brittle skull, but the revenant doesn't seem to notice. In panic, I heave mightily, pushing it away.

Leona's shotgun roars from my right, tearing the zombie's head into grisly ruin, spattering me in gore. It topples sideways to writhe grotesquely against the patched floor. My gut twists in revulsion.

Leona sags back against a stack of casks, one hand pressed over her heaving chest, her breath agonizingly loud in the stillness. Her eyes, rimmed white, remain locked upon the oozing corpse between us. This is the first time I've seen her shaken.

"Sweet heaven, I've never seen the like in person." She drags a hand down her face, casting about as if more monstrosities might lurch from the shadows. "Vampires and were-beasts are rare enough, but this?"

"Hoodoo always did favor parlor tricks." I toe what's left of the prospector. "Though I'll admit, this is new."

"Was that the 'special security' Vicente was so proud of?" Leona manages a shaky laugh. "If this is their best—"

"Don't get cocky." The purple glow from the corpse makes my teeth ache. "I reckon this is just the hello. Like as not the real welcome awaiting below is a damn sight less welcoming."

"Thank heaven you didn't feel the urge to use your special abilities." Leona eyes me, reloading her shotgun.

I wipe goo from my face with a bandanna. "Can't ride what's already dead. And I'd rather not use the buckle to invite Hoodoo's predations. Might be a good idea to conserve power."

"Should've eaten the guards at the bar when you had the chance."

"Maybe so." I tuck the bandanna away. "But you're the one preaching might for right these days."

Leona's head snaps toward the door. "Those shots'll bring company. We need to get to that tunnel."

The ventilation shaft we used before is sealed with a steel plate. They learned from our last visit. Nothing for it but the cellar door Edison found earlier.

We pick our way through the warehouse, past towering whiskey barrels into the cave section. Every shadow looks like movement. My shoulders ache from fighting not to check behind us.

The cellar hatch is waiting, mystical symbols carved deep in the timber. But the lock's busted, wood freshly splintered.

"Reckon that's where our friendly prospector came through," I say. "Nice of him to close the door behind himself."

Leona scowls at me and then bends to inspect the door. While she examines the heavy portal, a prickle of dread tingles my nape. Flights of imagination conjure undead lurking beyond the lamp's glow. If guards were coming, we'd hear boots on stone by now. Wouldn't we?

"Mick." Leona's voice breaks my thoughts. "Help me with this."

She takes position with her shotgun while I grab the hatch's iron ring. The door groans as I heave up, wedging a loose stone underneath. We freeze, listening.

Silence.

Another heave and the hatch swings up and over to lay on the floor, revealing pitch darkness below. I draw my revolver.

We stand clear of the edge, peering down. Both holding our breaths. Still nothing.

Leona's fierce smile flashes. "Cover me."

I wave her ahead, hissing, "Quickly."

Leona ejects the spent shell, then loads fresh. She slips through the gap, quiet as a cat. I pass her the lamp when she reaches for it, then follow her down.

The steep tunnel reeks of wet limestone and something worse. Whiskey smell's gone, replaced by rot and mineral tang that coats my tongue. Our lamp throws strange shadows on the rough-cut walls. The temperature drops with every step, but sweat still trickles down my spine. Everything feels wrong down here.

We push forward, checking each corner. This part of the tunnel's familiar from our last visit, but the emptiness sets my teeth on edge. No guards. No sound except our breathing and boots on stone.

The tunnel opens into a crossroads chamber. Leona stops short. "Does this look right to you?"

Thinking of our dead prospector friend and his purple glow, I reach for the Gleaner sight, trusting Edison's belief that what you are isn't enough to twig Hoodoo. I let my senses spread out slowly, like dipping toes in cold water.

Leona's Animus glows healthy pink beside me, but something else moves in the shadows ahead. Tendrils of sickly purple, like bruises in the dark. The Gleaner shows his necromancy clear as day.

"Ahh shit." I suck a shocked breath and bring my revolver up, then freeze. The figure approaching me could be one of the young women from the Imperial, but as she limps into the light, I see the truth. Her eyes have the flat milky sheen of a corpse. Shit, one of the missing prostitutes. Her clouded gaze fixes on me with neither malice nor recognition. Pitiful broken noises emerge around snapping teeth.

Behind me, Leona chokes out a curse. I tear my gaze from the corpse. More than half a dozen revenants shamble from the tunnels around us, grasping hands outstretched. Leona's shotgun booms twice in quick succession. One creature collapses messily, missing half its head. A second stumbles to its knees, a hole blown through its chest.

"The lady you're chatting with used to be Ada," Leona shouts. "I bet these others are the rest of the missing folk." She breaks open the gun and loads two more cartridges, positioning herself at my back. "Get to shooting, Mick!"

Mastering my horror I fire point blank into Ada-thing's left eye. She staggers but keeps coming until my second shot explodes the back of her skull. She collapses in a heap of dirty lace, bile scorching my throat at the sight. Three shots left. Two to the head to make them dead.

The monster Leona shot through the chest lurches toward me. Two more shots and it drops. Leona's shotgun booms twice nearby as I reach to reload.

Leona's harsh cry spins me around. Two revenants have her pinned, teeth snapping dangerously near her throat as she struggles with the shotgun's stock.

"LEONA!" I lunge forward, putting my last bullet into one attacker's thigh. Out of ammo, I grab the creature's tattered shirt and haul backward with everything I've got.

My effort loosens its grip on Leona, but pain blazes through my leg as another revenant—just a one-armed torso—claws up my body. Grave reek washes over me as we crash to the ground, the thing climbing heedlessly upward despite the damage I inflict with my pistol barrel.

Leona rears up with a bellow, gaining her feet. One assailant's head smashed to porridge beside her. The other clings tenaciously to her back. Her bared teeth glisten an instant before she whacks her passenger against the cavern wall. Its grip on her throat loosens and she bends, flinging it over her head and onto the ground. Specialized BMI training in action. The zombie rolls bonelessly before she rams its head with the shotgun butt.

No time for relief as my own attacker continues its campaign to eat my face. Drool sprays with each smack of my pistol barrel into its shriveled face. I reach for the Mortis Vorator power as a last resort.

Salvation explodes overhead, the blast lifting the zombie halfway off me to crumple, twitching over my legs. I kick free of its limp form, turning wide-eyed to Leona framed against darkness. I manage a jerky nod of thanks through heaving gulps of cleaner air.

The shadows behind Leona disgorge a fresh mob of corpses moving with shocking speed given their desiccation. Two retain a nightmarish semblance of femininity.

For Christ's sake, at this rate, we're never gonna reach Múcaro's cavern in time. Is this why Hoodoo doesn't give a fig about me Gleaning?

I find my feet as Leona charges to meet the new wave. Spinning, I release the revolver's empty cylinder and reload with shaking hands, the shotgun blasting over snarls and meaty impacts.

Cylinder slapped home, I sight down the barrel, legs braced wide. Two shots into the nearest ghoul's head spray blackened tissue. I shift and aim at the next, a strange calm settling over me. Wouldn't Ylva be impressed? I told her I knew how to do this.

Shot after shot, I topple the oncoming ranks, the revolver bucking in my hand. Beside me, Leona fights like a berserker, fists and shotgun smashing anything within reach. My heels crunch wetly over seeping bodies as I swing the hot revolver through the bitter smoke.

No more targets. Have we broken their sally?

I ease my throbbing trigger finger. My wrist and forearm scream from the abuse. Relief washes over me. Leona stands bent, head down, her hands braced on her knees, shoulders shaking. The prospector had just about knocked her off her nut. Did this attack finish the job?

She straightens and I see triumph on her face. "Damn, Mick. If those were a parlor trick..." The rest of her words are lost to guffaws.

Laughter starts bubbling low in my gut. "Well, it's a very good parlor trick..." I choke out. We both chortle, enjoying our victory and the fact of being alive. "You pulled my bacon out of the fire at least twice so far tonight."

"Thrice," she inserted.

"Well, no matter, I'm grateful." I slap her shoulder. "You ready to finish the job?"

"Dear friend." Sliding fresh cartridges into her shotgun, she replies, "Once more into the breach!"

Together, we turn toward the waiting blackness. Focusing my will, I pick up the sickly purple thread leading deep into the tunnels.

Chapter Thirty

WE DESCEND SINGLE FILE, both alert for threats. The tunnels reek of mold and decay, the darkness presses menacingly. By Leona's reckoning, we have less than an hour before the Equinox. It's not like we have a map. My only guide is the sickly violet thread of magic, tendrils of wrongness snaking deeper into subterranean shadow.

The rough-hewn walls glisten with efflorescent salts leached by endless seepage. Timber braces interrupt the carved passage at irregular intervals, some worryingly splintered. I ignore cold sweat trickling from nape to hips, recalling the ghoulish ambush that almost finished us. How many had Hoodoo murdered? Surely there was a limit to the number of bodies he could throw at us.

Rounding a bend, we enter a low arched-roof chamber partially reinforced by massive beams and tunnels snaking in multiple directions. Disconcertingly, the tainted violet thread bursts, bathing the chamber in purple hum. Nothing indicates which path to continue on. I halt, puzzled.

"What now?" Leona's voice is thin and maybe scared in the hush.

Before I answer, boots scrape stone behind us. We spin, weapons up. My heart stops.

"Morgan?!"

He stands there in the flickering light, but wrong. All wrong. His shirt hangs in bloody tatters. Ribs split wide, lungs visible through the gap. Where his heart should be, there's just an angry void glowing purple.

Leona curses, bringing her shotgun up.

Morgan staggers closer, left foot twisted at a nightmarish angle. No pain shows on his gaunt face—no anything shows. Just puppet strings of necromancy pulling dead flesh. Hoodoo's final insult to my friend.

At six paces, he stops, swaying. Those filmed eyes sweep over us, empty as the desert sky. Then his face splits in a grin like torn meat. His exposed lungs expand in a mockery of breath. One hand rises, pointing at my chest.

"Mary warned me." Blood foams from the wound at his throat. "I blame you."

The voice isn't his. Something in my chest cracks.

I step toward him, hand outstretched. Some stupid part of me still needing to help, to ease his suffering.

"Don't, Mick." Leona's calm tone cuts through the fog in my head. "It's a trick."

Wet giggles escape Morgan's lips, blood still bubbling. This thing wearing my friend's skin isn't Morgan. Not anymore.

"Caught in my snare at long last!" Hoodoo's familiar drawl croaks from Morgan's dead throat. "Welcome to your ringside seats for tonight's main event!" He spreads Morgan's arms wide, playing ringmaster at some hellish circus.

My head spins. Hoodoo's riding Morgan's corpse like a stolen horse. This is what he wanted me to find, this is why he let me use the Gleaner, why he gave up Vicente. All for this horror.

"Goddamn you twisted bastard!" Leona's voice could strip paint. "I will personally see you wriggle in a hemp four-in-hand."

The thing wearing Morgan sweeps an exaggerated bow, his ragged shirt trailing through congealed blood. "Thank you, ladies, so obliging of you to assist my plans." Morgan's features twist. That same violet sickness we saw on the zombies wraps around him like a shroud.

Bile floods my mouth. This is worse than the zombies. This is personal, intimate. Hoodoo using my friend's corpse to mock us. My hands ache to tear him apart.

Leona steps closer, knuckles white on her shotgun. Her face is carved from stone. "Step aside, Mick." Her voice is icy. "Let us grant this brave man dignity."

Hoodoo cackles through Morgan's ruined throat. "Such charming gallantry! But why would I leave when we've so many delights planned?" He bows to Leona but keeps those dead eyes fixed on me. "After all, tonight's entertainment is staged specially in darling Mick's honor."

"Yeah, thanks, but I didn't RSVP." Fury burns the softness from my voice. "You clearly went through some trouble on my account, though. Let's get on with it."

The puppet master prances Morgan's body closer. Leona snarls, shotgun steady at her shoulder. Morgan's slack face twists with Hoodoo's glee, turning my friend's features into something that'll haunt my dreams.

"Always impatient, our Mick!" Blood clots slide down Morgan's chest as he offers a courtly hand. "Terribly gauche skipping straight to the final course. What of the appetizer, your failure heaped raw upon the stage?"

"Don't listen to him, Mick!" Leona's warning cuts sharp. "He's trying to slow us down." Her finger tightens on the trigger. "I can silence its poison easily enough..."

His barb finds home anyway. Morgan died because I ignored every warning sign, every bit of good sense. Dragged him halfway across creation when he should've been home safe with Maria. My failure. My fault.

He clasps Morgan's weathered hands together, begging. "Mick, darling! You promised adventure awaited! Never dreamed we would reunite for my wake." He throws Morgan's head back, letting loose peals of wet laughter. "We shall have such capers, instead of doddering around my dull acres bleating at sheep!"

"Let me take him." Emotion roughens Leona's voice, her stance hard as iron. "He's said enough." The offer hangs between us like smoke. Maybe wisdom says end this torment quick.

"No!" The word tears free before I can stop it. Leona's face shows disbelief as I lower my gun and step forward. Beneath

Hoodoo's purple corruption, flickers of warm pink still pulse. Traces of Morgan's true Animus, echoes of his soul trapped in his own flesh. Getting him free is the last honorable thing I can do for my friend.

Ignoring Leona's hissed objections, I cross to within arm's reach of Morgan's corpse. The desecration turns my stomach, but I take one cold hand in mine. Feel for that spark of Morgan buried under the violet haze. I know these hands like my own. Death and Hoodoo's foulness can't break our bond.

There has to be a way to free Morgan's soul.

"Listen to me, Jones..." My voice is raw in the dead air. I grip those lifeless hands tight, fighting the chill creeping up my arms. "Know I would sooner ignite your bloody liquor production and burn this entire town down than watch you abuse this man further." I squeeze harder, feeling old strength even in death. "That is blood oath."

My words echo back from stone walls. Leona's breath hitches behind me, but she keeps quiet. Morgan's face shows nothing, but I hold on like my grip alone could free him.

Truth is, I don't know how to separate Hoodoo's will from Morgan's flesh. But Morgan's Animus needs freeing, and if anyone knows death's currents, it's me. I sink deeply into the Gleaner sight, the world shifting as my vision peels back the veil between worlds.

Morgan's body transforms before my eyes becoming a tapestry of energies. Threads of sickly violet magic wrap around fading wisps Morgan's true Animus, fighting Hoodoo's corruption. The purple strands pulse with malevolent intent, squeezing tighter with each throb.

Gentle as picking spider silk, I tease at the threads of energy. Never worked this delicate before. Like trying to unravel a rope one thread at a time, I start separating the strands holding spirit to flesh. Each violet thread feels oily and wrong against my senses, leaving a bitter taste at the back of my throat.

The moment I touch the first thread, Hoodoo's magic flares violently. Purple lightning shoots up my arms, burning through my veins like liquid fire. I gasp, my grip on Morgan's hands slips. Hoodoo's pushing back, but his power's spread thin.

"What's happening?" Leona's voice sounds distant over the pulse pounding in my ears.

I can't spare breath to answer. Sweat beads my forehead as I push deeper. The magical threads twist and writhe like live snakes, trying to bite. One slips from my grasp, lashing back to wrap tighter around what's left of Morgan's soul.

Something catches my attention, a second cord, thicker than the others, stretching from the buckle in my pocket toward Morgan's corpse. Both connected to Hoodoo like strings from a puppeteer. The cords pulse, feeding power back to their master. Working as quick as I dare, I follow that poisoned thread to its source. There—a knot of corruption where Hoodoo's will meets the buckle's magic, glowing like a pustule ready to burst.

A vise clamps around my skull. Pressure builds behind my eyes like they might pop. Somewhere far away, I hear Leona curse. Warm wetness trickles from my nose, the copper taste of blood on my lips. I ignore it, focusing harder.

My hands shake with the effort of untangling two sets of bonds at once, but I keep going. First Morgan's spirit, then the buckle. Thread by careful thread, I dismantle his foul work piece by piece.

The resistance doubles. My knees buckle as Hoodoo's magic pushes back—same crushing weight I felt in the town square when I faced him. Pain shoots through my temples like hot nails driving inward. Morgan's body convulses, head jerking as Hoodoo fights to maintain control.

Time's trickling away while I struggle. Behind me, Leona shifts restlessly, probably thinking I've lost my mind. Can't blame her—she can't see what I'm doing.

The pain intensifies. My vision clouding red. I can't breathe, can't think, raw determination keeping my grip on the magical threads. Doubt hits hard. What if this is stupid? What if Hoodoo's just letting me waste power we'll need later?

"Ain't this a familiar sight." The Reb materializes beside Morgan, adjusting his tattered kepi. "You standin' at death's door again, wonderin' if you got the grit to kick it down."

My concentration slips. Purple threads writhe from my grasp, reattaching to Morgan's Animus. I'm losing him. My arms go numb, magic burning through every nerve ending.

The Reb circles behind me. "That Yankee necromancer thinks he knows about death?" A cold chuckle brushes my ear. "Show him what a real death-dealer looks like, Kelly. It ain't about what you can take, it's about what you can bear to carry."

The pain blinds me. Blood trickles from both nostrils now, spattering Morgan's hands. I can't do this. Can't fight Hoodoo's power. My fingers loosen.

Morgan's eyelids flutter. Through blood-hazed vision, I catch the faintest glow of pink beneath the corruption, he's fighting alongside me and I ain't gonna fail him this time.

Gritting my teeth against the agony, I follow the power, past the barriers I've never dared breach. Somewhere, Hoodoo screams in rage. I feel it vibrate through the magical tethers. Grabbing every thread with fresh determination, I follow them to that weak spot I glimpsed earlier.

"You blind as a bat, Kelly?" The Reb's voice vibrates in agitation. "That necromancer's got his fingers in a bear trap." He points to the pulsing threads. "He ain't the master here."

I focus harder, watching the connection stretch thin as starlight. With one final surge of will, I tear through the knot binding Hoodoo to Morgan and the buckle.

Finally, something snaps, soundless, but I feel it vibrating right through my bones. Purple light sprays out like blood from a severed vein as Hoodoo's control breaks. Reality shivers, rights itself. The recoil feels like an elephant gun, throwing me backward.

"Mick?" Morgan's real voice. "Mick, you need to get moving!" Strong hands grip my shoulders. I stumble, nearly taking us both down. Morgan steadies me, concern creasing his brow.

"Easy now." That familiar rumbling chuckle steadies my wobbling legs. I stare dumb as a post. He's whole again, wounds gone like they never were. Impossible and wonderful, even if it can't last.

He looks at me, still cold as winter stone beneath my touch. No throb of life pulses. He's across death's threshold, just freed of Hoodoo's strings.

I don't want to move. Don't want this moment to end. My fingers clutch at his shirtsleeves like I could anchor him to this world through sheer stubbornness.

"Apologies for the awful theatrics..." His baritone sounds odd, muffled with my ear pressed so near his heart. The sob that wracks my chest comes unbidden, painful.

"Hush now, enough tears wasted on my sorry account." Morgan hugs me firmly until the storm passes. Smiling, he surveys his restored but lifeless flesh. "I might wish things otherwise, but at least we get a proper farewell."

I press his cold hand fiercely. "Morgan, I am so sorry. I led you into this mess. My bullheadedness got you killed."

He dismisses my guilt with a gruff wave. "I'm a man grown, Mick. Made my own choices." His expression grows serious as he glances down the tunnel. "But you need to make yours now. Their power is growing. I can feel it pulling at what's left of me."

Leona approaches, checking her shotgun. "I hate to cut this short, but we gotta get moving." She extends her hand to Morgan. "Mr. Smith, it's been an honor."

He engulfs her slender fingers without hesitation. "The lovely bartender! Seems Mick found a rattling new partner to finish this business."

Leona tips her head, accepting the praise. "I promise on my honor to ensure a proper burial for your bones."

"Not sure that matters much at this point." He winks at her. "Much as I appreciate the sentiment. But should you find the opportunity, Muneca's somewhere in Hoodoo's string. She's too good to end up ridden to death by those bandits."

She nods. "I'll do my best." She moves away, checking her shotgun, giving us space, but it's plain as day she's tamping down impatience.

Alone beside Morgan, I search for words equal to the loss. Nothing seems fit for our fellowship's span. My feet won't move, though every second matters.

"I guess this is the last time we will see each other." I push out, trying to imagine walking this world without him. The thought leaves my chest hollow.

Wordlessly, Morgan opens his arms once more, enfolding me. I fight tears while he holds fast, anchoring us to this last shred of now.

"I can't say for certain, but I suspect I'll always be with you, Mick." His body wavers slightly, edges blurring. "Time's short. Hoodoo's ritual is drawing power."

We move apart, my hands reluctant to release him. Morgan's form becomes indistinct, haze claiming him. My throat locks as he fades faster now.

"I was wrong to hold you back." His hands engulf mine one last time. "Remember, Mick, sometimes victory lies close as a heartbeat." He taps his chest. He offers that familiar half-smile. "When the moment comes, trust your power."

Blinding aura envelops him completely. I throw an arm across my face, then force my eyes open against the brilliance. It winks out, leaving ordinary darkness. Morgan's mortal remains slump to the ground.

Leona lightly steps beside me, her voice gentle. "Come. Morgan is well and truly gone. We gotta move."

I draw a shuddering breath. "Leona we've got him. We really do."

"What are you saying?"

"When I freed Morgan, it severed Hoodoo's connection to the buckle." I pat my pocket. "He thought showing me Morgan would break me, but his trick backfired."

Leona grabs my arm, eyes wide. A fierce grin spreads across her face. "We might have a chance at stopping this ritual."

For the first time since Morgan died, hope flares behind my eyes. "Since he can't stop my powers, it means Hoodoo gets to see firsthand what a wrathful Gleaner can do."

The ground shudders beneath our boots. A distant BOOM rattles through the tunnel, like God's own fist punching the mountain. Dirt and pebbles rain down, pattering across my shoulders. The timbers groan overhead.

Leona freezes mid-step, shotgun swinging toward the sound. "Is that the ritual workings?"

I cock my head, listening past the settling debris. Nothing follows but distant echoes. "I don't know, and it don't matter. No way to go but forward."

Leona straightens, nostrils flaring like she's scenting our quarry. "Damn right." She chambers a round with a satisfying rack of metal against metal.

Chapter Thirty-One

With Morgan's passing, the trail of malaise reasserted itself. Leona and I continue single file, the darkness and the gloom's weight palpable with imagined monsters. Leona creeps almost silently behind me, back ramrod straight, shotgun clutched tight.

The sickly violet thread snakes deeper into the ridge's belly. I don't recognize this path from our earlier adventure. I swallow hard, hoping mystical sense leads true.

Never before have my talents wrested back a necromancer's grip on his victim. That desperate bid nearly drained my Gleaner reserves, leaving me little more than a pissed off woman with a revolver against a death mage and a necromancer. I don't regret the expenditure and would have laid down my life to free Morgan, but do I have strength remaining to face what awaits? I should have eaten those dudes at the bar.

Like a stream bifurcating, the magic trail splits into multiple tributaries flowing into cracks and tunnels. I choose an opening and squeeze through, chasing the thread. Múcaro's cavern opens around us, ceiling soaring into darkness. Like before, our path deposits us above the floor in one of many crevices scattered around half the perimeter. I spot the tunnel we escaped through on our first adventure in the cavern. It's almost directly across from us at the cavern floor near the brass and steel tower.

The cavern is alive with power. Purple malaise spills through every crack and crevice flowing down the walls, swirling across the floor, flowing into pools glutted with writhing colors, coagulated life force glowing in the hues of fresh bruises.

The malevolent tower thrums, the tubes entwining its surface glow with each beat.

Two figures sway rhythmically before the empty, unchained reliquary next to a wooden slab, just as I saw in Vicente's memory. Ropes of imprisoned Animus climb the slab, fed by the pulsing turret. As before, the nearby table is covered in tools and bottles. The leather-bound manuscript still lies on a lectern near the reliquary. Múcaro's presence throbs against my senses, hungry and fathomless. His hands weave intricate symbols in time with his unrecognizable chanting. Hoodoo's lean form blocks our view of the body on the slab. I know it's not Morgan. Has some other poor slob been condemned to participate? As Múcaro's guttural voice rises in command, the body convulses, sigils blazing across its visible extremities. The tower's sickly light dims.

Leona gestures insistently, face set with determination. I meet her scowl. If we strike quickly while their focus holds tight... I nod sharply. As one, we let bullets and magic fly toward their unguarded backs.

A flash of movement—Múcaro's hand slicing through the air without even turning—and a shimmering dome materializes between us and the ritual. Our bullets and magic strike the barrier with a sound like hail on tin. Sparks erupt inches from my face, hurling me backward. The impact knocks the air from my lungs, stars bursting across my sight. Sound vanishes beneath a high-pitched whine needling my ears.

Dazed, I register Leona likewise sprawled against the rock wall, shotgun smoking uselessly in her hands. The barrier pulses with sickly light, revealing intricate runes etched in the air—Múcaro's handiwork, far more sophisticated than anything I've seen before. The death mage hasn't even broken his chanting rhythm, as if swatting away our attack required no more effort than brushing aside a fly.

I regain my feet, greeted by hated nasal tones burning through the whine. "Well, well, welcome, ladies! It's about time you got here. I was worried you had encountered misadventure..." I clench my jaw and meet his condescending stare through the forcefield's pearlescent magic. His grin widens, drinking my rage and humiliation.

Hoodoo claps, stepping sideways to provide a clear view of the body. "How rude of me not to properly introduce our distinguished guest of honor." His long arm stretches toward the slab, smile belluine. "After all, Mick and he share quite the storied past."

Horror and shock root me in place. The emaciated wreck—more mummified than man—is undeniably recognizable as Lafayette Baker! I reject the proof before my eyes. My mind conjures the memory of me burning his body ten years ago.

"Well, I'll be damned to perdition," the Reb coalesces from nothing, his uniform luminous against the cavern's purple glow. His sardonic smile is replaced with genuine horror. "Thought you crisped that devil to ash in Kansas City."

"I did," I say, though only I can hear him.

"Someone's been keeping mighty strange company," he mutters, nodding toward Múcaro. "That Owl fella's got death magic older than this country. Seen his kind once in Richmond—they don't play by Christian rules."

Leona gasps beside me, understanding creeping across her face.

"Oh yes, Lafayette survives, life everlasting as promised!" Hoodoo mockingly clasps his hands under his chin as if in prayer. His gaze flicks to Múcaro, who is maintaining a steady low stream of chanting. "Our lord merely required...restorative healing."

I can't tear my eyes from Lafayette's cadaverous face. His eyes, freakishly alive, bore into mine, promising retribution. I hold his gaze despite every instinct screaming to run for the tunnel's refuge.

"I collected his poor charred bones from the crash site as a memento. Can you imagine my delight when my good friend here"—gesturing to Múcaro—"told me Lafayette had already laid the groundwork for his resurrection? Together, they had assembled almost everything needed for the Ritual of Revivification, or Wua'l Wutzuachijl as he likes to call it."

Leona gasps. "Impossible. That's from the lost Scherze manuscript."

I nod slightly to encourage her. If Hoodoo's talking, we ain't dying.

"Clever girl," Hoodoo says. "Yes. My partner twisted it to our purposes. All we needed were his assassins and enough Animus to fuel it all." His smile is a death's head rictus. "Clyde Ball practically fell into our laps, just what we needed to restore flesh to Lafayette's bones."

"Then we had to wait, of course, to locate the rest of the assassins. Vicente's business ventures provided a ready supply of shifter blood, and of course the distillery delivered endless Animus to preserve our work." Hoodoo gestures to the tubes running to Lafayette from the tower.

I notice how Múcaro never takes his eyes off the ritual, his focus absolute, while Hoodoo preens and postures. Hoodoo's theatrics seem hollow by comparison.

"But here you are! Witness, Morgan will restore Lafayette to the vampire he was before your ill-conceived murder attempt."

Múcaro pauses his chanting and reaches into a simple wooden box next to the slab. He raises a bloody mass over his head, then lowers it to his mouth and kisses it reverently. It's a human heart, Morgan's heart. The glowing organ starts beating. At first roughly, a parched clicking sound like insect legs over dry bone. With its first pulse, Animus from the pools swirls up and around it, wending through its chambers. Each beat a mimicry of life blood. Its pulsing radiance transfixes me.

Ruby tendrils slither from the heart, reaching into the gaping cavity of Lafayette's chest. Seeking tentacles pierce, burrowing into fossilized tissues. Sibilant chanting spills from the death mage as he releases the organ into Lafayette's chest.

Leona's mindless cry of horror reflects my own frozen wail. Barely shifting her gaze, she seamlessly reloads the shotgun in preparation for whatever comes next.

The revenant twitches and sucks in breath, chest moving. I rack my brain for a plan, an action, something to stop this macabre drama.

Transfixed, we watch Lafayette's face regain its ruddy tones. Lips plump over yellowed teeth, collapsed nostrils expand, fresh gristle plumps beneath skin drawn tight, stretching as muscle extends over bone. The swirling Animus becomes a torrent blurring my view as Lafayette's transformation devours the magical vapor. The tower's pulse quickens to maintain the flow of energy. Within seconds, he is on his feet. Sinewy muscle ripples beneath renewed skin. Lafayette was a large man in life. Resurrected, he's immense. He raises his arms wide as his exultant laughter splits the air. In one greedy inhale, Lafayette sucks the magic out of the air, collapsing the magical field protecting the ritual space, giving us opportunity. My ears pop at the pressure change, and Hoodoo gasps and falls to his knees in reverence.

"Now!" I shout, but Leona is already in motion, raising the shotgun to her shoulder. I gather a blast of energy. The shotgun booms as I fling the power at the tableau below. Hope flickers.

And dies.

The Owl redirects bullets midair into the cavern walls. Stone chips and dust explodes near Leona. She throws one arm up, shielding her face. In the same moment, a second kinetic blast hurls her fully off her feet to crash limply against an outcrop on the far side of the cavern.

"Leona!" I scream, fearing her utterly broken by the impact. Lafayette charges with a burst of speed, swift and deadly. Hoodoo and Múcaro laugh behind him. I scramble for threads of Animus animating him, hoping to repeat the magic I used on Morgan. I can see the web encasing his form, but nothing is frayed. There is nothing I can grasp. Unlike Morgan, nothing ties him to an outside mage. Desperately, I twist the piddly power remaining to try and blast him, but like the Animus from the pools, he absorbs everything I conjure.

He pauses before me. "Mary Catherine." His voice croaks, straining unused vocal cords. "Has the painted cat come to redeem herself for the betrayal?" His skin is stark white, whole except for the open slash in his chest where Morgan's heart glows. The tentacles pulsing beneath alabaster. I would rip it from his chest given the chance.

I step back, hand searching for my pistol. "I require no redemption from you, Baker."

"But there is much I require from you," he rumbles and pounces, raking my coat before an iron-hard fist connects with my jaw in a savage blow. I crumple, stunned. Lafayette is upon me, on his knees, straddling my hips, my wrists anchored in one claw-like hand, immobilizing me completely.

And I can do nothing. The enchantment animating Lafayette steals any power I dredge through the Gleaner.

My face and jaw burn from the punch. Keep your head. Sampson has done worse to me. I can survive this. Wait for the moment. If I can get clear of the radius of his magic, we can still beat them.

I can't stop myself from fighting his restraint. He bends and buries his face in my throat, inhaling deeply. The grave stink of his hair assaults my nose. His beard scrapes my tender skin. He leans back to examine my face. Looking satisfied, he purrs, "Mmmmmm, so much darkness. It's quite delicious. I could devour it in one bite." He snaps his teeth.

Then almost tenderly, toying with my hair, he murmurs sweetly, "Your power will pay for your perfidy." He smiles indulgently.

I redouble my struggles. "The BMI knows about this operation. They will never tolerate another vampire on American soil."

Lafayette grins then. Rising, he hooks one arm under my knees, lifting me effortlessly. Nausea and vertigo war as he carries me like a naughty child. I twist, but his arms are like steel. I claw at his Animus, desperate for a single thread to pull but his power is impenetrable.

My frantic sight locks on Leona's crumpled body, her Animus a faint pink mist. She lives.

Lafayette slams me onto the slab. My head bounces against the stone surface, my teeth snap, piercing my tongue. I taste blood. From either side, Hoodoo and The Owl bind me. First, they bind my hands together, then wrestle my legs spread-eagled to secure them to the iron rings mounted in the stone surface.

"Your hand shall serve most graciously for this penultimate step," Lafayette continues conversationally, moving to stand at the foot of the slab. "Its past deeds balancing the scale of cosmic justice."

The Owl moves out of my view, but I can hear clinking of glass and metal, liquids pouring.

Hoodoo sidles up to my shoulder, brimming with malicious delight. "I suppose the honor of enlightening our guest falls to me while preparations continue, yes?" He glances at Lafayette, who nods once.

With an exaggerated bow in my direction, he gleefully acts the master of ceremonies. Pompous ass. "Allow me to explain precisely what grand destiny awaits the esteemed Warhorse.

"First, we are going to be taking your left hand. Like Clyde's head and Morgan's heart, it will bond to our lord to complete his transformation.

"Thereafter comes the true feast!" Hoodoo strokes his mustache. "At the moment the Equinox occurs in"—he pauses, glancing theatrically upward to judge phantom stars—"eleven minutes, our resplendent captain will ascend to divine status by drinking down that notorious dark magic you harbor."

Lafayette smirks from near my feet. "Just imagine, Mary Catherine, at the exact moment spring begins, your heart will beat its last. And I will be reborn as Gran Sangriento Dorado."

"Bloody Gold?" I snigger. "Not much of a sobriquet."

"No, you backcountry yack," Hoodoo sneers. "The Great Bloody Golden One."

"I will be the greatest vampire king the world has ever known!" Lafayette smashes his fists on the slab and thunders, "Like Alexander. Like Napoleon. Nadir Shah. The World will kneel before me." He hulks over me, creeping closer. "Prophecy is irrefutable. Belle set me on this path the night she turned me immortal. She recognized my destiny.

> *'Bathed in blood and righteous flame, felled by three of daring fame.*
>
> *The Golden One shall rise anew, when stars align, turning dark to light.*
>
> *As new dawn crests the vampire's bier, all creation shall cower in fear.*

Night eternal, for mortal men.'

Then, I had no idea how it would come to pass, but you put it all in motion. You see, don't you?" Bloody spittle gathers at the corners of his lips. "All of this was foretold. When you burned me. YOU, Mary Catherine, set my path to greatness."

"Yes," Hoodoo sketches a mocking bow and steps back. "Your life and power shall pave the very road to destiny. We remain profoundly grateful for your contribution."

"Fuck off." I sputter through bruised lips. "Overblown speechifying don't make you less ridiculous."

Lafayette smirks and grasps the rope binding my hands and traps it against the stone. The Owl joins Lafayette at my shoulder.

He extends a curved ritual knife, its blade catching the sickly purple light. The ancient metal seems to drink in the glow. He brings the tip to my chin, forcing my eyes to meet his dead stare. Nothing human lives in those obsidian depths.

"As the Americans like to say"—Múcaro's voice drops to a reverent whisper—"sacrifice fuels greatness."

My frantic sight locks on movement beyond Lafayette's shoulder. Leona's eyes meet mine for a fraction of a second.

The Owl raises the ritual blade high overhead, its shadow stretching across my face like a promise of oblivion. The chanting reaches a crescendo, the tower's pulse quickening to match. Time slows as the knife begins its downward arc.

The blade plunges toward me—

Chapter Thirty-Two

THE RITUAL BLADE ARCS down in a silver flash. Agony erupts as steel parts muscle and bone. My hot blood sprays the stones beneath. A shriek rips from my throat. Blinding pain devours all thought. Torment engulfs the severed stump, pumping blood onto the worn table. My vision washes a matching red, my blood painting Múcaro's hands crimson. I pull the stump against my chest.

Morgan's words flicker like distant lightning. "...victory close as a heartbeat..." The heart. His heart, now beating in Lafayette's chest. The thought slips away as another wave of pain crashes over me.

"Excellent, most excellent!" Lafayette's delighted purr churns my stomach. I twist wildly, seeking any escape. "Your suffering surpasses my most colorful imaginings, darling..." His fanged grin promises further savageries. I choke curses, spewing crimson flecks with each ragged breath.

Through agony, I realize my right hand is loose. I drag it to my chest as though to protect the stump. My palm slides inside my coat, finding the buckle tucked within. Capturing Leona's eye, my slick fingers grab it's rough edges and I fling her the charm.

"Leona! Get out, run!" My throw propels the buckle in an arc to her grasp. She snatches it from the air. Her head shakes in vehement denial even as the mages turn toward her.

"Go, damn you!" I roar hoarsely. Sorrow fractures my next breath. "Make the bastards pay for this!"

I feel the ward crash down, cutting me off from any future hope of reaching my power once the buckle leaves my hand.

Jaw set, Leona whirls clutching the amulet to her chest. She hurtles into shadows. With a violent oath, Lafayette points a claw after her fleeing form. "Stop her, Jones!"

He races toward the tunnel.

Lafayette rounds on me, patience exhausted. "No matter. The ritual shall proceed." He seizes my bloodied arm, pushing me sideways. I swoon, clamping my jaw against a scream as the stump flares agonizingly.

I lie dazed, distantly aware of the wet scrape of steel over stone. Lafayette extends his own hand upon the stone surface, casual as a gentleman proffering an invitation to dance. Effortlessly, Múcaro flicks the ritual blade, severing Lafayette's left hand. Inky fluid oozes sluggishly but no crimson. Dead flesh.

Lafayette angles his mutilated arm flat on the stone. Ghastly words slither from Múcaro's lips. Gorge rises in my throat as the death mage aligns my small hand to Lafayette's waiting wrist. I gag, stomach heaving. Múcaro's chanting climbs in pitch. Lafayette adds his own thrumming baritone. Their invocation continues to grow in volume. Rune-traced wrist bones meld seamlessly; flesh knits and shifts before my horrified eyes. Bit by bit, my severed hand assumes Lafayette's powerful dimensions, melding to his wrist.

Lafayette's new appendage spasms violently, each finger writhing in a travesty of rebirth. Veins bulge livid upon the mottled flesh seamlessly merging into Lafayette's marble forearm. Within seconds, his usurped hand blanches bloodless to match the hue of his flesh. The chanting ceases.

His new hand flexes smoothly into a fist. Lafayette's cry of exultation fills the stone chamber. "Your power becomes mine, witch! You have lost utterly..." A cold smile twists his face. Revulsion and despair war in my chest.

Múcaro's harsh words split the air. "We must finish to cement the working. The Equinox is nigh." His burning gaze rakes my shattered form. "The timing is exacting."

He places a large hourglass on the slab beside my head. "Her last heartbeat must correspond exactly to the last grain of sand falling." He pauses and observes the clock sitting on the lectern. The moment the clock finishes bonging the eleventh hour, he turns the glass over. "This counts six minutes. Heed its timing—"

Hoodoo bursts into the chamber, sweaty and flustered. "The lioness vanished. The damn tunnels branch like a warren. I've lost her trail completely."

"Incompetent fool," Lafayette hisses, fangs gleaming in the purple light. "One simple task—"

"It matters not," Múcaro interrupts, never pausing in his preparations. "That woman is inconsequential now. Celestial bodies will not pause."

The Reb materializes beside the hourglass, studying the falling sand. "Don't count your chickens just yet," he murmurs. His eyes trail to the rough wall of the caverns beyond the stalactites. "That cat's got more lives than you'd expect."

A shadow shifts. Leona, in lioness form, is creeping from the crevice we first entered above the ritual floor. Her position means the men gathered around the table where I lie all have their backs to her. She's above Múcaro. The death mage's attention is concentrated entirely on the spell, his awareness narrowed to the intricate magical weaving before him.

Múcaro stiffens suddenly, his chanting faltering for just a heartbeat. But it's too late. Leona launches herself, a golden blur of muscle and claw.

Múcaro spins, hands already weaving a defensive pattern, but Leona's weight crashes into him, driving him back from the slab. He rolls away from her, his robes tearing as flesh transmutes to feather and hollow bone as they tumble across the stone floor. Lafayette lunges toward them.

With a snarl, Leona leaps after the great owl that was Múcaro. He's surging upward, one wing trailing from the impact. Robes puddle on the stone as the owl disappears into the shadows of the cavern ceiling. With a frustrated growl, the lioness bounds after him, vanishing into the darkness.

"Ignore them, fool!" Lafayette's whip-crack tone halts Hoodoo's instinctive pursuit. "We don't need him to complete the magics!"

Lafayette turns, focus absolute upon me. "What matters her meddling? Your power already flows within me..."

He stalks to my side. I scream as fangs plunge deep into my throat. Life and magic pour from my veins. Desperate, I grasp for my power, but the ward leaves nothing for me to twist to halt his gorging.

"Yes, drink your fill, sire! I alone made this ascension possible. I kept you alive these long years. Soon you shall grant me the dark gift as reward!" Hoodoo's boot steps scrape closer. "See the witch laid low? My vengeance complete against your betrayer." His braying laughter is distant behind the rushing. "You shall raise me alongside to rule eternal night..."

Even as I spiral toward oblivion, I hate his stupid, flowery speech. Man never could just speak plain.

External awareness surrenders to disjointed images spanning my life. Glimpses of Juliana from our girlhood... Marching through cannon smoke... Caleb's face limned by love... Ylva's dancing eyes... Morgan's deep rumbling laugh... Morgan's heart. Memory flares, then dies, darkness devouring all.

The nebulous visions fade to inky void, carrying warmth and purpose away. No sensation remains of my physical form. All thought and feeling narrow swiftly to a single pinprick point of light barely visible in blackness. Then even that glimmer recedes.

Chapter Thirty-Three

I GASP, FIGHTING MY way to consciousness. Dank cavern and blood tang flood nauseatingly back. Lafayette's weight still pins me while he gorges. I shudder, life and magic hemorrhaging away.

Glancing at the hourglass, minutes remain. I sense the tipping point where cosmic tides turn. Morgan had hinted the ritual's heart might shatter at this crux...

Heart! Even as my strength ebbs, my right hand is pressed to Lafayette's open chest. Heat pulses against my fingertips. Morgan's stolen heart fused monstrously with this resurrected corpse. My friend who had steadied me through a decade of hardship, who never wavered in his loyalty, his heart trapped in this abomination. Right at my fingertips. If I'd had the breath, I would have laughed. How often was one granted the chance to literally rip out an enemy's heart?

I flex fingers, probing the graft binding the heart to this monster. The heart's tentacles have burrowed into Lafayette's flesh like grotesque roots, pulsing with stolen Vitae. I can just sense the web of magic weaving organ and corpse together. Morgan's words whisper through my fading consciousness: *The key lies close as a heartbeat.* This is what he meant.

What binds Life to Death? If I can just find the anchor point, the keystone where Múcaro's ritual magic converges with the stolen Animus and Morgan's heart... My fingers trace the contours, seeking that central thread. I feel it but it would take power. I can't do shit while the ward stands, choking my power like a hand around my throat.

I glance at the hourglass, again. A thimbleful of sand remains. Hoodoo inches closer, watching my face intently, waiting to celebrate the moment I cease. My vision darkens. I pray Leona got free and the BMI will burn this hellhole to the ground. Under the sound of Lafayette's slurping, the sound of hoofbeats reverberates. I'm hallucinating. Must be the memory of days spent on the road... And Edison... Edison will protect my family. The clop of galloping hooves on stone grows louder, my oxygen-deprived brain unable to sort reality from fantasy. Hoodoo's shadow scurries away. At least his face won't be the last thing I see.

My eyelids fall closed. Peace, finally. Even the hoofbeats in my dying brain sound comforting like riding home after a long campaign. Familiar. Safe.

Except they really are getting louder. And now there's vibration through the stone beneath me. My eyes snap open to Sampson bursting through the large tunnel feeding the chamber, Edison clinging to him like a flea, low over his neck, revolver flashing.

I try to shout a warning, but it emerges as a gurgle. Lafayette barely pauses. Leaving Hoodoo to confront the intruders, he sinks his fangs back into my neck racing to end me with the equinox.

Hoodoo raises an arm and screams, "HALT!" Idiot. Sampson gallops over the top of him, straight to the ward tower. Edison fires at the contraption, bullets ricocheting in every direction. Sampson rears and strikes the mechanical monstrosity. It teeters. He wheels and kicks both feet. The clang of iron-shod hoofs meeting steel plate resounds through the chamber. Edison tumbles over Sampson's head. The tower falls, crashing at the foot of the ritual table. Its light continues to pulse. Sampson charges it. Neck snaking like a band stallion, ears pinned back, he rears and stomps the device until it darkens and lies inert.

With the tower destroyed, my Gleaner is free to wash through my being like a sunrise. The world transforms as magical cords erupt in my vision.. Lafayette's chest is no longer flesh but a transparent vessel of swirling energies. The stolen heart blazing pink at its center, surrounded by writhing tendrils of violet corruption. Each magical thread visible, a constellation of stolen lives tethered to this central point.

Feeling the crest of the ritual approach, I fear it's too late. But with the tower's collapse, the Gleaner rises, its power surging through my fingertips buried in Lafayette's chest. The magic burns through my veins like lightning seeking ground. I gasp at the raw sensation of agony and ecstasy combined.

Concentrating, I sense the fetter fixing the heart to Lafayette's body. Not a physical bond but a complex magical knot. I throw myself into the magical currents, letting my awareness follow the tangled threads. A great web expands past the bounds of Lafayette's physical form, past the confines of the cavern. I see it all now. Múcaro's dark workings fed Lafayette with strands reaching across territories, each stolen moment of life flowing back to this monster. Every death, every corrupted buckle, every drop of tainted whiskey converging here, tied with a single anchor, a keystone binding the entire web.

The pain is blinding as I push deeper. This is power beyond any death I've ridden. My body convulses. Blood vessels burst in my eyes, but I can still see the magical architecture around me. I match my breath to my fading pulse, and mentally gather every ounce of strength into my right hand. The heart pulses beneath my fingers, a complex tangle of magic.

Sensing the crescendo in the stars above, I remember Morgan's final words: *Trust your power.* With a silent prayer, I clench my grip around the web of organ and magic and rip the keystone free as the last grain of the hourglass falls.

The magic fights back. Barbed tendrils of violet energy pierce my skin, trying to claim my Vitae in Lafayette's defense. A hideous wet sucking fills the chamber as the grafted organ jerks free, magical tentacles lashing my hand like whips. My palm burns where they strike, but I hold fast, fingers cramping around my prize.

Lafayette rears back, my lifeblood smearing his maw. He freezes above me for a single second, eyes widening in horrified comprehension. His skin, flush with stolen life moments before, begins to shrivel like paper in flame. Cracks spread across his face—hairline fissures that deepen with each heartbeat as the stolen Vitae abandons him. His elegant clothes hang loose on a frame rapidly collapsing in on itself. The vampire's cheeks hollow, eyes sinking into blackening sockets as his death reclaims him. A ghastly rasp escapes his withering throat as his ascendancy reverses, and the glutted power rushes out of his decaying form in a torrent.

Tidal waves of violet Animus cascade through me from him, flooding the cavern with raw power. The energy hits me like a physical blow, lifting me inches off the ritual slab. Violent aftershocks reverberate through my mind as each strand of the magical network snaps. Not only freeing the energy bound to Lafayette's physical being but the power siphoned from the entire region. Every malevolent conduit snaps, every buckle, bottle of whiskey or cursed grain from here to Georgetown breaks releasing stolen power.

Animus pools across the floor in shimmering violet puddles and washes the walls in a hideous glow. Before my eyes, the corrupted energy transmutes to bright pink in its freedom, spinning and dancing through the air before retreating through every crack and crevice like water from a bathtub drain. Without the magic constraining it, the stolen life forces are returning to whence they came.

My breath stops when my own stolen life returns, swamping eyes and ears and nose, sinking into my very pores. The life Lafayette took returns in a torrent, raw and wild. The pain in my left wrist transforms into prickling needles, then warmth, then wholeness as stolen life knits the wound, healing the stump to smooth, pink flesh.

For one blinding moment, I sense every life touched by the magic—prostitutes in Vegas, cattlemen in Trinidad, even Delilah, her shifting ability restored as her stolen Animus returns. Their relief and confusion wash over me before the connection is severed, leaving me gasping on the stone slab, clutching Morgan's freed heart to my chest.

The vampire crashes to the floor. Disoriented, I blink, trying to understand what is happening. Lafayette sprawls, unmoving. Hoodoo lies prone where Sampson trampled him. The Vitae healed my ragged wrist to a clean, painless stump. One hand gone, but I'm still breathing, seems a fair trade.

Edison clambers over the remains of the ward tower and rushes to me, circling wide of the villains' bodies. "Holy smokes, Mick!" His arms wrap around my shoulders. "That was way too close!"

I lean into his embrace before pulling away and ripping into him, "Didn't I tell you to get clear and get my horse clear! What do you mean rushing in here to save the day like that?" My voice breaks on the last words.

It's a strange feeling, scolding someone for saving your life. A minute ago, I was making peace with death, and now here I am clutching my best friend's heart and getting rescued by a green agent and my stubborn horse. The absurdity hits like whiskey on an empty stomach, warm and disorienting. After all the blood and terror, after Morgan's death and everything else we've lost, somehow we've stopped a ritual that would have destroyed half the territory. And I'm alive to see it. The relief is so enormous it feels like hysteria.

Edison pats my shoulder, eyeballing the bloody organ. "It just didn't set right. I told you Pete says, 'A good crew can't leave a job half done.'" He grins at me. "Plus, ole Sampson there kept trying to circle back. It became more than Johrun or I could do to keep him heading north. I figured maybe the horse had sense."

Movement draws our attention. Hoodoo has regained himself and crawls to Lafayette. Turning the body over, its milk-filmed eyes turn my way.

Lafayette croaks, "My power..." Desiccated hands rise, trembling. "Gone?! It cannot..." He reaches for me, despair etching his features. "Return what you have stolen, witch!"

I punish him the best way I know how. I ignore him.

"Damn, is that Baker?" Edison fumbles at his hips for his revolvers that came loose in the fall. They're somewhere amongst the wreckage.

"Never mind the guns." I lay the heart on the slab beside me. "Help me get loose." I start worrying the knots binding my ankles.

"There, there, lord, I will help you." Hoodoo tries to raise Lafayette to his feet. The vampire lunges weakly, fangs bared, attempting to latch onto Hoodoo's neck.

Hoodoo grapples with him making soothing sounds until he loses patience and with a savage oath, drops Lafayette back to the floor. Lafayette tries to bite Hoodoo's legs, desperate for sustenance.

"You dare?" Hoodoo backs away. "After all I have done, all I endured preserving your worthless hide?" His shoulders quake in outrage.

"Hold it right there, Jones," Edison shouts ineffectually.

Hoodoo barely spares him a glance. "Hush, the adults are talking..." He pulls his revolver and waves it dismissively in Edison's direction before turning back to Lafayette. "I kept your festering remains intact all these years, wasted my arts to restore your glory!" His voice climbs hysterically. "I sacrificed everything, damned my very soul and you would feed on ME!"

I struggle with the bindings at my ankles. "Jones, your machinations end here." What kind of knot is this? I pat my pockets for anything sharp. "Edison, do you have a knife?"

Hoodoo levels his gun at us and strides to the lectern to gather Múcaro's book, being careful to keep the wreckage of tower between himself and Sampson. Clutching the volume to his chest, he aims one last disgusted glare in my direction.

I straighten, hoping to slow him with what—moral indignation? I don't feel even a whisper of Gleaner power. Pulling out Lafayette's heart must have drained it to nothing. "Surrender, Jones! You will answer for the lives you destroyed. The BMI are already waiting."

Hoodoo chuckles. "Oh please, darling, we all can see that ploy lacks teeth." His gaze flickers dismissively over Edison and me. "Do give my regards to the old crowd." With that, he spins gracefully and sprints away into the darkness.

"Should we...?" Edison gestures vaguely toward the tunnel Hoodoo exited.

I shake my head. "Just saved the world. One villain at a time, Edison."

Likely that rat will slip whatever new net the BMI casts. But after stopping a vampire resurrection and having my hand lopped off, chasing a necromancer through dark tunnels doesn't seem that important.

First things first. I claw my right foot free. Then turn my attention to my pathetically diminished nemesis. So many destroyed so that Lafayette could spin his grand ambitions. I slide off the table to slump beside Lafayette as his frail weeping fills the chamber. Edison eyes him, no doubt wondering how to arrest the sorry heap. he is huddled on his side, knee's drawn up to his chest. I poke his shoulder, feels like a bag of sticks.

We stopped the ritual, thank Providence. And in doing so, we returned stolen Animus to its owners, though sadly too late for some. Half of New Mexico likely stood spared. But I suppose we have to do something with Lafayette.

Leona bounds into the chamber in her lion form, owl feathers clinging to her whiskers. Sampson snorts. Not even pausing for breath, she transforms into her human shape and surveys the chamber. She appears whole and hearty. Catching my mood she calmly asks, "You stopped the ritual, I see?"

I turn back to poking Lafayette. "Edison rode in at the last minute on Sampson and smashed the ward."

Her eyebrows climb to her hairline. "Damn kid can never follow orders."

He starts to protest, then recognizes the humor twinkling in her eyes.

"I would have liked to have seen that!" She says approaching Sampson. Pausing to scratch his jaw and blow in his nose.

"Mostly it was Sampson." Edison blushes, glancing to his boots.

Leona rifles through one of Sampson's saddle bags, eventually pulling one of Edison's shirts loose, and pulls it on.

"We'll convince him to regale us with details later," I say, standing and brushing my hand off on my pant leg. "I was otherwise occupied having my soul sucked and may have missed the finer points."

Leona climbs over the tower to join us near Lafayette. She stares down at him, lips pursed. "Múcaro is handled. That's some consolation..."

"Good. But Jones slipped the snare. And took the Scherze book with him."

"That's a problem for another day." Her expression darkens, and she tentatively reaches out to touch my shoulder. "I'm sorry I didn't get back sooner. They got your hand, I see?"

I hold up my stump. "At least it's my left hand."

"Is that really Lafayette?" Leona asks, nudging the bony heap beside me with her toe. It's barely recognizable as man shaped. His whimpering has fallen to pathetic mewling. As his body continues to atrophy, he's lost the ability for anything else. Even as we watch, he loses cohesion and collapses into a pile of bones and clothes.

"Yeah, that was Lafayette." I kick the pile, scattering dust and bone fragments across the room.

"Careful there." Leona smiles slyly. "That's evidence."

"Yeah." Edison joins in the ribbing. "We wouldn't want you to get in trouble with the BMI."

I scrub my right hand roughly over my face and take a breath. I feel an answering grin spreading across my face. "Right, with Lafayette gone and Múcaro dispatched, destroying the cursed grain could prevent the evil from spreading farther, I suppose..."

"My thoughts exactly!" Leona cheers. "Let's have a bonfire!"

"Aye. And we best do it swiftly," Edison responds. "No telling when the Bureau will show up."

Leona stares at the wreck of the ward device for a moment. Edison follows her gaze. "Is that our battery, allowing Múcaro's curse to store stolen Vitae, or did it just consume the power to fire the ward?"

"The signature is Múcaro's, without him, we may never know exactly how it worked." Edison runs a hand over the brass housing crumpled at the foot of the ritual table..

She pokes at a broken dial. "I think the question is do we want it out in the world?"

"Agent Freeman, you can't be suggesting we hide evidence from the BMI, can you?" Edison mock scowls at her.

"Yes, Agent Colt, I think I am."

I look back and forth between them. "Taking this permanently out of circulation gets my vote, if it matters. But first we need to secure our perimeter. There could still be bad men above and I need to tend to Sampson. How the hell did you get him here?"

"Remember that exit we found in our first escape from the cavern? It was built for horses. I used the dynamite from Mads's camp to blow the entry open, then just let Sampson run for it."

Leona glances at me, still smiling. "The big boom!"

I nod, grinning. "Guess we heard you coming."

Saying Edison had found a "horse friendly" route through the Imperial's mining tunnels was a major exaggeration. On the way out we had to remove the saddle twice because the ceiling wouldn't clear the saddle horn. I'm amazed Sampson was able to coax Edison through. My brave boys.

Finally breathing clean night air, we make our way back to the distillery.

Chapter Thirty-Four

THE SKY LIGHTENS TO a hazy gray as we trudge up Main Street toward the Imperial. It's hard to fathom that mere hours ago, Leona and I set out on what felt like a suicide mission. Yet here we are, battered and bruised, but breathing. Guess sometimes Providence sees fit to smile on even the most hopeless of causes.

I lead Sampson, his reins a comforting weight in my right hand. My left arm throbs lightly, the stump of my wrist a reminder of the price we paid for this victory. Edison and Leona flank me, shoulders brushing mine as we walk. The street's deserted, shutters drawn tight against the night's horrors. An uneasy silence blankets the town, broken only by the hollow clop of Sampson's hooves on the packed dirt.

As the Imperial comes into view, my chest tightens. The saloon's dark, not a flicker of light in the windows. Beside me, Edison tenses, hand drifting to his holster. "You reckon Hoodoo's holed up in there?"

I shake my head, mouth grim. "Nah. That snake's long gone, mark my words. Slithered off to whatever bolt hole he's got tucked away."

Leona cocks her head, nostrils flaring. "I don't smell blood," she says, voice low. "But something's off. The air tastes...strange."

We round the back of the saloon, approaching the distillery complex. The yard's lit by the first pale fingers of dawn, casting long shadows across the outbuildings. And that's when it hits me, a wall of stench that knocks me back on my heels.

"Sweet Jesus." I gasp, throwing a sleeve up to cover my nose. "What in the hell is that?"

Edison gags, doubling over. "Smells like a drunk pissed himself and died in it."

It's the sharp, eye-watering reek of whiskey, strong enough to make my head swim. I blink, taking in the scene before us. Is that snow? Popped corn, drifts of it piled against the grain sheds and warehouse like snowbanks. A cluster of Imperial residents gathered in the yard, Vilde and Marisol at the center.

And there, standing tall and proud amidst the chaos... Delilah.

My heart nearly stops at the sight of her. She's radiant, practically glowing in the weak light. Her blond hair gleams, and her eyes... Lord, her eyes are bright and clear, no longer haunted by the shadow of what was stolen from her.

"Mick!" She bounds toward me, laughing, arms out-stretched. "You did it, you magnificent bitch! You really did it!"

She catches me up in a fierce hug, and I wince as the jolt sends a bolt of pain up my left arm. Delilah pulls back, brow furrowed. "You're hurt," she says, gaze zeroing in on the stump where my hand used to be.

I grimace, shrugging. "Múcaro got a bit snippy, decided to take a souvenir before Leona ended him."

"I'm so sorry." She seems lost for words. "You saved me, Mick. Saved all of us."

"Was hardly me alone. It was all of us. None of us would have made it out alive without each of us," I rasp, throat tight. "But you...you're all right?"

She's grinning fit to bust. "I'm more than all right. I'm whole again, Mick. Whatever you did in that cave, whatever magic you worked...it gave me back my coyote. Gave us all back what was taken."

Tears prick my eyes, blurring my vision. I glance around the yard, taking in the faces of the Imperial folk. They're worn and haggard, sure, but their eyes...their eyes shine.

Marisol steps forward, sliding her arm around Vilde's waist. "We felt it," she says, voice hushed with wonder. "Felt the curse break, like a dam bursting. The whiskey casks in the warehouse, they just...exploded. Geysers of liquor shooting through the roof."

"And the corn!" Vilde chimes in, giggling. "Lordy, you should've seen it. Like the Fourth of July came early, kernels popping left and right. Sounded like a damn battlefield."

The cursed grain, destroyed by the very magic that made it. There's a twisted sort of poetry in that, a rightness.

"What about Hoodoo?" Vilde asks, sobering. "Did you catch the bastard?"

I trade a glance with Edison and Leona, jaw tight. "Slippery son of a bitch got away," I grit out. "Snatched up his devil book and rabbited while we were dealing with Lafayette."

Marisol spits, fierce as a mama bobcat. "Dammit. I was hoping to see that snake swing."

"You and me both," Leona mutters.

Edison clears his throat, shifting on his feet. "What about the BMI? They show up yet?"

Marisol shakes her head. "Not a peep. Might have been snow on the pass."

Leona snorts. "Twiddling their thumbs, more like..."

That earns a round of chuckles, strained but genuine. Gallows humor, the balm of the weary and bloodied. But we're alive. Against all odds and reason, we're alive. And that's a victory I aim to savor, BMI be damned.

I turn to Delilah, eyeing her speculatively. "So. You got your coyote back. That mean what I think it means?"

Her grin turns sly, mischief sparking in her dark eyes. "Why don't you see for yourself?"

And with that, she strips out of her dress, heedless of the whoops and catcalls from the gathered crowd. I barely have time to register the sleek length of her before she's shifting, blurring, body flowing like molten copper. In the space of a heartbeat, a coyote stands in her place, fur bristling and teeth bared in a wild, joyous grin.

The coyote that is Delilah throws back her head and howls, the sound ringing through the early morning stillness like a clarion bell. It's a cry of triumph, of defiance, of sheer, unmitigated relief.

The others take up the call, human voices joining the chorus until the very mountains shake with it. I add my own voice to the din, tears streaming down my cheeks. Beside me, Edison and Leona whoop and holler, caught up in the jubilant release.

And Sampson, bless his contrary hide, snorts and stomps and tosses his head, demanding attention. I loop an arm around his neck, burying my face in his mane. "We did it," I whisper, fierce and fervent. "We really did it."

He lips at my pocket, as if to say, "Of course we did. Now where are the carrots?"

I laugh, watery and weak, clinging to him like a lifeline. My friend, in a mad world, his solid warmth is an anchor, a reminder of who I am beneath the blood and bluster.

The celebration swirls on around us, laughter and tears mingling freely. There will be time enough for explanations, for planning our next move. Time enough to lick our wounds and gird our loins for the battles to come.

I meet Edison's eyes over Sampson's back, his face split in a grin bright as the rising sun. Leona presses close on my other side, Delilah winding sinuously between her legs. My lips curve, heart swelling till I fear it might burst.

We're gonna be just fine.

The BMI team arrives later that morning on an unscheduled train. Van Lew believed Ximena's pleas even if they are late to the party. She conscripted the entire train for official business, shutting down this leg of the Atchison Topeka Railway. I suspect Senator Thatcher had a hand in the scope of the response. As formidable as Commander Van Lew is, I doubt the wheels of commerce would grind to a halt on her authority alone. Leona and Edison met them at the station, then Leona escorted them through the distillery operation and caverns, clearly in her element, leading a team as the hero of the day. Edison slunk off, finding he didn't care for the spotlight as much as he expected.

The Bureau was extremely interested in studying the ward, no doubt greedy to get their hands on a magic suppression method on such an immense scale. But with the near-infinite stolen Animus powering the ward released, and the device stripped of its runes—Edison discovered them inside the panels when he went back and removed them with an abundance of caution—I doubt the Bureau's mages would ever make it function again. Small favor—some secrets are safer left buried.

Senator Richard Thatcher rolled in the second day to "thank the brave men and women who foiled the men responsible for his son's death." His words, not mine. Thatcher turned out to be an okay bloke for a politician. Sam Meechum, Leona's commander from Santa Fe, finagled a seat next to Thatcher at a dinner the ladies of the Imperial hosted at the senator's request. Meechum kept puffing himself up, trying to take credit for the Vegas operation, despite the fact he was the one who ignored Leona's intelligence for over a year. Thatcher got wise to Meechum's incompetence by the third time Meechum had to look at Leona to answer one of Thatcher's probing questions. At that point, the senator politely told Meechum to get lost and spent the rest of the evening listening to Leona's account of the entire adventure.

Later, Thatcher pulled some strings to help Delilah and Marisol assume ownership of the Imperial's saloon and hotel. The two women were eager to meet the future on their own terms after years of enduring Vicente's and Hoodoo's cruelty. I'm convinced they will prove far more gracious hosts.

By Sunday, neither Vilde's pigeons nor evidence of their demise had turned up and she was frantic. With Delilah's help, we tracked the little flock to one of Hoodoo's hidey-holes up near the Hot Springs Hotel. That rat Vicente had squirreled them away. I never saw a woman cry such ecstatic tears as Vilde, waltzing with her cooing beauties gathered close.

When talk turned to my own travel plans, I extended an impulsive invitation for Vilde to visit the homestead. After a lengthy obligation entangling her with the local BMI, Vilde was itching to disentangle herself from Vegas's excitement for a while. To my pleasure, she accepted eagerly, arranging to visit for two weeks in May. I couldn't wait to share that news with Gudrun and Ylva.

I'll admit to sneaking from Vegas as quick as manners allowed once the Bureau teams poured in those first days. Leona received well-deserved accolades for her perseverance exposing the insidious plot. Ever the good lieutenant, she hadn't balked when I refused a role liaising the mop-up effort with visiting brass. Edison endured plenty of his own gladhanding but eagerly shared the news with me when he received a summons from Trinidad demanding our return.

Edison and I bid our farewells to Leona, Delilah, Marisol, Ximena, and those allies, leaving Leona the stage to shape events to her best advantage. Leona helped us recover Muneca and Edison would ride her to Trinidad. I was eager to get away from all the official goings-on, and despite my hero status, cringed whenever a uniformed agent spoke directly to me. Besides, the sooner I traveled on, the quicker this shadowy chapter could close behind me.

Chapter Thirty-Five

THE ONCE-BUSTLING HALLS OF Holiday House stand near empty as Edison and I stride through. Seems the BMI's poured damn near every able body into the Vegas cleanup. Our boot heels echo loudly on the polished floorboards.

The cadet manning the front desk flashes us a grin as we pass. "Nice work out there," he stage-whispers with a wink. "Heard y'all kicked some serious Hoodoo ass."

I tip my hat, but my smile feels brittle. The prospect of facing Van Lew's got me twisted up. Ain't no telling which way her judgment's gonna fall, and I ain't exactly eager to find out.

Edison, bless his heart, radiates enough nervous energy to power a small city. Boy's practically vibrating out of his skin, stealing glances at me like he expects me to bolt any second. Can't say I blame him. I joked one too many times about following Hoodoo to Mexico.

But I'm here, standing tall as the floorboards creak under my boots. Ready to face the music.

Van Lew's door yawns open, and there she sits, prim as a preacher's wife in her starched collar and schoolmarm bun. But her eyes, sweet Jesus. Her eyes are sharp as a knife and dice me for stew meat. The room remains unchanged, still adorned with the same lace and pink velvet from our first meeting a lifetime ago.

Edison, standing a bit taller than when they last met, nods a greeting. "Reporting as requested, Commander."

"Agent Colt, Mrs. McClellan," Van Lew greets us, her voice surprisingly warm. "It's a relief to see you both alive and well."

"Wasn't our aim to worry you none, Commander," I say, easing into the velvet settee across from her. Edison perches beside me, spine ramrod straight.

Van Lew's gaze flicks to him, assessing. Dismissing.

"First, allow me to extend my deepest condolences for the loss of Mr. Jackson. He was a brave man and a true asset to your mission."

I swallow the lump in my throat, images of Morgan's final moments flashing through my mind. "Thank you, ma'am. He died a hero."

"Indeed, he did. Rest assured, the BMI will provide the promised compensation to his widow, as agreed upon. And I suppose congratulations are in order for your success in Vegas." Her eyes cut to me. "Uncovering that cabal in the distillery, avenging young Thatcher...quite the feather in the BMI's cap. We've been needing a win in the eyes of Washington."

Pride flares in my breast, bright and fleeting. We did good, Morgan, me, Edison, and Leona. Damn good. But I ain't foolish enough to crow, not with Van Lew's stare boring into my skull.

"Just doing our job, Commander," Edison pipes up. "Couldn't have done it without Mick's particular expertise, of course."

"Ah, yes. Mrs. McClellan's 'expertise.'" Van Lew's voice drips with something bitter. "Funny, I distinctly recall advising circumspection at the start of this operation. Warning that a repeat of the Kansas City debacle would not be tolerated."

My hackles rise, but I tamp it down, bite my tongue. "All due respect, ma'am, but I was downright surgical in Vegas. No innocents caught in the crossfire, not a one—"

"She's right, Commander," Edison butts in. "Lafayette Baker was too powerful, too far gone. We couldn't have stopped him without Mick's special abilities."

A muscle ticks in Van Lew's jaw. She sits back, drumming her fingers on the velvet arm of the settee. "And yet, Hoodoo Jones slipped through your fingers with the Scherze manuscript. Curious, that."

I fight the urge to squirm. Hoodoo Jones is a sore point I ain't proud of. "Bastard's slicker than a greased pig, Commander. He'll turn up—"

Van Lew's hand slices the air. "Oh, I've no doubt. But in the meantime, do you have any notion of the damage control it's taking to clean up your mess?"

Dread uncurls in my belly. "My mess?"

"Your destruction of Baker had far-reaching consequences, Mrs. McClellan. Exploding whiskey bottles clear to Cheyenne, reports flooding in from every jerkwater town in the territory. It's taken significant manpower to contain, to say nothing of the cost—"

"Hold up," I say, playing dumb. "Exploding bottles? I ain't never heard of such a thing." Damn it. I knew the backlash from the distillery was significant, but in my wildest dreams didn't imagine it would affect ALL of the Imperial whiskey in existence.

Van Lew fixes me with a glare that could wither the balls off a brass monkey. "Yes, well. Through the curse, Baker was connected to every drop of liquor from that distillery. When you destroyed him, it destabilized the curse. The trapped Vitae had to escape." She shakes her head, lips pursed. "The silver lining is that we've managed to put it about that there was an error in the bottling process. But covering up a magical disturbance of this magnitude? Let's just say it's proving quite inconvenient."

Fear churns. "Commander, I—"

"Oh, I'm aware it wasn't your intent to expose magic to the masses, Mrs. McClellan. But intent and outcome are two very different beasts." She steeples her fingers, gaze boring into me. "I trust you're aware of the penalties for such a breach?"

My blood runs cold as January rain. "Conscription," I rasp, mouth dry.

"Just so," Van Lew says, each word precise. "Whatever arrangement Alan Pinkerton saw fit to extend to you in the past, I think it's more than apparent that leniency was ill-advised."

Panic claws up my throat. Ain't no way in hell I'm letting the BMI leash me, put me on a choke chain and parade me around. I'll put a bullet in my own brain first, swear to God—

"However." Van Lew's voice cuts through the rising terror. "In light of your unique...capabilities, the BMI is prepared to offer an alternative."

My heart stutters behind my ribs. "What kind of alternative?"

She sits forward, gaze intent. "We'll use you on an 'as needed' basis, meaning when not on assignment, you can go about your life as a private citizen. You'll report to the San Francisco office in September to collaborate with the newly formed Anti-Death Magic Division."

It's more mercy than I dared hope for, but the bitter slick of it coats my tongue. "The ADMD? You want me working magic for the BMI?"

Van Lew's smile is thin. "Your skills saved the day in Vegas, Mrs. McClellan. Loath as I am to admit it, there may be some merit in...utilizing your particular talents in our ongoing efforts against unsanctioned death magic." Her gaze flicks over me. "You can thank Senator Thatcher for this beneficence. The man has a rather generous view of your potential."

I swallow bile, my chest tight. The notion of being in Thatcher's debt, of him pulling strings and greasing wheels on my behalf, makes me want to claw off my own skin. But what choice do I have? It's this or conscription, and I'll be damned if I let the BMI shackle me outright.

"September," I say, the words strange on my tongue. "I'll report to San Francisco in September."

"Excellent," Van Lew says briskly. "The BMI will assist in liquidating your assets and securing quarters in the city. I trust that will be all, Mrs. McClellan?"

It's a dismissal, clear as cut glass. I stand, legs nearly jelly, and manage a jerky nod. "Much obliged, Commander. Truly."

Her smile is reptilian. "Oh, the pleasure is all mine, I assure you. You may retrieve your pay and Mr. Smith's pay from the bursar's office. It's located in the dining room." Her gaze shifts, pinning Edison. "Agent Colt, a word in private, if you please."

He blinks, all wide-eyed confusion, but stands at attention. "Of course, Commander. Mick, I'll catch up."

I spare him a tight smile, not trusting my voice. Then I'm out the door, out of the house, gulping air. The sun's too bright after the dimness within, the clatter of Trinidad's busy streets jarring after the oppressive hush of Van Lew's office. I stagger a few steps, fetching up hard against the porch rail.

Sweet Jesus wept.

The BMI. The goddamn BMI, sinking their hooks into me after all these years. And me, like a dimwit calf, walking up the slaughter block. Some legendary outlaw I've turned out to be.

On the other hand, no more pigs. I am free of the homestead. San Francisco, here I come.

The screen door creaks, Edison stepping out onto the weathered boards. His face is drawn, brows pinched in consternation. I feel a pang. Boy didn't ask for any of this, for the unholy mess that comes part and parcel with Mick Kelly.

"Hey," I say, the word more exhale than sound. "She ream you out but good?"

His eyes are haunted. Lost. "Mick, I'm so sorry. I never meant for any of this to happen. I swear I didn't know—"

I wave him off. "'Course you didn't. Ain't your fault, Edison. I'm the one who brought this down on our heads, not you."

He presses his eyes with the heels of his hands, shoulders slumped in defeat. "Still. I should've done more, should've stood up to her—"

"And got yourself busted down to bootblack for your trouble?" I snort. "Nah. You did right keeping your trap shut. Ain't no sense in both of us being in the shithouse."

A clatter of hooves and the jingle of a harness draws my gaze. A sleek, black phaeton carriage comes barreling down the street, gleaming in the midday light. The matched pair of Morgans pulling it prance and snort, tossing their heads as if they know they're the prettiest things on four legs.

And holding the reins, looking for all the world like she's out for a Sunday drive...

"Louise Demarara," I mutter, disbelieving. "What in the hell...?"

Edison squints, shading his eyes. "Ain't that Robert's missus? The one with the brothel?"

I snort. "She ain't his missus, but yeah. That's her."

The carriage pulls up sharp, and Louise hops down, skirts swishing. She's a vision, all chestnut curls and creamy lace, a confection of silk and swagger. But it's her eyes that grab me, keen and glittering in her heart-shaped face.

"Mick Kelly," she calls, sauntering over. "Just the woman I was hoping to see."

I tense, wariness prickling up my spine. Last I heard, Louise was thick as thieves with Robert, and after the stunt he pulled with Hoodoo's grain...

"Louise," I say, cautious. "To what do I owe the pleasure?"

She smiles, red lips curving like a cat with cream. "I was hoping you might join me for a quick ride. I've got a new phaeton from Quilitch Carriage I've been dying to show off." Her gaze flicks to Edison, assessing. "Your partner's welcome to come along, of course."

I hesitate, torn. Part of me wants to tell her to go pound sand, that I want nothing to do with her or Robert or any of their ilk. But there's something in her face, a flicker of vulnerability beneath the brassy confidence...

"All right," I say before I can think better of it. "Lead the way."

Her grin widens, triumphant. She gestures to the carriage with a flourish. "Your chariot awaits."

Edison and I exchange a glance but clamber aboard. Before I'm settled on the plush velvet seat, Louise hops up, gathers the reins, and gives a sharp whistle. The horses leap forward, surging into a gallop.

"Hang on, my darlings!" she crows, laughter sparkling in her voice. "Let's see what these beauties can do!"

And we're off, careening down the street like bats out of hell. Pedestrians scatter, shouting curses that Louise blithely ignores. She handles the reins expertly, guiding the horses around corners and obstacles with a twitch of her wrists. Woman's gonna be ticketed for reckless driving.

It's exhilarating and terrifying in equal measure, the wind whipping tears from my eyes. Beside me, Edison whoops, face split in a manic grin. For a moment, I forget everything—the BMI, Hoodoo, the uncertain path stretching before me. There's only the rush of speed, the thunder of hoofbeats, the wild, unfettered joy of Louise's laughter.

As abruptly as it began, the ride is over. Louise pulls up on a rise overlooking the town, the horses shuffling and blowing. She sets the brake and turns to face us, expression somber.

"Mick," she says, quiet but sure. "I wanted to talk to you about Robert."

I stiffen, good humor evaporating. "What about him?"

She sighs, fiddling with the lace at her cuff. "I ended things with him. After what he did, getting involved with that Hoodoo character, putting your family at risk..." She shakes her head, mouth tight. "I couldn't abide it. And the fact that his foolishness impacted my business, my girls...well. Let's just say Robert and I are through."

I stare at her, nonplussed. "I... I'm sorry, Louise. I know you cared for him."

She waves a hand, dismissive. "Oh, don't be. Robert's a good man, but he's always been a bit too fond of his own cleverness. Gets him into trouble more often than not."

I snort. "You're telling me."

Her lips quirk, acknowledging the hit. "Anyway, I wanted you to know that I was not in on his little scheme. And that I don't hold you responsible for him having to pay the piper."

Something around my heart eases, a knot I didn't even know was there. "I appreciate that, Louise."

She nods, crisp. "Good. Because I've always admired you, Mick. Your grit. The way you never let anything keep you down for long. And I'd hate for a man to come between us, even a man as charming as Robert Tallmadge."

I laugh, surprised and a little flattered. "Well, when you put it like that..."

She grins, wicked. "I mean it, though. If you ever need anything, anything at all...you come to me. I've got resources aplenty, and I'm not afraid to use 'em."

I nod, throat thick. "Thank you, Louise. That means...well. More than I can say."

Her smile softens, understanding. Then she straightens, claps her hands. "Right then! We best get you two back to Holiday House. I'm sure you've got places to be, people to see."

As she gathers the reins, I catch Edison's eye. He cocks a brow, questioning. I shrug, a rueful twist to my lips. "Reckon we ought to head out to Morgan's place. Break the news to Maria, give her his share."

He nods, sober. "And his gun. And Muneca. Don't forget her."

"As if I could," I mutter. Muneca was as dear to him as his wife. It's only fitting to go home to her, now that he's...gone.

The thought aches like a rotten tooth, but I push it aside. Plenty of time for grieving later. For now, I've got a job to do.

The ride back to Holiday House passes in a blur, Louise keeping up a stream of innocuous chatter. As we pull up to the hitching post, she hops down, offers me a hand.

I take it, marveling at the daintiness of her fingers against my calloused palm. "Louise... I don't know what to say."

She squeezes my hand, quick and firm. "You don't need to say anything, honey. Just remember what I told you. My door's always open, come what may."

Then she's gone, a whirl of silk and sandalwood, leaving me blinking in her wake.

Edison sidles up beside me and bumps my shoulder companionably. "Hell of a woman," he remarks, admiring.

"That she is," I agree. I take a breath, squaring my shoulders. "All right then. Let's go give Maria the news."

He nods, falling into step beside me as we head for the livery. It's a small thing, having him at my back. But it steadies me just the same, a reminder that I ain't as alone as I sometimes feel.

We've got a long ride ahead of us before I can finally go home.

Chapter Thirty-Six

I LEFT EDISON IN town after we delivered the news of Morgan's death and his belongings to Maria. It went about as well as could be expected. She met us at the front door with a shotgun. She looked pointedly at my stump and then muttered something about it being no where near what I deserved. I left Edison to deliver the news and speak to her of Morgan's last days while I brushed down Muneca. True to her promise, I was not invited across the threshold.

Tomorrow Edison is going to catch the train to Dodge City to retrieve Johrun and Edwardo. We received word that they arrived in town with Abigail no worse for wear but with thrilling tales of their adventures. They are staying with Uncle Pete until Edison fetches them and escorts them home to Vegas via the railway. Modern travel is a miracle I am learning to appreciate.

The sun's low in the sky as I ride up to the homestead, Sampson's hooves kicking up dust on the well-worn trail. My heart's lighter than it's been in ages, a grin stretching my face till my cheeks ache. I'm coming home, and I'm bringing the best damn news my family's heard in years.

Sampson perks up as we approach, his ears pricking forward. The mules come trotting to the corral fence, whickering a greeting. Seems they're as happy to see us as I am to be back.

"Auntie!" Ylva's voice rings out, high and bright as a meadowlark. She comes pelting across the yard, feed bucket forgotten, blonde braids flying. "You're home!"

I swing down from the saddle, catching her up in a fierce, one-armed hug. The absence of my left hand throbs, a phantom pain. But I ignore it, focusing on the warm, wriggling weight of my niece in my embrace.

She pulls back, blue eyes wide and searching. "Did you have to do any shootin'? You ain't very good at shootin'."

I chuck her chin, mock scowling. "I'll have you know there was a bit of shootin', Miss Smarty-pants. And I hit what I was aimin' at, too."

"Well, I'll be damned." Gudrun's voice, warm and teasing, draws my gaze. She's striding across the field, red hair blazing in the dying light. But her steps falter as she takes in my bandaged stump, eyes widening in shock.

"Mick, your hand..."

I grimace, holding up my truncated arm. "Ran into a bit of trouble down south. But I'm all right."

Something in my throat catches at the open affection on her face. Ain't often Gudrun lets her soft side show. I meet her halfway, pulling her into a back-thumping embrace. "Takes more'n this to knock me down," I say, gruff to cover the sudden prickle in my eyes.

She holds me at arm's length, gaze raking over me like she's checking for more damage. "And Vilde? She's all right?"

"Right as rain," I assure her. "I'll tell y'all about it once I get this boy settled." I jerk my head at Sampson, who's eyeing the mules like he's fixing to go courting.

We make short work of untacking and brushing him down. Ylva fetches clean water while Gudrun and I heave hay into the corral. It's a relief to fall into the old rhythm, the simple satisfaction of caring for another creature. Grounds me in a way nothing else does.

Julianna's cry shatters the moment. "Mary Catherine Mc-Clellan, what in God's name happened to you?"

She's running full-tilt across the yard, skirts hiked up, face bleached. I catch her as she barrels into me, staggering under the impact.

"Jules, easy." I soothe, rubbing her back as she clings to me. "I'm all right, I promise. Just a little worse for wear, is all."

She jerks back, tear-streaked and furious. "A little worse for wear? Mary Catherine, your hand is gone!"

I wince, glancing down at the bandaged stump. It's a reminder of how close I came to losing everything, of the price I paid for my sins. But I can't let myself dwell on that, not now. Not when I have so much to be grateful for.

"It's a small price to pay," I say quietly, meeting her gaze. "For what we accomplished, for the lives we saved... I'd give my other hand gladly."

Julianna shakes her head, disbelieving. "How can you say that? How can you be so cavalier about losing a part of yourself?"

Ylva pipes up, voice small and scared. "Is it gonna grow back, Auntie? Like a lizard's tail?"

I laugh, startled and charmed in equal measure. "No, sweetling, I'm afraid not. But don't you worry none. I've got a few tricks up my sleeve yet."

Julianna sighs, scrubbing a hand over her face. "Lord knows that's true enough." She looks at me, eyes red-rimmed but clear. "All right then. Let's get you inside. And then you're going to tell us everything, you hear? No more secrets, Mary Catherine."

Cold dread trickles down my spine. I glance at Gudrun and Ylva, the words sticking in my throat.

Gudrun picks up on it first, placing a gentle hand on Ylva's shoulder. Julianna's face goes still and watchful.

"What happened?" she asks.

Instantly tears prick my eyes, I scrub them. "Morgan... Morgan didn't make it."

Gudrun's breath catches. Julianna pales, tears springing into her eyes. I pull them into a crushing hug, throat too tight for words. Morgan was family, blood or no. Losing him carves a hole in all of us.

Julianna is the first to pull away, swiping at her cheeks. "Are you square with the BMI?"

I blow out a breath. "About that. Seems I made a bit of a mess in Vegas, magically speaking. Van Lew was none too pleased."

Julianna stiffens, eyes going flinty. "They can't conscript you. They can't. Not after everything—"

"They ain't," I cut in. "Well, not exactly." I can't help the grin that spreads over my face. It's too big, too bright for the sorrowful moment, but I can't rein it in. "Jules, we're moving to San Francisco."

There's a beat of ringing silence. Then Gudrun whoops, scooping Ylva into a giddy twirl. "You hear that, baby girl? We're going to the city!"

Julianna gapes at me, face slack with shock. "What? How?"

I grab her hand, my own laughter bubbling up. "The BMI's gonna help us sell the homestead, get us set up in a place in the city. They need me to work with their Anti-Death Magic Division a few times a year, but other than that? We're free and clear."

"Free," Julianna breathes, a slow, incredulous smile breaking across her face. "Mary Catherine, do you know what this means?"

I squeeze her hands, giddy with it. "It means no more pig shit, for one."

She swats at me, giggling like a girl. "Language! But yes, that. And...and millinery shops, and streetcars, and gas lamps, and...and indoor plumbing!"

"And a proper schoolhouse," Gudrun chimes in, cuddling a beaming Ylva close. "Museums and a real library."

We grin at each other, giddy as kids at Christmas. It's everything we've dreamed of, everything we never thought we could have. A new life, a fresh start, far away from the hardscrabble grind of the homestead.

But even as joy fizzes through my veins, a cold thread of worry worms its way in. Because there's a detail I haven't shared, a loose end that could unravel everything.

Hoodoo Jones is still out there. And if I know that slippery bastard, he ain't done with me yet.

I shove the thought away, pasting on a bright smile. There'll be time enough to worry on that later. For now, I'm going to revel in my family's happiness, in the promise of a brighter tomorrow.

"C'mon," I say, tugging Julianna toward the door. "Let's go inside, get some supper going. Been too long since I had a proper home-cooked meal."

We troop into the cabin, Gudrun and Ylva chattering about all the city wonders they're going to see, the adventures they'll have. My heart swells at the lightness in their voices, the unbridled excitement on their faces.

This is what I'm fighting for. This is what makes it all worthwhile. My family, safe and happy and whole.

As I help Julianna with the supper fixings, I let myself imagine it. A snug little house in the city, with gas lamps and indoor plumbing and a proper range. Ylva in a smart school uniform, trotting off to lessons with her books under her arm. Julianna and Gudrun with their millinery shop, creating confections of lace and ribbon for the city ladies.

And me? I'll figure out a way to make it work with the BMI. A few jobs a year, putting my particular skills to use for the greater good. It won't be easy, juggling my obligations with my family and my past. But for them? I'd walk through hellfire. I'd face down a hundred Hoodoo Joneses. I'd do whatever it takes to keep them safe.

I catch Julianna's eye over the bubbling pot, her face soft and open in the lamplight. She smiles, and it's like the sun coming out after a long, hard winter.

Yeah. We're going to be just fine.

✦━━━━━━✦

Read on for a sneak peek of Mick's next adventure in San Francisco's Barbary Coast!
Necromancers and Navy Grog

Chapter 1:

Necromancers and Navy Grog

The morning fog was just starting to burn away as we crest the hill on 3rd Street, the bay and the wharf spread out before us. Masts of the ships crowding San Francisco Bay poke through the mist like the bare bones of dead leviathans in the distance.

We descend Berry Street into the crowd, the stink of Mission Creek rising to assault us. Its aggressive pungency amplified by the morning's low tide. The "Creek" is little more than an open sewer, carrying blood and offal and Lord knows what else from Butchertown. Sailors complain it will peel the paint off a hull in a day and swear you'd be dead in two minutes flat if you fell in.

"Tell me again why we're chasing ghost stories?" I say, lifting my skirt above the stinking muck with my good hand.

My temporary partner Loosh, Agent Aloysious Temple, pulls a handkerchief out of his breast pocket and dabs at his forehead, despite the cool morning. His breathing has been labored since we started out an hour ago. "Because Captain Garret needs to keep the brass happy. Because the mayor's sister-in-law swears to seeing the dead walking near Meiggs Wharf."

Loosh's been my unofficial nanny since I reported to my assignment at the Anti Death Magic Division of the Bureau of Magical Investigation last fall. I was bestowed upon him by my boss Garret who didn't like my history and had no idea what to do with me, a female agent. So, he tossed me at these pissant assignments trailing Loosh, a part time agent approaching retirement.

"The dead walking." I snort. "More likely a prank. Or worse case, some poor shanghaied bastard making a break for it".

No one gives us a second glance as we push our way through stevedores, sailors, and merchants. Wagons clatter over the cobblestones to our right. The ships and piers to our left swarm with sweat-drenched men loading, hauling unloading cargo, swearing singing, or conversing in what seems like every language known to man. I reckon a person could learn to curse creatively if they applied themselves for a single day of eavesdropping.

"Maybe," Loosh tucks the handkerchief away, his craggy face creasing into what passes for a smile these days. "Though, the description in the report was rather... colorful. 'Pale as fish belly, moving like a man with lead in his bones.'"

"Sounds like someone who's been locked in a ship's hold for a week or two," I say.

"Indeed," Loosh nods, smile widening. "Perhaps this is our opportunity to free some prodigal Odysseus, return him to the bosom of his loving family."

I shoot him a sideways look. Loosh's background as a Classic's professor sometimes leads him to flights of fancy. "Too much Homer before bed?"

"Never enough Homer dear girl!"

We continue to push through the mayhem, my blue riding skirt swishing against my boots. A concession to my sister Julianna's propriety. Technically there are ordinances on the city's books forbidding women to wear men's attire, but they're only enforced when someone in power gets pissy. Even so I wore the skirt to soothe my sister's sensibilities.

Loosh pulls a small notebook out of his coat pocket and scans it. I take advantage of the pause to steady myself against a stack of crates and use the hook replacing my left hand to adjust the stocking bunching at my ankle. The steel tip catches on the knit and threatens to tear. I'm sure Julianna would argue that's another reason for a nice ladylike prosthetic, easily concealed in a fashionable glove, but I prefer the utility of the hook. Terrible things, stockings, with their garters. Yet another nod to feminine decorum foisted upon me by dear sister.

A passing stevedore flashes me a grin. "Need a hand there, ma'am?"

I bark a laugh. "No hand needed, thanks all the same." I wave the hook in his direction, and he chuckles, shaking his head as he moves on. Stink aside, that's why I like the wharf. No one here gives a rat's ass about a missing hand or your past or your manners, or *feelings* as long as you do your job and mind your business.

Loosh glances around then indicates our destination is the organized bedlam of Pope & Talbot's lumberyard across the way. "Our witness is foreman there," he says."

The lumberyard is swarming with men and boys gawping at the schooner in the Talbot's slip, its crew working to unload a massive redwood log into the yard. It's easily eight feet across and a hundred feet long, dwarfing the men maneuvering it. The trunk hangs from complex rigging halfway between the ship and the work yard. I'm drawn closer to watch, I still can't quite believe trees this size are real, what after the scrub oak and pinion of home.

There's an eddy of activity on the ship's deck, workman's voices raise in pitch. An older man, maybe the captain, standing near the rail starts cursing "Back, BACK you idjits." He waves frantically at the men on the ground. Next thing the end of the redwood closest to the prow drops with a horrendous creak from the rigging. A rope snaps with a crack, sending the log swinging wildly.

Even as I gasp, the free end crashes to the dock below with a splintering screech. It bounces once before coming to rest. Shouts fill the air. I feel death coming for some poor soul under that log. I glance back for Loosh, see if we should go in. I've lost site of him as the crowd gathering at my back, drawn to the excitement of the accident.

Turning I fight my way clear of the crowd to see Loosh disappearing into an alley.

I curse under my breath and shoulder my way through the growing mob. Men press forward to get a look at the damage, their voices rising in excitement and concern. I push past them, my skirts catching on rough hands and tool belts.

"Loosh!" I call, but my voice is swallowed by the din.

I break free of the crowd and sprint toward the mouth of the alley where I last saw him. The narrow passage between two warehouses is dark, crates stacked haphazardly. My eyes adjust to the gloom as the excited cries fade behind me.

But ahead voices. Low and urgent.

I slow my pace, my boots silent on the packed dirt. A familiar hum slips past my defenses starts up in my bones. I've developed an unwelcome sensitivity to old death that's plagued me for months, a gift from the ritual in New Mexico last year. Now I sense death magic residue like a dog smells rot. Can't turn it off, can't ignore it. Just one more way that business marked me.

"Told you he'd be sniffing around today," a voice drifts from deeper in the alley. "Boss wants to see him."

"Don't see why we can't just gut him here and be done with it."

My blood turns cold. I edge forward, keeping to the shadows cast by the overhanging eaves. The alley opens into a small courtyard behind the warehouses, cluttered with broken crates and rusted iron.

There's Loosh, his white hair stark against the dingy wall, his bowler at his feet. Three men in filthy clothes have him cornered. Hollow-eyed and gaunt, with the pallor of people who hadn't seen sunlight in weeks.

Hop heads, sure enough. But not the usual sort. Hoppies ain't violent. And they surely don't go dragging Bureau agents down alleys.

"Now gentlemen," Loosh's saying, his voice steady despite the circumstances. "I'm certain we can reach some sort of accommodation. Perhaps we could discuss this over a drink?"

"Ain't gonna be no discussion," the tallest one answers. "Boss says bring you, so that's what we're doing."

The humming in my bones gets louder. There's magical corruption here. It clings to these men like smoke.

I step into the courtyard. "Afternoon, boys."

They whirl toward me, and I get a good look at their faces. Sweet Christ. Whatever they've been smoking, it ain't just opium. Their skin has a waxy sheen. But their eyes burn with an intensity that has nothing to do with poppy dreams. I wonder if these fellows account for the zombie sightings we've been hearing about.

"Well now," The tall grins. His mouth a graveyard of blackened stumps where teeth should be. "Look what wandered in. Pretty little thing, ain't she?"

"I ain't little," I say, keeping my voice level. "You best let him go,"

Another one pipes up, burn scars stretching over his skin. He takes a step toward me. "You got spirit. Boss might like that."

"I doubt it." I blink slowly. "Let *Agent* Temple go," I continue, hoping the reality of law enforcement will send them scurrying. "The Bureau of Magical Investigations doesn't take kindly to folks roughing up their men."

The three exchange startled glances. Scarface's eyes widen. "BMI? Shit. You're with the Beemers?"

Loosh winces, shooting me a look that could curdle milk. I realize my mistake too late. He wanted to stay on the low down.

"Boss just said grab the old man from Meiggs," Toothless mutters to the others. "Didn't say nothing about him being no law."

The humming in my bones shifts, becomes more urgent. Whatever's wrong with these men, it's amplifying. The corruption I'm sensing isn't old. It's alive, slowly, eating them from the inside.

"Walk away, lady," Tall and Toothless says. "This ain't your business."

"Afraid it is."

"Mary Catherine, perhaps discretion—" Loosh starts, his voice tight.

Ignoring him I launch myself before anyone can react. The Bureau doesn't allow me to carry firearms, but I've got other advantages.

My hook catches Scarface across the jaw, tearing flesh. He staggers back, blood streaming down his chin. The other two rush me at once. Damn it, I expected them to run as soon as I fought back. Hop heads never stand and fight.

I duck under a wild swing from Toothless, grab the short one by his greasy hair, and slam his face into my knee. The crack of his nose breaking echoes off the warehouse walls. He drops like a sack of grain. My knee numbs from the impact.

They're faster than they should be. Stronger too. Toothless backhands me across the face hard enough to rattle my teeth. Maybe I was too hasty in my approach? I stumble, my vision blurring for a moment.

"Mary Catherine!" Loosh shouts.

A fist catches me in the ribs. Pain explodes through my side, and I grunt, rolling with the blow. Whatever's in their systems, it's made them vicious and fearless.

Loosh grabs a broken crate slat from the ground and swings it at Scar Face. It connects with his shoulder and splinters. He barely flinches.

"Hold her!" Toothless yells.

Scar Face lunges for me. I sidestep, but my heel catches on my damned skirts. I go down hard on my ass, my palm scraping against the ground.

He's on me in an instant, his hands around my throat. His fingers are ice cold, and when I look into his eyes, I freeze. They're not just hollow. They're empty, emotionless. Like looking into a well at midnight.

"Should've minded your own business," he snarls.

I drive my hook up under his ribs. The metal punctures something soft, and he gasps. "Stupid bitch," his grip loosens.

I scramble backward out from underneath him until my shoulders hit the wall and pull myself to my feet, scanning for Toothless. The humming in my bones is so loud now it's like standing next to a steam engine.

Toothless is grappling with Loosh across the courtyard tying to pin him against the wall. Loosh's got 30 lbs. and at least six inches on the hoppy, but Loosh is old and tired. The hoppy's hands close on Loosh's throat I do the only thing I can think of. I run at Toothless and tackle him low.

He stumbles, off balance, and crashes into the cargo hook protruding from the warehouse wall behind him. The curved iron punches through his back and out his chest, just below his collarbone.

For a moment, he hangs there, suspended on the hook like a piece of meat. Then his eyes roll back, and breath rattles out of him. Before the moment passes I lay my hand on his chest and call the Gleaning.

Chapter 2

The moment my palm touches his chest, my world narrows, he and I connect. His animus flares beneath my hand, sickly pink threaded with violet, pulsing like a bruise. Wrong. Corrupted. The Gleaner wakes, thirsty for the death, eager.

Toothless's final breath breaks foul across my face and I'm falling through the moment of his dying.

Sprawled on a filthy mattress in a basement that reeks of piss and rotting fish. My bones ache. My teeth hurt. Everything hurts.

Need it need it need it.

The craving tears through me like broken glass. Not just for opium. Something else. Something that makes the poppy seem like candy.

Flash.

I'm standing in a doorway, rain pelting my face. A man in expensive clothes steps from a carriage. His face a blur but eyes violet in the lamplight. Wrong color. Wrong everything. But he's got what I need.

"You want more?" His voice slides over me like oil. "You bring him to me."

Another flash

I'm stalking Loosh, noting his habits. The way he favors his left leg. How he stops to catch his breath. The route he takes through the wharf.

The violet-eyed man presses something into my palm. It burns cold against my skin. "This will make you strong. Fast."

I take it and swallow it whole.

The hunger gnaws at my insides. I'd sell my mother for another taste. I'd kill for it. I will kill for it.

My link to Toothless snaps as his Animus Mortis rushes through me, hot and bitter. Corrupted. This isn't clean death. It's poisoned by whatever was in that vial. The energy scrapes against my nerves like sandpaper, leaving me shaking and nauseous.

The courtyard spins. My knees buckle, and I hit the ground hard, bile rising in my throat.

Every living thing's got Animus. Call it a soul if you're feeling poetic. It's tethered to the body by invisible chains. When something dies, those chains snap. That breaking, that split second between alive and gone, releases a surge of pure energy. Animus Mortis, the scholars call it. Death energy.

My Gleaner, this knack I was born with, it lets me ride that breaking. Absorb it. Store it up like bullets in a chamber, ready to unleash as pure kinetic force when I need it. Been doing it since I was a girl.

Something, a flicker of movement at the periphery of my vision. Just a shadow, slipping away like a wisp of smoke. The hoppy's shade? It hovers just out of reach. It's a dance of hunger and loss, a fleeting echo of a life snuffed out in darkness. Trouble with Gleaning is, in addition to the dying bastard's memories flooding through me whether I want them or not, sometimes their shades stick around to haunt me after.

But Toothless ain't gonna stick around, got nothing tethering him to the physical plane; he's shadow in death as he was in life. I blink rapidly, shaking him off.

The other two hoppies need dealing with. Scarface maybe fifteen feet down the alley, is dragging himself toward the mouth. The short one's closer, groaning through his broken nose. Both well within my reach if they try something stupid. I can project force about fifty feet when I'm fresh, farther if I'm willing to burn myself out. Right now, with what I just took from Toothless, I'm raring to go.

"Mary Catherine!" Loosh's voice seems to come from miles away.

I retch into the dirt, my body trying to purge the tainted energy. But the power surges through my veins, hot and electric. I feel every heartbeat in a three-block radius, sense the fear and excitement from the crowd still gathered over at Talbots. My muscles sing with stolen strength.

Hands grip my shoulders. "Agent McClellan, look at me."

Loosh's face swims into focus, flushed and slick with sweat. His breathing is ragged gasps, and his hands shake against my shoulders.

"What the fuck was that about, Loosh?" My voice comes out raw. "Those men knew you. They were hunting you."

His face pales beneath the flush. "I... what do you mean? They were just—"

"Don't." I struggle to my feet, the world still tilting. "I heard them. 'Boss wants to see him.'"

His eyes dart away from mine. "I haven't the faintest idea what you mean."

"Come on Loosh." I gesture at the body hanging from the cargo hook, then at Scarface who's clutching his bleeding chest while trying to crawl away. "These weren't random thugs looking for an easy mark. They knew you. They mentioned following you from Meiggs Wharf."

Loosh's face goes pale beneath the red flush. "Perhaps they mistook me for someone else."

I study his face. But before I can press him further, Scarface makes it to his feet and starts limping toward the alley mouth, blood seeping from his chest. I'm on him in three strides, bumping the back of his knee and knocking him to the ground.

Loosh fumbles in his coat pocket for his manacles. His hands shake so badly he drops them twice before managing to hand them off. Scarface groans as the metal cuts into his wrist. The short one just stares at nothing, blood crusted around his broken nose.

"We need to get these two to Captain Garrett," I say, hauling Broken Nose to his feet. "Let him sort out who sent them and why."

"Mary Catherine, wait." Loosh's voice creaks. "Perhaps we should reconsider."

I stare at him. "Reconsider what exactly?"

"Well, it's just..." He wrings his hands, his eyes darting between the prisoners and the mouth of the alley. "Captain Garrett has been under considerable pressure lately. From the mayor's office, from the city council. Perhaps it would be better if we simply turned these men over to the regular police. Let them handle it as an assault."

"Assault?" I can't keep the disbelief out of my voice. "Loosh, these men were magically corrupted. I can smell it on them. Feel it. This is exactly what the Anti Death Magic Division is supposed to handle."

"Yes but think of the paperwork. The questions. The complications. You'll have to explain to Garrett how one of the suspects died and you...benefited." He's speaking faster now, the words tumbling over each other. "Wouldn't it be simpler to just... let us investigate ourselves?"

I study his face. The man who tries to teach me Latin and shares beers at Calpurnia's looks older than his sixty years. Fragile? Frightened?

The humming in my bones has faded to a whisper, but I still sense the corruption clinging to our prisoners. Whatever they'd been dosed with, it ain't natural. And it ain't gone.

But Loosh never complained about being saddled with me. Never made me feel like dead weight or a charity case. When other agents whispered about me, the Gleaner who killed a federal marshal, Loosh treated me like a partner. Like someone worth talking to.

I study his face. This is the terror of a man who knows he's in over his head.

I owe him this much, help him get out from under whatever he's gotten himself into.

"Regular police," I say finally. "Random assault."

"Thank you. Truly. I know this puts you in a difficult position."

I help him hoist Scarface to his feet. The man's jaw hangs at an odd angle where my hook caught him, but he's conscious enough to shuffle forward when I shove him toward the alley mouth.

"This better not come back to bite me in the ass. And you're gonna tell me everything."

"I will but later. It's a long story and I've got to take care of something in Sausalito this afternoon. Monday, we'll sit down together and I'll tell you everything. I give you my word."

His word. For some reason, that doesn't comfort me as much as it should. I push doubts away and smile, "Fine, you're buying the beer."

We march our prisoners out of the alley and back into the chaos of the wharf. The crowd around Pope & Talbot's has dispersed, leaving only a few men working to clear debris from the fallen log. No one pays us any mind as we make our way to 4th Street and then via cab to the police station on Battery Street. Loosh has a friend there and there will be no hard questions asked.

But I can't shake the feeling that I'm making a mistake. The visions from the dead hoppy keep circling through my head. The shadow figure with his vials of purple liquid.

Whatever's happening, it ain't finished. And Loosh knows more about it than he's letting on.

✦━━━━━━━✦

Necromancers and Navy Grog is coming in Spring 2026!

But while you wait...
Ever cross paths with a Trail Wraith?
In 1869, wagon trains are ravaged on the Santa Fe Trail. Mick
Kelly and her crew, Morgan, Clyde and Uncle Pete, are sent to
clean up what the Bureau thinks is a magical outlaw problem.
Bodies say otherwise. Survivors don't talk sense. Something
ancient is moving across the plains, feeding on fear and blood.

Luckily the trail has a protector.
It just isn't human.
The *Phantasm Prism* is a prequel to *Bad Magic and Whiskey*
Download your free copy of *The Phantasm Prism*

THANK YOU

Thanks for riding along with Mick Kelly through a world of death magic, double-crosses, and the ghosts. *Bad Magic and Whiskey* was the first book I ever started, but took the long way home to finish.

I began writing this story at the end of 2022, right before I was laid off from a job I'd held for seventeen years. That shake-up sent me into a full-on identity spiral. I'd always thought of myself as a rebel. Punk rock. A creative. Not someone who stayed put in corporate leadership for nearly two decades. But there I was. And when people, trying to be helpful, told me repeatedly that it would be impossible to find a new job at my age? I felt it. Deeply.

Those questions of relevance, identity, and second chances became the beating heart of Mick's story. She's scarred, stubborn, and still figuring it all out. She's not me, but her journey was shaped by mine.

Along the way, I took a detour to write *The Phantasm Prism*, a short novel meant to introduce Mick's world. (Grab a free copy here or at melissajacobsonauthor.com. Morgan, Clyde and Uncle Pete are all there in their prime!) It was supposed to be a quick little freebie but it became a major turning point. Writing that book helped me see *this* one more clearly. I learned so much that I came back to *Bad Magic and Whiskey* with sharper tools and a stronger voice. And I think the story is better for it.

I'd love it if you'd take a moment to leave a review; on Goodreads, Amazon, Barnes & Noble, Kobo or wherever you discovered *Bad Magic and Whiskey*. Reviews are a big shot of **Big Magic** for indie authors. Reviews are the most powerful way to help new readers find stories like this one, and they help writers like me keep going. Reviews are more heady than a shot of good whiskey.

And yes, I read them. Every single one.

The next story in the Bad Magic series is *Necromancers and Navy Grog.* Mick heads to San Francisco's Barbary Coast. Expect necromancers and mythical creatures in a supernatural noir with a cast of dangerous women who refuse to play by anyone's rules.

If you'd like to hear when the next book drops (and maybe snag a few extras along the way), come join me at melissajaco bsonauthor.com. I'd love to keep in touch.

Thanks for spending your time with me and Mick.

Melissa

Acknowledgements

I blame my husband Jason for the completion of this novel. He encouraged me, supported me, set up the publishing company, sent me to 20 Books Vegas, reassured me everything would be all right, cheer leaded, talked me off cliffs, discussed plot and character motivations, read multiple versions of the book, unloaded the dishwasher, found a critique group and in general pushed to make my dream a reality. The nerve of that guy.

But seriously, I am so lucky to have people in my life who love and support me, this book would never have happened without them.

In addition to Jason, I owe thanks to friend and fellow author T.A. Caldwell, my gorgeous, sweet, brilliant daughter Candace, the Littleton Rocky Mountain Fiction Writers Critique Group, and my dear friend, the frighteningly talented Jaz DeWillis for help getting my cover back on track. And of course, my mom.

This book has been through a lot. A full developmental edit that completely changed the arc of the story. Thank you, Damien Pitter! Find him at damienpitter.com. Two professional line edits, thank you Lawrence Editing. And a final FINAL proof, thank you Hosang Quality Editing. There were also multiple beta reads and more rewrites than I can count. Any remaining errors are my own! Typos are my superpower, I can seemingly introduce into text I haven't touched. The novel is far from perfect despite all the help! But I'm growing as an author thanks to everyone who made this possible.

BAD MAGIC

Historical Urban Fantasy of the American West

Bad Magic is a historical urban fantasy series set in Post Civil War America, told through the eyes of Mick Kelly, a middle-aged death mage with a long memory, and a dark past.

In the haunted edges of 19th-century America, supernatural danger blends with real history. Magic lingers in the grit of frontier towns, the shadows of railroad cities, and the quiet places where the past refuses to stay buried. These are character-driven stories about a woman who survived the worst, the ghosts she carries, and the reckonings that comes calling when bad magic rises again.

Explore the series today!

melissajacobsonauthor.com/about-bad-magic-series/